2001

Dear Reader,

One August, fifteen years ago, I was visiting my sister to serve as birthing coach for a baby who was three weeks overdue. We were just outside New Orleans, and I was anxious for her to go into labor so I could get out of that heat and humidity and return home. One day, desperate, I decided that the process of labor could be accelerated by a really bumpy road, so I got in the car with my sister, her three children, and my daughter and drove to her in-laws' family compound.

As we pulled up, my sister told me to park the car by the trees and, even before I turned it off, the children bolted out and ran up a hill to the swimming pool.

I reached up to turn off the ignition and my gaze was drawn to a majestic oak tree, dripping with Spanish moss. This tree was huge and ancient, and I felt like I was frozen in shock as a strange energy seemed to pass from that tree, through the ground, to rush up my legs. I felt scared as a heavy wave of grief crushed down on me and extremely foolish as tears came into my eyes. My sister, who was still in the car, turned to me and, when I looked at her, said, "You've been here before, haven't you?" I didn't answer. However, as incredible as it might sound, the entire afternoon I could "feel" that tree. When I finally returned to my home, I vowed never to talk of such bizarre reactions to a tree, of all things. Well, I've learned never to say never. I'm not just talking about it. I've written about it.

I hope you enjoy this time travel into the past, where the heroine rediscovers the magic of childhood, opens up to an extraordinary man who rekindles the wonder of passion, and learns a simple truth: the only treasures that really last are our memories and the love with which we keep them. See you on the next adventure!

Kindest regards,

Constance O'Day

Constance O'Day-Flannery

Time After Time

AVON BOOKS

An Imprint of HarperCollinsPublishers

This is a work of fiction. Names, characters, places, and incidents are products of the author's imagination or are used fictitiously and are not to be construed as real. Any resemblance to actual events, locales, organizations, or persons, living or dead, is entirely coincidental.

AVON BOOKS
An Imprint of HarperCollins*Publishers*
10 East 53rd Street
New York, New York 10022-5299

This book is dedicated to the memories of

my father, Francis Edward Aloysius Xavier O'Day . . .

whose words began my own journey of the heart

and my uncle, Frank Scheib . . .

my gentle Knight in Shining Armor

who taught me about honorable men

and my sister, Virginia O'Day McLellan . . .

who took me to that tree and, later,

mirrored for me the dignity in the circle of life

Prologue

"Oh, Kelly . . . you look wonderful!"

Maybe it happens to everyone . . . that moment of wondering what the heck you're doing with your life . . . and suddenly it hits you that for most of it you've been floating along in a sea of indecision, allowing others to direct the flow. Kelly Brennan was having just such a moment as she stared at her reflection in the antique floor mirror, and she would have laughed if it hadn't been so pathetic.

"You're a vision in that dress, dear."

Yards and yards of green satin wrapped around her like a runny key lime pie. She was a vision, all right. Ruffles of stiff organza at her shoulders made her feel like a Brazilian football player in drag. And atop her auburn hair, the matching straw hat looked more like a wilted mushroom. How could anyone have picked such a hideous bridesmaid dress, and how could anyone have agreed to wear it? Guess that's what happens if you can't say *no* to an old college roommate when she asks you to stand up for her. So these were a wimp's rewards.

Smiling politely, Kelly turned to the bride's mother. "Thank you, Mrs. Whelan."

"I'm so happy for Melissa. I think this time she's found her Mr. Perfect." Peggy Whelan looked into the mirror and adjusted her tasteful cream-colored silk jacket.

"I hope so," Kelly whispered, wondering why she was the only one in this wedding party who looked so ridiculous. Had Mel been on drugs when she'd picked out this dress?

Why couldn't she just have said thank you for asking, but no thanks? Surely, there must be someone else in your life upon whom to bestow such an honor.

Obviously, there wasn't.

"Now I expect you to catch the bouquet, Kelly. Next wedding will be yours. It's your turn."

Kelly winced as memories came unbidden, yet managed a tight smile. "I was married."

Mrs. Whelan looked startled for a second, then returned her smile. "Oh yes, I forgot. Well, time to begin again, dear."

Kelly couldn't answer as she pushed away painful thoughts of Michael. It had taken too many years to accept that she was no longer married. She had to keep holding those memories as far below the surface as she could. Especially now. She turned to the window of the lovely old Southern mansion that had been rented for the occasion and stared out at the elaborate garden below.

Watching the last-minute guests arrive, she fought the urge to rip the stupid dress from her body and run away from all the madness. What had possessed her to agree to be a bridesmaid to a woman she'd only sent Christmas cards to for the last fifteen years? Why couldn't she just tell Mel's mother that marriage wasn't the be-all and end-all of a woman's life? And that there were no guarantees? At the very least, her daughter's third marriage should have shown her that.

Turning around to the woman who was still surveying her own reflection in the mirror, Kelly mumbled with a bit of unusual defiance, "What I mean to say, Mrs. Whelan, is, I don't know that I'll ever marry again."

The woman again seemed startled, then appeared decidedly relieved not to have to answer as Melissa came floating into the room on a cloud of white organza.

"Oh Mom, guess what? Damon just gave me my wedding present! A house! In the Garden District!"

Mrs. Whelan squealed along with her daughter, and Kelly was forgotten in the celebration. And, at that moment, Kelly swore she was going to change. Surely, this was the straw that had broken her wimpy back. She was going to learn to say *no* . . . and mean it!

"Are you ready?" Mel asked, beaming at Kelly. "You look . . . really sweet," she added with a tone of satisfaction.

"Sweet?" Kelly asked with a laugh as she looked down to her wide skirt. "Ya know, Mel, this color—"

"I told you I wanted it to look like an old-fashioned Southern ball gown." The interruption was obviously timed to halt any complaints. "And it does . . . doesn't it, Mother?"

Peggy nodded. "Sweet."

Suddenly, Kelly wondered if Mel was attempting to get back at her for something in college. What else could warrant this ridiculous costume?

"Well, it's time," Mel announced with a gusty sigh, glancing at herself once more in the long mirror.

Kelly had to admit that Mel looked pretty, even though wearing a formal white wedding gown for the third time might be overdoing it just a bit. Still, it was Mel's day and, like it or not, she was involved, so they might as well get it over with. Realizing how terrible that thought was, Kelly smiled at her old friend while trying to bring back memories of their closeness in college. "I wish you everything your heart desires, Mel. Be happy."

Melissa seemed to soften as she turned from the mirror. "Thanks, Kelly. I think this one's a winner."

"Well, of course he is," Peggy chimed in, picking up the delicate spray of white freesia and handing it to her daughter. "He just presented you with a house in New Orleans' Garden District!"

Mel laughed and held her bouquet to her waist. "All right, how do I look?"

"Beautiful," Peggy pronounced.

"Beautiful," Kelly whispered in agreement.

"Then we're ready. Let's get this show on the road, ladies!"

Kelly wondered if the guests were prepared for her to lead the bridal procession. When was the last time anyone had seen a walking key lime pie?

The reception was even more elaborate than the wedding, if not a bit exaggerated for Mel's newly acquired affinity with Southern culture. Catered by one of New Orleans' leading chefs, French and Cajun cuisines were the fare, and everything had been impeccably arranged under six large white canopies. White-and-yellow freesia arrangements were on every table and in front of several columns around the bandstand, where musicians in black tuxedos played. Long tables were heavily draped in white linen and dressed with the finest china, real silver, and cut crystal. The guest list was as impressive as the wine list, and Kelly was bored to tears.

She knew no one, yet found it at least got her off the hook from making conversation about monetary gains and other small gossip about family and friends. She had done her duty and witnessed Mel's wedding. She had danced with the best man, a lawyer and friend of Damon's with a very thick Southern accent who blatantly hit on her, even though his wife was sitting not ten feet away.

Kelly smiled as genuinely as she could, making her way through haughty cliques of strangers, and felt that overwhelming sensation that one doesn't quite fit in . . . and it wasn't just the dress. Through stems of twirling parasols and under bouquets of painted straw bonnets, women eyed her from head to toe while their husbands, charmingly Southern, bowed at her passing, even if they couldn't quite meet her gaze.

She'd lost her appetite much earlier in the morning, probably from wearing the lime-colored dress, and now she was fed up with the entire charade. . . . Enough was enough. She needed to be alone, and headed toward the dark canopy of trees at the edge of the garden, figuring it would at least provide some relief from the bayou heat and humidity.

Removing her straw-mushroom hat, Kelly made her way aimlessly under the umbrella of branches laden with Spanish moss and felt her flushed cheeks settle with the cool breeze. Why did she suddenly feel as though she were struggling with something? Was it Peggy's remarks to her earlier that brought back memories? Was it Mel's wedding, reminding her of her own so many years ago? Again, unbidden, the flashing scenes came rushing back at her. She pictured herself, right out of college, so young and so naive . . . never having a clue that in less than two years her entire life would be filled with such debilitating pain and loss that she couldn't get out of bed for weeks. . . .

Michael.

Her chest tightened with a dull pain. Her throat felt like it was closing.

How she had loved him. How he had loved her.

She still loved him. It was the reason she remained alone. She dated occasionally, yet knew it was unfair to compare every man to Michael, for they all came up far short. What else can a woman, who has had the love of her life taken instantly from her, do when she's just twenty-three years old?

Shrugging as she walked farther into the wooded area, Kelly twisted the brim of her hat and mentally pondered answers to her own question. She either dies, or she keeps herself preoccupied with something else. Okay, she was too much of a wimp to die, so she plunged herself into work, becoming a slave to it, and could now claim to be financially secure and the proud owner of a small travel agency. Sure, she helped other people fulfill their dreams, while her own . . . ?

Oh, what's the use, she thought, walking farther into a sun-dappled clearing. She didn't need to try very hard, for she could still see him in her mind's eye; finely chiseled, tall, dark, with laughing blue eyes . . . smiling at her as he walked in the front door of their small apartment. A tiny smile played at her lips. How just the thought of him softened her heart. They were so close they didn't need words to know what the other was thinking. They had a comfortable, silent language. One look could simply say it all. And then came that April morning, when a policeman said her husband had been shot in a convenience-store robbery. By the time she arrived at the hospital, she was already a widow. He had just been in the wrong place at the wrong time, they told her. Such a cliché.

Through the deadened silence that enveloped her, Kelly felt that all-too-familiar pain rip at her heart and, dropping her hat, she clutched her chest.

Shaking her head, as if the action might wipe out the memories she had kept at bay so long, she stiffened and mentally demanded she not dredge it all up again, and yet . . . she couldn't deny he still haunted her life. There wasn't a day that she didn't feel his presence. Most of the time, she forced herself into a state of automatic pilot, half-awake, just pretending to be alive. Without Michael, her life felt superficial. Maybe that was why the fight had gone out of her, why she couldn't say no to anyone . . . not a last-minute client or old college roommate.

Still, she couldn't deny she'd made a choice, for if she'd given in to the rage she would have run into the night screaming at the gross injustice and completely lost her mind. Instead, she closed it all off and shut down. And where had it gotten her?

She glanced down to the wide skirt of her gown and wanted to laugh out loud at the absurdity of it all. It got her right here, looking like an absolute idiot, in a lime green, old-fashioned Southern ball gown wandering around in some back bayou woods in Louisiana.

Hearing the faint music begin again, Kelly knew she should probably head back, though she really didn't want to rejoin the party. What she really wanted was to go to her hotel, change into a pair of jeans, and try to reschedule her return flight back East for this evening instead of the following afternoon. Yet she didn't want to appear rude or to disappoint her friend, and, if she were completely honest with herself, she would admit she still hadn't mastered the fine art of saying *no*.

Someday, she would stop being such a pushover.

Turning back to the grove of old trees, she was awed by one in particular, just twenty feet away. It was like a post-card picture. The massive oak tree was at least eight feet wide at the base of its trunk. Large, spreading, leafy branches loomed above, dripping with silver-green velvet moss. Breathtakingly ancient and beautiful, the tree was compelling. She felt an inexplicable urge to get closer, just to touch it. As Kelly stepped nearer, she was suddenly forced to stop as an overwhelming jolt ran through her. Her jaw dropped in surprise, and she again clutched her chest. It was so unexpected . . . *something,* like an electrical charge, appeared to have emanated from the tree, traveled through the ground and raced up her legs, settling in her heart.

Uncontrollable tears began to trickle down her cheeks, and she felt foolish for not knowing why . . . and then it hit her. It was grief. Swells of grief washed over her, and still she couldn't name the source. It wasn't Michael. Or it was Michael *and* something else, something so intense she had to tear her gaze away and turn back to the sounds from the wedding reception.

Composing herself by focusing on the distant white canopies, Kelly wiped at her eyes, feeling the searing sensation lessen.

Having calmed herself, Kelly became aware of the heavy air around her. It was very still, yet she heard a strong breeze rustle through the leaves of the ancient tree right behind her. Her thoughts made the small hairs on the nape of her neck stand on end. Was the tree making its presence known to her again? She must surely be having a nervous breakdown or something to think such a thing. With shaky fingers, she grabbed up the hem of her skirt and figured the dress had really been her breaking point after all. Stepping away, she felt a deep sense of urgency pressing between her shoulder blades, as if the tree were calling her back, and doggedly tried to ignore it.

Just get back to the party, she told herself. *Don't even think about it. It's only a tree. Whatever just happened isn't real. Imagination. That's it.* She was a grown woman, and such things were ridiculous. A tree doesn't transmit *feelings*!

A part of her was angry with herself for being scared. Wait a minute! Hadn't she made up her mind that she wouldn't be a wimp, that she would be able to say *no* and mean it? As crazy as it would have sounded to anyone else, Kelly knew that she had to do one thing for herself before she left these woods.

Taking a deep breath, she grabbed up the yards of material surrounding her and turned around with firm determination. Stomping right back up to the tree, she planted her feet in the soft, leaf-covered earth, placed her hands on her hips, then glared up its huge trunk and into the greenery above. If she had to begin with a tree . . . even if it was limb to limb . . . then so be it! It was a start.

"No!" Her defiant word muffled off into the shaded woods.

Somehow, in the following silence, she felt better.

Almost in a display of good sportsmanship, Kelly let out her breath slowly and lifted her hand to the aged trunk. It wasn't so scary now. In fact, the rough bark felt almost comforting. Shaking her head and exhausted with emotion, she leaned against it, wondering why she had ever been afraid. Must have been that trip down memory lane. It was just an old tree, a sentinel of history, that had probably been around for over a hundred years. She almost laughed at her vivid imagination. Sentinel of history? Where had *that* come from?

No sooner had the question popped into her mind when it appeared her enormous companion was beginning to fade right before her eyes, as her hand *disappeared* . . . then her arm . . . then her shoulder. Instantly, she was seized by an intense drawing sensation that pulled her off balance giving her the uncanny impression of falling *through the tree,* feeling its age, its moisture, its musky essence and its weariness of just existing for so many years. . . . It happened so quickly she felt helpless to stop it.

Sparks of electricity buzzed through her body again, causing a dizzying nausea, and Kelly blinked her eyes as she suddenly found herself on her knees. Her body felt incredibly drained, and she began to shake. How had she fallen? When? Had she passed out? She started to whimper, as fear of the unknown began racing through her system. What the hell had just happened?

Get up, she mentally instructed herself. She struggled to stand upright through her twisted skirt. Dizziness immediately assaulted her again and, slamming her eyes shut, she grabbed her head as if to hold it all together. Once more Kelly reached out to lean against the wide trunk for assistance in rising when she found herself falling again, this time to her side.

"Oomph . . ." The sound forced out as her body hit hard against the ground. For just a few moments, she lay there alone and in shock as she tried to regain her breath. Eyes wide-open, she stared up at the cloudy blue sky and asked once more, this time aloud, "What . . . the . . . hell . . . is . . . going . . . on . . . here?" Rising slowly and leaning on one elbow, she shifted her head to look at the tree, and her brain froze when she realized why she'd fallen.

There was no tree.

Her head turned in all directions, her eyes darted about desperately to find it, or any of the other magnificent trees that had drawn her to the woods in the first place. All the trees around her now looked much younger, less substantial. Crazy thoughts crashed in her mind all at once . . . Okay, so maybe she *was* having a nervous breakdown! Or maybe something was wrong with her brain . . . perhaps she had heatstroke. She hadn't had anything but coffee all morning, and a light salad on the plane the night before. The heat and humidity of the Louisiana bayou could fry your nerves. That had to be it. Or maybe she was dreaming. Sure, that was it, she was dreaming. None of this could be real . . . because trees don't just damn well disappear!

With that final thought, Kelly forced her brain to stop thinking and closed her eyes. She held her breath and waited, sure she would wake up at any moment. Only an eerie silence followed her pause, and her brain began churning again. Where's the band music from the reception? The clinking of glasses? The muffled chatter and laughter of the guests?

"Oh, come out of it!" Kelly commanded herself aloud, relieved to realize she hadn't gone deaf altogether, when suddenly, a rustling in the woods grabbed her attention. Her eyes shot open, and she turned toward the noise. What began to emerge slowly from behind a young oak tree made her gape in even more stupefaction as she lay frozen on the ground.

Eye to eye their gazes locked, and even as Kelly heard the words, nothing in her life could have prepared her for them. . . .

"I gotcha! You *is* a fairy, *ain'tcha?*"

One

Kelly pushed herself into a sitting position and stared at the child, who was still peeking around the tree trunk and eyeing her with such wonder that Kelly almost laughed. "No, I most certainly am not . . . a fairy," she mumbled, while brushing dirt from her face and pushing back the long strands of hair from her eyes.

"Oh yes you is," the child insisted in an excited voice. "And I caught ya! Now you have to grant me three wishes." Pointing a small finger at Kelly, the youngster added, "I knows the rules!"

This time Kelly couldn't hold back the laugh as she sat and looked across the few feet separating them. She didn't know if it was a boy or a girl since the child, around ten years old, was dressed like a character from *Huckleberry Finn*, even down to the broken overall strap hanging down his or her chest. "Look, I'm not a fairy, and I can't grant you any wishes," she said in a gentle voice as she got to her feet and dusted the leaves and dirt from the wide skirt of her gown. "Now, I really have to get back to the party."

"What party?" the child asked, cautiously sliding around

to the front of the tree. "A fairy party? Where is it? Can I come, too?"

Kelly shook her head and snickered at the absurdity. Was this child backward? She looked around the woods, wondering how she could have gotten herself turned around, and where was the house? "It's . . . it's a wedding reception," Kelly muttered, turning around and around, searching for her way back. "It's at a house, an old house. The . . ." she tried to remember the name. "The Tyler Mansion."

"Ain't no Tylers 'round here," the child stated firmly. "Just me and Mammy Clara . . . and my daddy."

Kelly stared at the child. "What's your name?"

"You first!" A small chin stuck out with determination.

"Okay," she relented. The kid was probably taught not to give it out to strangers. "I'm Kelly Brennan. Now, it's your turn."

"Lizzie Gilmore." The child let go of the tree and stepped forward. "Now ya gots to grant me three wishes. I know your name!"

So this blond-haired wild child was a girl. Kelly fought for patience and released her breath slowly and deliberately. "Nice to meet you, but look, Lizzie, I'm not a fairy, and I can't grant you anything." She paused, inhaling as she looked around the woods again, then added, "Especially since I'm the one who's lost here." Kelly looked down at the child, who was bravely moving closer. "Besides, I think it's leprechauns that grant wishes. Anyway, I have to find my way back to the wedding party."

The girl looked at Kelly's gown, and asked, "You gettin' hitched?"

She couldn't hide the grin. "No. I was in a wedding party." Kelly placed her hands on her knees and leaned down to the child. "Now, if you just point me in the right direction to the Tyler house, I'll—"

"I told ya, there ain't no Tylers 'round these parts," the impish child interrupted. Grabbing a tiny handful of Kelly's skirt, she added, "I reckon you is lost, but you's mine now. I'll take ya home and keep ya . . . then yer gonna have ta pay up."

Pay up? Oh, the wishes . . . Kelly began nodding in mock agreement. "Okay, but first, do you think you could help me? If you'd take me to a phone, that would be a start."

"A what?" The young girl looked puzzled.

"You know, a telephone . . . so I can call for help." She started to walk away in what she figured was the right direction and felt the child tugging behind her.

"Oh no, you ain't disappearin' on me, now that I gots ya!"

"Lizzie . . ." She stopped and turned around.

"No!" The child again stuck out her chin, then folded her arms over her chest to emphasize her point further. "You ain't playin' fair!"

Kelly realized this youngster didn't have a problem saying *no*, and a part of her had to admire the girl's spirit. "Look, I can't play. I have to get back. I'm going to be missed."

After a momentary pout of silence, the child reached into an overall pocket. "Ya hungry?" she asked, pulling out some purple berries and holding them up. "Picked fresh this mornin'," she added with a grin, and looked imploringly at Kelly. "I'll share 'em with ya . . ."

Kelly recognized a calculated bribe when she heard one, yet the look on this child's face softened her heart, and she had to smile again. "No, Lizzie, but thanks. I'm not really hungry. I just need to find someone who can help me."

"Well, I can help y'all."

Kelly lowered one eyebrow in apprehensive faith and looked down to the little girl. "You can?"

"Yep, I sure could," the child stated confidently. "But ya gotta do somethin' first."

"Oh, *not* the wishes again . . . I told you—"

"No, no . . . I tell ya my wishes later." She began to whisper and gestured for Kelly to come closer.

Kelly leaned forward. "Okay, Lizzie, tell me what I have to do first before you can help me."

Looking around suspiciously, as though to ensure no one would overhear the secret, the child continued to whisper. "Yer kinda big like this, but see, I was figgurin' if y'all just git real tiny-like, I could put ya in my pocket and take ya home."

Unable to answer, Kelly blinked repeatedly. What was wrong with this kid? Too many stories? Bad blood? What was she thinking when she hoped this child might be able to help her? Abruptly, Kelly took a deep breath, straightened and surveyed her choices. She then asked the most ludicrous question. "Lizzie, how far is your home?"

The girl held out her left arm and pointed. "Down this way a piece. But ya gots to git smaller, 'cause my daddy don't believe in no fairies, and he ain't gonna let me keep ya."

"I can't get smaller," Kelly found herself whispering, trying desperately to reason with the imaginative child. "Look, if I just spoke to your father, maybe he could help me and—"

"Oh no," Lizzie interrupted, making her point by shaking her blond curls vigorously. "Ya can't talk to Daddy. He won't hear nothin' about no fairies."

Kelly felt her controlled patience weakening as quickly as the clouds were darkening the early-afternoon sky. "For the last time, Lizzie—"

"But I'll bet my Mammy Clara would talk to ya. She believes in y'all."

"Okay, now we're getting somewhere." This child was truly confusing. "So your mother might help?"

"Well, she might help ya, but she's an angel now. She only comes to visit me when I'm scared . . . and she ain't here right now, 'cause I ain't scared of no fairies, ya hear?"

Kelly blinked several times before whispering, "I'm sorry. I thought you said—"

"I said Mammy Clara would talk to ya." Lizzie popped a few berries into her mouth. "But she ain't my momma."

"Oh." What else could she say? "Well, do you think you could take me to her? I really have to find a telephone."

"Mammy Clara ain't gonna find no such thing, 'cause there ain't no such thing that I ever heard of . . . and if I ain't never heard of it, sure as rain, Mammy Clara ain't heard of no telly-fone neither."

What was it that made this child so confounding? "Yes,

speaking of rain, I think it's going to start soon, and I don't want to get wet in this dress. Just take me to your Mammy Clara. Please, Lizzie?"

"Oh, yeah," the child agreed knowingly, and began wiping her berry-stained fingers on her overall pant legs. "I guess yer wings don't work when they gets wet, huh?"

"Oh, geez . . ." Kelly blew out her breath and closed her eyes. *Please, give me strength,* she silently pleaded to anything. She wished she could fly away! After her moment of silent reflection, she admitted it wasn't an option, so probably the best way to deal with the situation was to play along with Lizzie's little-girl fantasy. Kelly figured reverse psychology had some advantages.

"You ain't gettin' ready to fly away now, is ya?"

"My kingdom for a pair of wings, Lizzie . . . alas, as much as I wish I could, I left my spare set back at the fairy castle. We'll have to walk from here, all right?"

Kelly watched as the child's expression slowly transformed from a suspicious squint into a mischievous grin and delighted giggles. Feeling a bit triumphant at her own progress with the exasperating child, she couldn't help but grin.

"Okay, now . . . promise to grant me my wishes. Fair's fair. I found ya, and ya gots to keep up yer end of it. I told ya, I know the rules."

Sheesh . . . this kid didn't miss a beat. Kelly was beginning to wonder who was leading whom. "Okay, I'll try to grant your wishes, Lizzie, as long as they're within reason. Just take me to your Mammy Clara or any other adult now, okay?" *Mammy* Clara? What the heck was that about? Sounded like something from *Gone With the Wind!*

"First ya gots to promise."

Sighing, Kelly muttered, "Yes, I promise." Though what she was promising she had no idea, nor how she would fulfill this kid's wishes. She would do something really nice for her when she got back to the hotel. Send her flowers and some toys, or something. Small price to pay for getting out of the woods, avoiding the impending rain, and finding her way back to civilization.

Lizzie came closer with a huge smile plastered over her dirty face. "All righty. Now here's my first wish. You ready?"

Shrugging her shoulders, Kelly nodded. "Go for it."

"I been thinkin' on this, ever since Will Hoskins told me a story 'bout how if ya capture a fairy, they gotta grant yer wishes and so I knows my first one already."

"What is it?" Anything to get them started out of the woods.

"I want . . . *three more wishes*. That would give me . . ." Lizzie held up a hand that was stained purple from the berries. "Five more wishes!"

Lizzie appeared so thrilled she had gotten something over on her that Kelly couldn't help laughing. It was the oldest one in the book. So she'd have to buy five presents now. Big deal. "You got it, Lizzie. Now, let's go."

"You ain't mad, 'cause I tricked ya?"

Shaking her head, Kelly murmured, "My madness is yet to be determined."

"What's that mean?" Lizzie demanded as she stood in front of her.

"Pretty much, it means I must have been crazy to fly," Kelly muttered as she waved her hands out to the woods, "almost fifteen hundred miles, just to be a part of a wedding for someone I hardly know anymore—"

"I knew you could fly!"

"I meant in an airplane." Grabbing her skirt with both hands, she continued, "I must have been even crazier to put on this dress. . . ." Kelly sighed with resignation, "and now I know I've surely lost it, because I've agreed to be a little girl's fantasy fairy." Looking back down at the child, she added, "All I need now is an official diagnosis."

Lizzie laughed again, with her short, charming giggle that seemed to dissolve the angst right out of her. "You ain't crazy," the child confirmed as she held out her stained hand.

She placed hers inside the child's and felt the girl's tight grip.

"You's the queen of fairies, and I'm gonna keep ya!"

Kelly's smile broadened. *And a child shall lead them*, she

mused to herself, as they walked on through the woods. What was the point of arguing with her? Obviously, Lizzie was poor, not well educated, and living in some kind of fantasy world. Just keep playing along, Kelly told herself, until you find some help.

Above them, the sky was becoming ominously gray and the warning scent of rain was getting stronger. Kelly felt her chest tighten once more as the melee began pounding in her head.

None of it made any sense. How does a huge tree just disappear? Why did the woods look the same, yet younger? Where was the Tyler Mansion? The music? She hadn't wandered *that* far from the reception! Where had this child come from, and where was she allowing herself to be led? Had she truly lost it? Did she pass out from heat exhaustion? Was she still lying on the ground under an ancient tree and just dreaming all this? It was too much for Kelly's tired brain, so she decided to focus on the child's incessant chatter as they continued walking.

"Mammy Clara ain't gonna believe me *until* she sees ya, but . . . ya gotta grant me one of my wishes first. I still gots five more comin', an' fair's fair."

"What do you want, Lizzie?" Kelly asked, wondering why the child was holding on to her hand so tightly. Was she afraid she'd run away?

"All righty, what I want may be a hard one, but you's a fairy and y'all can do magic."

"Lizzie . . ." Kelly really wanted to stop her from thinking anything so ridiculous, yet the child kept right on talking.

". . . . for my first wish I want my daddy to say I can keep ya. You can make some magic for that, can'tcha?"

Kelly chuckled at the way the child's mind was working. "You're really masterminding this, aren't you?"

Lizzie lifted her head and stared up, a quizzical expression on her face. "What's that mean? How come ya talk so funny?"

"I don't talk funny. I'm from the North, that's all. I have a different accent, and what I meant was—"

"You's a *Yankee fairy*?"

Kelly couldn't help laughing. "I guess I am."

Lizzie suddenly dropped her hand as though she had been scalded. "Will Hoskins says the goddamned Yankees killed his uncle in the war and there wouldn't have been no yellow fever to kill my momma if Yankees didn't bring it with 'em." The child had stopped walking and was now glaring at her.

Kelly took a deep breath. Something truly was wrong with this kid. "What are you talking about? What war? What yellow fever?"

"The war everybody is always so mad about and the yellow fever Mammy Clara says killed my momma. If yer a Yankee, *you* done that!" the child accused with a scowl, while waving her finger.

"Lizzie, I didn't do anything to anyone. I just live up North and came down here for a friend's wedding. That's all. Sounds to me as though this Will Hoskins fellow is filling your head with quite a few stories. There is no war and yellow fever comes from mosquitoes, or something like that, not people. And finally, nice little girls don't go around saying *goddamned Yankee*, either."

"I'm not nice," Lizzie said with defiance. "Who wants to be nice?"

Now, there's a question, Kelly thought. Nice hadn't gotten her very far either. "Well, never mind. Let's just get to your house and then I promise I'll give you a gift in return, though it may take a few days for it to arrive."

"You can't do magic, like right now?"

Kelly shook her head. "Nope. It takes time."

"What kind of fairy are you?"

"I'm not a fairy. I'm a woman."

"You just said you flew, and I saw you fall out of the air. You wasn't there and then ya was. It was magic. I saw it happen right before my very eyes, and ain't nobody can tell me what I saw, but me!"

"Okay, okay," Kelly soothed, trying not to upset the child any more. "I don't know what happened either. That's why I'd like to speak with an adult." Feeling a couple droplets land on her shoulders, she looked up at the sky, and added, "Can you walk a little faster, Lizzie?"

Lizzie grabbed her wrist again and began a faster pace. "I knows what happened. I captured a Yankee fairy, and now you's gonna pay up."

Holding up the hem of her gown with her free hand, Kelly marched quickly behind the child. Why couldn't she break through to her? Perhaps when she got to Lizzie's house, she would find some sanity . . . and a chance to get out of the rain that was beginning to come down more heavily. Kelly could now see the woods' edge and a dirt road ahead of them.

"Is it much farther, Lizzie?"

"Naw," the child answered. "Just down the road a piece this ways, hey . . ." She stopped and put her hands on her hips. "You sure ya can't git tiny 'fore we get there?"

"Nope, I can't get tiny, but I'll tell you this . . . if I get any more wet, I may just be growing out of a shrinking dress." Rain began pelting them harder without the cover of tree limbs, and Kelly shaded her eyes with her hands. "C'mon, Lizzie . . . I'll race you!"

"Oh no, yer tryin' to trick me and get—"

"No, Lizzie, really . . . I can't fly away," Kelly interrupted, thinking quickly. "You caught me, and it's just like you say, fair's fair. I have to stay with you now . . . to grant your wishes."

Before Kelly could even take her first step, Lizzie chimed, "Okay, one-two-three-*go*!" And bolted down the dirt road laughing uproariously.

"Why you . . ." Kelly gulped, and began running. "Hey, what happened to *fair's fair*?" she called out as she saw the child make a sharp right dash behind a picket fence overgrown with honeysuckle.

She slowed to a jog at the spot where Lizzie had disappeared. In a huge field, where she could see Lizzie still running, Kelly saw a two-story house with a wide wraparound porch. Grabbing up her skirt again, she quickened her stride. Getting closer to the house, she could see it was in disrepair, as though no one had put any care into it for many years. White paint was peeling from the clapboard siding, and azaleas were choked by weeds in wide garden beds. A black shutter hung lopsided from one hinge at an upstairs window. Kelly thought it had to have been beautiful at one time, but right now it didn't look too promising.

"This is your house?" she puffed as she caught up to Lizzie, who was now waiting in the side yard.

"Shhh," Lizzie instructed with a finger to her lips. "We'll go 'round back and I'll git Mammy Clara, then ya gots to give me my first wish. Make my daddy let me keep ya."

"Honey, you can't keep—"

"I found ya, so yer mine now. 'Sides, I won the race. Fair's fair!"

She was too close to help from an adult now to argue with this child any more. "Right. Fair's fair," Kelly softly whispered down to the child, then prodded, "okay, let's go."

"We gots to be real quiet so's not to disturb Daddy. If'n he finds ya, there'll be hell to pay for us both."

Nodding, Kelly allowed herself to be led by the child with a mouth on her that belied her innocent age. Whatever it took to find help, she reminded herself.

Walking around the large house, Kelly could see it once had been really lovely as more flowers struggled to peek through the strangulation of weeds. The whole place looked unloved, as though someone had turned their back on it. She saw an old-fashioned water pump close to the house and a chicken coop at the back of the yard, and, beyond that, what looked to be an outhouse. *Wow, these people really are living the simple life. Well, who am I to judge?* Kelly mentally reproached herself. *Yeah, I appear out of nowhere asking for help, looking like something the cat dragged in from the rain, wearing a lime-colored bridesmaid's gown and pretending to be an imaginative child's "fairy." Could it get any more bizarre?*

"You wait here," Lizzie commanded as she leapt up the stairs onto a small porch and paused before what had to be the back door of the old house.

Stepping under the eave of the roof, Kelly nodded and began an attempt to make herself somewhat presentable by smoothing her wet hair behind her ears. She watched as

Lizzie flung back the wooden door and bounded into the house, leaving the door open behind her.

"Mammy Clara! You ain't never gonna believe what happened, but ya gots to believe me 'cause it's the truth and now I needs your help and you—"

"Calm down, chile." Kelly heard the woman's voice chide. "What have you got churnin' in that head a yours now?"

"Mammy Clara . . . I found me a fairy!"

Sheesh, I am going to have to come up with some fantastic presents for that kid to make up for the disappointment, she thought. Kelly nearly laughed out loud.

"A fairy, you say?" The woman's voice was soft and Southern and very patient.

"In the woods. She just done appeared to me, and I caught her!"

"Chile, chile . . ."

"I'm tellin' the truth! Mammy Clara, I am! And she's right there, if'n ya don't believe me! Go on and look . . . but you gotta promise not to tell Daddy!"

Kelly heard soft footsteps and began readying herself with a smile for the introduction.

"Now slow down, Lizzie, I'm goin'. I'm not as quick as . . ." The woman's voice trailed off as her eyes met Kelly's. ". . . I used to be . . . Lord have mercy."

Kelly stood in equal shock as the small, older black woman appeared in the doorway wearing a green kerchief wound tightly around her head and knotted at the top. She was dressed in a white blouse, with the sleeves rolled up, exposing arms covered in white powder. Her long brown skirt and white apron were covered in the dust as well. The woman continued to stare wide-eyed as Lizzie peeked out from behind her.

"See? I told ya!" the child blurted excitedly.

"Hello," Kelly murmured, sticking her hand out while trying to keep her truly perplexed reaction from becoming evident. Why was the woman dressed like that? *Well, she's probably thinking the same thing of me,* Kelly mentally admonished herself. "Um, hi. My name is Kelly Brennan. I, ah . . . I met Lizzie in the woods," she paused, thinking the woman's silence and expression seemed decidedly as though she'd just seen a ghost. "Ah, I'm afraid I'm lost," Kelly continued, "could you tell me how to get back to the Tyler Mansion?"

"Lordy, lordy," the woman slowly mumbled, and held the door open wider. "Gave me a shock to see you standin' there. I'm sorry, thought you was someone else for a moment."

Seeing the way the woman was scrutinizing her, Kelly brushed the skirt of her gown and explained, "I was in a wedding."

"Come in out of the rain and set yourself down Miz Brennan."

"Thank you," Kelly said with a grateful smile as she walked up the three steps into the kitchen. Lizzie grabbed her hand and led her into the room. It was warm and cozy, and Kelly could see that the woman had been baking, as bowls and flour were spread out over the table. "I'm sorry to interrupt you like this," Kelly said turning back to the woman, "but I'm not from around here, and I seem to have gotten a little lost. Lizzie was kind enough to bring me—"

"I brought her home 'cause she's gonna grant me my wishes, Mammy Clara. That's the rules, and fair is—"

"Hush, chile, and let the lady speak," the woman gently reprimanded Lizzie while wiping her hands on her apron.

Kelly smiled to the woman and went on. "I just need to use your phone to call a cab, then I'll be on my way."

"You promised!" Lizzie nearly screeched until she realized she hadn't followed her own advice. *"You promised you wouldn't go!"* she added, correcting herself with a whisper.

"Elizabeth! Hush now and let us give this lady some room to breathe." The woman pulled out a chair at the table and looked to Kelly. "Set yourself down, Miz Brennan. Can I get you some lemon water?"

Gingerly seating herself, Kelly smiled again to the older woman, then glanced at Lizzie, who was now glaring back at her, as though she'd been betrayed. "Yes, that would be very nice, thank you."

The woman lifted a dish towel from a pitcher and filled a glass with opaque water. Kelly unconsciously licked her lips as it was placed in front of her at the table. "Thank you very much," she murmured again, not realizing just how thirsty she was until that moment. The water tasted heavenly, without that chemical aftertaste she was so used to. It probably came from a well, maybe from that old-fashioned pump in the backyard Kelly remembered seeing.

"Now, what's this you be wantin' to use?" the woman asked with interest as she placed her hands on her hips, as though very tired.

"Your telephone, if I may. I need to call a cab, or if you could just kindly point me in the direction of the Tyler Mansion . . ."

"I done told her twice already there ain't no such Tyler place, an' she won't listen."

"I said, hush," the woman firmly scolded the child. Kelly was pleased to see that Lizzie might finally mind someone as she pouted while crossing her arms over her chest.

Turning back to Kelly, the woman named Clara said, "So far as I know, there ain't no such place in these here parts, Miz. This here's the only home for quite some ways. How far you come?"

"Oh, but it can't be that far away. I didn't really walk any great distance before I met Lizzie. But I seem to have gotten turned around at this huge tree . . . it was at least eight feet across and dripping with Spanish moss . . . in this small wooded area . . . and the wedding I was attending was right around there . . . The Tyler Mansion. It's a huge place. You must know it."

The woman appeared decidedly confused and shook her head.

"Okay, it's an old place, kind of like a hotel, that's rented for parties and . . ." Kelly paused. The silent, glazed look on the woman's face convinced her to backtrack to her original question. "You do have a phone, don't you?"

Kelly watched as Clara continued staring at her while mouthing the strange word as though saying it would help her understand what one was.

"A *telephone.*" Kelly said the word with emphasis to make sure she was understood.

"Tele-phone, tele-phone . . ." Clara said, shaking her head. "I'm sorry, Miz Brennan, I don't rightly know what that is."

Where the hell was she? In a place where time stood still? No phone? She'd heard stories about people who withdrew from civilization, but this was nuts. How could anyone on the planet not know what a phone was?

"I knows about a tele-graph," Clara said, as though it might be helpful.

"She's a Yankee!" Lizzie whispered, as if it were some dark secret that explained their difficulty in communicating.

"Ain't no reason to be rude, Lizzie." Turning her attention back to Kelly, she charmingly smiled. "Nearest town is over seven miles away," the woman said, and paused, looking down at Kelly's green-dyed satin pumps. She then added, "I can see you ain't been walkin' too far in them shoes, so just how did you come by here, Miz Brennan?"

"Please, call me Kelly. I've told you, I was in a wedding party at the Tyler Mansion and I walked into the woods for a few minutes and then . . ." And then what? Fell through a disappearing tree?

"And then she just came outta nowhere, Mammy Clara. She said she was flyin'! I found her, and she belongs to me. I'm keepin' her!"

Both women looked at Lizzie, who was sticking her dirty hand into the dough in the bowl.

Quick as an arrow, Clara flipped her towel at the child's arm and Lizzie pulled back in surprise. "Don't you be stickin' them hands in my sweet-roll dough."

"Yes'm." Lizzie rubbed her arm, then stuck out her chin. "But I'm keepin' her just the same. Ain't no one can take her from me now. I captured the fairy queen, and she's gotta grant me all my wishes."

"Lizzie . . ." Again, Kelly pleaded with the child for reasoning. "I'm not a fairy."

"How'd you do it then, if'n ya ain't got magic?" Lizzie continued the cross-examination.

Kelly just shook her head in frustration with the stubborn child.

"I saw ya fall through the air. Weren't nobody there, and then ya was. That's magic."

"Look, I . . . I don't know what happened." She glanced imploringly to the older woman. "Can you please try to tell her?"

Clara wiped her hands on her apron again and sighed. "Well I just don't know, Miz Kelly. This chile's got a good imagination, but I ain't never known her to lie. She's like her momma that way," the woman paused and her voice softened as she added, "God rest her soul."

"You can't believe I'm . . . *a fairy!" What is it with these people?*

"Well Miz Kelly, my senses is tellin' me there's somethin' here that just ain't right. I ain't never heard of them things you been talkin' 'bout . . . no Tyler Mansion, no big ole mossy tree in these woods, and no telly phone . . ." The woman paused, giving Kelly the once-over again, then remarked, "And I surely never seen a dress an' shoes like that before." The woman pulled a chair out from under the table and slowly sat down across from Kelly. "You best tell Clara everything that happened . . . everything you can remember," she added confidently.

"I knew you'd believe me!" Lizzie hollered, jumping up and down. "She's the fairy queen, I tell ya!"

Clara reached out to grab one of Lizzie's arms as she exuberantly spun around in circles. "Chile, if you don't stop your pounding your da—" As the woman's word dropped off, Kelly's attention was immediately drawn away from Lizzie and to the spooked look on Clara's face.

"I caught her, and now I can get my—"

"What's this ruckus in here? Mammy Clara, I'm trying to work. Can't you keep this child quiet for—"

Lizzie's exuberant disruption had obscured the sound of a door opening and footsteps entering. Kelly turned in the direction of the stern voice, and what she saw took her breath away.

"Uh-huh," Clara whispered officiously. "Like I was sayin',

your daddy is gonna be madder than a swarm a bees at a honey gatherin'."

Their gazes locked, and Kelly watched as the man's scowl was instantly replaced with a look of such bewilderment it sent shivers down her spine. Her mouth dropped open in shock. Her heart slammed into her chest wall. Her brain told her it couldn't be. Her heart yelled that it couldn't be anything else.

Tall with dark straight hair brushed back from his face, he stood in the doorway and continued to stare at her with those wide blue eyes . . . eyes she would know anywhere.

It was Michael.

Two

Stunned, Kelly gripped the edge of the wooden table and whispered his name in disbelief. . . .

"Michael . . . ?"

Clara came around the table and stood beside her. "Mistah Daniel, this here is Miz Kelly Brennan. Your Lizzie came upon her lost in the woods and brought her here."

The man glanced to Lizzie and then back at Kelly. "Who are you?" he demanded, as though still shocked by her appearance in his home.

Kelly took a deep breath, realizing that Clara had called him Daniel. Of course it couldn't be Michael. Michael was dead and . . . and this man just resembled her late husband, that's all. She really was on the other side of the looking glass if she thought her dead husband was living in the deep South, raising a child and . . .

"Who are you?" he repeated, with greater resonance.

She blinked several times and dryly swallowed before answering. "I . . . I'm Kelly Brennan, and I was telling Clara that I was attending a wedding at the Tyler Mansion, not too far from here, when I walked away into the woods for a few moments and I must have turned myself around. Now I'm lost. If someone could just help me get back, I would be most grateful." There. She'd gotten it out all in one breath.

The man walked out of the shadow of the doorway and closer to her. Kelly reached for the glass of lemon water and raised it to her lips. Why was her hand trembling, she wondered, pressing the glass closely to her chest to try and conceal the movement.

"I am not aware of any Tylers around here," he said formally. "Only in New Orleans."

Kelly could feel the man's intensity as he stood not ten feet away and continued staring at her. She supposed he rarely saw a woman in his kitchen dressed in an absolutely crazy-looking gown and mumbling about being lost.

Could she blame him for staring?

On closer inspection, she could see he was older than Michael, maybe in his late thirties, with fine lines around his brooding blue eyes. There were threads of gray at his temples, and his mouth wasn't as gentle as her late husband's. His clothes weren't like anything Michael would wear either. A black vest hung unbuttoned over a loose, collarless white-linen shirt, and his dark, baggy trousers were well wrinkled, as though he'd been sitting in them for quite some time. Everything, including his demeanor, appeared to droop tiredly from his tall frame, probably making him look much older than his actual years. Still, from afar and in the shadows, the resemblance to Michael was enough to be a shock. In a flash of emotion, everything she had buried, threatened to come to the surface, and she held the glass tighter to her chest, as if the action might ease the pounding of her heart.

"The closest town is seven miles from here," the man continued in a serious voice. "Oakville?"

"No, no," Kelly shook her head, in an attempt to dislodge the past and gather her wits. "It's not that far from here. I know I didn't wander seven miles. The Tyler Mansion is an old Southern house you can rent for parties . . . it's a huge place—"

He shook his head slowly, still staring into her eyes. "I'm

very sorry, Miss . . . Miss Brennan, I've never heard of anyone named Tyler in this parish. And there is no mansion that you speak of . . . perhaps you're thinking of someone in New Orleans?"

He was handsome in a distracted way, and his softly accented words seemed polite.

"I told her that, Daddy. Ain't no Tyler house in these here parts!"

"Lizzie . . . How many times do I have to tell you that if you speak, speak correctly?"

The child seemed to shrink under her father's reprimand, and she slid behind Clara's skirt. "Yes, sir."

Suddenly feeling very protective of Lizzie, Kelly interjected, "Your daughter has been very kind to me, Mr. Gilmore."

He seemed to ignore her compliment as he turned, looking out the window to the rain. Sighing heavily, he responded, "You are welcome to rest here, Miss Brennan. It's getting too dark to start traveling now, and it looks as though we're in for a storm." He paused, then inhaled sharply, as though pulling himself out of a momentary trance, and looked back to her. "Clara will see to your comfort, and tomorrow a packet will take you to New Orleans. Perhaps you can find what you are seeking there." Bowing slightly, he quickly turned to leave the room.

"Excuse me," she called after him.

When he stopped, Kelly went on, "Thank you for the hospitality, but I can't stay here. I have to get back to my party. Don't you have a telephone, or a car, or something?"

Only the pelting rain against the house penetrated the silence that followed her words. The sound became almost deafening as his pause lingered. Kelly sensed his actions indicated he was more than distracted about something, for he seemed troubled, maybe by her presence, and that only strengthened her resolve to leave. The sooner, the better.

"You know, a means of communication?" Her voice fell off softly.

Turning his head only slightly to address her, he finally answered. "We don't have any of these things you speak of,

Miss Brennan. You are welcome for supper and to spend the night with us, if you wish. Beyond that . . . I cannot help you."

He walked through the door and closed it firmly behind him.

"You did it," Lizzie whispered with great excitement as she crept closer to Kelly. "You got Daddy to let you stay!"

Kelly was still staring at the closed door. How rude! Well, he wasn't exactly rude, just uninterested, as though her predicament was beneath him.

"Mistah Daniel got a whole lotta things on his mind," Clara said, as though reading Kelly's thought. "And he ain't used to company, is all. Been a while since we had some here," the kind woman added with a smile.

"I can tell," Kelly answered. "Well, I can't stay, so I guess I'll just start walking when the rain lets up."

Clara leaned her hands on the table, and asked, "Where you gonna walk to, Miz Kelly? Ain't nothing but the bayou with them gators and water mocs out there. You best spend the night, then go with the packet when it comes tomorrow."

Kelly felt like her mind was reeling, as if her world, the sane world, was slipping away. "I can't stay here, Clara."

"Sure enough you can. I'll open a room and make up a bed for you. You gonna want to eat before this night is over, Miz Kelly, and I be cookin' fried chicken for supper."

"You promised!" Lizzie accused. "You said you would stay!"

She had almost forgotten about the child. Staring into Lizzie's eyes, she said, "Honey, I told you I have to get back and—"

"I hope them gators git you then!" Lizzie pouted, stomping her foot loudly on the old wooden floor.

Kelly looked up to Clara. "You were kidding about them, right?"

The woman shook her head as she went back to kneading her dough. "Them gators is out there, all right . . . but if I was you, I'd be more worried 'bout the water mocs."

Kelly nearly jumped at the sound the wad of dough made when the woman slapped it on the table with emphasis.

"I nevah liked snakes . . . and they likes to come up, outta everywhere 'round here when it's rainin'," Clara continued, beginning to roll the dry, flaky dough with vigor. "And I reckon, the quickest way to Oakville is back through them woods you say you already came from." She nodded to Kelly, and added, "You understand what I'm sayin' here, Miz?"

Kelly shuddered and nodded in return. She hated snakes, too, and just the thought of walking all alone in a place that had snakes and alligators was enough to make up her mind. What else was she to do? She had no idea where she was or how to get back to civilization, and her plane didn't take off until late tomorrow afternoon. Glancing out the kitchen window to the darkened sky and pouring rain, she figured she had to spend the night somewhere. . . .

"Okay, I'll stay," she said to the sulking Lizzie. "But just for one night."

The child's eyes lit with pleasure, and Kelly couldn't help smiling at her. "You sure your father's not going to be upset?" Just thinking of the man and his resemblance to Michael caused a shiver of yearning to race through her body. It reminded her of when Michael would kiss the back of her neck. Now, that was surely craziness!

Clara spoke up as she slapped another mound of dough onto the floured board. "Aw, Mistah Daniel's bark is worse than his bite," she said reassuringly. " 'Bout time this old house had some company . . . besides, 'tween these two"— the woman tilted her head to indicate the child standing behind her, and the door where Mr. Gilmore had just walked out, she continued—"I could use hearin' a different voice." Picking up the rolling pin and pointing it toward Kelly, she added, "Maybe you showin' up is like this chile says . . . some magic."

"I knew'd you believe me, Mammy Clara," Lizzie spouted with glee.

"Chile, I believe in a whole lotta things there ain't no way of explainin'," the older woman declared as she began spreading the dough. "Miz Kelly says she's lost. You say you found her. I been around long enough to know I ain't got all the answers." Then she added with a soothing tone, "But what I do know is ain't nothin' happenin' here, or anywhere else for that matter, that ain't got a reason." Clara paused, then looked back up at Kelly and smiled comfortingly. "You is supposed to be here, Miz Kelly, so's you might as well make the best of it while you is."

Kelly didn't know how to respond to the woman. Blinking for a few seconds, she pondered the concept. She was *supposed* to be lost, in a wet, lime green gown, in the middle of nowhere and basically forced to impose upon a somewhat backward family? Where's the magic in that? She didn't want to know the reason why. It was just too bizarre.

"Lizzie Gilmore, if you wants to join your daddy and Miz Kelly for supper, you best git a move on and git you a bath. 'Cause you already know, ain't no way your daddy is gonna allow you at his table lookin' like that."

"A bath?" Lizzie asked in horror, as she stared at Clara.

"Uh-huh." The older woman nodded as she continued cutting harder into the flattened dough with a tin cup. "And a dress."

"I ain't wearin' no dress!"

"Then you ain't settin' at the table. You can eat right here in the kitchen like you do every night. Ain't no skin off my back which way you choose."

Lizzie scowled and crossed her arms over her chest.

"It'd be a shame, is all, you eatin' in here . . . seein' as we got company tonight," Clara murmured as though absent-mindedly. "Maybe Miz Kelly would help you," she added with a wink.

"Oh, yes," Kelly piped up. "Whatever I can do to help." It had also dawned on her that she didn't have her purse, or anything else to prove who she was, so helping Lizzie with her bath seemed like small payment for dinner and lodging. "I can set the table and help you with the cooking and—"

"I does the cooking 'round here," Clara said with a wider smile on her face as she grabbed the door handle of the cast-iron oven with her apron. "If you wants to set the table and help that sorry excuse of a girl over there with a bath, I'd sure appreciate the help."

"Of course," Kelly said, as she stood up and brushed a strand of hair back behind her ear. "Where's the bathroom?"

Bent over the stove, Clara stopped stoking the fire. Standing, she looked at Kelly with a quizzical expression. "The room for the bath is right here. Lizzie"—she prodded the child with a nudge on her back—"show Miz Brennan where the tub is. The two of you can manage."

With a great show of resentment, Lizzie stomped over to a door and threw open the wide panels. "It's in there," she said with disgust, and pointed through the doorway.

Kelly couldn't believe it when she peeked into the small closet. An oval copper tub . . . on wheels, and there wasn't a faucet in sight.

This was going to be something.

"You mean there isn't any running water in the house?" Kelly asked in a hushed voice. She knew it was impolite, yet her curiosity was getting the better of her. Why were these people living like this? Okay, so maybe they couldn't afford kitchen appliances, but how did people survive with no telephone, electricity, or plumbing? This was the new millennium, after all.

"We got running water, right there," Clara said, pointing to an old-fashioned pump. Kelly had noticed it earlier, but thought it was an antique decoration.

"I mean in a bathroom. You know, a tub and faucets with hot running water."

Clara shook her head. "Where you from, Miz Kelly, that has hot water running?"

Kelly chuckled. "I'm from the modern world . . . the year 2001?"

Clara slowly straightened her back and repeated the question as though she'd totally misunderstood the answer. "Where you say?"

"The year 2001. You know, the new millennium?" This was a joke, right?

The older woman's wide-eyed stare almost made Kelly laugh out loud.

"Miz Kelly," Clara whispered as if in confidentiality toward someone who was about to be involuntarily committed to an asylum, "this here is the year 1888."

She shook her head, now beginning to laugh. "No . . . it can't . . . I mean you're just . . . confused, or something. I happen to know the year. Everyone knows the year, Clara—2001. Nobody could forget the millennium, all the celebrations . . . remember?"

"Miz Kelly," Clara repeated in an insistent voice, "this here's the year 1888, and I'm certain of that. 'Cause it's been twenty-five years since I lost my man and my boy Clevis in the war, and ten years since this chile's momma died of the yellow fever. I may not know 'bout a lotta things, but I knows how long we all been grievin' in this here house. That's somethin' nobody forgets."

Kelly sank back down onto her chair. There was a strange look in Clara's eyes and a tone to her voice that seemed to pierce right through Kelly's mind and soul. It scared her, and a terrible feeling of dread frizzled along her nerve endings. This old woman was telling the truth, at least *her* truth. "Wait a minute, Clara," she whispered in a frightened voice. "This can't be happening. You can't be living in 1888!"

"And why not? I know where I am," Clara said pointedly with one eyebrow raised.

"Because that's . . ." She did the mental calculation. ". . . that's a hundred and thirteen years ago! It . . . it's crazy!"

"You flew through time!" Lizzie proclaimed. "And I caught ya! Ain't this like that book Daddy was telling you about, Mammy Clara . . . huh, ain't it?"

"Hush, chile . . . can't you see Miz Kelly is upset now?" Clara wiped her hands on her apron and came to stand in front of Kelly. "Don't trouble yourself with this now, Miz Brennan. You can't dwell on it . . . you gots to get up and busy yourself. I know I ain't crazy, and so far I don't think you is either. This here's the year 1888, and if what you're sayin' and what Lizzie says is true . . . maybe you is being blessed somehow, and meant to be here with us. Don't you go losin' it on me, until we figure out what to do with you."

Kelly stared at them and would have laughed, except they both looked so serious. She could write off the child's excited fantasies, but Clara seemed so normal, so steady and calm. What was this woman thinking? "You can't be serious. You can't truly believe I . . . I've *time traveled* from the year 2001 to 1888! That's . . . absolutely ludicrous!"

"Don't know what that word means, but that don't matter. There ain't nothin' or nobody here that's crazy, Miz Kelly," Clara stated firmly. I believe this chile when she says you came outta nowhere, and I believe you is from where you say. I ain't got no reasons not to. 'Sides, I knows my man still watches close over me, and I'd a known by now if you was trouble, and you ain't. But there's a storm brewin' outside that's just chock-full a trouble, and I reckon there ain't no hurry in you gettin' back out there in it."

Kelly found herself speechless and only able to shake her head in denial of what she was hearing. As though sensing her confusion, the older woman gently took Kelly's hands into hers and spoke more tenderly. "Gettin' busy right now is what we needs to do. Take our minds off a things a while. It'll all unravel in its own good time, Miz Kelly. Right now, if you could help this chile look like the little girl she really is, maybe her daddy will pay more attention to her. Maybe that'd bring him back to life some, and then this ole woman can finally release them both and go *home*." Clara emphasized the final word.

Still stunned, Kelly stared into the woman's eyes, then desperately muttered, "I have no clue what you're talking about."

Clara's smile was meant to be reassuring.

As nice a woman as she seemed to be, the gesture wasn't comforting.

"I know you don't, Miz Kelly. I ain't got the answers, but I've seen too many things out in these woods that ain't nobody can explain. Still, you gots to have faith . . . you is where you is supposed to be." The kind old woman squeezed Kelly's hands, then let them go.

"Come on, Clara . . . you're obviously an intelligent woman. *Time travel?* You must understand that's imposs—"

"Only thing I understand right now is this chile needs a bath, and I'm gettin' too old to carry this by myself. This arthur in my hip ain't gettin' any better," Clara said as she patted her right side. "I been prayin' too many long years and it's 'bout time the Lord heard me. You comin' along is some kind a magic for me." The woman turned back to the stove and began taking her own advice to keep busy. "The pot for boilin' the water is on the wall there." She indicated with a nod as Kelly watched her put the first batch of rolls into the old oven. "Bring it on over here and fill it, then we'll get it to warmin' on the stove."

Kelly kept blinking her eyes, really trying to keep her own faith that this nightmare would end. On top of everything she'd already gone through today, now an old black woman with arthritis has been praying for help and she thinks she's found it? How nuts was that? Unable to think of any way to get back to civilization at the moment, Kelly made up her mind not to discuss it any further. No sense in adding to the insanity. She would help out and in the morning find her way back to reality. It was either that or face the alligators and snakes.

Slowly rising from the table again, Kelly looked at Lizzie, and said, "C'mon, let's get your bath started."

Talk about a fiasco.

When she originally agreed to help, Kelly had no idea she was going to get a crash course in pioneer life. She had hand-pumped the water into a large pot, boiled it on an antique stove fueled by wood, carried it across the room, and dumped it in the tub. After the fourth potful, she figured it was just the right amount to clean a little girl. How dirty could she really be?

Then began the race.

Around and around the kitchen table and then around Mammy Clara, who at that point simply kept on cooking and mumbling, "Thank you, Lord" under her breath. To Lizzie, this had obviously turned into a grand game. When Kelly had finally caught the child, she picked her up and carried her like a sack of potatoes across the room, then plopped her down in the tub, fully clothed. She'd won.

But it wasn't over yet. She had to wrestle the kid to remove her dirty overalls, while at the same time, keep her safely in the tub. Scrubbing mud and berry stains from nearly every inch of the little girl's body, Kelly had been soaked by deliberate splashes of water, got soap in her eyes, and now her knees were sore from being on the floor to keep the girl in the tub.

Finally, Kelly surrendered and leaned against the wall.

"Okay, Lizzie. I think you're clean enough. You can get out now."

"Aw, do I hafta?" the child asked, sitting quietly.

Kelly exhaled deeply and looked down at the very wet floor. "Sweet surrender," she sighed. "I'd say you won the second round, kiddo."

Lizzie beamed at Kelly. Scrubbed clean, the child looked rather angelic.

"Supper's almost ready. Best be hurrin' along now, chile," Mammy Clara called out.

Reluctantly, Lizzie rose out of the cloudy water and began shaking her arms, spraying more droplets around. Kelly grabbed the towel that Clara had brought over during Lizzie's "rinse stage" and quickly wrapped it around her. As she helped to dry the child, Kelly felt a surge of tenderness start to rise up within her. The innocence of the child's clean, young body stirred a deep compassion. She was just a child, a troubled child. Imagine losing a mother so young. No wonder Lizzie was such a toughie.

"Okay, where are your clothes?"

Lizzie scowled. "I ain't wearin' no dress," she mumbled.

"Oh, yes you is," Clara again called out over her shoulder. The old woman was standing at the stove, frying chicken in a sizzling skillet. "If'n you don't, you is gonna miss all the interestin' conversation you didn't hear 'cause you was too stubborn and settin' in this here kitchen eatin' your supper."

Lizzie, wrapped in the long towel, stomped her bare foot. "Dresses are stupid. I'm just eatin'. What difference does it make what clothes I got on to do that?"

"That pretty yellow one your daddy just brought back from New Orleans would be best," Clara responded, as though that was the answer to the child's question.

Lizzie grabbed up the dragging towel around her and stormed out of the room, just as another distant roll of thunder accompanied her mood.

"Should I help her?" Kelly asked, brushing the back of her hand across her forehead.

"Oh, she can dress her own self. She just puts up a fuss. You done the hardest part, Miz Kelly. But when she comes back down, you could fix her hair. That would be a help."

"Of course," Kelly answered, staring down at the tub and her soaking wet dress. It wasn't enough being rained on, then waterlogged from bathing a rambunctious child . . . she was now sweating from all the exertion and the heat of the kitchen. She quickly reconsidered her fleeting thought. A bath for herself would have to wait until she got back to her hotel. "Ah, how do you empty this?"

Clara turned around and stared at her. "You sure is a puzzle, Miz Kelly. You push it to the door and you unplug it."

"You do?" How the heck would she know something like that? In her sane world there was indoor plumbing, and air-conditioning. *No, don't think*, she told herself. *Keep busy until you can fall into a bed and sleep*. In the morning she would leave this place and regain sanity. Right now she would take Clara's advice and not go there.

Determined, Kelly pushed the copper tub to the door and, after she opened it, she unplugged the drain and watched as the water ran out onto the first step and down into the ground. Raising her face, she looked out to the darkening sky and deeply inhaled the cool, rainy breeze. What did it matter if her dress was watermarked, if her hair was hanging in sweat-stained streaks? Nothing mattered right now, except the sound of the rain. She closed her eyes and exhaled slowly.

Immediately, her mind ran the picture of Lizzie's father walking into the kitchen. Dear God, at first glance she really thought she had seen Michael . . . for just a moment. What was with that? Later she could tell herself that both had been tall and dark-haired, same strong lean build, same high cheekbones and square jaw. It was structural resemblance, that's all. Actually, on closer inspection, Daniel Gilmore was nothing at all like her late husband . . . yet, just being in his presence had been enough to reawaken those surges of yearning. How long had it been since she was held in a man's strong and warm embrace? How long since she'd felt that deep comfort? A tiny flicker of resentment passed through her that Daniel Gilmore had given life to what was better off buried.

"You can leave that tub there a while," Clara called out from behind her. "That breeze is finally coolin' off this kitchen."

Glad for the distraction, Kelly turned around and placed her hands on her hips. "Okay, what else can I do to help you?"

Clara looked up from her frying pan and grinned at Kelly. "You can set the supper table, if'n you'd like. Everything you need is in the drawers of the cabinet out there." She pointed a long fork toward the door where Lizzie had disappeared.

"All right," Kelly said, making up her mind. It would keep her busy and help Clara.

As she entered the dining room, she swore she overheard Clara saying, "I just knew the Lord was gonna answer all my prayers."

That was another thing Kelly wouldn't think about . . . Clara's weird thoughts about her being sent to this place to help these people. Nothing could be further from the truth. She didn't know exactly how she got here, but she was certain she was leaving in the morning! Kelly walked through a small hallway and looked to her left. The dining room.

Even with the storm and fading light of late afternoon filtering through lace curtains on two tall windows, Kelly could still see it was a marked change from the kitchen. Decorated in classic Victorian period furnishings, it was as if the room had been frozen in time. Kelly suddenly realized the irony in her passing thought and cringed. *Don't go there girl*, she reprimanded herself.

Looking up, she saw a large crystal chandelier hanging from the high ceiling. Her hand fumbled around the wall by the door for an electrical switch, yet she couldn't find one.

No electricity in here either? Shrugging, she spotted a cabinet she figured must be the one that Clara said held everything she needed. As she walked across the room, Kelly sensed the house had definitely had a strong female influence at one time.

The walls were papered in a beige background with intricate vines and fluted flowers of yellow and blue bursting out. White-paneled wainscoating with high baseboards met the waxed wooden floor. A massive mahogany table, heavily polished with ornately carved turrets on each corner, set on top of a large Turkish rug graced the center of the room. Around it were eight high, fan back chairs with leather seat covers and nailhead trim. It was a little too dark for her taste, but she had to admit it was lovely in a plantation setting.

Kelly stood before the tall china cabinet and looked through the beveled-glass doors. She caught a quick breath and hesitated. The entire inside glistened with finery. Etched crystal goblets of all shapes and sizes and various cut-glass bowls filled the shelves. There were even four glass salt troughs, with tiny silver scoops, and a couple of other silver gadgets whose use was lost on Kelly. Two sets of dishes were neatly stacked, with plates carefully leaning against the back mirror in display. It was really quite an impressive collection of antiques.

"Are you sure you want me to set the table with these dishes from the cabinet, Clara?"

She waited for the woman's response. "Sho'nuff, Miz Kelly. What's in there is what we use when we gots company."

Kelly bent over, grasped the poured-glass knob, and pulled open the wide bottom drawer. It was full of beautifully embroidered linen and lace tablecloths. She ran her fingers gently over the top one. Leaving that drawer open, she opened the one above it and lifted a felt cloth that covered the silver flatware. This room and all these things were obviously intended for serious entertaining.

Since the table was so long, she decided to set it all at one end; the head of the table would, of course, be for Mr. Gilmore. Thinking of the man, she turned and looked at the double wooden doors that must separate this room from the rest of the house. She would get a closer look at him later, when she wasn't in shock . . . just to put to rest the notion that he resembled her Michael. Suddenly, her body shuddered.

Keep busy, she told herself again, and pulled out the white-on-white embroidered-linen tablecloth. Within minutes she found herself absorbed in the project of setting the table. Gingerly removing the china from the cabinet, she chose the pattern with delicate blue flowers and gold-embossed trim. She laid the heavy silverware out in respective courses and placed two etched-crystal glasses at each setting; the larger for water, the smaller, she figured, just in case wine was served with dinner. Kelly paused for a moment, then removed one glass from Lizzie's place and put it carefully back into the cabinet. Turning to the table, she stopped and had to smile at herself when she realized she actually enjoyed what she was doing. It had definitely been too long since she'd had an opportunity to use her own good things. Why, she suddenly wondered, were good things only used for company, and not for herself?

The thick aroma of fried chicken now filled the air, and her stomach rumbled with hunger. Truly grateful to be taken in on a stormy night, Kelly resolved to be as much help as possible for the hospitality being shown to her.

"I can't get these darn snarls outta my hair."

Spinning around, she spotted Lizzie standing at the doorway with a wide comb stuck in her damp blond ringlets. The child was dressed in a long, pale yellow dress with a wide white-satin sash. The ends were hanging to the floor.

She actually looked . . . pretty.

"What a lovely dress," Kelly exclaimed as she walked closer to the child. Lizzie could have been in Mel's wedding and quite frankly looked better than she did. Strange that the child was wearing such a long party dress, but then Clara said they didn't have much company, and maybe Lizzie was dressing for the occasion.

"Hmm . . ." was all Lizzie would comment.

"Here, turn around and let me tie your bow."

Lizzie turned slowly and Kelly picked up the satin ends. After fluffing out the bow, she said, "Now, let's see what we can do with that hair. Come into the kitchen, and I'll comb it for you."

"It'll hurt."

"Not the way I'll do it," Kelly promised.

"Daddy ain't gonna like the way you set the table, but I think it's right pretty."

Kelly glanced once more at the room as they passed and was pleased with the view. The table looked very nice indeed. No one had given her any specific instructions. She did the best she could given what she had to work with. If Mr. Gilmore didn't like it . . . tough.

She shuddered with the thought of him again. There was something so impatient about the man, as though he barely tolerated his daughter and that irked Kelly. Lizzie might be a handful, but she was still a good child. "C'mon, kiddo . . . let's untangle that mop."

Seated at the table, with Lizzie standing between her legs, surrounded by lime green watermarked satin, Kelly gently began at the end of the snarls and worked her way up to the child's scalp. It didn't take as long as she thought it would, and Kelly had to admit that Lizzie was very patient. Clara was putting the dinner onto platters and humming softly as the rain pounded outside the door. The scene was quite pleasant, much calmer than earlier, and Kelly was grateful for the respite.

"Okay . . . shall we just let your hair dry, or should I pull it back into a little pony tail? Do you have any rubber bands, Clara?"

The older woman looked at her strangely. "Rubba—what you talking about, Miz Kelly? Tsk, Lizzie, you g'on upstairs and bring down a white ribbon so's Miz Kelly can tie your hair up proper. Now scoot! Supper's about to go on the table."

Sighing, Lizzie stomped away, muttering something about stupid rules.

"Don't you pay that chile no mind, Miz Kelly," Clara whispered, arranging the fried chicken on a silver platter.

"Under all that vinegar is a sweet one. She ain't had it easy in this house. Ain't got nobody for company, but me, really."

"She mentioned Will somebody," Kelly said, standing and walking to the door she'd left open for the bath to drain. The wind was stronger and had begun blowing rain into the house. "Would you like me to close this door now?" Kelly asked as she moved the tub.

"Why yes, Miz Kelly, thank you. I reckon it's cooled off in here enough," Clara said, placing the lid on the platter. "Did you say you knows 'bout the Hoskins boy?"

"Lizzie mentioned some things he had told her. I just figured he was a friend."

"Uh-huh," the woman responded thoughtfully as she turned back to the oven. "Well I knows I ain't got the right to pass judgment on nobody, but I gots to be honest with myself and especially with those I love," Clara insisted as she removed the last baked rolls and placed them on the table. "That chile would do better to stay away from that Hoskins boy. There ain't no friends in any of that family, is my opinion."

"I don't understand. Did he hurt her or something?"

"Well, I'd say so," Clara continued without flinching as she removed the steaming bundles from the iron sheet with her bare hands. "Fillin' any good chile's head with ideas 'bout hate and war is an awful crime. Lord knows it, too."

Kelly suddenly recalled Lizzie's comments about *Yankees* while they were walking through the woods. "Oh, yes, I see what you mean now. She did say a couple of things that were, well . . . questionable in this day and age. And quite frankly, I was a bit shocked with her colorful use of language," Kelly whispered, adding with a wink, "if you catch my drift."

"Mmm," Clara replied knowingly as she dropped the last roll into a huge bowl. "Well, I gots enough to do 'round here, and what with this arthur in my hip, I can't be runnin' off to catch that chile every minute of my day." Covering the bowl with a white-linen towel, she mumbled under her breath, "If'n her daddy paid her more attention, that chile wouldn't be runnin' 'bout with the likes of Will Hoskins."

Kelly nodded with a weak smile. What could she say? This was a private family matter. Regardless of how much she found herself growing fond of Lizzie, she couldn't see the point in becoming embroiled in somebody else's problems. She had her own to deal with. Like getting back to civilization and flying home tomorrow. Time travel, indeed! Kelly cared, but she couldn't save anyone. She'd learned that a long time ago.

Clara picked up the bowl of rolls and added, "So, I just prays for 'em all. That's the most I can do now."

"Here, let me help you carry these out to the table," Kelly offered, placing the comb on a shelf by the tub.

"I sure do appreciate everything you've done, Miz Kelly."

Kelly reached for the server with chicken in it, figuring it would be the heaviest and she'd save Clara the trouble of carrying it. "No problem, Clar—" She was right. It must have weighed thirty pounds. "My goodness," Kelly exclaimed, laughing as she strained. "You'd think there was an army coming to dinner tonight!"

Clara spun around quickly. "There'll be no talk a armies or war 'round this table, you hear, Miz Kelly?" the woman whispered harshly. "Mistah Daniel won't have it. No suh, he won't." She set the bowl down hard on the dining-room table. "Can't say as I blame him, neither."

Slightly taken aback, Kelly stood blinking at the woman. "Okay, Clara. I'm sorry, I meant it as a joke, really."

"There ain't no jokin' 'bout that war," the woman continued as she helped Kelly put the platter down on the table. "Sure did 'nuff damage 'round here."

Instinctively Kelly followed the woman back into the kitchen as she rambled on. "It's been over now twenty-three years, but some, they just don't know how to let things go." Clara picked up two pitchers of lemon water. "I'd surely appreciate it if you would bring them string beans and potatoes out now, Miz Kelly," she said with a more friendly smile.

Kelly was still trying to figure the math in her head. There had been no war in 1977. The last war she could recall that America was involved in was the Persian Gulf War. She also knew the Vietnam War ended more than twenty-three years ago. Kelly watched as the woman hurried out of the kitchen.

"Which war are you referring to, Clara?" she asked as she picked up the dishes.

There was a long pause before the response came back from the dining room. "The War of Northern Aggression Miz Kelly. The Civil War they called it."

Trying very hard to change the annoyed expression she knew was slowly creeping over her face, Kelly looked out the kitchen window and focused on tree limbs bowing in the heavy wind. Clara was a nice lady, and she would humor her, but Kelly was beginning to think the whole day was turning into an episode of the *Twilight Zone*, and she refused to play a part in it anymore.

"Don't know why they called it a Civil War . . . wasn't nothin' civil 'bout it," Clara said as she came back into the kitchen. "But you know what I say, Miz Kelly?" the woman asked, staring directly into Kelly's eyes.

"No, what do you say, Clara?"

" 'Bout time everybody 'round here stopped hangin' on to the past and got on with their lives." The old woman patted Kelly on her arm as though she was now dismissed.

How utterly profound.

"You couldn't be more right," Kelly agreed as she walked out.

Three

"One, one thousand, two, one thousand, three, one thou—*there!*" Lizzie screeched as the thunder cracked and rolled overhead.

"Uh-huh . . . this arthur been tellin' me it's gonna be a strong one, all right." Clara breathed heavily, rubbing her side again. "And it's hurricane season. Sure hope that bayou don't flood again. Lordy, what a mess that was last year."

Kelly placed the bowls on the dining-room table and glanced over at Lizzie, who was standing by the open double doors. Nervously twisting the white ribbon around her little fingers, she looked up at Kelly. The poor kid had an expression on her face that looked as if she didn't know whether to laugh with delight or burst out crying.

"C'mere, Lizzie. I'll tie the ribbon in your hair." She smiled reassuringly at the child, who grinned widely in return as Kelly used the satin ribbon as a hair band.

"Miz Kelly, I thanks you a hundred times for all your help today. I sure appreciate it."

"No problem, Clara. It's the least I could do for all the hospitality."

"Daddy . . ."

Kelly looked up as a great flash of lightning filled the room and illuminated the man in the doorway.

"Evenin', Mistah Daniel. Supper's on the table," Clara said as she passed the man and closed the double doors behind him.

As thunder reverberated around them, she knew it wasn't just the storm. Kelly could swear there was another energy that entered the room with him. Was she the only one who felt it? She stared at him, feeling once more those unwelcome surges of yearning. Just being around the man was causing havoc with her senses. Her entire body was tingling with . . . what? Attraction? She certainly didn't need this right now, yet she couldn't deny what her body was telling her. It went beyond irritating to scary. Why him? Just because he barely resembled her dead husband? She had to pull herself together!

He had brushed his straight, brown hair back from his face and was wearing an old-fashioned jacket and a thick tie. Kelly acknowledged he certainly was handsome, in a haunting sort of way, and was about to greet him when he surveyed the table and scowled.

"Who did this?" he demanded.

Tying off the ribbon to Lizzie's hair, Kelly glanced at Clara and swallowed tightly. "I did. I'm sorry if I set it incorrectly."

"You did a beautiful job," Clara remarked, quickly coming to her defense. "And I surely am grateful for the help I had 'round here today." Looking up at her boss, she stuck out her chin and handed him a box. "We gots a guest for supper, Mistah Daniel, and the candles needs lightin'. I ain't been bent over that stove all day to have it served in the dark like slop."

He took the box from Clara and withdrew a long match. "I was just asking, Clara."

"Well, you been answered," she shot back.

Kelly almost wanted to laugh at how well Clara put this man in his place. There was no doubt who was running this house at dinnertime.

"How come there's another place?" Lizzie asked, pointing across the table.

Kelly's gaze connected with the man's, as though again she'd done something wrong. "Well, there are four of us." She looked to Clara.

The older woman's eyes softened for a moment as she reached for the place setting and began removing it. "I'll be eatin' in the kitchen, but I thanks you, Miz Kelly."

The finality in the old woman's voice made it very clear. Kelly couldn't help but feel badly as she watched Clara gather up the dishes and walk back into the kitchen. It seemed so unfair to have Clara eat alone in the kitchen during such a storm, but then it wasn't her place to say anything more.

"You may sit down now, Elizabeth," the man said as he finished lighting the candles.

"Yes, sir," Lizzie meekly answered, pulling out the chair in front of her.

Kelly sat next to Lizzie and put her napkin on her lap. The child watched Kelly's movements and did the same. She could tell Lizzie didn't eat this formally with her father very often. Smiling down to Lizzie, she waited until Daniel Gilmore took his place at the head of the table.

Once seated, he seemed uncomfortable as they all waited in silence.

"Ain't we gonna say grace?"

"*Aren't we going* to say grace," father corrected daughter, and then seemed even more agitated. "Yes. You may say it, Elizabeth."

"Okay," Lizzie answered, bowing her head.

Kelly did the same.

"We be most grateful for this food," she began in a timid voice. "And for bringing Miz Kelly Brennan to us and for Mammy Clara and her hip not flarin' up worse than it is, and for . . ." she hesitated, ". . . and for Daddy."

Kelly smiled and lifted her head to look at Daniel Gilmore. "Amen." For just a moment their gazes met, and Kelly felt her stomach flutter with excitement as Daniel stared deeply into her eyes.

He appeared embarrassed as he looked away and muttered, "Amen."

Lizzie looked most pleased. "Amen."

Recovering quickly, Kelly grinned at the child. What was that about with her father?

"Shall we begin?" Daniel finally said, reaching for the platter of chicken.

He held it toward Kelly. "Thank you, Mr. Gilmore," she said in a surprisingly steady voice. Now was not the time to figure out what the man's stare meant. She placed a breast on her plate and when Lizzie held up hers, she asked, "Which piece would you like, sweetie?"

"I likes the bosoms, too."

"You also would *like* a *breast*, Elizabeth," Daniel Gilmore once more corrected.

"Okay. That's what I like."

Kelly wanted to laugh, but she bit her lip and served Lizzie the other breast. Handing the platter back to the man, her fingers brushed his and she heard him quickly inhale, as if he was shocked by the contact. "Everything smells wonderful. Thank you again for your hospitality, Mr. Gilmore," she breathed, determined to concentrate on her dinner and stop analyzing everything.

"Glad we could be of some assistance to you, ma'am," he answered, taking the platter without looking at her again.

Mentally shrugging, she continued to serve herself and Lizzie, who was seated next to her. Mashed potatoes with perfect gravy, string beans seasoned with bacon fat and chopped onions, and Clara's fresh rolls completed the meal. A true Southern meal. Kelly's stomach growled loudly, and Lizzie giggled.

"Excuse me," Kelly said in embarrassment. "I didn't realize how hungry I am."

"Me too," Lizzie said, looking to her father, as though for his reaction.

None came.

When everyone was finally served, they began eating through a prolonged silence . . . until Daniel Gilmore broke it.

"Do *not* pick up your chicken with your hands, Elizabeth! Have you no manners at all?"

Startled, Kelly glanced to her side and saw the child quickly drop the chicken back onto her plate.

"I always eat it with my hands," she mumbled, as a blush crept up on her round cheeks.

Kelly instinctively reached over and took Lizzie's napkin and wiped her hands. "Here, honey . . . I'll show you how to cut it, okay?"

Lizzie's chin started to quiver, as though she was about to cry, and Kelly quickly changed the subject while cutting the chicken breast on Lizzie's plate. "You have such a lovely home, Mr. Gilmore. Have you lived here long?"

The man sighed, as though he knew he had created a scene and embarrassed his daughter in the process. "Thank you, Miss Brennan. This home has been in my family for generations."

Minutes went by without any conversation, yet the tension between them was almost palatable.

So much for small talk.

Undeterred, Kelly swallowed the delicious mashed potatoes, and said, "This is only my second trip to the South and I'm very impressed with your hospitality. I don't know what I would have done if your daughter hadn't found me."

The man simply nodded as he chewed and continued staring at his plate.

This is a hard man to have a conversation with, Kelly thought. Another flash of lightning brightened the room. Okay, how about the weather? "It's quite a storm out there. Do you suppose it will last long?"

The man waited until the thunder stopped rolling before giving his answer. "I can't really say, Miss Brennan. It's hurricane season."

Kelly jabbed her fork into some beans. "Not again." She sighed. "I'm supposed to fly home tomorrow."

"Uh-oh."

Kelly glanced up from her plate to Lizzie. When she saw the child's expression, Kelly turned to the man, who was now staring at her.

Daniel Gilmore's mouth was opened in shock. Holding his fork in midair, he rasped, "I beg your pardon?"

Kelly smiled politely. "I was just saying I hope there aren't any cancellations due to the storm. The last time I flew to New Orleans, the same thing happened."

"You *flew* . . . into New Orleans?"

"Uh-oh," Lizzie muttered again, while kicking Kelly under the table.

"Yes. I flew from Philadelphia to New Orleans and back again." Smiling through clenched teeth, Kelly glanced down at Lizzie and squinted a nonverbal warning to stop kicking her.

"Daddy, tell her she's gotta stay. I caught her—"

"Elizabeth! Stop interrupting with your nonsense!"

Kelly was stunned as she observed the tense scene. She thought she should try and diffuse the situation. "Listen, Lizzie's just a little confused," she replied, desperately trying to represent the child. "She's got this fanciful idea that I'm a—"

"Madam . . . people cannot *fly!*" He put his fork back onto his plate and glared at her.

The room flared again with bright white light and, from the corner of her eye, Kelly could see Lizzie was now trembling. She didn't like him taking that tone with his daughter, and she definitely wasn't about to let him speak to her that way. Enough was enough.

"Mr. Gilmore. I certainly know how I arrived in New Orleans. I'm a travel agent and arrange for people to 'fly the friendly skies' all the time!"

The immediate crash of thunder that followed her last words rocked everything in the room, and Kelly nearly jumped out of her chair.

In the silence that followed, she dumbly watched as the man stood up and placed his napkin on the table. Taking a deep breath, as though calming himself, he looked down to his daughter. "Elizabeth, it's time for you to go to bed," he said softly. Turning away, he called out over his shoulder. "Clara, supper was delicious. I'll take my coffee in the study as usual."

"Yes, suh," came the prompt answer from the kitchen.

Kelly blinked and shook her head. Dinner was over? No one had finished! The whole scene was too surreal.

"Look, I'm sorry if I've said anything to offend you. I was just—"

"Good night, Miss Brennan," he interrupted her. Then, without even turning back around, he hesitated in the doorway, and added, "I trust you'll sleep well and feel much better in the morning." He closed the doors firmly behind him.

What was wrong with that guy?

"I believe this is just your size, Miz Kelly," Clara remarked, handing her a folded white-cotton nightgown.

Standing in the bedroom Clara had opened for her, Kelly accepted the delicate nightgown and smiled. "Thank you so much for everything, Clara. You've been very kind. I really hope I haven't made things more difficult for everyone."

The old woman grinned and shook her head as she walked to the bed and turned back the thick coverlet. "Aw, you still broodin' cause Mistah Daniel excused himself from supper and left you and Lizzie alone?" Clara chuckled and deep lines of laughter appeared around her lovely dark eyes. "I reckon Mistah Daniel's world is bein' shaken up, and he don't like it too much. But a little shakin's good for everybody, I always say. I likes it, and I likes you, Miz Kelly. Was kind of you to help with the dishes, too."

"It was the least I could do."

"Most wouldn't," Clara said as she walked toward the door. "You think you gonna be comfortable here for the night?"

Hearing another crash of thunder, Kelly looked around the bedroom. "Absolutely."

"All right then, sleep well."

"Good night, Clara."

"Night, Miz Kelly. May the angels be watchin' over us all here tonight."

Kelly smiled back. "Thank you."

When the door was closed, she placed the nightgown on the bed and knew the first thing she was going to take off . . .

her shoes. "Ohhh, gawd." She sighed out loud. Relief swept up her legs as she felt her bare foot touch the cool wooden floor. Why Mel had chosen such heavy, clunky-heeled pumps was beyond her, but she figured her friend didn't expect that Kelly would be trudging across a bayou in them. With both hands, Kelly reached around her back for the dress zipper. After a few moments of fumbling, she let out another deep sigh as the thing slid down her body and onto the floor. Stepping out of the rumpled pile, she had to admit she thought the entire ensemble was . . . well, downright ugly.

"Sorry Mel," she whispered, wanting to kick it across the room. Even in her friend's defense, she couldn't deny it still looked like a runny key lime pie. Especially now.

Kelly removed the wide underslip, picked up the dress, and placed them both on a wing chair by the window. Never had she been so glad to get out of something! Well, except for her panty hose, which had been practically ripped to shreds while trekking through the woods with Lizzie. She had taken the opportunity to remove them after dinner when she had to "use the facilities." What an experience that was, Kelly recalled with a shudder. And in the rain, too!

She wished she could wash out her underwear, but that was obviously out of the question. She'd just have to put everything back on again tomorrow. Oh well, she knew she wouldn't be wearing it much longer, and she vowed then and there, when she got back to her hotel, the entire costume would be thrown out.

What a complete disaster this whole trip had become. If she'd only had the courage from the very beginning to say no, to tell Mel how she truly felt . . . she would never have been in this situation. Then Kelly wondered just what Mel must be thinking of her disappearance.

Another streak of lightning followed by the roar of thunder had Kelly hurrying to finish preparing for bed. It was a little too spooky to be there on such a night with nothing but a candle on the nightstand. Sliding the soft thin cotton gown over her head, Kelly smelled roses and wondered if the drawer where it had been kept was scented. Somehow it re-

minded her of the floral lining her mother had used when she
was young. Shrugging off the thought, she folded her underwear and placed them on the chair with her other clothes.

Aching as she climbed up on the high bed, Kelly tried not
to moan out loud, but was unsuccessful. Slowly, she pulled
the cover up over her body, and when her head sank into the
feather pillow, she released a final sigh of contentment. After
the day that she'd had, this was sheer heaven . . .

And then her mind started to destroy her peace. What *was*
Mel thinking? Had the police been notified yet? Usually, she
was so organized, so independent . . . and now she was nothing but trouble.

Once more in her mind she saw Daniel Gilmore as he
reprimanded Lizzie, then reproached her when she stuck up
for the child. Okay, so maybe the kid had an overactive
imagination. That didn't harm anyone. In actuality, it was
kind of endearing. This time, Kelly smiled as she thought of
Lizzie believing she was a fairy. *Bless her little heart for
helping a stranger in need.*

Why couldn't Mr. Gilmore see those qualities in his own
daughter? What the heck had she said at dinner that seemed
to upset the man so much? Okay, she was an unexpected
guest, but that didn't give him license to be rude. And what
was with the way he barely excused himself from the table,
as though he couldn't bear to sit with either of them any
longer?

Yeah . . . in this house it seemed she was trouble.

Well, tomorrow she would mind her own business, thank
them all, and be on her way, rain or shine. She would get
back to New Orleans, contact Mel's mother and apologize,
pack her clothes at the hotel, get on her plane, and get out of
the South. She couldn't wait to be in her own home again.
This was the most bizarre trip she'd ever made.

Imagine, these people pretending that they'd never heard
of an airplane or modern technology.

They *had* to be pretending . . . right?

Shaking those thoughts out of her head, she reached over
and blew out the candle. She would listen to the storm and
fall asleep. Once she had loved lying in the dark and listen-

ing to rain on the roof. It had made her feel so safe and secure. When was the last time she'd felt safe? Too many years ago, when her world had been filled with love. Oh, don't go there now. Glancing to the lace-curtained window, she sighed deeply and closed her eyes.

What she needed to do was clear her mind of everything and just make it to the morning. She followed her breath, in and out, in and out, concentrating on the lift of her stomach, feeling the muscles in her legs ease, in her back, her chest, her shoulders and neck relaxing and—

Her eyes snapped open. What was that noise?

She held her breath and listened again.

Through the wind and the sound of branches rubbing against the side of the house, Kelly swore she heard someone crying on the other side of the wall. Lizzie. Tough little Lizzie was scared and crying? Somehow, that made her heart ache with sympathy. Poor kid was all alone. Her father certainly didn't seem to give her much comfort, and her only friend in the house, Clara, was sleeping downstairs and probably couldn't hear her.

Kelly pushed herself into a sitting position and within moments made up her mind. So what if she didn't have a robe? Who would see her, save the child? Slipping out of bed, Kelly pushed her hair off her face and walked to the door. She owed Lizzie a lot. If it wasn't for that kid, she might be out there in that storm, still trying to find her way back.

Opening the door, Kelly walked into the dark hallway and tiptoed through it. She knocked softly on Lizzie's door, then opened it.

"Momma!"

"Shh, honey. It's Kelly. Are you okay?"

She heard Lizzie sniffle and, in the next flash of lightning, Kelly watched her bolt upright in bed. Making her way to the child, Kelly whispered, "This storm is pretty strong, huh? I could use some company. Do you mind if I sit down with you for a little while?"

"I thought you was my momma. She comes sometimes when I'm scared."

Not wanting to get into *that,* whatever it meant, Kelly sat on the edge of the bed and looked out the window. "You think it's a hurricane, like Clara says?"

"If'n it is, then we gonna be flooded again," Lizzie whispered in a brave voice as she sniffled. "I don't like that 'cause then you see dead birds and coons and snakes floatin' and—"

"Well, let's not think of that," Kelly interrupted, stifling her own shudder as she folded her arms over her chest. "What if I tell you a story?"

Lizzie rubbed her hands over her face, brushing away tears, then asked, "A fairy tale?"

This kid was sure fixated on fairies. "All right, but you have to lie down and rest. I don't want Clara to think I'm keeping you up, okay?"

"Oh-kay," Lizzie said with a soft sigh as she sank back down into her pillow. "Which one you gonna tell me, 'cause I know I ain't heard them all."

"Hmm . . . how about this one? I used to climb trees when I was a girl like you and—"

"I climb trees, too, but don't tell Daddy."

"No, I won't," Kelly promised. "When I climbed them, I used to take a book and shove it down my top. Then, I'd find a nice strong branch near the top and gently sway in the breeze as I read." She sighed with the memory. "Anyway, one of my favorite stories was *Peter Pan.* Do you know it?"

Lizzie shook her head. "Is it about fairies?"

Kelly smothered a chuckle. "It's about a very famous fairy. Her name is Tinker Bell."

"Tell me that one!"

"You have to promise to close your eyes and try to picture it as I'm telling it, okay?"

"Oh-kay," Lizzie said, and closed her eyes.

Grinning, Kelly reached over and stroked Lizzie's hair back from her forehead. "Once upon a time, there was a little boy named Peter Pan, who ran away to Never-Never Land to escape growing up."

"He didn't want to grow up?" Lizzie whispered.

"No . . . he wanted to stay a child forever and play and play, which he did in Never-Never Land."

"What was it like . . . this land?"

"Hmm . . . it was magical. Everything a child could want to play with was there. I remember one of my favorite characters was Tiger Lily, an Indian princess."

"That's a pretty name. My momma's name was Lily. I saw a picture of a tiger once in one of Daddy's books."

Kelly nodded. "Well, one night Peter Pan, who could fly through the air . . ." She stopped for a moment and wondered if she'd picked the best story to tell this child, whose mind was already filled with fantasies about people flying.

"Go on," Lizzie urged.

Figuring she couldn't stop now, Kelly continued. "One night Peter came to three children in their bedroom . . . Wendy, John, and Michael Darling."

"That was their name? Darling?"

"Yes."

"That's a funny name. Darling." Lizzie giggled.

Kelly chuckled along with her. "Anyway, he invited them to go with him to Never-Never Land and told them they could fly. They didn't believe him until the fairy, Tinker Bell, appeared and sprinkled them with magic fairy dust. This enabled them to—"

"You got fairy dust? Can you make me fly, too?" Lizzie interrupted.

This was definitely *not* going in the right direction.

"No, sweetie, I don't. Honey, I can't fly either. I tried to tell you that. Maybe I should tell you another story. Ever hear 'The Princess and the Pea'?"

"I wanna know how you say you flew here and now you say you can't. Is it cause I caught you?"

"Hmm . . . Lizzie, you ever hear of an airplane? A big metal machine that carries people through the sky?" She held out her arms, like the wings of a plane.

"Nope."

"You've had to have seen planes in the air . . . in the sky. You aren't that far from the airport."

"What air-port? You Yankee fairies sure talk funny."

"It's a place where . . ." Kelly's words dropped off in stunned silence. This kid really had no idea what she was talking about. "Forget it. I'll tell you the story of 'The Princess and the Pea.' "

"No, I wanna hear about Peter Pan and Wendy and Michael and John. They could fly after the fairy sprinkled them with the magic dust?"

How smart was this to continue? She'd have to be very careful how she told it, or Lizzie would get it into her head that she, too, could fly. "Now, this is just a story, Lizzie. Real people can't fly."

"I knows that! Only fairies . . . like you."

"Honey . . ."

"I *saw* you. Ain't no good tellin' me you can't. You plopped down right there in front of me."

A chill ran up Kelly's spine, and it had nothing to do with the storm outside. What if something weird really did happen? Where was that huge tree? What if she had somehow traveled back in time? Would it explain why these people were living like this?

Shaking the crazy thought out of her head, Kelly said, "Okay, let's drop that and continue with the story. But you promised you'd close your eyes. No more questions, all right? Just lie there and listen."

"All right." Lizzie sighed deeply and closed her eyes again.

Reaching out, Kelly stroked Lizzie's hair and began again. "None of these children are real, Lizzie. It's just a story."

"I know. I'm glad you're here. Glad my daddy let me keep you."

She heard the raging storm outside and sighed as she looked down to the child by her side. "I am too, honey." Taking a deep breath, she continued, "Well, into the room Tinker Bell came flying. She was so tiny, with wings of shimmering light, and she reached into her bag and sprinkled Wendy and her brothers with her magical fairy dust. Peter told them they had to really believe they could fly before it would work, and soon all the children were floating up to the ceiling, light as air."

"Like my momma, when she comes to me."

"So Peter invites the children to Never-Never Land with him and Tinker Bell. They all held hands tightly, so they would stay together, and Peter led them out through the bedroom window and off into the night . . ." She didn't know how to answer Lizzie, especially when she talked about her mother appearing to her and figured it was best just to get back to the fairy tale. On and on she whispered the childhood story, making it up when she forgot parts of it. Her voice got lower and softer, and she continued to stroke Lizzie's head, listening to the child's steady breathing.

When she was sure Lizzie was again asleep, she simply sat on the edge of the bed and looked out to the storm. What had really happened to bring her into this house? If she believed Clara and Lizzie, then she would have to accept she'd time traveled back into the past. It was absurd, crazy. She would have to speak to Daniel Gilmore tomorrow, as much as she'd like to avoid the moody, strange man, at least he seemed rational and logical. Just the thought of him sent another involuntary shiver down her spine. What a cold fish! He might barely resemble her late husband, but his heart was nothing at all like Michael's. Daniel Gilmore's very soul seemed welded closed.

Staring at the charred walls in the corner of the dimly lit room, he stiffened with the onslaught of memories. Nearly ten years had passed since he'd thrown the oil lantern in a fit of rage, hoping the entire place would burn down. And at the time he had wanted to go with it, for to remain in this world without his beloved Lillian had seemed a living hell to him then.

Sighing, Daniel now knew deep down he was grateful Clara had heard the bursting lamp and rushed in with a pail of water on that fateful night. She'd only left for a moment to put his child in her cradle when he had allowed grief to overwhelm him. Shaking his head with regret and disbelief at his own actions, he recalled the old woman's kindness.

She'd stayed by his side the entire time as he had dug his wife's grave and laid her to rest on that chilly fall day. Gently rocking his small baby in her arms, she'd remained silent and strong while he had wept through more useless prayers. In the weeks following his wife's death, he'd mostly sat in a numbed daze. He was certain if it hadn't been for Clara taking over in nearly every capacity, he'd have gone mad, and his daughter surely would have starved.

He softly smiled and felt truly blessed for the incredible person Clara was in his life.

Slowly, he stood from the stripped horsehair mattress and glanced around the space he and his wife had once shared. After she was gone, he'd insisted it remain untouched, leaving everything exactly as his wife had left it. Clara would come in and dust occasionally.

Running his fingers in reverence over one of the tall, carved bedposts, he recalled his wife's joy as they had unpacked the cargo boxes. How she loved the dark walnut collection he'd had shipped from England when they moved to the States and into his family home. Even while seven months pregnant with their child, she had been tireless in decorating and arranging everything "just so," she'd said. She had wanted to make their home a sanctuary of love for everyone.

Turning to the long oval mirror in the wardrobe door, he imagined her standing behind him, as she had done so many times, brushing off his jacket shoulders after putting the last finishing touches on his tie. He never could get the damned things right. He had called them "nothing but society's nooses" and she had laughed, responding in a low, sexy tone that he was *the most stunningly handsome hanged man she'd ever seen.* He exhaled quietly as he remembered laughing out loud when she'd said it. She had then wrapped her arms around his waist, squeezed him tightly, and simply whispered, "And you're mine."

He took in a tight breath through his teeth and closed his eyes as the memories flooded his soul. He could hear her voice so clearly, as though she were right there in the room with him . . . only now he couldn't feel anything more than the longing ache in his chest.

It was then the tears came, and he couldn't stop them.

"I'm so sorry, Lilly."

Clearing the hoarse whisper from his throat, he pinched the bridge of his nose and gritted his back teeth. He had never shown her red eyes.

Hauntingly mirrored by the single candle flame, he blinked through the stinging wetness at his solitary figure as more memories engulfed him. Her laughter, nights of exquisite lovemaking . . . talking until dawn of his dreams, sharing books and ideas . . . how she believed in him and supported everything he wanted . . . he owed her so much . . . and yet what did she gain from his ambitions? A harrowing sickness and a death too soon.

Eternal rest. It was such a stupid cliché.

The anguish of her suffering gripped his heart again. He still blamed himself for it. Had he never insisted they come to the South . . . had he returned her to England where her family and friends were . . . had he thought of more than himself and loved her with as much strength and integrity as she had loved him, she might still be here to raise their daughter and be the family he so desired now. He certainly knew what he had once. And he was deeply aware of what he had still. . . .

Yet, all he really knew how to be was a faithful and loving husband. He'd never quite learned how to be a father to their daughter. He knew it wasn't that he didn't try; he provided everything a precious little girl could want.

Except a mother.

And Elizabeth is growing so quickly, he worried silently. All these years gone now, without a mother's soft touch and tender way. . . .

I fear I have done our child no justice, my love.

"Oh, Lilly," he whispered up toward the raging night sky. "I'm so sorry for what I did . . . for everything."

He listened. If only the rain could be divine forgiveness to wash away his guilt.

Kelly sighed with exhaustion and slowly rose from Lizzie's bed. Looking around the shadow-cast room, she could make out a dollhouse on what appeared to be a small table, a rocking horse and a large toy box, its lid brimming open with more toys. It all seemed odd in a way, Kelly thought as she rubbed the muscles in her lower back. Lizzie had not struck her as the type of young girl even interested in these things. She seemed more inclined to climb a tree and run barefoot through the bayou than wear a dress and play "tea party." Well, at least it showed Daniel Gilmore wanted to provide something for his daughter, but it wasn't enough, Kelly suspected. It was obvious to her that toys would never replace what it appeared the child so longed for . . . a parent's love.

Tiptoeing from the room, she glanced back at the angelic sleeping child and smiled with satisfaction. Pleased with herself for putting her back to sleep, Kelly slowly opened the heavy wooden door, wincing as it creaked with the movement. Silence followed as she slipped through and quietly latched it behind her. She couldn't wait to climb back into her bed and find some peace this night.

Tomorrow she'd get her answers.

Just as she placed her hand on the knob of her own bedroom door, she caught a glimpse of faint light coming from across the hall. She turned to look closer and saw it was coming from a door that was slightly ajar. Waiting and listening, she heard shuffling noises coming from inside the room.

None of your business, she told herself. Maybe it was Lizzie's father's room, and she should just get into her own right now and get to sleep. *That's it,* she thought . . . *just get back in bed and put this day behind you . . . a wedding you shouldn't have attended, getting lost in the woods, mistaken for a fairy, captured by a child, forced by a storm to stay with people who have no idea about modern conveniences and talk about spirits appearing and . . .*

As she turned the doorknob to her room, there was a loud gasp behind her. Spinning around in fright, she could make out the silhouette of a man standing in the opposite doorway. Her heart felt like it jumped into her throat. Her stomach clenched in fear. Blood raced through her body until she felt it pounding in her fingertips and rushing in her ears.

"You!" He breathed the word with anguish and longing.

Kelly was frozen with a mixture of surprise and fear as the lightning flashed and thunder rattled the floorboards beneath her bare feet. She had no time to react as he reached out to her. Pulling her into his arms, he clasped her tightly to his chest and brought his mouth down on hers with such yearning, such passion, that she found herself accepting his kiss and moaning with a gratification she had long forgotten.

Inhaling deeply he repeated, *"You,"* against her mouth, then began kissing her temple, her neck, the slope of her shoulder.

Instantly, warm threads of pleasure raced through her, and she was shocked by her reaction. Her mouth was tingling with the faint taste of brandy. Her skin seemed to come alive with excitement and anticipation as a desire began stirring up a wildfire everywhere he touched.

Forcing her mind to work, Kelly brought her hands up to push against his chest.

Groaning with disappointment, he seemed surprised, as though she'd thrown a bucket of cold water onto him. His body stiffened, and his hands released her.

"Mr. Gilmore! *Please!*"

She heard him breathing heavily and, even through the darkness, she could see his shocked expression. "Oh my God . . . I beg your pardon, Miss Brennan. I . . . I am mortified by my own actions."

Kelly pushed her hair back from her face and muttered, "Well . . . um . . ." What could she say? She couldn't condone what had just happened, yet she was still reeling from the kiss, the first kiss in many, many years that felt as though it had awakened something in her she thought had died when she was twenty-three.

"I . . . I saw you standing there, in that nightgown, and for a moment I thought . . . well, I thought you were someone else." He took a deep steadying breath.

In an instant, she remembered Clara thinking she looked like someone, and it was then Kelly knew he meant his wife, his dead wife. This was becoming too uncanny for, in the darkness, he again reminded her of Michael.

"Where did you get that nightgown?"

Was it his wife's? "Clara gave it to me," she muttered, hoping her answer wouldn't cause any more trouble than she'd already created. She should be angry. She should let him have it, yet in that kiss she could find nothing to be angry about. Trying to bring some semblance of sanity back to the situation, she crossed her arms over her chest. "I . . . I'm sorry if I frightened you."

"You didn't," he replied with more than a tinge of sadness to his voice. He ran his fingers through his dark hair. "You just . . . surprised me."

She couldn't help it. She giggled in nervousness. "Well, you certainly surprised me, Mr. Gilmore." Okay, she couldn't be angry.

He smiled, for the very first time, and even in the darkness it touched something in her mind and heart.

"Please call me Daniel, and, again, I implore your forgiveness. I most certainly am not the type of man who accosts his houseguests in the middle of the night."

"I didn't think you were." Now, why in the world did she want him to take her back into his strong warm arms? Craziness. Would it never end? "Lizzie was upset by the storm, and I just sat with her until she fell back asleep. I guess I shouldn't have been wandering around your home in the dark." She was rambling now, but who could blame her?

He'd kissed her. Just like that! *Kissed her . . . and she'd liked it!*

He turned around and glanced back into the room he had left. "Allow me to get the candle."

She watched as he reentered the room and picked up a single candelabra. As he came back into the hallway, he handed the light to her. "Would you mind?" he asked. "I keep this door locked."

"Oh, not at all," she answered, taking hold of the candlestick.

As he closed the door and began to lock it, Kelly bent so he could see better in the candle's glow. How crazy was this? She should be angry . . . really angry, yet she wasn't at all. In fact, if she were honest, she would just admit that every cell in her body was still tingling from his touch, the way his lips captured hers with such passion that she'd almost—

"It was my wife's room," he murmured, his voice soft and gentle.

Leaning so closely to him, Kelly found she liked the sound of it. Much better than his usual gruffness.

He stood up again and Kelly rose in unison.

"This is a most awkward situation, Miss Brennan."

She inhaled deeply as she stared into his eyes. The candlelight was casting shadows around them, and the air seemed charged with a wild energy.

"Call me Kelly," she whispered, suddenly wanting to hear him say it. "My husband died when I was much younger. I sympathize with your loss."

"Thank you," he said and then paused. "You were married?"

"Yes," she whispered, realizing this was a very strange conversation to be having in the middle of the night in a darkened hallway. "He died when I was twenty-three. Honestly, I don't know that I've ever really gotten over it."

"Well, again, forgive me, I had no idea," he said slowly, staring back into her eyes, as though seeing something in them he hadn't seen before. "Was it the war?"

"The war? No. It was . . . an accident. Something that never should have happened."

She was old enough to know when an attraction existed, and it threw her for a loop. What the hell was she doing? This can't happen now and especially with *him!*

"I guess I should say good night," she muttered, blinking to break the electrical charge that now appeared to encircle them both.

"I'm sorry I left you and Elizabeth at the table. I've been . . . I haven't been myself for some time," he admitted, as though not wanting to leave.

She stared at the contours of his bare neck, the way his white shirt lay open and exposed it. She really was going to have to stop this! "It's all right. Having an unexpected guest can be unnerving." She wasn't about to tell him that the kiss was wonderful and needed no apology. He'd think she was wanton . . . which even she was beginning to consider herself as the shivers of delight continued to rush through her. She could still feel the sensation of his body pressed tightly against hers only moments before. *Wanton?* Who even thought in words like that?

"You're cold, and I'm keeping you from your bed."

Somehow, she knew neither of them wanted to leave, but one of them must. "Yes, well, good night, Daniel," she said, hesitating slightly before turning to her door. "Oh!" she spun back around. "Here, your candle. I already have one in my room."

She felt his warm fingers gently cover hers as he stopped her from handing it back to him. A long moment of silence burned between them as they stared into each others eyes in the flickering light.

"You keep it, Miss Kelly," he whispered. "I know my way around this house blindfolded."

She smiled. He said her name . . . and she loved how it sounded coming from his lips, lips that had felt so inviting, so impassioned, so . . . What *was* wrong with her?

"Well, good night then." He smiled tenderly in return.

"Good night," she whispered again, and quickly opened the door to her bedroom.

Closing it behind her, she leaned back against it and sighed heavily. She looked around the small room again and sensed a familiarity she hadn't felt before. How could she possibly know this place . . . this house and, somehow, him? She blew out the candle and walked directly to the bed.

"Okay," she muttered to the dark room as she slipped in between the sheets again. "This is beyond crazy. Now I'm definitely into bizarre."

Four

Kelly wrapped the borrowed tan shawl closer around her and shivered as she looked out the kitchen window. "It's a hurricane, isn't it?"

"Sure does seem like it to me," Clara answered. "Don't look like you be goin' anywhere too soon, Miz Kelly. And this hip is hurtin' somethin' awful. The badder the weather, the badder this arthur, so's I be thinkin' it's a hurricane."

Spinning around, Kelly said, "Why don't you sit down, Clara? I can serve you breakfast."

Clara stared at her in the candlelight. It was morning, yet the sky was so darkened by clouds that they still needed candles for illumination.

"What?" Kelly demanded with a laugh at the older woman's shocked expression.

"You can't be servin' me, Miz Kelly," Clara whispered, even though Lizzie and Daniel hadn't yet made an appearance and they were all alone this stormy morning.

"And why not?" Kelly looked to the stove. "You've already made coffee, and I can make great scrambled eggs. Do you have any cheese?"

Clara nodded, then shook her head as she gingerly sank down onto a chair at the kitchen table. "You sure is the strangest white woman I ever done met," she stated, rubbing her hip with a weathered hand.

Kelly laughed. "It's the least I can do in repayment for all the kindness you've shown me."

Clara slapped the table and pushed herself upright, as though thinking better of her decision to rest. "Mistah Daniel ain't gonna like it. No, not at all."

"Well, Mister Daniel isn't here, is he? Now, *sit*," Kelly said with a grin of affection. It amazed her how quickly she had come to feel comfortable with this old woman. "How do you take your coffee?"

She poured some of the strong brew into thick mugs and turned around, still waiting for Clara to answer. "Do you use cream? Sugar?"

"You gonna fix it for me?" Clara asked, still appearing shocked.

"Of course. Why wouldn't I? Now, where's the cream and sugar?"

"Cream's in the icebox, there," Clara pointed to a short wooden chest by the kitchen door. "With the rest of the vittles I'll be cookin' all day. Don't think the iceman's gonna make it through this storm for some time, and I can't be lettin' it all spoil," the old woman added with a sigh.

Kelly froze for a moment. The *iceman*? Lifting the lid, Kelly was surprised to see a very melted piece of ice sitting in the tin-lined bin, draining through a hole in the center.

"In the bottom, Miz Kelly," Clara corrected politely.

"Oh," Kelly muttered, dropping the lid. "Wow. This is quite an antique. But I guess without any electricity, it comes in pretty handy." She bent over and opened the small cabinet door. Grabbing a ceramic pitcher and checking to be insure it was full of cream, she then set it on the table. "Now point me to the sugar."

Clara did, and soon Kelly was placing the mug of coffee in front of her. "Let's just sit and have our coffee in peace," Kelly said with a grin as she sat down opposite Clara and began fixing her own coffee. "You know, Clara . . . I've heard that the barometric pressure during rain will increase joint and muscle pain. A chiropractor told me all about it when I hurt my back a few years ago. That might explain why your hip hurts more now . . . because of the intensity of the storm."

Clara slowly stirred her coffee. "You sure do talk strange, Miz Kelly. I ain't never met nobody like you in my whole and entire life. Imagine . . . me settin' here at the table with a white woman discussin' from ailments to the weather."

"Oh, Clara, surely you've sat with . . . well, I mean, with a white woman before," Kelly whispered while trying to adjust to the strong chicory taste of the coffee.

"I sat with Lizzie's momma when she lay dying, and I sat with the woman who came from the church in town and told me my man was killed in the war, but I ain't never in my life sat like this . . . friendly like, sharin' a cup of coffee. They do this up North?"

Kelly stared at the old woman and wanted to put her arm around her thin shoulders.

"Of course. And I'm sure they do it here in the South, too, Clara. You just have been back in the woods and . . ." Now, that seemed rude. Kelly whispered, "I'm sorry."

"What you sorry about?"

"Well, to imply that you have been sort of isolated here. I guess you don't get to see many people."

"That's a fact, but it don't matter none. I don't think many white women would sit down with an e-man-ci-pated slave and share a cup of coffee with them, no matter how i-sol-ated it be."

Kelly stared into the old woman's eyes and suddenly wanted to cry.

"You looks like you seen a ghost, Miz Kelly."

"What did you say?"

"I says you looks like you seein' a ghost."

"I mean be . . . before," Kelly stammered. "About an emancipated slave."

"Sure 'nough, that's what they call us now. What you think I was?" The old woman's eyes twinkled with mischief. "The Queen of Sheba, lost in some bayou?" Clara cackled while picking up her mug.

"You were a slave?" Kelly whispered in disbelief.

Nodding, Clara sipped her coffee. "Was born on a sugar plantation up the Mississippi and—"

"Clara! *Please!*" Kelly interrupted. "That can't be true. None of this can possibly be true."

"Well now, Miz Kelly, I thinks I knows where I was born," Clara answered calmly.

Kelly blankly stared at the woman. "But slaves? Clara, slavery was abolished after the—" She stopped when she realized the words about to leave her mouth. She wouldn't say it. She wouldn't buy into this whole charade.

"Well, least there's somethin' you understand 'bout the South, Miz Kelly." The woman smiled as though knowing what Kelly wished unrevealed. "I been with Mistah Daniel ever since he brought Miz Lillian with him here in 1876. But after she died in 1878, I stayed on to help him bring up that chile upstairs sleepin' right now. Um, um, um . . . twelve years now I been with him."

Abruptly standing, Kelly announced, "I'm going to make breakfast." Walking briskly back to the icebox she took out the cheese and butter. Keeping her back to the old woman, Kelly went to the stove. Earlier, she'd noticed a small wire mesh basket on the counter with eggs in it, and from helping clean the dinner dishes the night before, she knew where the bowls and frying pans were kept. She realized the clatter she'd begun to make, so she took a deep breath to calm herself. "Just keep busy," she whispered.

"You know, when I was told my Lucius weren't comin' back from the war, I musta gone on for days thinkin' he'd be walkin' through the door anytime."

Kelly heard Clara's voice, but she really didn't want to know any more of the old woman's recollections. It was just too preposterous to accept.

"I just wouldn't believe it either," the old woman continued ironically. "But when I was told I was *free*," Clara emphasized the word as though she were still getting accustomed to it, "I done had to accept it. My man and my boy was gone from this world, and I was on my own."

The long, heavy silence in the air between them was too much for Kelly to bear.

"I know the exact feeling, Clara." Kelly really didn't want to share any more or she knew she'd become embroiled in this crazy unfolding drama.

"I had a feelin' you'd understand, Miz Kelly. It's a hard thing to let go of somethin' you believe in so strong and love so much."

"Yes, it is." She could sympathize, but she couldn't accept what this woman was obviously trying to imply.

"And I know it's best when you accept it," Clara said softly.

Kelly didn't answer her. She couldn't.

"I don't know how you got to be here, Miz Kelly, but you is here . . . and the year is 1888. And you best not be tellin' too many people what you be thinkin', cause they ain't gonna have the patience I do for the things you can't never explain."

Kelly spun around and ripped Clara's shawl from her shoulders. Throwing it over the back of a chair, she said, "Clara, I appreciate everything you've done for me, but I refuse to believe that it's 1888! What you're talking about is *impossible*!"

"But you is here, ain't ya?" the old woman remarked knowingly as she stared out the window and sipped her coffee again.

It was only words, spoken so softly that Kelly had to strain to hear them, yet they had the effect of a sledgehammer upon her brain. "Clara," she whispered back, "as God is my judge, I swear I don't know where I am anymore . . . but it can't be a hundred and thirteen years back in time!"

"Lordy, Lordy, but life can be confusin'." Clara swallowed her coffee and smiled up at Kelly sympathetically. "Maybe it's good you busyin' yourself makin' them eggs. Best not to be thinkin' on things that ain't got no answers."

"Oh, there's an answer, Clara, and as soon as I get to New Orleans I'll find it," Kelly replied, turning back to the stove. Breaking the eggs into the large bowl, she added, "That's where normalcy is . . . like a modern stove, a bathroom, a telephone . . . a *plane* to get back to my own home."

"Well, I reckon you ain't gonna get none of them things today, and that'd be for sure. Where is your home, Miz Kelly?"

That was a safe subject, Kelly thought. No more talk about ex-slaves and such nonsense. "I live in Philadelphia, Clara."

"Phil-a del-phia," Clara repeated slowly. "What's it like up North? I think I gots some relatives that made it up there."

"It's . . . very nice," Kelly said, not knowing how to describe an entire city. "Different than here. May I borrow your apron?" She turned back to the old woman, who was still sitting at the long wooden table.

"There's a clean one in that drawer." Clara pointed to a series of built-in drawers along the far wall. "The middle one," she directed.

Kelly opened it and pulled out a plain white-linen apron. "Though why I think I'm going to save this dress is beyond me. It's ruined."

Clara chuckled. "You sure is right, Miz Kelly. Ain't no one gonna be able to get those watermarks outta that. Maybe I could ask Mistah Daniel if you could wear some of his wife's clothes. I reckon they's just your size and been settin' up in that room for years now . . . ain't been touched. Kinda a shame, since some is brand-new."

"No, don't ask him," Kelly advised. "He was a little shocked I was wearing the nightgown."

"And how'd he know 'bout that?"

Kelly was glad she was still turned away from Clara. She didn't want the woman to see the blush creeping into her cheeks when she thought about that stunning kiss in the night. Just the memory was enough to make her shiver. "Well, last night Lizzie was scared in the storm and I went to her and told her a story. After she fell asleep I was going back to my room and Daniel . . . er, Mister Daniel came out of his wife's room—"

"Oh, Lordy, he weren't mad you was wearin' it?"

"Well, not *mad,* he was . . . surprised, mostly," Kelly said, tying the apron behind her.

"Well, well . . . now ain't that a good sign."

From the corner of her eye, Kelly glanced at Clara and could see a wide grin on the woman's face. "Why is that?"

"That room's been locked up like some holy place ever since Miz Lillian done gone. Only time I go in there is to clean it. That man been grievin' way too hard and way too long, I say. 'Bout time for some new ways in this house."

"Hmm," was all Kelly could reply. What difference did it make to her what happened in this house? She was merely a guest, a reluctant guest at that. She beat the eggs and left the fork in the bowl. She grated the cheese into another bowl. She buttered the cast-iron pan and turned back to the table, really wanting to sit down again and finish her coffee.

"Come on," Clara said with a chuckle, as though reading her mind. "I ain't gonna spook you with any more talk about being a slave. Lordy, though, if I can say it, I don't know why you can't hear it."

Grinning, Kelly returned to her chair and sank down onto it. "Clara, you can't imagine how confusing all of this is to me. It's like I left one world and entered another."

"Well, I don't know 'bout any of that, but what I do know is that you is here for a reason. I asked the Lord for some help and you arrived . . . and look at you . . . makin' breakfast for this ole, tired, fool of a woman. Can't rightly remember the last time someone cooked for me."

"I don't think you're a fool, Clara."

"Course I am," she answered with a smile. "Who else but a fool would live with such a sad man and a hellion child?"

"Why do you stay?"

" 'Cause Mistah Daniel offered me a place and a paying job when I was down and out, after I lost everybody I ever loved to the war and then the yellow jack. 'Cause I made a promise to Miz Lillian to watch over them both but, Lord above, I am tired."

"How old are you, Clara? If that's not a rude question?"

"It ain't rude, but I don't rightly know. Near as I can figure I must be around seventy and two years on this Earth."

"You don't know?" Kelly found it hard to believe that someone wouldn't know their own age.

"My momma was sold off when I was around four and I ain't been able to keep track since. Some of them years seems to just fold together on me."

Kelly simply stared at her.

"I can tell you thinks I'm lyin', but you better know I ain't got one good reason in this here world to lie to you or to anyone else. I am what I am. Same as you, Miz Kelly. Our stories may be different, but we both know our truth. I believes you when you say you is from a time I ain't never heard of, with things I ain't never seen. I been here too many years and seen things that would make some shake in their boots, but I'm still here, and I'm still believin'."

Kelly sipped her coffee and tried to organize the myriad thoughts racing through her brain. It was useless. She was feeling as though she were on information overload, and it was probably best to focus on one thing. Just continue talking, she silently rationalized. "Like what things have you seen, Clara?"

"I seen peoples that have passed on to the next life standing right in front of me and I've heard voices in them woods that tells of troubles and the mean things people can do to one another. I once seen—"

"Lizzie says she sees her mother when she's afraid," Kelly interrupted.

Nodding, Clara said, "Seen her, too. Ain't nothing to be scared about, Miz Kelly."

"I'm not scared," she lied. "I'm just confused."

Clara again chuckled. "Like I said, life sure can be confusin' at times. This here is just one of them times."

"It sure is, Clara," she said with a deep sigh. "It sure is."

The door behind her was flung open, and Lizzie came bounding into the room.

"Oh, goody, you're still here!" the child proclaimed as she stared at Kelly.

"Yes, I'm still here," Kelly almost reluctantly muttered into her coffee.

"It's a hurricane, Mammy Clara, ain't it?" Lizzie demanded, going right to the stove and looking into the bowls.

"Sit," Kelly directed Clara when she saw the woman begin to rise. "I can take care of this." Walking to the stove, she put her hand on the girl's shoulder, and said, "Good morning, Lizzie Gilmore."

Lizzie looked up and grinned. "Mornin', Miss Kelly. I'm hungry."

"I guessed that already. If you want, I'll teach you to make scrambled eggs with me."

"You will?"

Nodding, Kelly said, "Get an apron."

She watched as Lizzie ran to the drawers, and Clara rose from the table.

"I'm only gonna bring the dishes," she said, "so's we have something to eat offa. You can heat up them sweet rolls from last night too, if you want."

"Great idea," Kelly pronounced, beginning to feel quite pleased with the way the morning was actually turning out.

Soon all three were busily preparing breakfast. Lizzie appeared to be thrilled for being given a job to do, and Clara was humming while setting the table. It was then, in the midst of such domestic bliss that Daniel Gilmore entered and stopped at the doorway.

"Good morning."

All three women turned to him.

"I'm makin' breakfast, Daddy!" Lizzie announced, her apron nearly dragging on the floor.

"I can see," he said, coming into the room and surveying the scene further.

"An' Miss Kelly's teachin' me to make scrambled eggs."

"Good morning . . . Daniel." Kelly said his first name on purpose. He had opened an intimate door last night, and she wasn't about to close it. Besides, the man she had met last night in that darkened hallway was far preferable to the cold one who seemed to roam the rest of the house.

"Good morning, Miss Kelly." He actually smiled at her.

"I insisted upon making breakfast," Kelly added almost shyly while looking to Clara.

"Mornin', Mistah Daniel," Clara called out as she placed

a saucer of butter on the table and a small bowl of what looked to be jam. "Miz Kelly is sure one fine woman, she is. You ready for your coffee?"

Startled by Clara's statement, Kelly watched as Daniel stood at the table.

"Yes, I am, Clara."

She looked at the older woman and smiled with genuine fondness. "Now you just sit back down, Clara, and let me serve."

Kelly turned her attention back to the stove. "Hurry, Lizzie . . . don't let them burn or get too hard. Here . . ." She placed her hand over the child's and together they scrambled the eggs.

"Daddy don't eat in the kitchen with me and Mammy Clara," Lizzie whispered up to her.

Kelly paused for only a moment before pouring another cup of coffee and turning back to the room. "Won't you join us at the table, Daniel? The kitchen is so warm and cozy on this stormy morning." She could see him hesitate for a moment.

Daniel put his hand on the back of a chair and said, "I'd be honored, Miss Kelly."

She smiled as she handed him his coffee, and was startled when his fingers brushed hers. A shiver of sensual excitement rushed over her body, just as the night before, and she quickly glanced up into his eyes. What she saw almost took away her breath. He was looking at her with such tenderness she had to remind herself that she was supposed to be serving breakfast.

Turning quickly back to the stove, she said to Lizzie, "Okay, I think we're about finished. Let's hurry and put the eggs on the platter and I'll take the rolls out of the oven. They should be warm by now." Dear Lord, what the heck was going on with her and that man? It was almost as though they shared some secret. Yeah, he'd kissed her. Yeah, she'd enjoyed it. But it was more than that . . . and it was weird.

Minutes later all four of them were seated at the table.

"This is mighty fine, Miz Kelly," Clara pronounced. "Can't remember when I've had such good eggs. I'd be rightly pleased if you taught me how you made 'em.'"

"I can teach you, Mammy Clara," Lizzie piped up. "Miss Kelly showed me and—"

"Wait until you finish chewing, Elizabeth, before speaking," Daniel admonished, and then smiled to Kelly. "They are very good, Miss Kelly. Thank you for preparing them. It is our place to serve you, though, as our guest."

"I done told her that, Mistah Daniel, but Miz Kelly has her own ideas."

"Yes, I do," Kelly answered, very pleased everyone was enjoying breakfast. She had to admit the eggs turned out pretty well, even if using that old-fashioned stove was a challenge since she couldn't control the heat.

"Independent thinking is to be commended," Daniel remarked, while smiling at Kelly. "Makes for progress. Most of our inventions were fueled by it."

"Like that place you worked on, Daddy? That . . . ex-position?" Lizzie said the last word as though she wasn't sure it was right.

Daniel smiled at his daughter. "Well done, Elizabeth. I'm glad you remembered. That was four years ago." He looked at Kelly and explained, "The World Industrial and Cotton Centennial Exposition: 1884. I helped to design the horticultural hall in Audubon Park."

"I beg your pardon." Kelly was hoping she hadn't heard correctly.

"Yes, we may not be as advanced in electricity as the North, Miss Kelly, but we could boast of a ninety-foot glass tower illuminated by electric lights that could be seen twenty miles away."

"I'm sorry, what year did you say?"

"Mmm, Mmm, Mmm . . . but these eggs is sure the best I've ever had," Clara interrupted. "You is definitely gonna have to teach me how to make these, Miz Kelly."

Kelly looked at the woman and knew she was trying to divert the conversation, but this was far too important. "Mr. Gilmore," Kelly said, ignoring Clara's ploy and using the formal address to Daniel, "what year did you say?"

"Four years ago, Miss Kelly—1884. President Arthur,

from Washington, opened the Exposition with the flick of an electrical switch. Why, it covered over thirty-three acres and had more elevators than exist in the rest of the world. It was quite a sight."

Kelly placed her fork on her plate. "Excuse me. Eighteen eighty-four?"

"Why, yes. I'm sorry, I don't understand your confusion. It was reported in all the major newspapers at the time. I worked for three years on the project, heading the architectural team."

"You must mean 1984," she whispered, feeling her heart pounding in her chest. This can't be happening!

"Nineteen eighty-four?" Daniel chuckled. "Surely, you jest."

Kelly stared down at her food. She heard the storm raging outside, the crackle of the fire in the stove, even Lizzie's breathing . . .

"You ready for another cup of coffee, Mistah Daniel, Miz Kelly?" Clara asked, standing up and reaching for their cups.

"I'll do it!" Kelly said in a forceful voice as she stood abruptly. Just keep busy, her mind again directed. Don't think about it. "Please sit down and rest your hip, Clara." Without waiting for a reply, she took both Daniel's and Clara's mugs to the stove.

It can't be possible, she told herself. *People don't just travel back in time! No matter what these people say, such things can't happen.* She came from a sane world, a place where everyone knew it was the new millennium, not from a place where people were stuck living in the past and . . . God, she wanted to get home!

She returned to the table and placed the mugs back in front of Daniel and Clara. No one had spoken in the short time it took to refill the coffee. She sat back down and stared at her plate. Suddenly, her appetite had disappeared.

"You feelin' all right, Miz Kelly?" Clara asked in a soft whisper.

She nodded, and from the corner of her eye, she saw Daniel rise.

"If you are finished, Miss Kelly, would you please join me in my study?"

Glancing up, she saw him pick up his mug and wait for her answer. She couldn't tell what was on his mind from his noncommittal expression. "Of course," she answered.

"Uh-oh," Lizzie muttered, being very quiet for once.

Kelly rose and straightened her skirt. "Excuse me," she said to Clara, who was smiling sympathetically at her again.

She followed Daniel from the kitchen and through the dining room. Entering a small hallway, they passed the staircase, and Kelly once again tried to peek into what she figured was the living room, just as Daniel stopped and opened a door.

"Here we are. Please, come in, Miss Kelly, and pardon the disarray of my study. I wasn't quite expecting a visitor, but I took the liberty of assuming this would be a more private and quiet place for us to talk."

"Oh, certainly, and why don't you just call me Kelly." She smiled, nodded, and stepped through the doorway. Three walls of the room were lined with bookshelves from ceiling to floor. Stuffed with an array of leather-and cloth-bound volumes, the office was impressive, and she figured if the man had read all these books, he was obviously very well educated.

"Please, sit down and make yourself comfortable," he said, and indicated a large wing chair.

"Thank you." Kelly sat down and folded her hands in her lap. Looking around the dimly illuminated room, she could see a bin stuffed with many large rolls of paper beside an antique drafting table in front of the one long window.

"So you're an architect, Daniel?" Kelly thought she'd make conversation, as she felt a bit uncomfortable in the silence, especially with him still behind her as he lit an oil lamp sconce on the wall over her head. The room filled with a soft glow, and she could make out stacks of papers and more books on every flat surface available.

"Yes, I am," he answered, blowing out the wooden match and tossing it into a brass ashtray on a table next to her. Striking another, he lit a lamp on the desk directly across from her.

"So, what's on your mind, Daniel?"

"That is precisely the question I was going to ask you, Miss Kelly," he replied as he walked around the massive desk and sat down in a high-backed leather chair. "You appeared a bit faint when I mentioned the exposition I worked on."

"It wasn't the exposition," she muttered. "It's the year of it."

"Eighteen eighty-four?"

"You said that was four years ago."

"And it was."

"That can't be possible."

"And why not?"

"Because that would make this 1888 and that, Daniel Gilmore, is definitely *not* possible."

It was his turn to stare. "You'll need to explain that statement to me, madam."

She felt like laughing at the absurdity of this conversation, but knew it wouldn't help her case. "Look," she began, "obviously, you, like Clara, believe that it's a hundred and thirteen years ago. I mean, I'll give you credit. You've got the setting down pat here in the woods. No indoor plumbing, except for the cold water in the kitchen," she said, and continued pointing out the items on her fingers. "No electricity, central heating, much less air-conditioning. No radio or TV. No telephones, no cars, no computers. Not one single modern convenience or anything normal people have to communicate with the outside world." She held up her counted fingers and open hands to him.

"What are you talking about?"

She had to admire the way he kept up the charade. In fact, he looked stunned.

"I'm talking about the real world, Daniel, where I come from," she said, slapping her opened palms down on her thighs to emphasize her point. "The one where you flip a switch and lights come on in a room, where you turn a thermostat and heat comes out of vents. Where you cook on a gas stove and you turn on a television to hear the news and weather . . . where . . . where you have a damn telephone to call anywhere in the world, let alone the next town to get a cab to drive you to the airport so you can fly home and get back to normalcy." She took a deep breath. "That's what I'm talking about."

He leaned forward, settling his elbows on the leather desk blotter. "You're really going to have to explain to me what some of these things are that you're talking about. I know of electricity, as I already mentioned, I know telephones are used in some parts of the East Coast and are expected to cover the country one day . . . as for now, there is a telegraph office in New Orleans . . . but ray-dee-oh, tel-eh-vision . . . flying . . . air-conditioning?" He leaned back in his chair and shook his head with a look of utter amazement on his face.

This time she did laugh, but it was mostly at herself for being in this situation where she *had* to explain common, everyday things! "Look, you must know about television. A box, powered by electricity that allows you to view programs . . . comedies, dramas, musicals, the news, the weather, you can even get the stock-market reports on it. Kelly paused then added, "And I already explained the flying part last night, right before you walked out of the dining room."

"People cannot fly, Miss Kelly," he whispered as he continued eyeing her in disbelief.

"I know that. Try telling it to your daughter." She sighed with exasperation. "I was talking about airplanes . . . ah, big airships that carry people in the sky." She shook her head and glanced down at the floor. "I can't believe I'm talking to someone like this. Come on, Daniel," she said, looking back up pleadingly. "Surely you've seen airplanes flying in and out of the airport in New Orleans." She stared him directly in the eye and waited for even the slightest sign of comprehension on the man's face.

Nothing. He simply held his confounded gaze.

"Daniel, where I come from, people are living in the twenty-first century, where we have all those things and much, much more. You know, the year 2001?" she asserted, nodding her head imploringly.

Okay, now the man looked as though something had begun to sink in.

"You're saying, you live in the year 2001?"

"Well of course!" she replied, wondering why he appeared to be just grasping the concept.

"The year 2001?" he repeated.

"Yes."

"Unbelievable." He exhaled. "You believe this?"

"Well, I can't believe I'm with people who are pretending that it's a hundred and thirteen years ago, so I guess we're even. But when I get to New Orleans, all this will be resolved. I just have to wait out this hurricane."

"I don't think it's a hurricane," Daniel muttered, looking behind him to the stacks of books lining the wall. "More of a tropical storm," he added almost absentmindedly. "Ah, here it is." He pulled a book from the shelf and handed it to her from across the desk.

"What is it?" she asked, accepting the cloth bound volume.

"Read the title."

She did . . . and it was her turn to be stunned.

Looking Backward: 2000–1887.

The author's name was Edward Bellamy.

"Is this some kind of a joke?" she demanded, as her hands began shaking.

"No, not at all. I thought you might recognize it. It's a recent publication, sent to me by a friend in Boston. Another, shall we say . . . progressive thinker." He nodded at her with a wink before adding, "Of course it is fiction, yet I found it to be very interesting."

Kelly suddenly felt nauseated.

"It's a story about a man who travels forward in time, to the year 2000. I'd be interested to know what you think, Miss Kelly, and it might help to answer some of your questions. A few of mine too, I might add." He smiled slightly with near tenderness and Kelly was suddenly reminded of their kiss.

"Yes, I'd really like some answers, but do you seriously believe I'm going to find them in this book?" she implored, wishing her shaking body would sit still and she could put that kiss out of her mind.

"It's a perfect day to read," he said, glancing out to the rain. "Perhaps after you finish, we could discuss it . . . and your assertions."

Kelly opened the book to the copyright page and read the year the book was published. 1888, The World Publishing Company, Cleveland, Ohio. She quickly closed the book. Running her hand over the cover, she noted it appeared nearly new. How could such an antique edition be in such good condition?

"This is crazy," she muttered under her breath.

"You're right. It is an abstruse concept," Daniel said, rising from his chair and looking down at her. "But I would be very interested to know your thoughts, Miss Kelly."

Glancing up at him, she knew he didn't understand how she'd meant it. She was thinking she had to be crazy to believe these people would go to such lengths as to provide books, much less an entire setting of a historical time, to convince a total stranger it was the year 1888. But why?

She realized her mouth was hanging open, and she swallowed dryly. "Right. Well," she paused, clutching the book to her chest. "I guess I'd better start reading." Standing, she added, "Like you said, nothing better to do on a rainy day."

Walking toward the door, he quickly stepped in front of her and opened it. For a few timeless moments they stared at each other's eyes, at each other's mouths, and she knew he was thinking about what had taken place the night before. Every feminine instinct was telling her that if she moved closer, he would kiss her again. She couldn't let it happen just because they each reminded the other of a lost love . . . even if her body was crying out for more. Without another word, she merely nodded, and headed for the stairs. She simply had to be alone to find some way of quelling her darkening fears, for what she was thinking she knew bordered on madness.

Her own.

But . . . was it possible?

Had she somehow traveled back in time?

And how the hell was she going to get back home?

Five

I t was a romance novel. At its core, it was a *time-travel romance novel*!

Kelly sat on the bed and read. She lay on the bed and continued to read. She sat in the chair, on the rug . . . but couldn't seem to put down the book, though at times she was lost in the social mores and had to read a paragraph over and over until she understood it better.

"Yes . . . *yes!*" she cried out as the protagonist fought for his sanity when realizing he had time traveled. Stuck out in the woods, away from modern civilization, she had some idea how he felt though she refused to accept Clara's notion of time jumping. It was fiction, after all!

The author had created a fascinating story, what he termed a "fairy tale of social felicity," about a man named Julian West who travels forward in time from 1887 to 2000 and the so-called amazing discoveries he finds. Kelly was actually surprised at how accurate the author was about some things, such as music being piped into bedrooms while she laughed at others, like rain never touching the pavement and underestimating the population in the year 2000.

West, the time traveler, is dumbfounded by his discoveries, but what really bowls him over is old-fashioned love. That appears in the character of Edith Leete, who happens to be related to the woman West planned to marry back in 1887.

It was tedious reading in parts and Kelly really had to concentrate, for West finds himself in a social-industrial utopia, where everyone contributes through their work to the "Great Trust." The nation, not government, is the sole capitalist and employer.

There are no wars, no military, no class distinctions of richer or poorer, better than, less than. There was only one class . . . human. Everyone receives a good education and is encouraged to find and nurture their talent, thus contributing to society and enjoying their work experience. Everyone is paid equally, the waiter and the artist, the doctor and the street sweeper, and all are valued for their contribution.

Hardly the twenty-first century.

It was still quite a visionary piece of work, the science of wealth and happiness, and Kelly was amazed at how well the author had dealt with every aspect of life, yet it *was* a fairy tale of social felicity, for the year 2000 wasn't anything like this writer had envisioned. His work of fiction was nevertheless brilliant, and to think that it had been written over a hundred years ago blew her away.

When she finally finished reading, Kelly realized it was late afternoon and she was hungry, really hungry. Her stomach growled as an added reminder. She smelled something delicious cooking and sighed when she closed the book. Glancing out the window, she saw that the storm was easing. Great, she would be able to leave tomorrow. What a relief it would be to get back home on familiar ground. Lying on the bed and looking up to the ceiling, Kelly wondered about the incredible events of the last twenty-four hours. Whatever had happened to her she was here, now, in this home . . . and Daniel was waiting for her response to this book. She had liked the love story and wondered what such a serious man as Daniel would have thought of it.

Love. It seemed the great unifying force, no matter what the era.

Anxious to discuss the book with Daniel while it was still fresh in her mind, Kelly stood up and brushed the hair back from her face. Thank goodness Lizzie had given her a comb last night, for without a shower she figured she must look as grungy as she felt.

"Well, nothing to be done about it," she muttered, pulling the sharp teeth through the tangles of her hair. "Ouch!" She'd just have to make do. Seemed to be the story of her life, ever since she'd put on this horrid dress. She certainly didn't wind up in utopia! Shrugging, Kelly put down the comb and walked out of the room. Making her way through the house in search of Daniel, she decided that if he really wanted to know what life is like in the year 2001 . . . she would gladly set him straight.

"Come in."

Taking a deep breath, Kelly opened the door to his office and stepped inside. He looked up from papers scattered on his desk and stared at her as she crossed the space between them. Trying not to give credence to the growing attraction within her whenever she looked at the man, Kelly placed the book on his desk and said, "Very interesting, but Bellamy doesn't get it right. In the year 2000, rain still hits the pavement, socialism has not become the way of life, capitalism is more powerful than ever, and government is bigger than ever. Taking care of our fellowman is still seen as a burden, and class distinction is still a reality. Obviously, you know this book is a fantasy."

"You've finished?" he asked with surprise, gathering his papers together and sitting back in his chair while gifting her with a wide smile.

"It wasn't that long, and I'm a fast reader," she answered, sitting down in the wing chair opposite him. Why did he have to look so handsome when she must surely look a mess?

"So you found it interesting?"

"Interesting? Yes. Tough to follow in parts? Oh, yes. I liked the love story more than the science fiction," she admitted. "I guess love is the one thing that hasn't changed much over the ages." Embarrassed with her comment, she continued quickly, "Bellamy was right about music being piped into bedrooms, all rooms. It's not through telephone wires though. It's from a radio, or a stereo that's carried by wire and heard through speakers. Unless one is listening to something on a computer. Then it does travel through telephone wire. There's nothing unusual about that, except if one is writing from the point of view of someone living in 1887."

"What other point of view is there?"

She chuckled, going along with his fantasy. "Umm, the point of view of someone who has actually lived in the year 2000 . . . like *me*!"

"Surely, Miss Kelly, you are making a joke and—"

"First of all, you can drop the formal Miss Kelly," she interrupted. "Just call me by my name. And I am not making a joke, Daniel. In my world, the real world, I listen to music all the time, in my home, in my car, in stores, even on an air-plane. Yes, even that very airplane that brought me from Philadelphia to New Orleans."

"Air-plane?" His expression was confused and his complexion was suffused with color. "Again, you are claiming that you can fly?"

"I can't fly, the plane flies, and I had a seat on it. Look, you know what a telegraph is, right?"

He nodded.

"Okay, I can't explain an airplane, much less the techni-cal definition of radio, but it has something to do with the air being filled with electrical signals." She paused, thinking how she could state these facts to a man who claimed to be over one hundred years behind.

"Frequencies," she continued, "from transmitters. With-out a receiver to collect them and an amplifier to increase their strength, they remain unheard . . . but they're still out there. We move through them all the time. It's all too techni-cal for me, but I know what I know." She had a momentary thought that she'd taken so much for granted in her life. She didn't know how things worked; they just did. "Look at it this way, what if you tried to tell someone who lived in . . . say, the 1600s, about a train when the only transportation they know is a horse and carriage? This big iron horse uses wood and coal to propel an engine and drag cars behind it? That hundreds of people can ride on it at once and it would cut down travel time by weeks and months? Would they believe you, Daniel?"

His eyes were wide with confusion. "I don't know. Probably not."

"Right, and that's my dilemma, for you and Clara and even Lizzie claim to be living over a hundred years ago." She leaned forward. "But it just isn't so. This is the year 2001. I ought to know."

"And I ought to know where and when I am living."

She smiled. "Daniel, all three of you live out here in the bayou, isolated from everyone else in the world and—"

"I have an office and a home in New Orleans, Miss Kelly. I am not some backwoods ignorant man."

"Oh, well, I wasn't implying you were," she answered, knowing that was exactly how it must have sounded. "So you've been to New Orleans recently?"

Again, he nodded. "Last week."

"And you didn't see automobiles, airplanes, faxes, computers . . . ?"

"I honestly have no idea what you are talking about."

"What about a credit card? Even Bellamy mentioned it in his book."

"I only know what I read, that credit cards are issued by the nation and you exchange it like coupons for goods."

She couldn't help the laughter. "Credit cards in the year 2001 are paid for with cash and interest as high as twenty percent is sometimes charged to it."

He was shocked. "Twenty percent! Why that's usury!"

"Well, if that means robbery, then you're right, but what about cars, automobiles? You can't walk down a city street without the risk of being run over by one."

He simply stared at her.

"Televisions? Computers?"

He blinked.

"McDonald's? The golden arches?"

No signs of recognition.

"You had to have seen this stuff when you went into the city."

"I sincerely don't know what you are talking about."

She stared at him. "C'mon, Daniel. This isn't funny. How could you have been to one of the largest cities in the country and *not* have seen any of those things? I mean, we're talking about modern technology. It's everywhere!"

"Certain places are wired for electricity, a great advance, and as I said, telephones are becoming known, though private ownership is rare, but these other things you speak of . . . automobiles, computers . . . what are they?"

"You expect me to explain computers?" She laughed with exasperation. "It's . . . I don't know . . . a device that performs logical operations when programmed. It's stored information. The Information Superhighway, via telephone wires?" Staring into his eyes, she silently pleaded for some sign of recognition. Still, none came.

She wasn't getting anywhere. "Well, what I really found interesting is the way Bellamy handled the subject of women in his book," she said, thinking to change the subject from technology.

He smiled. "I thought you might enjoy that part."

Kelly straightened her shoulders. "It makes sense, doesn't it? In his utopia, where all men and women are entitled to the same rights and the same financial security . . . when a woman doesn't have to worry about being able to provide the day-to-day necessities for herself and her children, when she knows that she is able to do that on her own, she's then free to choose a mate for those things that are admirable like integrity, intelligence, compassion, wit. Security doesn't enter into it. And since man is basically motivated by his urge to . . ." Okay how was she to put this one? She cleared her throat. ". . . by his urge to mate, he drops those characteristics that are undesirable like aggression and greed and cultivates the more humane qualities, if he wants to . . . well, be intimate with a woman."

Daniel grinned and crossed his arms over his chest. "So you think women really do have the power to change the world?"

She thought about it for a moment, then blurted out, "Yes, if they just don't breed with arrogant bastards."

Yikes! Did I just say that?

He burst out laughing. "You are quite a progressive thinker, madam."

Embarrassed, Kelly took a deep breath, and said, "Look, I just want to get somewhere where I can find a telephone and get back to my own home. I'll leave the progressive thinking to Mr. Bellamy. I'm not a crusader for anything right now, save getting back to Philadelphia." She looked out the window. "The rain seems to be easing, so I should be able to leave tomorrow. And I don't think we should be having any more of these strange conversations about futuristic novels or technology, because we're not getting anywhere with this and—"

"But I know about telephones," he interrupted, looking very interested in continuing the conversation. ". . . twelve years ago, at the Centennial Fair in Philadelphia, Alexander Bell's machine converted sounds waves to electrical currents."

It was her turn to stare in disbelief. Twelve years ago at the Centennial Fair? "Now I don't know what you're talking about. The last centennial in Philadelphia was the *Bi*centennial in 1976. I was twelve years old."

"You really claim to be from the future?"

"I don't just claim it, Daniel. I know it! Even if I don't have anything with me to prove it."

He again crossed his arms over his chest and stared back at her. "Let's just pretend that such a thing is possible. Why here? Why now?"

Her eyes widened. "Like I know the answer to that? And I'm not saying I'm from the future. I'm from the real world where it *is* the year 2001. To you, that might seem like the future, but to me it's reality. This"—she waved her hand around the office—"this is not normal, Daniel. This is weird."

"Weird?"

"Yes. To be living back here with an old woman raising your daughter, without anything modern in sight." She'd had enough of this debate. It was time to change the subject as she'd suggested. "Tell me, does Lizzie even read and write?"

"Of course she does. I have taught her."

"Then she needs to be around children her own age, in school. Doesn't the state have laws about that?"

The muscle in his jaw seemed to clench, and Kelly realized she had overstepped her bounds. "I'm sorry," she whispered. "It's none of my business. It's just that she appears to be so intelligent and yet . . ."

"And yet she speaks like she's uneducated," Daniel finished, letting out his breath. "I know. Even though she has been to New Orleans on several occasions, even attended Sunday school, it's something I am attempting to rectify."

"How? By admonishing her all the time? Don't you realize she's terrified of angering you? And yet she adores you? All she wants from you is a little attention, and not negative attention. Did you ever think she could use a hug?"

He appeared embarrassed by the last part of her words. "I know. She's spent too much time with Clara."

"I don't know that Clara could be a bad influence. What about Will Hoskins?" Kelly asked. "He seems to be filling her head with all sorts of nonsense."

"How do you know about him?"

"Lizzie told me he was the one who informed her about capturing fairies and making them pay up with granting wishes. When I get to New Orleans I'll buy her some presents and have them sent here, but she needs to know that fairies aren't real, that I'm just a woman who got lost, and she found me. Not that I'm ungrateful for riding out this hurricane with all of you, but I wouldn't want the child to believe such nonsense."

"It wasn't a hurricane. If it had been, you wouldn't be able to leave tomorrow. We would be flooded. I'm sure the packet will come in the morning, and it will take you into the city."

"What is the packet?" She'd heard him say that before.

"A boat that makes regular runs into New Orleans. Delivers mail, supplies and such."

"How far away is it?"

He smiled. "The bayou is right at the end of the property."

"So I can do this tomorrow, you think? Get into New Orleans?"

"Yes. You should be there by noon."

She sighed, as though a great weight had been lifted from her shoulders. "Good." Then she thought about how she was going to pay for this ride into the city. "Daniel, I have something delicate to ask of you," she said in a hesitant voice. This was not going to be easy.

"And what is that, Miss Kelly?" He seemed amused by her, as though what they had been speaking about was an everyday conversation.

She cleared her throat and just said it. "I don't have my purse with me. Could you possibly lend me the cost of this packet ride into New Orleans? I promise you I will send it back with the presents for Lizzie. It's just that I'm in this situation right now, and—"

"I would be happy to arrange your transportation," he interrupted and saved her further embarrassment.

She stared into his blue eyes and swore she saw something else in them . . . some affection, tenderness, something that made her pulse race, and she had to look down at her lap to regain her composure. All of these emotions were totally misplaced. They barely knew each other! "Thank you . . . Daniel."

"It's the least I can do for a time traveler."

She glanced up to him and saw he was smiling. "You don't believe me, do you?"

"Do you believe me?"

She slowly shook her head. "No, I don't. I can't. For if you and Clara and Lizzie are correct . . . well, then I'm having a nervous breakdown, or I'm delusional, and I know I'm not. I know what I know. I don't belong here. I belong in my world."

He simply nodded. "And going to New Orleans tomorrow will settle this for you?"

"Yes. I'll get back to my hotel, throw out this horrid dress, get into my own clothes again, and check the airline schedules to fly back home to Philadelphia. That's my plan."

"Interesting. Fly home to Philadelphia. I can see why my daughter might think you are . . . someone possessed of magical powers."

"I don't think we should discuss that anymore, do you? We'll never agree, Daniel."

"And do you have family in Philadelphia?"

She nodded. "Just cousins now. My parents are no longer alive."

"I am sorry."

Kelly smiled. "So am I. I miss my mother. My father died when I was young, and my mother raised me. We had a very close relationship and then when . . . when my husband died, well, I thought I was all alone in the world. Not a very healthy place to be."

Suddenly, as she glanced up and saw sympathy in Daniel's eyes, Kelly's began to fill up with moisture, and she couldn't explain why.

He came around the front of the desk and leaned back against it. Smiling into her eyes, he whispered, "You haven't had a very easy time of it, have you, Kelly?"

It was just what she didn't need . . . sympathy. For too many years she had fought to stay strong. She felt her chest well up with emotion, and her throat burn from trying to hold back the tears. "Thank you, Daniel, but . . ." She couldn't continue. The words just wouldn't come.

"I know I don't have any right to say this, Kelly . . . but I would like to help you, if you would permit me."

She reached up and brushed a tear away from her cheek. "Help me? You've given a stranger shelter, and I thank you, Daniel, but nothing will help until I get back to the real world. All of this can't be real. It can't!"

He reached into his pocket and handed her a handkerchief. "Here. If you're going to cry, then do it. I'm not uncomfortable with a woman's tears."

In spite of everything, she almost laughed. "I don't cry," she muttered, taking the handkerchief and swiping at her eyes.

"Well, it appears you do, madam."

She glanced up at him and shrugged. "Yeah . . . well . . . in *normal* circumstances I don't cry . . . but nothing about this is normal."

He grinned, creating tiny smile lines around his wonderful blue eyes. Kelly almost groaned, as that spark of attraction again seemed to center on her solar plexus and swiftly travel through her body.

"I agree, nothing about this is normal," he said in a low voice. "When I first saw you sitting in the kitchen yesterday, for just a moment, you took away my breath. You . . . remind me of . . ." His words dropped off, as though he couldn't even speak it.

She did it for him. "I reminded you of your wife."

His eyes widened with surprise. "How did you know?"

"Clara told me. Don't look so stunned, Daniel. When I first saw you, I called you by my husband's name."

"That's right, you did call me Michael, I believe."

She nodded. "That was his name. You have the same features and build. Now, what are the chances of a widow and widower meeting like this, meeting two people who bear a resemblance to their dead spouses, under these circumstances? See what I mean about this not being normal?"

He continued to stare at her. "It is . . . odd, to say the least."

"Odd." She couldn't help chuckling while sniffling away any remaining tears. "That's one way to put it."

"Again, I apologize for last night. It was . . ." He seemed uncomfortable as he searched for a word.

"Weird." She supplied it and watched as his eyes sparkled. She wondered if it was from the memory of their kiss.

"Well, I should see if I can help Clara with dinner," Kelly announced as she stood up. "I suppose we could discuss the other aspects of the book later, if you wish." No way was she going to get into a conversation about this crazy attraction taking place between them. She was leaving tomorrow and would never see any of them again and . . . why didn't he move away when she stood up?

He straightened from leaning back on the desk yet barely

two feet separated them now. They stared into each other's eyes and Kelly sensed his chest rising and falling as he breathed.

"I don't understand this," he whispered, acknowledging what was taking place between them.

"I don't either," Kelly whispered back, wishing somehow she could, for the electricity was charging the small space between, drawing their bodies closer. At any moment, she thought he might kiss her again . . . and God help her, she wanted it!

It *was* craziness!

Blinking quickly, she took a deep breath and held her hand up. "This can't happen," she breathed, fighting the sexual attraction.

"I know."

"I mean, I'm leaving tomorrow and . . . and I'll never see you again."

"I know."

"You're a stranger, and I've never done anything like this before."

"I know."

"Stop saying *I know*," she pleaded.

"Yet, you don't feel like a stranger," he whispered, his eyes bright with wonder. "It's as though I already know you . . . as if we have done this before, felt this before."

"I know," she whispered back, and realized now *she* was saying it! "You understand this is absolute craziness?"

"I would say I know, but I've been told not to," he answered, now staring at her mouth as he took her hand and ever so gently stroked her fingers, then her palm. "I cannot explain this . . . this attraction. We've just met, and yet this seems so natural, so right."

She sighed as shivers of delight raced from her hand through her body and murmured, "We must both be crazy then, for I'm feeling the same thing."

"It's a divine madness, Kelly Brennan, and—"

Staring even more intensely into her eyes, he slowly leaned closer and Kelly felt his breath upon her mouth. She was drawn, too, as though some magnetic force was working between them, and neither had the power to stop the inevitable. "Divine madness," she repeated in an awe-filled whisper, watching as his gaze lowered to her lips. In an unconscious invitation her tongue wet her bottom lip and, with a low moan, Daniel closed the remaining space.

As his soft, warm skin grazed lightly against hers, he whispered, "Just to taste you . . ." and Kelly could no longer contain her own moan of desire. Daniel's mouth captured hers fully . . . promising more, so much more, and Kelly felt the strength nearly leave her legs as anticipation grew to ache between her thighs. Sighs of exquisite yearning mingled with their heavy breath and—

"Daddy!"

They each froze, as if caught in a compromising situation. She felt as though their passion was left suspended between them like the straight-line beep of a heart monitor when they broke apart as the office door was flung open. Lizzie stood there staring at them. Kelly resisted touching her mouth, though her lips still tingled and ached for what had been lost. She simply *had* to get control of herself! How could she have allowed this to happen again with a man she barely knew? It was madness.

"Clara said to tell you it's time for supper. And she said to tell you, too, Miss Kelly."

Embarrassed, Kelly glanced at Daniel and muttered, "I'm starved. I'll see if I can help in any way."

"I already helped," Lizzie piped up, looking very pleased.

"Then I'm sure it's going to be delicious," Kelly said, quickly moving past Daniel and touching Lizzie's shoulder as she left the room. "You look very pretty," she added, seeing that Lizzie was now wearing an old-fashioned light blue dress with puffy sleeves. "Doesn't she, Daniel?" She wanted the father to acknowledge his daughter.

He appeared to be shaken, both by his daughter's interruption and Kelly's question. And perhaps also by that stunning kiss. "Yes, Elizabeth looks lovely," he said with a smile to the child.

Kelly nodded and turned to leave. What had she almost done? If Lizzie hadn't knocked on the door, she would have thrown herself completely into his arms! Shocked at her own behavior, she smoothed down her dress and headed for the kitchen.

As she passed the dining room, she saw Clara lighting the candles on the chandelier.

"Here, let me," she said, walking into the room and taking the match from Clara's fingers. "I'm so sorry I didn't help with dinner. I was reading, and then I—"

"Ain't no reason to be apologizin', Miz Kelly," Clara said with a grin. "Cookin' kept that chile busy all day. Looks like you started somethin' this morning with your scrambled eggs. Seems Lizzie is takin' a real likin' to it."

"Maybe she can help you now," Kelly murmured as she lit the last candle. Blowing out the match, she smiled at the older woman. "That is, if she is a help, and not just underfoot."

Clara chuckled. "We'll see how long it lasts once the sun comes back out and that chile can run wild again."

Kelly laughed. Indeed, there was a wild streak in Lizzie, yet Kelly couldn't help but admire the young girl for it. "Everything looks wonderful, Clara," Kelly pronounced as she viewed the abundance of food on the table. Ham. Whipped sweet potatoes with brown sugar and butter. String beans in a tomato creole sauce. At the sight of food, her mouth started to water, and her stomach again churned with hunger. "After all this work, I wish you would eat with us, Clara."

"I'm happy to eat in the peace of my kitchen, Miz Kelly, but I thanks you for thinkin' of me. Breakfast was real nice this mornin', wasn't it?"

Nodding, Kelly said, "I'm finding being around you is what's nice, Clara. You're some woman."

Clara wrinkled up her nose and laughed while waving away Kelly. "Go on now with you, Miz Kelly! Too many compliments will spoil me."

"Maybe it's time you were spoiled, Clara." The equality she had read about in the book came back with a force. Too bad that part of the book was fiction.

"Who is spoiling whom?" Daniel asked as he walked into the dining room with his hand on Lizzie's right shoulder.

"I think Clara is spoiling us with this wonderful dinner and I say it's time someone spoiled her," Kelly answered with affection for the older woman, deciding to firmly put the incident in the study behind her.

"Now, you just hush, Miz Kelly, before Mistah Daniel thinks I put you up to this mischief."

"This is entirely my idea. In fact, after dinner, I think we should all do the dishes tonight and give you a break, Clara." Turning to the startled man, she continued, "What do you think, Daniel? A little physical labor might just be the thing for all of us, and Clara can rest her hip."

Daniel continued to seem startled as Clara said in a shocked voice, "Mistah Daniel can't be doin' no dishes!"

"And why not?" Kelly asked in amusement. "His hands seem perfectly fine to me."

When she saw Daniel's eyes widen even further with her statement, Kelly could feel herself blushing. "What I meant was—"

"I think I could manage a few dishes, Miss Kelly," he interrupted to save her from further embarrassment. "I also have read Mr. Bellamy's words about all contributing for the benefit of all. We shall practice it tonight."

Thankful for the rescue, Kelly returned his smile and again felt her heart melting. What was it with this man and her bizarre reaction to him? What kind of power did he have over her?

"Shall we be seated?"

"Yes, suh, Mistah Daniel. Y'all enjoy your supper."

Clara walked out of the dining room and Kelly watched as Daniel gently directed Lizzie to the chair she had used the night before. She couldn't help smiling at the child's tiny grin. If nothing else, before she left this family she wanted to make sure Daniel realized how much his daughter loved him . . . and needed him. What she was now witnessing was a far cry from last night's debacle.

After seating his daughter, Daniel came around the table and held out the chair for Kelly. "Thank you," Kelly murmured as she sat down and could feel his breath upon the top of her head.

"You are very welcome, Miss Kelly."

Damn, even his voice was sending shivers along her skin. She really was going to have to pull her act together. Kelly glanced across the table at Lizzie and grinned as she picked up her napkin. "I know! Let's pretend this is an oh-so-proper dinner party and we have to use our very best manners. We'll pick up our napkins, like so . . ." And she held hers gracefully as she slipped it onto her lap. "Want to play, Lizzie?"

The child looked at her father questionably as she touched her own napkin.

Daniel glanced at Kelly, and there was a moment of silent communication as though he knew exactly what Kelly was trying to do. "Why, that's a fine idea, Miss Kelly."

Lizzie's mouth broke into a wide smile as she grabbed her napkin.

"Try it like this, Lizzie," Kelly said, bringing her own up and gracefully placing it on her lap again. "Remember, this is supposed to be fun."

"Ain't never been fun before," Lizzie mumbled, trying to mimic Kelly's placement of the napkin.

"Elizabeth, there is no such word as ain't," Daniel said, after placing his napkin on his lap. "It's slang and—"

"And for tonight," Kelly interrupted before it became a lecture, "we won't be using it, for we're just oh-so-proper," she said with an exaggerated air of dignity in her voice before adding, "Is that not correct, Miss Elizabeth?"

Lizzie giggled and lifted her chin. "That is correct, Miss Kelly. We're oh-so-proper."

Grinning, Kelly said, "Perhaps your father might lead us tonight in grace?"

"Oh yes, Daddy. Lead us."

Kelly winked at the child, and whispered, "Well done."

"Hmm, why is it I fear I have become quite the amusement for you two lovely ladies?" Daniel protested with good nature.

"Surely not I, sir," Kelly said in mock protest.

"Surely not I, suh," Lizzie repeated in her softly accented voice while she theatrically held her hand to her heart, as though the very thought was unthinkable.

Oh, nice touch, Kelly thought while biting her lip to stop a laugh. She glanced at Daniel who appeared to be holding back a laugh of his own. He smiled slightly at his daughter, mixed with a look of fair warning as though the child should underplay the overacting. Lizzie shrugged her shoulders and grinned sheepishly at them in return.

They all burst out laughing.

"Perhaps it would behoove us to assume a respectful attitude as I'm about to say grace," Daniel finally breathed seriously.

Kelly nodded to Lizzie and the two of them bowed their heads.

"We give thanks for the bounty before us," Daniel began. "We are grateful for the many blessings bestowed upon us and we pray for continued blessings upon those who are seated here, especially our honored guest."

Kelly glanced up and saw that Daniel was smiling at her with such tenderness she wanted to reach over and caress his cheek. She then looked to Lizzie, saying, "Shall we begin serving, Miss Elizabeth?"

"First we have to say amen, or it don't . . . er, doesn't work."

"You're absolutely correct, Elizabeth," her father said affectionately. "Amen."

"Amen," Kelly added.

"*A*men," Lizzie said with finality. The child then lifted her chin again, and said to Kelly, "Now we can serve. I cooked this here food all day and I don't want it to get cold."

Kelly and Daniel looked at each other and burst out laughing again.

"Why, Elizabeth . . . you sound just like a woman," her father declared.

Lizzie looked very pleased.

The dinner proceeded without a single slipup. A few times Lizzie needed some direction but on the whole it was a very good show of manners all around. Daniel was pleased. Lizzie had fun. And Kelly found herself getting more and more drawn into this family.

When Clara came in later to clear the table, it was Daniel

who shooed her out as he stood up. "I believe tonight has been declared the dawn of a new age. You shall be 'spoiled,' as Miss Kelly has stated. We shall wash the dishes and clean your kitchen, Clara. Off with you now . . . and do as you wish."

Clara looked stunned. "You was serious?"

Kelly laughed, and Lizzie giggled at the older woman's shock. "Rest easy, Clara," Kelly answered. "I've done lots of dishes in my life, and I promise I won't let Mister Daniel break any."

Clara started laughing. "Mistah Daniel's gonna do my dishes?"

Nodding, Kelly glanced at Lizzie, and said, "He's quite capable of it. Lizzie and I will dry them and put them away. We women know our way around a kitchen and we'll help him if he gets overwhelmed." She looked at the man with a sly grin.

Daniel laughed, and said, "Now it is certain I am providing the amusement this night." He pulled back Kelly's chair as she rose from the table.

Kelly walked over to the old woman and placed her hand on her back as she led her from the dining room and out of earshot of the others. "Allow us to do this, Clara," she whispered. "If it makes you feel better, it's not just for you. This is another great opportunity for Daniel and Lizzie to get to know each other better and have some fun doing it."

Clara glanced up at her. "Dishes is fun?"

Grinning, Kelly answered, "For someone who never does them, it can be . . . especially if I'm around to make sure of it."

"You is one strange woman, Miz Kelly. Look at all you've done, and you has only been here one full day. Makes my head spin to think of what it might be like if'n you was to stay longer."

Kelly stared at the woman and merely blinked. What was that supposed to mean?

"I'm leaving, Clara. Tomorrow morning."

"Yeah, I figured you would," the old woman said with a

tired smile. "Best I take advantage of this *spoilin'* while I can."

Kelly watched Clara walk away from the kitchen and had to admit these three people were working their way into her heart, and she didn't want it. Not now.

She needed to get home. . . .

That was what she wanted. Wasn't it?

Six

"You mean you have never done dishes in your life?"
Daniel stood in front of the sink and looked at the soapy water in a basin. "No, truly, I haven't."

Kelly tried to repress her amused tone. "How old are you?"

"I am forty-one years of age, and I don't understand what you find so amusing when—"

"How can anyone make it to forty-one years without ever having washed a dish?" she interrupted, no longer able to hold back the laughter. "You don't exactly practice Mr. Bellamy's version of egalitarianism, do you?"

Now he laughed. "What you read in that book, madam, was fiction. And it was about the future. I've always had servants, or if I ate publicly, the dishes were taken away. Why should that be such a surprise to you?"

"Servants, huh?" Kelly asked with a grin as she looked at Lizzie and winked. "Well, let's show your dad how the other half lives. Come on, Lizzie, help me roll up your father's shirtsleeves. He's about to do some honest labor and appreciate all the effort that went into feeding him tonight."

"*Honest labor*, you say," Daniel parodied. "Ladies, I'll have you know, these hands have seen plenty of blisters and calluses in their day." He held his hands out for inspection.

Pulling his hand toward her, Kelly began unbuttoning his cuff link. "Must have been quite a few days ago," she mumbled loud enough to bring a wider smile to Daniel's face.

Lizzie grabbed her father's other hand and followed the lead. Kelly held out her palm and Lizzie dropped the cuff link into it. Placing both into the pocket of her apron, Kelly then began rolling up Daniel's sleeve. "Like this, Lizzie," she pointed out. "Make it tight to keep it up, because your father's going to be up to his elbows in dirty dishwater."

The child giggled, and Daniel eyed Kelly. "You are enjoying this, aren't you?" he asked softly with a smirk.

Both females nodded. "I always enjoy watching a man work, especially when it's anything domestic," Kelly said with a playful grin, and looked back down to her task.

"Domesticity is a woman's art," Daniel declared. "I don't mind helping, but I hope you appreciate that tonight, I am acceding purely for your amusement," he added, allowing Kelly and Lizzie to roll up his shirtsleeves.

Staring at the fine dark hairs on Daniel's arm, Kelly was acutely aware of how long it had been since she'd touched a man's skin and hurried to finish before *those* memories started her thinking about those kisses they had shared. Yes, she had shared them with him, and it still shocked her. She patted the sleeve, then turned to help Lizzie. When she looked back up into his eyes she saw he was staring and smiling at her. She hoped he wouldn't notice the flush that was creeping around her ears.

"So you think keeping a home and washing dishes is solely a woman's job?" Kelly asked to break the penetrating silence between them.

"Of course," he answered, rubbing his hands together as he looked back to the basin of water. "It's one of the natural laws of life." He paused before adding, "Though I'm certain it can't be too difficult."

Okay, now he was deliberately goading her, Kelly thought, as she bit her lip to keep from smiling. "You're absolutely right, Daniel," she admitted, pausing to allow the man a momentary sense of victory before adding, "It isn't difficult at all . . . I'm certain even a man could handle it." Kelly then stared at him, anticipating his reaction of defeat.

He glanced at her and grinned even more. "Now, tell me you are a suffragist too."

"What's that, Daddy?" Lizzie blurted with her hands on her hips.

"Yes, do tell your daughter what a suffragette is, Daniel."

He cleared his throat. "It's . . . well, Elizabeth, there is a movement of women who want the same rights as men and—"

"What are rights?"

"It means how one is treated under the law, Elizabeth. The privileges one is accorded."

Kelly shook her head. "What a suffragette means, Lizzie, is a term for a woman who fought to change laws that would allow all women the same rights as a man, including the right to vote. If it weren't for those women, you and I might not have many rights today."

"I don't get it," the child grumbled, and squinched her eyebrows in frustration.

"Neither do I," Daniel whispered and winked to his daughter. "Just what are you talking about?" he asked, picking up a dish and putting it into the basin. "Women can't vote."

Kelly glared at him. "I voted in the last three presidential elections."

"If you did, it was not done legally," he murmured, washing the dish and holding it up for inspection.

"Daniel . . . I voted legally."

He turned his head and looked directly into her eyes. "You are, by far, the most fascinating woman I have ever met, Miss Kelly Brennan."

Kelly blinked. "Flattery will get you nowhere, Mr. Gilmore," she warned, grabbing a linen towel off the table. Okay, so maybe that wasn't entirely the truth, she mentally admitted, but she wasn't about to let him think he could get out of this debate with flagrant charm.

"Let's get back to the point. Women have lived under a patriarchal system of government and religion for thousands of years and yet, since suffrage, women are embracing change, pioneering new territory, raising our daughters differently because of it and making sure our voices are heard." There. She'd let him chew on that for a minute.

It had been a very long time since she'd had a verbal sparring match with a man. She recalled how Michael would tease her with challenges, yet he was always respectful. The entire scene was becoming too reminiscent of another time in her life . . . a time when her heart was wide-open and the joy of love flowed through it. What was happening to her?

"So, you are saying that women have been given the right to vote?"

His deep voice snapped her back from her romantic notion. "Yes . . . it happened in the early part of the twentieth century. Legally, in the Nineteenth Amendment."

He handed her the dish. "You say it with such conviction, I could almost believe you."

"Believe me," she said, taking the dish and holding it in the towel. "I'm not making any of this up."

"Making what up?" Lizzie demanded.

Kelly turned to the child. "That I am a woman who has equal rights to any man."

"I can climb a tree better'n Will Hoskins," Lizzie volunteered.

"There you go," Kelly said with a grin.

"You climb trees, Elizabeth?" her father quickly asked, as he handed his daughter a fork to dry.

Lizzie looked startled and glanced up at Kelly.

"Dry them really well, Lizzie . . . they're silver and will tarnish if you don't." Turning her attention back to the handsome man at the sink, she remarked, "I climbed trees when I was her age. Many girls do."

"Well, it's not very ladylike," Daniel muttered, handing Kelly another plate.

She shrugged her shoulders. "It's fun. Didn't you climb trees, Daniel?"

"Of course, but I'm . . ." He hesitated for a moment before glancing at Kelly. "I'm walking right into this, aren't I?"

Chuckling, Kelly nodded. "Why should it be fun for boys and not fun for girls? Because of some arbitrary rules of society?"

"We live by rules of society," Daniel answered, stacking the flatware on the sideboard for Lizzie to dry. "Without them, we would be barbarians."

Kelly shrugged. "We might just have a few too many rules. Especially if young girls can't enjoy the same freedoms as young boys, without being judged by those who are so programmed by what others might think. They've forgotten about the freedom to just have innocent fun." Kelly paused before she dried the dish. "Um, you missed a spot," she added, handing the dish back to Daniel.

"This is an impassioned subject for you, Kelly," he said, taking the dish back with a smile. "You *are* a suffragist."

"Well, I've never thought of myself as one, since I thought that movement was specifically about voting. But you might be right."

"Am I one, Daddy?"

He looked down to his daughter, and his smile widened. "I have no doubt you will be one day, Elizabeth."

Lizzie seemed very pleased by her father's remark. "Well, if Miss Kelly is one, then I wanna be one, too."

Kelly and Daniel laughed together.

"Contributing to the delinquency of a minor, are you Miss Brennan?" Daniel asked.

"Oh, believe me, Mr. Gilmore, your daughter has contributed much to the delinquency of a major," Kelly joked, then added in a whisper, "She really is quite a young lady, though." She smiled down to Lizzie, who was intensely inspecting the spoon she'd dried. Once more Kelly was reminded that the fondness she was feeling for this family just didn't make sense.

"Yes, her speech and her manners have greatly improved since your arrival."

Kelly winked at Lizzie. "It's been fun. And we're just oh-so-proper, aren't we, Lizzie?"

"Oh, yes, we are," Lizzie pronounced, holding the towel to her chest with a dramatic flair and lifting her chin playfully.

Kelly chuckled at the little actress.

Finished with the flatware, Lizzie picked up a china bread plate and Kelly, readying herself to help, watched in horror as it slipped through the child's fingers and crashed to the wooden floor.

"Elizabeth!" Daniel instantly scolded his daughter as he reached down to pick up broken pieces. "Do you know how old this china is? It was your grandmother's, and one day it was to be yours. How could you be so careless?"

Lizzie's face reddened, and her chin started to quiver. Suddenly, she dropped the dish towel on the table and ran out of the kitchen.

"Why did you yell at her?" Kelly demanded as she knelt to help pick up the shattered china. "It was an accident."

Daniel's face looked pained. "I . . . I just reacted."

"You don't think she wanted to break it, do you? She was being so very careful."

"Yes, yes, I know it was an accident."

"Then why did you have to yell at her?" Kelly again demanded, handing the tiny pieces to him. "Can't you see how much she really wants to please you? You're her only parent, and she loves you."

"I didn't mean to yell," Daniel insisted.

"You should apologize. Tell her you aren't angry."

"Apologize to a child?" He seemed surprised as he stood up and looked down at her.

Rising, Kelly nodded. "Why not? You don't really believe you have to maintain power over her like that, do you? Yes, she's a child. Yours. All she wants from you is your love and a little attention."

He didn't reply as he threw away the broken dish.

"Daniel, I'm telling you that it would make a huge difference in your daughter's life if you just went upstairs now and talked about this. Don't let her sit up there in her room all alone, thinking she's some horrible kid. She's not. It was an accident, that's all."

"It's a shame you don't have any children of your own, Kelly," he said in a low voice. "If I may be so bold to say, you would make a fine mother."

Embarrassment flooded over her, and Kelly smiled a little. "Well, thank you, Daniel. Who knows what's in store for me?" She turned to the sink and shooed him away. "I'll finish the dishes. You go upstairs to Lizzie."

"Now?"

"Right now. Before it gets any bigger in her mind. *Go!*" She handed him her dish towel.

Wiping his hands, he looked into her eyes, and quietly said, "Thank you."

Kelly nodded and turned her attention to the remaining dishes as he placed the towel next to her and walked across the room. When did she get so bossy and protective about the child? Sighing, Kelly smiled sadly. It was too bad . . . they had been having so much fun until Lizzie dropped the plate. Poor kid, she probably felt rotten about it. Kelly could see the tension in Daniel's back as he left the room. Apparently, he was feeling rotten about it, too. There was more than shattered pieces of china that needed mending.

Ascending the stairs slowly, Daniel felt embarrassment and regret for his reaction creep over him. Why had he gotten so angry? He cared for and loved his daughter incredibly. He really felt he'd tried so many times to become close to her, but for some reason, in his mind, all his efforts became miserable failures. Then suddenly, Miss Kelly Brennan an extraordinary stranger, "flies" into all of their lives and he is now greatly concerned with how he might prove he truly loved his daughter. He shook his head in brief amusement, mostly at himself. Just what was it that woman possessed to captivate him so much? Suddenly, he felt that things he'd buried long ago were reawakening. Was it she who inspired him to begin caring more deeply and seeing things clearly again? Did she truly possess some kind of magic as his daughter insisted? He paused at the top of the staircase. It was all so remarkable to him. He was beginning to feel his heart again.

Could he be so bold as to hope for more?

Knocking softly on his daughter's bedroom door, he turned the handle and poked his head in. "Elizabeth, I must speak with you."

"You done real well, Miz Kelly."

Startled, Kelly spun around from the cabinet where she was putting away some of the dried bowls. Clara was standing in the doorway of her bedroom off the kitchen, dressed in a long brown robe. The kerchief was off her head, and her gray hair was braided down her back. She looked so old, so fragile. "Clara . . . I didn't know you were there."

"I heard that plate crash, and I was afraid all hell was gonna break loose." The woman grinned and shuffled into the room. "No harm done, far as I can see."

"Lizzie accidentally broke a bread plate. It couldn't be saved."

"Things break," Clara muttered, holding on to the back of a chair. "I see how Mistah Daniel listens to you, and that's a good thing. If that came from one little ole plate breakin', then I say it was a good thing it done broke. 'Bout time he starts hearin' the truth again."

"The truth?"

"That his child needs him. We sure is gonna miss you when you go, Miz Kelly."

"Yes . . . and I think I'm going to miss all of you, too. Isn't that funny?"

"Sure 'nough, it is. Life is funny. I knows if I couldn't laugh, I woulda died, so I just shake my head and keep on laughin'."

Grinning, Kelly looked with affection to the older woman. "I'd like to write to you, Clara. Would that be all right?"

"Write to me . . . in a letter?"

"Yes. I'd like to stay in touch if that's okay."

"Well, I don't suppose Mistah Daniel would mind readin' me your letter, cause I ain't never learnt to read or write myself, Miz Kelly."

She found it hard to believe that anyone, even someone as

old as Clara, didn't know how to read, but it wasn't her business. "Then I'll send you a card every once in a while and we can stay in touch."

"That would be very nice," Clara said with a sigh. "I ain't never had a letter before."

Kelly didn't know how to answer her. How could someone *never* have received a letter? A single piece of mail? "Well, when I get to New Orleans, I'll be sure to send something with Lizzie's gifts." Suddenly, she wondered if Mrs. Whelan had her purse. It had been left at the Tyler Mansion, in the bedroom where she had dressed. At least the hotel had a credit-card imprint, and she'd just have to call and get another if her purse was lost. Thank heavens she'd left her plane ticket in the safety-deposit box in the hotel room.

"I appreciate your kindness, Miz Kelly. I knows that chile upstairs is gonna miss you."

Kelly turned back to the sink and continued washing the last of the pots and pans. "I know," she murmured. "I'll miss her, too."

Clara picked up the discarded dish towel from the table and came to stand next to Kelly. "I reckon we'll all be a bit changed for havin' you come here. Just like Lizzie says . . . you brought some magic with you."

"Oh, Clara . . ." She handed over a skillet. "That's very kind of you to say, but I don't know about any magic."

Clara wiped the pan and remarked, "Well, Mistah Daniel is upstairs with his chile. First time I ever seen him do that. I'd say there's some magic afoot."

Kelly grinned. "Surely, it's not the first time."

"First time for that man to tell her he's sorry. You made him see that. Weren't somethin' I could have done."

"Why is he so distant with Lizzie? She really isn't a bad child."

"Course she isn't. Now this is just my opinion, but seems it's got more to do with her momma than with her. That man's been grievin' somethin' awful way too long, and that chile reminds him of Miz Lillian. I thinks it's the pain he ain't dealt with all these years." Clara paused and sighed. "Lord knows, we've all had our share of pain."

Kelly understood pain, gut-wrenching emotion that can paralyze. Even she'd been trying to deny her own for too many years. "Sometimes, we just can't deal with it, Clara. We'd drown in it if we tried."

"That sure 'nuff is true. Sounds to me like you spent some time with this your own self, Miz Kelly."

"Yes," she murmured, finally finished with the dishes and extremely grateful Clara had dried and put away the last of the pots and pans. Weariness was quickly descending upon her. Tomorrow was a big day, and she might as well get some rest. She looked at Clara and smiled with affection. "I think anyone who's alive has dealt with pain."

"Now, ain't that the truth?" Clara handed her the dish towel.

Wiping her hands, Kelly said, "I guess it's just part of the human experience. Maybe that's why we appreciate happiness so much? Can you have one without the other?"

"I don't rightly know, Miz Kelly. Surely I don't, but seems to me that we is meant to be happy, just lots a stuff holds us back." Clara picked up the oil lamp from the table and, handing it to Kelly, added with a warm smile, "Now you go on to bed. I can see you is tired. We'll say our good-byes in the mornin'."

"I will really miss you, Clara. Do you mind if I hug you?"

The older woman again looked shocked. "You wants to hug me?"

"If you don't mind," Kelly said with a big grin.

Beaming, Clara put the lamp down and opened her arms. "Mind? It'd be a sheer pleasure to hug you, Miz Kelly."

Kelly felt the warm comfort of Clara's arms, a comfort that had been missing in her life for some time. Her eyes began to fill with emotion as she reluctantly broke away. "Thank you, Clara. I'll see you in the morning."

"Dream sweet and rest well, Miz Kelly."

"You too . . ." she whispered, and quickly turned to leave the kitchen before she got too emotional.

"Oh, Miz Kelly, you don't need the lamp?"

Whispering over her shoulder she replied, "No. Thank you, Clara. I know the way."

From behind her, Kelly heard the puff of breath that extinguished the amber glow. Walking through the darkened house, Kelly was again stunned by the way she had become so attached to this family in such a short time. Why was that? Reaching for the newel post, she ran her fingertips, almost reverently, over the ornate carvings. As she slowly climbed the stairs and ran her hand along the banister, the oddest sensation came over her. It seemed all too comfortable. She was in a home, not a sterile apartment where the only sounds came from a stereo, a television, or an occasional guest.

Reaching the top landing, she dismissed the puzzling thoughts and made her way through the shadowed hallway to her bedroom door. Quietly turning the knob, she entered and instinctively made her way through the dark to the night table. She felt for the box of matches and withdrew one. Lighting the oil lamp, she watched as the flame grew larger.

She actually felt a pang of regret that she was leaving in the morning and wanted to laugh at herself. Clara and Lizzie claimed she had magic, but it was as if this strange family placed some kind of magic spell over her. When she thought about leaving it was with an odd mixture of anticipation to get back and a weird reluctance. Better to get to bed and not dwell on what she couldn't understand. Untying the apron, she was about to place it on the bed, when she felt the weight of something heavy in the pocket. Immediately, she knew it was Daniel's cuff links. She pulled them out and held them in her hand as she sat on the edge of the mattress.

They were squares of gold, with the initials *DG* engraved on each. Inspecting them closer, Kelly could see they were real gold, and she knew they were valuable. She glanced to the door, wondering if it was too late to return them tonight. Should she just wait until morning? Something, some strange feeling in her solar plexus that radiated up to her heart, was telling her to return them now. Did she dare? She knew from earlier in the day when Clara was making the beds which room was Daniel's. Surely he wasn't asleep yet. He'd probably just finished talking to Lizzie, for there was no sound on the other side of the wall.

Standing up, she clutched the cuff links in her fist and walked out of the room. She could feel her heart beating faster as she made her way down the darkened hall. All she was doing was returning his property. Right? *Right*?

"Oh stop it," she muttered. She simply had to refrain from second-guessing herself around this man. She was leaving tomorrow and would never see him again. What difference did it make what he thought of her? A tiny voice told her it mattered far too much.

Taking a deep breath, Kelly brought up her hand and knocked lightly on his bedroom door. Why was she so nervous? She was a grown woman and had interacted with men before and was only returning something. It wasn't like she was coming to him to—

The door opened and Kelly finally let out her breath. "Hi," she breathed with a small smile of apology. "I'm sorry to bother you so late, but . . ." Nervous, she looked down to her hand and willed it to open. "I found these in my apron and thought I should return them at once."

"Thank you," he whispered, holding out his hand. "I only remembered myself a few moments ago. I was going to wait until morning before asking for them."

Embarrassed, Kelly dropped them into his palm, inhaling when her fingers touched his. "Yes, well, I considered that, too, but thought you might want them." He was still dressed, even his sleeves were still rolled up, so she figured she'd been right to return them.

"Well, you didn't disturb me. As a matter of fact, I was just thinking about you."

She glanced into his eyes. "You were?"

His smile widened, as though he knew his remark must have embarrassed her. "Yes. I wanted to thank you again for insisting I speak with Elizabeth. You were quite right."

"Good. I mean . . . I just sensed it would be best," she paused before adding, "for everyone."

"It was," he said, and smiled. "I don't know why my patience is so short with her. She was crying in her room when I entered. I could see it made a difference that I followed her and settled it without letting more time go by between us."

"Lizzie really is a sweetie. She wants to please you so much."

He sighed with resignation. "I don't suppose I appear to be a good parent to you."

She shook her head. "Oh, I can see you care about her, Daniel. I just don't think you understand little girls."

"Now, that's an understatement. You wouldn't have any advice for a willing student, would you?"

She returned his smile. "Just love her, Daniel. Show her you love her. That's really all she wants."

He nodded. "You have a rare clarity of thinking, Miss Kelly Brennan. I appreciate it, and I'm very pleased you've come into our lives."

She chuckled. "Well, you didn't seem all too pleased when you first saw me."

"I was shocked."

"You explained. What a difference a day makes, huh?"

He leaned against the doorjamb and, looking down at the cuff links in his hand, sighed. "You will leave us tomorrow then?"

"Yes. I must get back home."

He looked back up at her. "And you will fly there?" It was his turn to chuckle.

Instead of being annoyed, Kelly smiled with him for the teasing note in his voice was very pleasing. "Yes, Daniel. I'll fly on an airplane to Philadelphia."

"You have a wondrous imagination."

"Well, thank you, but it doesn't take a good imagination to know a few facts about daily life."

They stared at each other in silence, and Kelly swore she could feel that same energy pulling at her, drawing her closer to him. To save disgracing herself, she cleared her throat and crossed her arms over her waist. "Okay, I should get back to my room now. Good night, Daniel."

"Allow me to light the way for you," he said, quickly turning back to his bedroom and picking up a lamp.

"No, really . . . I'm fine. Don't bother. I can—"

"It's no bother, Kelly. As your host, I insist."

She simply nodded and turned back to her room. Daniel

followed her, holding the lamp high to illuminate the way. It was a short distance, and when they reached her door, Kelly turned around to thank him.

He was standing so close to her that she leaned against the door to make more room.

"Thanks. Well, good night, Daniel."

"Don't worry . . . I won't accost you again in the hallway." Once more, he was teasing her.

"I wasn't worried," she murmured, though a small part of her was dying to feel his arms around her and to taste his kiss again. Craziness.

"By the way, I've decided to accompany you tomorrow morning. I have business in the city and am anxious to see these wonders you speak of so often. May I escort you to your hotel?"

Startled by his announcement, Kelly nodded, and a strand of hair fell over her eye. "Oh, sure. That would be okay, I guess." With her arms still crossed over her waist, she shook her head slightly to move the hair back. It wasn't working.

Without warning, he reached up and gently brushed the stray strand behind her ear while smiling at her with such tenderness she had to stifle a moan while a tingle of excitement created goose bumps all over her skin.

Impulsively turning her head toward his lingering hand, she breathed, "Thanks."

He slowly lowered his hand and spoke softly. "Good night, Miss Kelly Brennan. Sleep well."

"Good night," she whispered, and quickly turned to open the door. She didn't even trust herself to look at him again. It was all she could do to close it behind her. Leaning against it, she finally moaned, then spun around to lock it.

It was not to keep him out.

It was to keep her in.

Lizzie stamped her foot loudly on the wooden floor. "How can you leave? You didn't grant me all my wishes!"

Kelly looked at the child and tried to smile, as she stood in the kitchen. "Oh, Lizzie . . . honey, I can't grant wishes. I told you that, but I'll send you some gifts from New Orleans and—"

"I don't want any gifts!" the child protested. "I found you, and you're mine!"

"Honey, I have to go home. I told you when we met that was what I was trying to do. I'll tell you what . . . I'll write to you, okay? You and I can be pen pals. How about that?"

"What's a pen pal?" Lizzie's fists were placed firmly on her hips. She didn't look placated at all.

"Friends who write letters to each other. We are friends, aren't we, Lizzie?"

"You really leavin' me, after you promised? You said fair's fair, and I could keep you."

This was tougher than she'd thought. "Lizzie, I will miss you, but I have to get home. I always said that."

"You got children there?"

"Well, no."

"You have family there?"

"I have cousins."

"Cousins don't count. You ain't got no one, so you can stay here with us. You like it here, right?" Tears were coming into the child's eyes.

"Of course I like it here with you, but—"

"Lizzie Gilmore, you let Miz Kelly leave now without a fuss," Clara interrupted, gently putting her hand on the youngster's shoulder. "She said she would write you a letter, and you can keep in touch that way."

Lizzie shrugged off Clara's hand and stared into Kelly's eyes. "You never granted me all my wishes," she accused again.

Sighing, Kelly asked, "What would you like? Toys? A new doll? Clothes? Games?"

"I wanna use up all my wishes right now."

"Okay," Kelly murmured hesitantly.

"I want . . . I want . . . I want . . . I want . . . I want you to come back. There! Five wishes all at once!"

Kelly merely blinked. She didn't know what to say. Finally, realizing she had to somehow answer, she murmured, "Well, I'll try and return for a visit, Lizzie."

"You gotta promise, and this time you gotta mean it."

"Okay, I promise someday I will return for a visit. How's that?"

"Answer Miz Kelly, chile, then run and say good-bye to your daddy."

"You mean it?" Lizzie looked Kelly squarely in the eye and demanded truth.

Nodding, Kelly said, "Yes, I mean it. I'll be back." She was startled to realize that she *was* telling the truth. One day she would return and see Lizzie and Clara and Daniel. She could probably combine it with a business trip.

"Fairies' promise?" Lizzie asked, holding out her curled pinky in invitation.

Grinning, Kelly locked her finger into the small hand then pulled the child into her arms. "Oh, c'mere, you big toughie. Give me a hug."

Lizzie clung to her, and Kelly heard her whisper, "I want you to stay."

Bending down, she kissed the top of Lizzie's head, and whispered back, "I'll see you again. I promise."

Lizzie tore out of her arms and ran from the house to where her father was waiting. Poor kid, she was taking this pretty hard. Kelly turned to Clara and smiled with sadness. "I didn't know it would be this difficult to say good-bye." She could feel tears beginning to well in her own eyes, and her throat began to burn with emotion.

"You sure is one fine woman," Clara stated with a big smile. "Been a pleasure to know you, Miz Kelly."

Shaking her head, Kelly gathered the old woman into her arms and whispered, "The pleasure has been mine, Clara." She sniffled back her tears. "You are a jewel."

Clara patted her back and chuckled. "No wonder I likes you so much, with such sweet talk!"

Kelly left the house to join Daniel and Lizzie, who were holding hands, and she felt another surge of gratification. Perhaps her presence here had a purpose, as Clara insisted. Kelly was sure Daniel and Lizzie were becoming closer, and if she'd had anything to do with it, then in a way she was even more grateful for the turn of events. What an adventure, she mused to herself, as Lizzie reached out to take hold of her hand.

With the child connecting them, the three walked toward a small dock at the bank of the river. There, a flatboat was waiting, and Kelly was surprised to see more men dressed in old-fashioned clothing on and around it. A black chimney stack smoked, and she could smell the distinct aroma of burning wood. She figured it must be a steam engine, and then wondered why these people insisted upon living in such archaic fashion. Shrugging, she decided she wouldn't give it any more credence than a culture of people lost in romantic nostalgia.

Daniel helped her board and, as she stood at the side and watched Clara join Lizzie on the bank, Kelly kept waving. She really was going to miss them more than she ever thought possible.

Suddenly Lizzie started running as the boat took on speed.

"We'll be pen pals!" she shouted, waving wildly.

Kelly swallowed back the tears and waved even wider. "I promise!" she yelled back. "Pen pals!"

Lizzie began running along the wooded shoreline, darting in between trees, trying to keep up while shouting, "And you'll come back!"

"Yes . . ." She gulped down the lump in her throat. "I promise!"

Kelly kept waving, swallowing back her tears, until the boat rounded a bend. She could no longer see Clara, and she watched Lizzie's tiny figure slump onto a rock in exhausted defeat. Kelly moved her trembling hand to her mouth and blew the child a kiss. She didn't know if Lizzie could make out what she was doing, for the small girl didn't move. Kelly continued staring until Lizzie was merely a shadow that blended into the woods.

"Come. Sit down," Daniel murmured, touching her arm.

Sniffling, Kelly turned her head and smiled sadly. "It seems your daughter has had a profound effect on me, Mr. Gilmore."

"I am certain those feelings are mutual, Miss Kelly," he

answered with a sympathetic smile as he motioned behind him. "Why don't you sit down?"

Kelly looked at the two rows of wooden benches that were fastened to the boat's middle. She picked up the hem of her gown and stepped over coiled rope and around several wooden boxes. There were two other men on a bench, also dressed in old-fashioned clothes, and she noticed that Daniel nodded in recognition.

"Neighbors," he whispered, as he sat down next to her on the other wooden bench. "I'm sure there will be gossip up and down the river concerning your appearance." He chuckled, as though the prospect of gossip was amusing.

"Considering how I look, they might just think I'm a leftover from Mardi Gras."

"You know about Mardi Gras?"

"Of course," she answered as she looked out to the passing scenery. Low branches at the shoreline nearly dipped into the water. "Everyone's heard of Mardi Gras. I do a lot of business arranging trips to New Orleans for it."

"Arrange trips?"

She nodded. "I told you about my business. I'm a travel agent. I own the agency."

"You arrange travel?"

"Yes. I help people who want to travel around the world book reservations and—" She turned to look at him. "You've never heard of a travel agent?"

"I have heard of transportation agents, but for a woman to own such an agency is astounding."

"Why? You don't think a woman can handle it?"

He chuckled. "Oh, I am not getting into that discussion again. I learned my lesson last night."

She grinned. "What I find astounding is that you have this antiquated opinion of women. When we get to New Orleans you'll see."

"What will I see?"

She laughed. "How can you claim to work there and deny what is there for all the world to see? Like modern buildings, electricity, women working in every capacity from politics and police work to construction and owning their own businesses."

"Why would a woman want to work in construction?" He seemed shocked.

She made an involuntary noise with her mouth, as though shocked by his question. "Because they like working outdoors? Because the pay is better? There are many reasons, Daniel. The most important one is because they can, if they are drawn to it. I guess those suffragettes started something, huh?" She squinted her eyes. "Oh my God, is that really an alligator?"

He looked where she was pointing and nodded as the reptile slid into the water from a muddy bank. "Yes. Now, tell me more about this . . . this world of the future you claim to be from, for I must prepare you . . . it does not exist here."

She turned and stared into his eyes and felt a deep foreboding welling up in her chest.

"It has to, Daniel," she whispered, trying to keep her voice even. "For if it doesn't, then, God help me . . . I'm beyond lost."

Seven

Kelly saw the city in the distance, and her heart clenched in fear at the absence of tall buildings. Where were the big hotels, the Trade Mart, the Riverwalk, all the development of the city? She saw two steamboats and a few barges on the river, but nothing modern. Her brain refused to believe what her eyes were seeing.

"There must be another way," she muttered to herself, yet she could see the famous crescent of the shoreline, the distinctive spires of St. Louis Cathedral, and knew she was on the Mississippi now. "Daniel, this can't be New Orleans!"

"But it is," he insisted as she clutched his arm. "This is New Orleans."

"No, it can't be!" she protested. "It's . . . it's not the same. Everything modern is gone."

"We're a very modern city. Certain places have electricity and—"

"Daniel!" she interrupted, tugging on his jacket sleeve. "Something is very wrong!"

"Calm down, Miss Kelly," he said in a serious voice, as he patted her hand. "We'll figure everything out when we get—"

"Where's the Trade Mart? All the hotels, *my* hotel?" she nearly shrieked, not caring if the other passengers were staring at her. "If my hotel is gone, then so is my luggage and my ticket and . . ." She stared at the outmoded city skyline and lowered her voice. ". . . and my way home."

"Now, now . . ." Daniel consoled her. "I would never leave you stranded. We'll find some help, and you will return to your home. Have you no relatives in the North that we might telegraph for assistance?"

"Relatives? Telegraph?" She stared at him, thinking he too was crazy. "I don't know their addresses off the top of my head. Everything was in my purse."

He took a deep breath and stared at the city. "Not to worry, dear lady. Everything will be all right," he continued, lowering his voice, "you are merely seeing things as they are, as I tried to warn you yesterday when we had our discussion. This is the world of now, of 1888."

Her jaw dropped in shock as his words resounded within her brain, and that terrible feeling of dread again raced across her nerve endings. As they neared the docking area, she could see burly stevedores transferring bales of cotton and wooden crates from ships. The men who were dressed more formally looked like Daniel, wearing long dark jackets and top hats. It was as though she were entering a world where everyone was in costume. Including herself!

"This can't be happening," she muttered, terrified that it was. She wanted to refuse it all, to scream out her denial, as she clutched her forehead and shook her head slowly. "I think I am having a nervous breakdown."

"Please, Miss Kelly . . . sit back down and compose yourself. Soon, we'll be docking and then you can—"

"Can *what*?" she interrupted, fighting for some semblance of sanity. "Where's my time? The time I came from?"

Daniel held her shoulders and literally pulled her back down to the bench. "Kelly, you must pull yourself together," he whispered sternly, as though trying to break through her near hysteria. "No one has lied to you or tricked you. This is where you find yourself, and you must come to peace with it."

"Peace!" she gritted out, still clutching his arm. "Something truly crazy has happened to me. I don't belong here, Daniel!"

"You shall come with me and together we can resolve this situation, but you mustn't draw any more attention to yourself, Kelly, for no one will understand, and it may create more difficulty for us."

She nodded, realizing as the small boat pulled into the landing that she was now totally dependent upon this man, a man that she had thought was living in the past . . . but *the past was real*! "Okay," she whispered, more shaken than she had ever been in her life as she saw in the distance several women wearing long gowns and carrying parasols.

Insanity! It couldn't have happened. People just don't time travel!

Something was very, very wrong . . . and she hadn't the slightest idea of how to make any of it right. Did she have a nervous breakdown by that old tree? Was she lying on the ground and dreaming all this? For to believe that she was living a hundred and thirteen years ago was just too much for any human being to accept!

She felt like she was sleepwalking as she rose and followed the other passengers off the small boat. Accepting Daniel's assistance, she passed black men dressed in pants and shirts made of rough cotton who were transferring cargo from a barge. Horses and carriages lined the busy dock. Broughams and landaus with liveried drivers sitting erect were awaiting their passengers. *How did she even know those terms? What was happening?*

Everything was moving, living . . . it was so *real*!

Around mounds of steaming manure Daniel led her through the carriages, through the throng of people who occasionally glanced at her, to a hired carriage while Kelly was too shaken to do more than stare at the passing scenery as she sat on the leather seat. This was happening . . . whatever "this" was, and she remained silent, for she feared if she opened her mouth a scream of denial would tear from her body and she just might pass out. She recognized the French Quarter with its lacy iron grillwork, yet where were the automobiles? Even the trolley was gone! The women were dressed in elaborate costumes with trains and bustles on their backsides. They were holding parasols and had servants behind them carrying parcels. Men in dark suits with wide ties made room for them on the sidewalk and tipped their hats as they passed.

"Here, we are," Daniel said, as the carriage came to a stop in front of a stately old building.

She merely nodded, stunned by what she could no longer deny. This wasn't the New Orleans she had flown into days ago. This was . . . something else, and she wasn't sure of anything any longer. She was truly dumbfounded as she accepted his hand and stood in the street that was brimming with life as passing women stared at her, at her pathetically soiled dress, as though she were below them in rank and didn't belong on the same street. Some inner core of dignity sparked into life, and she tilted her chin up a little, though she couldn't look them in the eye for to do so might mean all of this was real. And it couldn't be real. *It just couldn't!*

"Come," Daniel said gently, shielding her from the stares of those who passed. "Let's get out of the street."

She allowed him to lead her up the steps and through one side of a double wooden door. Kelly was surprised to be in the foyer of what appeared to be a home. A large arrangement of flowers was beautifully presented in a tall urn upon a circular table. The floor was marble and she was standing upon an exquisite oriental rug.

"This is your office?" she asked stupidly, as she stared at the tasteful wallpaper and the oil paintings that lined the curved staircase.

"This is my home and my office," he answered as a tall black man in a formal, old-fashioned suit came into the foyer.

"We didn't expect you so soon, suh. Welcome back."

"Hello, Andrew. I returned early as I have business in the city."

The man nodded, and said, "Your mail is on your desk, suh. May I take your hat?"

Kelly watched as Daniel handed over his top hat, and Andrew accepted it.

"Andrew, please show Miss Brennan to the garden, and we'll have tea served there. Also, tell Delia to prepare a guest room, as Miss Brennan will be staying. Thank you."

"Yes, suh, Mistah Daniel." He nodded to his employer and turned to Kelly. "If you would follow me, Miz Brennan?"

Kelly glanced at Daniel, and he smiled while nodding. "You'll be all right. I will join you shortly. Forgive me, but I have some urgent business I must attend to."

In silence, Kelly followed Andrew past the staircase to a pair of French doors. Through the etched and beveled glass she could see greenery beyond. When the butler threw open the door, she nearly gasped aloud when she saw the exquisite sanctuary hidden in the middle of this house. She stepped out into the small paradise.

Plants of virtually every distinction unfurled their lushness with blooms of vibrant color. Sweet fragrances filled the air and her senses. She closed her eyes momentarily and took a deep breath. The gentle sound of water trickling beckoned her to find its source. Turning, she opened her eyes to see that a sculptured white-marble fountain added to the serenity. The form was of a mother and child in contented embrace. It was a far cry from the stark city she'd been hurried through only moments before.

"Here you are, Miss Brennan. I'll be right back with your tea."

"Thank you," Kelly murmured, carefully sitting down in a comfortable wicker chair. As she sank back into the soft cushion, she finally let out the whole of her breath and just stared around her. Glancing up, she could see rooms with little terraces that overlooked the incredible courtyard.

"Where am I?" she whispered to herself, actually pinching her arm to make sure she was awake. Unfortunately, she was. Where was her world? Her hotel? Her things? Had the police been called? Surely when she didn't return to the wedding reception, some alarm went out . . . What would happen when she didn't return to Philly? What about her business, everything she had worked so hard for in the last eight years? What about her *life*?

She found her brain was on overload from the many impossible questions and the futility of finding answers to any of them. It was as if she had stepped out of her life and was now in suspended animation.

"Here's your tea, ma'am."

Andrew carried a silver tea service and placed it on a wicker table at her side. Kelly could see there were powdered-sugar pastries on an ornate china plate. "Thank you. Andrew, is it?" she asked, wanting to address him by name.

"Yes, ma'am. May I get you anything else while you wait for Mister Gilmore?"

"Well, maybe you can tell me something . . ."

"I'd certainly try, ma'am."

"Okay, Andrew . . . what year is it now?"

The servant merely blinked at her for a few moments as though recovering from a rap on his skull. "Why, the year is 1888, ma'am . . . as best I know." The man shook his head with confidence before adding, "Will there be anything else, Miss Brennan?"

Kelly dropped her head slowly and took a deep breath. "No, nothing else. Thank you, Andrew." That really wasn't the answer she needed to hear.

She looked up to watch the tall man leave her, closing the French doors behind him. What in the world was she going to do? Her brain refused to function with the enormity of her situation, so she turned to the table and looked at the teapot. Sighing, she poured herself a cup. Just keep busy. That had been Clara's advice, and Kelly found herself following it again.

Adding two lumps of what appeared to be unrefined sugar, she slowly stirred. The sound of the spoon spinning around and around became mesmerizing. As the silver against the delicate china softly chimed, she actually began to feel herself calming.

She focused on the rising steam and laid the spoon on the saucer. She couldn't think. After sipping the tea, she placed the cup back down and picked up one of the pastries. She knew what they were. Beignets. New Orleans was famous for the confection. Biting into one, she chewed and again refused to think. Eat, that's what she would do . . . best to keep up her strength for whatever awaited her. Knowing she was resorting to food in her panic, Kelly almost didn't pick up the second one. Almost. She was midway through it when she heard footsteps behind her.

Turning quickly, she saw Daniel approaching. He was holding what appeared to be a letter in his hand, and he placed it in his jacket pocket as he smiled at her.

"Are you feeling any better?"

Her mouth full, Kelly merely tried to smile back as she shrugged her shoulders. It was a poor effort. She grabbed the finely pressed napkin and dotted her lips. Finally swallowing, she said, "Daniel . . . we have to talk."

He tried to hide his grin but was unable. "You . . . you have some confectioners' sugar on your chin."

She wiped it.

"And your nose."

She wiped that.

He couldn't suppress a chuckle as he came closer and held out his hand for the napkin. "Please, allow me."

She felt like a child as he gently, ever so gently, wiped her cheek, then smiled down at her again. "There."

"Thank you," she whispered, embarrassed to have been caught scarfing down his food and probably looking like a glutton, too.

He sat next to her in the matching chair and sighed with weariness. "Now, we can speak at length about your . . . situation."

"That's just it," she exclaimed. "What *is* my situation? How could any of this have happened? It's as if I've . . . I've time traveled, like in that book, only the other way around." Just saying it sounded so crazy.

"Kelly, I really don't know how to answer you. You have remarkable knowledge for someone, anyone, man or woman, about the future. You are so convincing that I could almost believe when you say you come from the year 2001 and—"

"I *do*, Daniel! You have to believe me!"

"But it's so incredible, Kelly. So fanciful . . . like in that work of fiction. There are laws, natural laws that govern everything and—"

"Daniel," she interrupted again, "I don't give a damn about laws. There must be exceptions to them. I can't explain it. I can't prove it. I only know it must have happened to me. There could be no other explanation for all this. You've got to believe me. Please . . . just consider I might be telling the truth."

He was staring at her, and the look on his face told her that he must see the desperation in her eyes. *Who cares*, she thought . . . she was desperate! "*Please?*"

"How could such a thing happen?" He shook his head in disbelief.

"Okay," she said as calmly as she could manage, since she was fighting for her sanity here. "I'll tell you everything I know. Please, just listen. I have no reason to lie to you or to make up a story. Anyway, what happened is so fantastic, I could never have thought of it on my own. I was in a wedding for a friend of mine from college. That's why I'm dressed like this," she said, waving her hand to her soiled skirt.

"So far, I'm following you," he said, then held up his palm to stop her. "But, what college?"

"LaSalle University."

"I've never heard of it. Is it in Philadelphia?"

"Yes. None of that matters," she said in a barely controlled voice. "All that was a long time ago anyway. Fifteen years ago, and that's why I never should have agreed to be in my friend's wedding. We hadn't even seen each other in all that time, just sent Christmas cards, so there really wasn't a reason for me to come all this way . . . except I couldn't say no to her."

"So this is why you came to New Orleans?"

"Yes. I had a hotel room here in the city, and I rented a car to drive to the Tyler Mansion, where the wedding was held. Then I walked away from the reception and—"

"Excuse me again."

She sighed. "Yes?"

"What is a car?"

"What?"

"You said you rented a car. I am trying to keep up with you."

She would have laughed except she was desperate for him to believe her. Someone had to! "I told you about them last night. Automobiles. Okay, think of it as a horseless carriage. That's what it was called when it was first introduced. You drive it at . . . at great speeds and it runs on gasoline. Do you know what gasoline is?"

He shook his head.

"It's oil . . . refined from oil."

"I know what oil is," he said, pushing his hair back from his forehead. "And you are saying that carriages use this as some sort of fuel to propel it forward, instead of horses?" He leaned forward and rested his elbows on his knees as he concentrated on her words.

"Yes, that's it. It has a small but powerful combustion engine. It's fueled by gasoline, oil, water, and now computers. And don't dare ask me about computers again. Please, just allow me to tell you what happened to me."

"And these cars just *move*?"

"Yes, at great speeds. Some over a hundred miles an hour."

"Impossible!" he gasped, sitting upright.

"It's *not* impossible. I've been driving them since I was a teenager. Just take my word for it right now, okay?"

Shaking his head in awe, he whispered, "I'm sorry I interrupted. Do continue . . ."

Nodding, Kelly drew in her breath, and said, "Well, anyway, I just wanted to get away from the noise and the people. That's why I walked away from the wedding reception. It wasn't that far. There was this tree. Very old. I was drawn to it and . . ." She hesitated. ". . . I know this is going to sound crazy, but this tree . . . it was . . . well, like it communicated with me, or something."

"I beg your pardon? Communicated? A tree?"

"I know," she said, nodding in agreement. "I, too, thought it was crazy, but something about this tree made me so sad. It was like grief just traveled from it and into me."

"Into you?"

"Yes, *into* me," she said with emphasis while placing her hand over her heart. "I tried walking away, and then I thought, no . . . I'm not going to allow this to happen so . . . well, I walked up to it and told it to stop." She tried to grin, for she knew how that must sound to this very sensible man. "Then I leaned on it. You know, just my shoulder and arm, and then all of a sudden I got light-headed as my shoulder and then my arm started to disappear into the massive trunk."

"What?" His mouth gaped open in greater disbelief.

"Look, I know how this sounds, but it's true! Just stay with me for a few more minutes, all right?"

He simply nodded. At least he didn't jump up and call the authorities to haul her away . . . yet.

"Okay, so then I must have passed through the tree because I could actually feel its sap, its age, and then the next thing I knew I was on the ground and the tree was gone and your daughter came out of the woods and found me. She thought I was a fairy because she claims one minute I wasn't there and the next I was, that I just appeared in front of her. She said it was like magic." Kelly watched as the skeptical look on Daniel's face became more evident. She gestured with her hands again for him to wait before he said anything or came to any premature opinions.

"Okay, I've never believed in magic either, but since I've gotten here, I'm not certain any longer what I believe, Daniel . . . but I *know* I'm not a fairy. So, that leaves time travel, and it terrifies me to believe that . . . because if that's what has happened . . . I'm truly . . . lost in time."

Her hand was shaking as she picked up the teacup and gulped more warm liquid.

"I don't know what to say," he whispered, sitting back and looking up as a bird swooped down and landed at the fountain.

"Me, either," she whispered back. "I don't know what to do. I have a life waiting for me a hundred and thirteen years into the future. This isn't my time, Daniel!"

"So you've said," he murmured. "I can help you get back to Philadelphia, but not to the future." He turned to her and stared. "Kelly, this is utterly unbelievable."

"I'm asking you to believe the unbelievable, then, because that's exactly what happened, Daniel. I don't know what to do. If I went to Philadelphia, it would still be 1888 and then what? I'm . . . stranded."

As the word entered her mind, a feeling of terror seized her heart. "I'm stranded in time," she mumbled. The tears she had been holding back since that walk in the woods had turned into this nightmare burst forth, and she covered her eyes as she turned her head away from him.

"Now, now," Daniel soothed, and touched her arm in sympathy. "We will think of something."

Sniffling, she dabbed her eyes with the napkin and turned back to him. "What will I do? How will I support myself? How will I *live*?"

"Right now we don't have to have all the answers, do we?" he asked gently. "I would suggest that it may be best if you rest now. You've had a pretty rough morning. Your room should be prepared, and I will ask the servants to draw a bath for you to refresh yourself," he said while standing, then added, "Tonight at supper we can continue this discussion. I regret that presently I must attend to some personal matters and step out for a while."

"You'll allow me to stay here?" She hated that her voice sounded like a child's.

"But of course. Where else would you go? You think I'd cast you out?"

She shook her head and looked down. "I . . . I just don't know anything anymore," she whispered, and bit down on her bottom lip to keep the tears that were welling in her eyes from trickling down her cheeks again. "I've never been in a situation like this . . ." She almost laughed at the absurdity of her words, then went on, ". . . what I mean is, so dependent on someone." She looked up at him. "Thank you. I won't stay long. I promise. I'll . . . I'll figure out something."

"No more talk about leaving until you are well rested.

This is only your second visit to New Orleans, so perhaps you aren't familiar with our Southern hospitality. You may stay as long as it is needed, Kelly."

She tried to smile. "I'm so grateful, Daniel. You're a very kind gentleman."

He grinned, embarrassed by her words. "I am a man who needs to leave you to your bath, madam. Rest easy, Miss Kelly Brennan. You may be in 1888, but you are in the home of a Southerner . . . and we take very good care of our guests." He waved her toward the French doors.

She walked toward the house as he followed behind her. Opening the door, he called for Andrew. The servant appeared out of nowhere, and she barely listened as Daniel instructed the man.

Turning to her, he said, "Andrew will show you to your room. I hope that later, when you are well rested, you will feel up to joining me for supper tonight."

"Yes," she murmured. "And thank you again . . . for everything, Daniel."

His smile was tender. "You are most welcome, Miss Kelly." Bowing slightly, he left her in the hallway.

"If you would follow me, Miss Kelly?"

Andrew led her through the lovely townhouse, up the stairs, and into a beautiful bedroom with a heavy mahogany sleigh bed, stenciled wallpaper, a bouquet of artificial flowers under a dome of glass, a large wardrobe, and a dresser of burled walnut with a pink marble top.

"I hope you find everything comfortable, ma'am."

"It's lovely," she whispered, looking at the thick comforter on the bed and aching to throw herself onto it and pretend none of this was happening.

"Your bath will be drawn shortly, and there is a water closet right here for your convenience."

Kelly walked into the bedroom and opened the door on the opposite wall.

It was a bathroom!

She held her hand over her mouth, yet couldn't suppress her startled yet grateful laughter. "Oh, thank you!" The tears returned to her eyes and she clenched her teeth together to stop them. Surely she was having a nervous breakdown if a bathroom could be the best part of her day!

"Delia will be up to assist you right away, ma'am."

"All right," she murmured, walking into the antique bathroom with an awe reserved for places of worship. She was so grateful for the tub with claw feet, the wooden seat of the toilet, and the wall box with a long attached chain. It was heaven . . .

"Ma'am?"

She turned toward the door and a young woman in a long black dress with a frilly white apron was standing in the arch of the doorway. She even wore a tiny white cap, edged in lace.

"I'm Delia, ma'am."

Kelly smiled. "Hello, Delia. My name is Kelly."

"Yes, Miss Kelly. I will draw your bath now, if you'd like."

"Please . . . you have no idea how wonderful that sounds."

"Yes, ma'am."

Kelly left the bathroom to the maid and wandered through the bedroom, once more admiring the comfortable furnishings. Pulling back a curtain, she looked out the French doors to a small terrace overlooking the garden. From behind her, she heard water running in the bathroom, and her entire body seemed heavy with anticipation. She simply couldn't believe she was here, in this home, in this time, and again the tears crept close to the surface.

Knowing it wouldn't do to lose it right now, she sat down in a soft chair, slipped her shoes off, and sighed with mental and physical exhaustion. She felt like she had been run over by a truck.

She watched as Andrew and another maid helped Delia to carry in buckets of hot water, probably to add to the cool water of the tub. What did she know anymore? Her brain felt like it might explode if she tried to figure out even one more thing. She closed her eyes and took deep breaths in an effort to calm down. There was no use in trying to make sense of it. Her entire life had been turned inside out, and she was alone. Was she delusional? Could all of it be just a night-mare?

"Ma'am?"

Opening her eyes, she saw Delia standing in front of her. She was middle-aged, and her skin was a smooth mocha that highlighted her lovely brown eyes.

"May I help you undress?"

Kelly stifled a moan as she slowly stood up and shook her head. "I can manage, thank you. The bath is ready?"

"Yes, ma'am. Would you like anything else?"

"Just the bath, Delia." She smiled slightly and walked toward the bathroom while reaching behind her to unzip her dress.

"May I?"

Startled, Kelly looked over her shoulder as Delia offered to help.

"I have never seen such a fastener," the woman murmured, slowly pulling the zipper down. "It's so simple."

When the gown was released, Kelly turned to her and said, "It's called a zipper, Delia."

"Zip-per," Delia said slowly, as though memorizing the term. "What a wonderful thing."

"I guess it is," Kelly answered, once more realizing how she had taken so many simple things for granted. And now she was here, in this time, where even a zipper was a wonder!

"Enjoy your bath, Miss Kelly." Delia curtsied and turned to leave.

Kelly almost stopped her and asked about the year, then thought better of it. She now knew no matter how many people she asked, the answer would always be the same. No one here, or anywhere else, would say 2001.

She had time traveled.

Don't think about it, she mentally scolded while remembering Clara's wise advice. Shaking her head as the door closed, she allowed the gown to fall to the floor and then removed her wide slip. She wriggled out of her ruined panty hose, her underwear, and walked nude into the bathroom. She saw two huge towels folded on a small table by the tub, along with vials of oils and a bowl that contained round balls of soap. Picking up the natural sponge from the table, she tossed it into the tub and then entered herself.

As she sank into the warm water and allowed it to penetrate into her pores, she shivered once and then lowered her head as she clasped the sponge in her hand. It began slowly, leaking from the corners of her eyes, and this time she didn't try to stop it. She was all alone. It was as though sanity had deserted her. She had . . . nothing. Soon deep sobs wracked her body, and she allowed it to come out, for she no longer had the strength to hold any of it back. She cried for herself. She cried for everyone she knew. She cried for the life she had left, her home, her friends, her employees, and she cried because somehow, through some twist of fate, this terrible thing had happened to her and she was helpless . . . for the first time since she was a child . . . she was helpless and alone.

Somewhere, from some distant part of her mind came the thought that she wasn't alone. Not right now. Daniel was here, and that thought stopped her for just a moment. She blinked away the moisture from her eyes and brought up the wet sponge to wipe her face.

Daniel.

How weird was that? To have a man that resembled her late husband be the one she was dependent upon now? To be in his lovely town house and being pampered? To have the only man who had stirred anything in her for the last eight years to be living in a different century!

Way too bizarre, she thought, reaching for a ball of soap. She brought it to her nose and inhaled. It was scented with jasmine. Sniffling, she decided that she might as well make the most of the situation. Who knew when she'd be able to have another bath? What if Daniel sent her away? Yes, he was a Southerner and had mentioned hospitality, but for how long would he allow her to stay? Could she find a job in this time? Women weren't even allowed to vote yet! There had to be something she could do, she worried. She hadn't a clue, and the tears returned in full force. One thing she knew, she wasn't going to fit in 1888, not if she was handcuffed by outdated social rules about women.

She thought she heard a noise in the bedroom and quickly stopped crying, afraid the servants would hear her. Frustrated, desperate, depleted of strength, Kelly sank back into the water, allowing it to cover her shoulders, her face, and finally her hair.

She stayed under, listening to the muffled drone of her heartbeat and wishing that she would disappear . . . pass out, wake up under that tree and rejoin the wedding reception. How long could she remain underwater? How long would it take to die?

No!

She shot up through the water and gasped for breath as she wiped the moisture from her eyelids.

She didn't want to die!

Considering her circumstances, that revelation surprised her. She sat for just a moment and digested the fact that she certainly had learned to say no and mean it. As bad as everything seemed, she wanted to survive it. Maybe she would find a way back. Maybe it wasn't so desperate. It had happened instantaneously, and it could reverse itself just as quickly. Maybe all she had to do was wait it out!

It was something to grab on to . . . a slim ray of hope, in an otherwise dismal situation.

"Okay," she muttered. "If I'm here, then somebody, something, somewhere, better help me out now." She didn't know where she directed her voice. Was it inward? Outward? Both? She only knew that some force beyond her knowledge had sent her back in time, and she was demanding that force now show some guidance.

A surprising reserve of inner strength infused her body, and she looked at the soap she still clutched in her fist. She lathered it between her hands and started washing her hair. First things first, she told herself. She would get clean. She might even pamper herself with oil afterward. Then she was going to wrap herself in a long towel and fall into that enticing bed and sleep. Yes, sweet sleep.

That was it . . . she needed to take care of herself until the way to return was shown to her. Clara was right. Worrying wasn't going to help. Besides, it just took too much out of her to keep doing it. As she rinsed her hair, Kelly vowed to put a lid on worry and just take it moment by moment. There were no rules any longer, none that applied to her. She had never heard of anyone time traveling, but then again . . . who would talk about it publicly if they had? She couldn't be the only person this had happened to in the whole world. There had to be a way out of it. Right? *Right?*

"Stop it," she muttered, picking up the sponge and lathering it. For right now, no more worrying. She concentrated on washing herself, scrubbing every inch of skin until she was reddened by the process. Finally clean, Kelly stood up and reached for a towel. It was so large that she could easily wrap it around her. She dried herself off, then opened one of the vials. Again, she smelled jasmine, and she poured oil onto her palm. She rubbed it into her arms and shoulders and repeated the process on her legs and feet. When she was done, she rewrapped herself in the towel and used a smaller one to wrap around her hair.

If nothing else, she was clean again.

That was an improvement.

When she walked out of the bathroom, she saw that her clothes were no longer on the floor. Curious, she opened the wardrobe and saw her heels had been neatly placed on the bottom shelf, but her clothes were missing. *Great*, she thought . . . *Delia must have taken them away to be cleaned* . . . and now she had nothing. Looking into the mirror on the inside of the door, she thought, save for the towels, she was as naked in life as the day she had been born. And she felt just as helpless.

Kelly reminded herself of her new credo and shrugged off the worry. She closed the wardrobe and turned to the bed.

Sleep . . . that was really all she wanted.

She pulled back the lace coverlet and climbed up. What did it matter if she just kept the towel on her hair? She wouldn't dampen the beautifully embroidered pillowcases. Pulling the cover back up over her, Kelly felt like she was in a warm cocoon and, sighing deeply, closed her eyes and willed herself to fall asleep.

All she wanted right now was oblivion.

Everything would look better when she woke up. It simply had to. . . .

Eight

"Miss Kelly?"

She didn't want to wake up, yet she heard the soft voice calling her name and, reluctantly, opened her eyes. Kelly vaguely recognized the woman in a maid's costume standing at the side of the bed, smiling down at her.

"I'm sorry to wake you, ma'am . . . but I thought you might want to see what Mister Daniel brought home for you."

Blinking furiously to wake up and make sense of her surroundings, Kelly pushed herself upright against the pillows and quickly realized the bath towel she'd wrapped around herself was undone. Grabbing the coverlet, she held it over her breasts as the woman's name came back to her.

"Have I slept long, Delia?"

The maid smiled and said, "Around five hours. Mister Daniel said to let you sleep, but I thought you might want to look at these before dinner." She waved her hand to the foot of the bed.

Confused, Kelly focused on the pile of boxes stacked at least three feet high. Well, she might still be dreaming, but this was certainly a surprise! "Mister Daniel bought these for me?" she asked in disbelief, as a surprising wave of pleasure raced through her body. That she could feel pleasure at all considering her circumstances added to her shock. "Yes, ma'am. He said you lost all your things in the storm. Sure was a bad one, all right. Lucky thing you weren't hurt."

"Yes," Kelly murmured, realizing that Daniel was protecting her. "It was a bad storm." She turned her anticipation back to the boxes. "What's in them?"

Delia opened the lid to the first one, smaller and thinner than the others. "Oh," the woman said with appreciation and handed the box to Kelly.

Kelly accepted it. A beautiful comb and brush was lying inside layers of tissue paper, along with rolls of satin ribbon in shades of white, yellow and blue. She brought out the brush and turned it over. Mother-of-pearl was inlaid with silver, and she ran the bristles over her palm. "How lovely," she whispered. The towel she had wrapped around her hair had come loose when she'd sat up, and she realized her hair had dried in hundreds of fine ringlets. She could certainly use these! "This was so thoughtful of him," she said to Delia.

"Mister Daniel is a good man," Delia replied, and opened the next box. The maid merely handed it over.

Curious, Kelly looked inside and saw three pairs of white-cotton stockings rolled up amid lacy garters, and what appeared to be . . . underwear. She pulled out a white-cotton chemise and what looked like lacy knickers with a waistband of silk and tiny pearl buttons. Bursting out laughing, Kelly shook her head and could just imagine Daniel asking a salesclerk for them. "Oh, what a precious man."

"Oh, Miss Kelly . . . just look at this!"

Kelly glanced up to see Delia lifting a white-silk negligee with a gathering of lace and silk at the collar and wide sleeves. The material was embroidered with a fine white stitching of flowers. Tiny pearl buttons ran down the front and a white-satin ribbon at the waist completed the elegant costume. "Wow . . ." was all Kelly could breathe as she held out her hands and touched the exquisite material. "It's so beautiful!"

"Sure is," Delia said, gathering the negligee and holding it out in invitation. "You should try it on," the young woman insisted.

Kelly slipped from the bed and held the towel in place as she turned around, while Delia placed the gorgeous creation over her shoulders. Dropping the towel, she lifted her arms into the billowy sleeves and brought the edges together. As she turned back, Delia reached out and picked up the long satin ribbon and tied a perfect bow at her waist.

It was so soft against her skin as she walked a few steps and experienced the fluid movement of the silk. She had never worn anything so beautiful in her life. Well, her business certainly had provided her with the money for fine things, and she had indulged herself in more than a few, yet this . . . this robe was so feminine, meant to be worn by a woman who was aware of her charms . . . and that was something Kelly realized she had lost in the last eight years.

Delia walked over to the wardrobe and opened a door. On the other side of it was the mirror. "Come look, Miss Kelly," the woman offered with a wide grin. "Don't you look just like a fairy princess!"

"Oh please, Delia . . . don't even say that," Kelly softly chided. "I've had enough of fairy tales!" The irony of the woman's statement made Kelly shake her head with refusal to accept the notion.

"My apologies, Miss Kelly. I didn't mean—"

"It's okay, Delia. I only meant that . . . well, it doesn't matter." Kelly smiled to the young woman. "It is beautiful, isn't it?" she said, holding the fabric out at her sides.

Slowly moving across the room, she felt so feminine she wanted to giggle. When she stood in front of the mirror, she simply looked at her reflection and watched as her mouth opened in shock. She appeared . . . almost beautiful. Who would believe after everything she had just gone through that she could look like this? Her hair was rumpled, almost wild, yet the contrast of the white silk against her auburn hair made her blue eyes sparkle and her cheeks appear flushed.

Delia left her at the mirror and opened the rest of the

boxes, laying out three other fantastic costumes on the bed. Hesitantly, she left the startling reflection and turned around to admire a striped dress of dark blue satin and fawn with a high-necked bodice that appeared to be fully boned. Small double puffs were at the top of the long sleeves. A twisted ribbon of deep cream silk was sewn in place at the waist with tiny buttons leading up to the throat, where a brooch of pearls was neatly attached. The costume was in two pieces. The bodice and the skirt.

"Wow. I can't believe he bought all this for me."

"Look at this one," Delia whispered, fluffing out the skirt of a deep purple shot-silk taffeta creation with a thick braiding of black at the cuffs and the hem. It looked like the kind of dresses the women were wearing when she'd seen them on the street. The last dress of soft dove gray was short-sleeved with a low square neckline, and a crossing of silk under the breasts, allowing the remaining material to fall in a gossamer drape to the floor. It all reminded Kelly of gowns a princess would wear.

She sank to the side of the bed and just stared at the beautiful clothes Daniel had purchased for her. Never would she have asked him, nor would she have thought he would voluntarily do something so generous, so thoughtful. Again, she felt a tugging at her heart, that unexplainable attraction to the man, and tears of gratitude ran down her cheeks. Standing up, she quickly wiped at her eyes before Delia could see them.

"What time is dinner?" she asked, brushing her hand through her hair. "I have a lot to do to get ready."

"Oh, you have time, Miss Kelly," Delia answered, picking up the gowns and hanging them in the wardrobe. "Mister Daniel said you weren't to be rushed. When you're ready, I'll help you get dressed."

Again, her heart expanded with gratitude, and she smiled at the woman. "Which dress should I wear?"

"Why, that's up to you, ma'am, but I think this one is the prettiest." Delia ran her slender fingers over the soft gray gown with appreciation.

"It is gorgeous, isn't it?"

"Yes, ma'am, it sure is."

Making up her mind, Kelly nodded. "Okay, I'll wear it. I hope it fits."

"It should," Delia replied, laying it out on the bed and smoothing down the skirt. "Mister Daniel had me wrap up the gown you were wearing and he took it to the dressmaker to find out your size."

"He took my clothes?" Kelly felt embarrassment at the thought.

"Just your gown, ma'am. Everything else will be returned to you, all clean in the morning."

"Oh . . ." She felt a little better, but still . . . She'd worn that dress for three days and could just imagine Daniel showing it to a strange woman. And just what exactly, she wondered, had he explained to the dressmaker?

"Would you like me to dress your hair, ma'am?"

"Dress my hair?" Kelly asked stupidly.

"We can pull it back with ribbon," Delia offered, "or I could use a hot iron on it to style it more formally."

Sighing, Kelly looked at her reflection once more in the mirror and ran her fingers through the tight ringlets. "I guess I could use some help. Thank you, Delia."

"It's my pleasure, ma'am . . ."

What a difference a nap made. She had fallen asleep, wishing for oblivion, and now here she stood, anticipating dinner with the first man in ages to make her pulse race. Maybe this *not* worrying was working?

He stood at the French doors and looked out to the garden . . . and to her. For just a moment, his breath caught at the back of his throat. In the moonlight and soft glow of the lanterns, he could have momentarily mistaken her for Lillian. He watched as she strolled over to the overhanging branch of an olive tree and reached out to cradle the leaves in her fingers. She was so beautiful, and he was glad she'd chosen to wear the gray gown, for as soon as the dressmaker had shown it to him, he was certain Kelly would be exquisite in it. He congratulated himself, not only for his choice, but also for having the courage to walk into the establishment and proceed with his purchases. He'd had to invent a story about Kelly losing all her things in the storm and was thankful that it had been accepted so readily by everyone. Still, when the dressmaker had questioned him about the strange metal fastener in the back of the dress that slid up and down the material so smoothly, he'd concocted something about newest Parisian inventions. But the question had made him ponder her assertions about the future. How was it possible that he might just be entertaining a time traveler? He was an educated man, a man of logic and reason . . . and yet, here she was.

What was this strange pull of attraction? It was more than a desire to relive his past. Inhaling deeply as he watched her move away from the branch and wander through his garden, Daniel felt something deep and exciting stirring within him again and marveled that it should happen with this woman . . . a woman who claimed to be from the future. Everything about Kelly was absolutely extraordinary.

And, moreover, he'd come to the conclusion that Kelly Brennan wasn't delusional . . . something truly incredible, yet true, had happened to her. Yet how fortuitous that something had brought her to him . . . and at just the right time, for now he had a thing even more unimaginable to propose to her, and he wasn't sure if she was ready to hear it. However, time was of the essence, and he couldn't afford to waste another moment.

Walking into the garden, he stifled the groan that nearly left his throat when she looked in his direction and smiled. His heart started to thump wildly inside his chest with each step he took closer to her. Dear God, but she was beautiful . . . and it wasn't that she simply reminded him of Lillian. That was merely a glimpse of the surface. He admired her intelligence, her courage, the way she could be so passionate about her fantastic story of time traveling. If it were true, and he had no means of proving it otherwise, then she had surely arrived at a fortuitous time. He thought of the letter in his breast pocket and bowed slightly as he said, "You are a vision of loveliness, madam. Thank you for joining me this evening."

He watched as she blushed prettily and murmured, "Thank you, Daniel . . . for everything. The clothes are beautiful and you are very generous. I don't know how I can repay you, but I'll try and get a job and—"

He held his hand up to stop any further words. "Seeing you, with a smile upon your face, is repayment enough." He paused, finding himself momentarily speechless as he gazed at her bathed in the moon's soft glow. She truly was spectacular.

Suddenly, a low, growling rumble rose between them and she looked down, as though his stare had been too intense. "Oh, Kelly . . . I'm sorry if I've made you uncomfortable," he whispered. Damn. It was going to be a struggle to keep his wits about himself this night.

"Oh no, I'm sorry. It was my stomach—"

"Well . . ." he breathed, saving her from any further embarrassment. "I had hoped you were hungry, as the chef has promised us a feast tonight."

She grinned. "I'm famished."

He offered his arm. "Then may I escort you to the table?"

She placed her hand on his arm, and whispered, "You are a very charming man, Daniel Gilmore. I don't mean to imply anything, but you seem completely different here in the city."

"Alas, I fear I gave you a poor first impression, madam." He looked down at her as he opened the French doors to the house, and added, "I shall strive to be charming in your presence," he said sincerely.

He found that he loved to see her smile, the way her eyes twinkled with merriment, the way her perfect lips lifted so sweetly.

"I think I'm going to enjoy Southern hospitality," she murmured, as they entered the house.

The elegance and sophistication of his town house compared to the country house appeared to mesmerize Kelly as she finished the delicious French food that had been prepared.

"I was much too hungry, Daniel, to be polite and leave anything," she said with a sigh of contentment, as she sat back and grinned at him.

Their conversation throughout dinner had been light, as he briefly brought her up to date about life in the past. It only served to convince him further that she must have come from some futuristic society, as she already knew much of what was presently happening in history and she foretold of a few amazing things to come in the not-so-distant future.

Very pleased with the way the entire evening was progressing, Daniel also leaned back and smiled across the table to her. "I admire a woman with a good appetite, Miss Kelly, and if I may be so bold, I would assume the look of satisfaction on your face would imply you have recovered quite well from this morning's events."

Her small laugh was charming. "I must have looked a fright. I'm glad I couldn't see myself, and I apologize that you were subjected to my appearance for days." She placed her hands in her lap and sighed. "And yes . . . somehow, incredibly, I do feel better."

Her comment reminded him of the Latin credo he followed: *Carpe diem*. The time was perfect and he took a deep breath for courage. What he was about to propose would surely shock her. "There is something I wish to discuss with you. Would you care to take brandy with me in the garden?"

"That sounds like a lovely ending to a perfect meal."

He stood from the table and walked around to her chair. Assisting her to rise, he closed his eyes momentarily as he inhaled the scent of jasmine when she stood. He instantly opened his eyes as she turned and politely smiled at him.

"Thank you."

Nodding, he offered his arm, and they began walking through the house. He was acutely aware of everything about her as she walked next to him. She was more than radiant this night. The way her hair cascaded down to her creamy shoulders. The brilliance of her eyes and the way she'd looked at him during dinner. She seemed to possess a transcendental air, and he couldn't deny that his whole body was responding.

An ache of desire rushed through him with sudden risqué thoughts, and he knew he had to repress them. He had to remind himself she was a guest in his house and to refrain from these thoughts and the others that had plagued him since he'd mistaken her in the hallway that first night. The night he'd first kissed her. Though even remembering that made his blood race through his body and the ache deepen.

"It's so lovely out here," she murmured, as Andrew followed them with a tray containing a crystal decanter with two matching crystal brandy snifters.

"That will be all, Andrew," Daniel said, as the manservant stood waiting for further instructions. "Thank you."

"Good night, suh. Madam." Bowing, he left.

"Everyone here has been so incredibly nice and helpful to me. You certainly have a good staff in this house, Daniel," Kelly observed when they were alone. "And it's such a lovely home. Especially here in the garden."

He watched her look out to the hanging lanterns that dotted the garden as she smiled.

"It has been in my family for generations," he answered. "And, I was fortunate when I returned from England to have found reliable people to maintain it."

"You were in England?"

Daniel poured the brandy into the glasses and handed her one. As her fingers lightly touched his, he drew in a sharp breath. How even the slightest touch from this woman had such a powerful effect was incomprehensible to him. "Yes," he said, clearing his throat. "When I was ten years old, my father had the foresight to take the family to England to wait out the war. He was not a proponent of seccession and felt the South didn't have a chance to win over the North's industrialization."

"So that's why you don't have a strong-Southern accent."

Smiling, he said, "I was educated in England, and was also married there."

She nodded to him. "So you came back after the war."

"Actually, my wife and I came back for the Centennial Celebration in Philadelphia in 1876. I had persuaded my wife, who was English, to come here and see where I was born." He paused for a moment then added, "It was here that Elizabeth was also born."

"Do you ever bring Lizzie into town?" she asked, motioning to the house, then added, "Here to this home?"

"Not often. She seems to prefer the country life, I fear."

Kelly smiled sweetly and Daniel clenched his fists as though the act would help summon up his courage. Now was the time. "As a matter of fact, it is Elizabeth that I wish to discuss, Miss Kelly. And . . . a situation that has just this day come to my attention."

"What is it, Daniel. Can I help? It's the least I can do . . . considering all that you've done for me."

He motioned to a chair. "Please, sit down."

She did and chuckled. "This sounds serious."

"It is," he replied lowly.

Her voice immediately sounded contrite. "I'm sorry. What's wrong?"

Reaching into the breast pocket of his dinner jacket, he withdrew the envelope that seemed to burn a hole next to his heart. "Just today I received this letter from my in-laws. It was postmarked over a month ago, and it states they are coming for a visit." He tried to calm the tone of desperation from his voice. Inhaling, he continued, "Their schedule had them leaving England two weeks ago. They are en route to New Orleans as we speak."

"And this troubles you?"

"Yes . . . greatly. You see, they have never met Elizabeth, and they state they are most anxious to know her."

"Well, they are her grandparents."

"Yes, but Elizabeth's grandparents are . . ." He searched for a diplomatic way to elaborate. ". . . very . . . proper. Let's just say they will more than likely be appalled by the way my daughter has been raised."

"I see," she murmured, then sipped her brandy.

"I'm not sure what they will do," he paused, draining his own glass. He sat down in the chair opposite her and looked into her eyes, hoping for understanding. "But if I know my in-laws well, I fear they will try to take Elizabeth back with them to England for a proper education." He turned toward her and continued earnestly, "You see, to them, she will appear a wild disgrace. As it already is, they were not pleased with me for taking their daughter away from England . . . and, needless to say, having Lillian die in this country has not endeared me to them any further," he said, stifling the sigh in his throat.

"How long do you have?"

"Probably not more than two weeks."

"Can I help? I could try and instruct Lizzie and—"

"Indeed, you may very well be able to help. I have a proposition, one that came to me this afternoon. Pray do not think me mad, Miss Kelly."

Her smile was endearing and gave him the courage he'd been seeking.

"Daniel, if what you heard from me this afternoon doesn't make you think I am mad," she said softly, "then you can say whatever you wish. I promise I won't think less of you. Now, what is it that you propose?"

"A marriage." At her sharp intake of breath, he quickly added, "One of convenience, of course. When my in-laws arrive and see that I am married and Elizabeth has a new mother, they will not even think to ask for her." He watched as Kelly's eyes grew wide with shock, and wished circumstances were different, that this attraction between them could deepen with time. But that was one thing he was running out of, so he hurried to finish. "You, yourself, said this morning that you are alone and have no idea where to go or what to do. I can provide for you for as long as you wish. Throughout the years I have made successful investments, increasing my family's good fortune, and am a wealthy man. And if you desire to leave after they have returned to England, we can quietly have the marriage annulled and I will provide you with compensation, enough that you can comfortably relocate anywhere you wish." There! It was out.

His heart was pounding madly within his chest as he waited for her reaction. Why was it that he feared he had more to lose if she refused? Why couldn't he admit that he wanted to keep her with him?

"Marriage!"

The word barely squeaked out of her mouth, and Kelly thought again that her world just tilted and she needed to find a balance. Glad she was seated, she managed to ask, "You are serious?"

"Most assuredly, Miss Kelly. Quite serious. I know I don't present the best picture of a father to you, but I love my daughter and will do what is necessary to ensure she stays with me."

"Can't you just refuse, if they try to take her? Wouldn't the law support you?" This was way too incredible to digest! He wanted to marry her? Okay, so it was in name only . . . but marriage! Even if she had time traveled, this was just too unbelievable . . .

"The law would support me, but do I really want to take this public? A fight in the courts with my in-laws? To put Elizabeth in the center of such a display would only cause her harm. I know I am to blame for the way she has been raised. I know a young girl should have been educated in the ways of gentility but—"

"Now you want to do damage control," she interrupted, for she could see he was struggling.

"That's a curious way to put it, but yes. Have I severely offended you?"

Breathing heavily in an attempt to digest his remarkable proposition, Kelly shook her head. "You haven't offended me, just surprised me." She laughed nervously. "Marriage!"

He stood up. "I have offended you, madam. I sincerely apologize. Though I have thought of little else since this morning, I spoke in haste and would never wish to—"

"You haven't offended me," she interrupted, standing also. "This has been quite a day. That's all. I . . . I can't answer you right now."

"Of course," he said, nodding. "Please take your time and think about it. I shall wish you good night, madam, and pray you forgive me. I did warn that you might think me mad."

She struggled to smile. "Perhaps we're both mad, Daniel. Good night." Rushing out of the garden and through the house, she kept thinking . . . *I can't marry a man who's almost a stranger! I simply can't . . .*

Yet when she closed the door to her bedroom and leaned back against it, she stared blindly into the room and realized he didn't feel like a stranger at all . . . and spending this time with him and Lizzie would be far better than wandering around alone a hundred and thirteen years in the past.

A soft knock on the other side of the door almost made her jump in fright. "Yes?"

"Miss Kelly, do you need help before you retire?"

Why did a sudden thread of disappointment that it was Delia race through her body? "Thank you, Delia, but I can manage," she said through the door.

"Yes, madam."

Kelly heard the woman's footsteps in the hallway and turned back to the room. Quickly, she undressed and hung up the beautiful gown. After she slipped into the negligee, she looked in the mirror. Could she do it? She already felt a connection to him that couldn't be logically explained. And the thought of being his wife, even in name only, wasn't totally appalling. In fact, if she were honest . . . it was downright appealing.

"You must be nuts, Kelly Brennan," she said to herself, and walked away from the reflection. How could she even consider marrying a man that she barely knew, and yet she *knew* him on some level that even she couldn't understand. Yet he thought she looked like his wife; she hoped that wasn't also a motive. If she was even considering this, and insanely agreed . . . she would be accepted for who she was, not as another woman from the past.

Nodding as though to confirm her thoughts, she shrugged. She had to admit that he reminded her of Michael. Did she believe in past lives? Futures lives? Reincarnation? But Daniel wasn't really like Michael. How could they be alike when over a hundred years had separated them?

Opening the French doors to the terrace, she walked outside and watched as Andrew blew out the lanterns in the garden. Breathing in the night air, she wrapped her arms around her waist and stared up to the stars.

How could any of this have happened to her?

She stilled her chaotic mind for just a few moments and

proceeded to calm herself so she could think clearly. It was then she realized that in all the time she'd spent here, she had only just now thought of Michael. It was nearly a revelation to her. Somehow, it was as though that terrible longing within her heart was easing.

Was she actually opening herself up again to the possibility of another man in her life? And if she were, did it have to happen like this? She shook her head slightly and almost laughed at herself. It didn't matter right now . . . what did matter was that she had a decision to make.

Daniel had said the marriage would be in name only. She was torn between relief and curiosity, and that surprised her. Why shouldn't she marry him? What did she have going for her in this time? What would she do if she left? Where would she go? No matter where she went, she was ill prepared for life alone in 1888.

To her left she felt a presence and turned her head slightly.

He was wearing a smoking jacket and leaning on the iron railing as he brought a long thin cigar to his mouth. He was also staring up into the sky. Kelly slowly pulled back toward the door and watched him. Her chest became warm as tingles of excitement raced through her veins. Just looking at him caused an ache within her as she remembered what it was like to be held in that man's arms and the passion within him as he'd kissed her.

Thinking about it made her knees weak.

Suddenly she knew she didn't want to leave him. She wanted to see Lizzie again and Clara, too. She wanted to feel protected while being thrown into a time when women didn't have the right to vote, the right to own property, hardly any rights at all.

Taking a deep breath, she eased her way back to the lacy iron railing. If she didn't do it now, she would lose her nerve.

"Daniel!" She called his name in a loud whisper.

She watched his silhouetted form spin around. He seemed startled and looked as though he was squinting to see her in the moonlight. "Kelly?"

"Yes," she called back, still trying to keep her voice as low as possible.

"Are you all right?"

"Yes," she called again. "My answer"—she drew in a deep breath—"to your proposal . . . is yes!"

There was a moment of stillness, and she held her hand to her heart while waiting for his response.

His voice, when it came, was low and almost sexy.

"Thank you. You honor me."

She nodded and had no idea if he could see her doing it. "Well . . ." she stammered. "Okay . . . we'll discuss it in more detail tomorrow morning."

"All right . . ." he whispered back.

She didn't trust herself to say more. "Good night."

"Sleep well," he called out. "And Kelly?"

She turned around in the patio doorway. "Yes?"

"I promise you won't be disappointed . . . er, with your decision, I mean."

She couldn't even respond. She knew what he meant. Whether she chose to leave on her own or agree to his proposition. Yet, in the instant before she called out to him, just the thought of being in his arms again made his words take on an entirely different meaning. All she could do was nervously wave and step back into her room.

Staring at the bed, she brought her hand up over her mouth in shock.

"What have you done now?" she mumbled to herself against her fingers.

She was getting married!

Nine

"Do you, Kelly Maureen Brennan, take this man, Daniel Beauregard Gilmore, to be your lawful wedded husband, for better or for worse, for richer or for poorer, in sickness and in health?"

Beauregard? She was so rattled and nervous she almost giggled. Swallowing down the hysteria, she nodded. "I do."

"Do you promise to love, honor and obey him?"

Obey . . . ? Now, wait a minute.

"I don't know about obey," she muttered, acutely aware that the two witnesses present, the minister's wife and a friend of Daniel's, in addition to all the house servants, were staring at her.

Daniel, dressed in a formal gray suit with an elaborate cravat, leaned down and whispered with a slight grin, "It is merely a formality."

"I know," she whispered back, clutching the spray of white roses to her waist. "But that word, obey, was eliminated from the wedding vows years ago and—"

"Do you wish to continue?" the minister interrupted in an officious tone.

She was wearing the blue-and-cream-striped dress with the high neck, and Kelly felt like it was strangling her as she croaked out, "I do." Her heart was hammering inside the tightly boned bodice, and she wanted to gasp for air as Daniel slipped a gold band onto her finger. She was really doing this!

The minister looked contented and turned his attention to Daniel. "And do you, Daniel Beauregard Gilmore, take this woman, Kelly Maureen Brennan, to be your lawful wedded wife, for better or for worse, for richer or for poorer, in sickness . . ."

The words droned on as Kelly tried to remain calm. She was getting married to a man she hardly knew! She had to admit that Daniel worked fast. Bouquets of white roses were tastefully placed about the garden. It looked quite festive, and she almost wanted to laugh when she thought about Mel's wedding. Here she was in New Orleans and getting married, too!

"I do," Daniel said in a solemn voice.

That brought Kelly's attention back to the ceremony, and her hand shook as she slipped a matching gold band onto his ring finger.

"By the power vested to me by the state of Louisiana and the sanctity of the church, I now pronounce you husband and wife. May your union be fruitful."

Smiling, Daniel looked at her and she could merely blink in astonishment as he bent his head and lightly kissed her lips. She'd been stifling the nervous laugh that wanted to escape for the absurdity of it all. They were married!

"Congratulations," the minister said, and Kelly looked back at him in dismay.

"Thank you," Daniel answered, shaking the man's hand. He then turned and thanked their witnesses, while Kelly continued to stand, shell-shocked.

A married woman . . . again! After all this time. *Time!* Hell, she didn't even know the meaning of the word anymore.

"Please join us for a small reception," Daniel said to the

group, nodding at Andrew and Delia and the other servant.

Kelly watched as the servants rushed into the house and the minister's wife came up to her and smiled widely. She wished she could remember her name.

"I must congratulate you, Mrs. Gilmore. It is now official that one of New Orleans' most eligible bachelors has been expunged from *the list*." The woman gave a nod with the inflection in her last words, then added, "I would imagine when word of this marriage circulates, more than a few ladies will be, shall we say, distraught."

"Really?" Kelly didn't know how else to answer.

"Well, of course you wouldn't know of such things, being as you're not from this city, but indeed, Mister Gilmore has managed for years to evade such a day as today, though not for lack of the efforts of many a New Orleans family." She reached out and patted Kelly's arm. "I'm certain it will be great conversation in the social circle to imagine how you ever managed it. Again, congratulations."

Kelly could tell the woman was harmless and merely trying to make conversation. "Thank you," she replied, pausing to think of a diplomatic response, then simply murmured, "When he asked, I just said yes." She figured if she stuck to the truth, it would be best.

The nameless woman laughed. "And what good fortune to be the one being asked by such a fine man. How long will you remain in the city? Are you planning a wedding trip? I would so love to present you to our church's social club. Do you have a fondness for gardening?"

"Gardening?" she asked as Daniel rejoined her.

"We are planning to renovate our country home," Daniel interjected. "I do believe my wife's gardening skills will be put to good use there, as I must confess I've let the place become rather overgrown through the years."

Kelly was struck again into silence as his words, *my wife,* resounded in her brain.

"Ah, Mister Gilmore . . . is not a man blessed to have a woman's soft touch in his life? I wish you both much happiness."

"Yes, thank you, Mrs. Holden," he said, looking down at Kelly. "I recognize my blessing, and I'm certain we will both be very happy."

It was all too much for Kelly, as with his words her mind wandered far from social clubs and gardening. Realizing she must look like a social simpleton, she took a deep breath, and finally said, "Thank you, Mrs. Holden, for all your kind words."

"You seem a bit overwhelmed, my dear." Mrs. Holden looked on her kindly.

"I think I am," Kelly answered with a smile.

"The institution of marriage can do that," the male witness said, as he and the minister joined the small circle.

That was an ironic use of terms, Kelly thought. She'd been wondering if she'd lost her mind since the very beginning of her fateful trip.

"Pray, do not frighten my new bride with your cynical bachelor's viewpoint, Alexander," Daniel said with a laugh, "I'll have it known that I have never taken the sanctity of marriage lightly, old friend . . . it is a very serious matter to me, indeed."

She was glad to hear him say that, for she felt the same way. It was a serious matter and yet, now she couldn't help but wonder how sanctified this union was, as it was "in name only." There had to be honor in the decision they'd made and the vows they had just spoken. The reasons flew through her mind again. It was for the sake of a child's life with her family, for the sake of a woman's whole life, even the sake of a lonely man . . . it was for everyone's benefit. Wasn't it?

Andrew approached the group with a tray of champagne glasses. After each had accepted one, the man named Alexander held his high, and announced, "I propose a toast to the exultant couple. May you both enjoy a long life of happiness in wedded bliss, dear friend and wife."

"Hear, hear!" Everyone toasted them and sipped in agreement. That word again hit Kelly like a punch to her solar plexus. Wife. Okay, she was a bride, but no one in attendance knew this marriage was simply a business deal, so all the congratulations rang hollow. She was to tutor Lizzie, presenting a stable family to the child's grandparents and in return, Daniel was to provide her with security. Security . . . that word made her stomach muscles tighten. It was no reason for a marriage, and she felt almost disappointed. As crazy as it seemed, deep down, she truly wished this day meant something more.

Daniel led her into the house, and their guests followed. She sat through a light lunch, listening to their conversation, smiling at appropriate times, but was acutely aware that Daniel was holding up her end of the social obligation. She just couldn't seem to get past the fact that all these people were living a hundred and thirteen years ago, and she was among them, pretending to be one of them. It seemed so unnatural.

Right . . . like marrying one *was* natural?

Determined to push past her comfort zone, she swallowed a bite of the delicious wedding cake and placed her fork on the plate. If she married to play a role, then she might as well get started.

"Mrs. Holden, thank you for your kindness today. I'm not certain how long we shall remain in the city, for we're both anxious to see Elizabeth again, but when we do return I would be most honored to visit your social club." Kelly figured it would be a good place to observe how women of this time conducted themselves. She knew her New Millennium Woman would not go over big in the nineteenth century and had better learn how not to stick out like a sore thumb.

"Why, certainly, Mrs. Gilmore. We would be honored by your presence."

Daniel looked across the table and smiled with approval.

It was still a struggle for Kelly to become accustomed to hearing her married name.

"How is young Elizabeth?" Alexander asked, sitting back in his chair and dabbing a napkin to his lips.

"She is well," Daniel answered.

"It's a shame we haven't seen her in Sunday school," the minister said seriously, then quickly added, "She is . . . quite spirited." It was obvious the man's intentions were to add humor with his final words.

"Well certainly," Kelly interjected, not quite caring for the way the man was so liberal with his opinion. "She is quite spirited, for how could a child that loves nature as much as she does, not be filled with spirit? Is it not all around her?"

Immediately, the wine stopped pouring and the sound of silverware on china made it quite clear to Kelly that her question startled everyone. She mentally groaned. Obviously, she'd said enough to compromise her newly found social grace.

"*Touché*, madam!" Alexander proclaimed with a raise of his wineglass. "I am sure our good minister will agree it is in nature that the divine is so clearly present."

Kelly smiled gratefully to the man, who seemed such a good friend of Daniel's.

"Well, yes, that is so, but I was merely stating it would only serve to benefit the child by continuing her redemption and that we would be pleased to see her regularly attending Sunday school with the other children once again."

"You are entirely correct, Reverend Holden," Daniel commented firmly. "I was quite remiss in allowing her absence for so long. I assure you, Elizabeth will make an appearance in Sunday school very soon. You have my word on it, sir."

Kelly politely smiled at the minister. "Yes, I look forward to Elizabeth joining us here when we return again. I rather miss her now, as I do so enjoy her company." Hopefully, that would smooth an end to the tense conversation.

Only the Reverend Holden and his wife appeared surprised by her words. Apparently, they considered Lizzie a real hellion. Kelly almost laughed out loud when she imagined Lizzie dealing with the stodgy cleric in the past. Such a free-spirited and imaginative child . . . it must have made quite a scene!

Soon afterward, the luncheon ended, and Kelly was her most gracious self as they bid good-bye to the Reverend Holden and his wife. Standing curbside while Alexander boarded his carriage, she watched as the man sat down. He pulled Daniel aside and whispered something that seemed to sound as though he approved of his friend's choice in a wife. She was not within clear earshot, but she saw Daniel almost blush when he stood away from the carriage.

Honestly, to have Alexander's approval pleased her, for it was obvious how fond Daniel was of him and, she had to admit, she too really liked the man for the way he had come to her rescue with the minister.

As they walked back to the house, Kelly remembered how Daniel had to swallow a bit of pride to admit in front of everyone he'd relatively failed as a parent. How hard that must have been for him, she thought with sympathy.

"Well, I believe we handled that fairly well, don't you?" Daniel asked, as the front door closed and they were finally alone.

"Yes, *fairly* being the key word here," Kelly said, smiling sheepishly up to him. "Actually, I think I may have upset the Reverend Holden and . . . I am sorry about that, but I just didn't care for the way he spoke about Lizzie and—"

"It is really of no consequence, Kelly," Daniel interrupted her words. "I am concerned with the dictates of social circles only for the sake of my daughter. Quite honestly, I'm sorry Alex spoke up before I could. However, know now that I wasn't speaking lightly when I said Elizabeth would join the Sunday school when she comes to the city. It will be important to show her grandparents that she is exposed and involved with some religious endeavor. They will expect it."

"Hmm," was all Kelly would say to that. She'd let Daniel handle telling Lizzie.

"Now I ask you, Mrs. Gilmore . . . how shall we spend the remainder of this, our wedding day?"

Startled, it was Kelly's turn to blush, for his question brought up a very vivid answer that was certainly not appropriate for a business arrangement. Why did he have to be so handsome? If it had to be a business arrangement, why couldn't he look like Elmer Fudd?

"I was thinking that . . . if it's possible, we might go shopping? I promised Lizzie presents, and if it's all right with you, I would also like to return Clara's kindness to me with something from the city."

"Then shopping it is," Daniel proclaimed with a laugh. "And how wonderful that it will start tongues to wagging when all of New Orleans see us shopping on the day of our nuptials."

Kelly smiled back at his mischievous grin. Maybe the man really didn't care about social standards. In fact, right now it seemed as though he'd abandoned them with glee.

"Well, we only have today," Kelly reminded him. "You did say you wanted to return to the country tomorrow."

"Yes, it would be best if we began preparing Elizabeth for her grandparents' arrival as soon as possible," he replied in a more serious tone.

Nodding, Kelly looked down to her dress, and said, "Well, I guess I'm ready. Let's give 'em somethin' to talk about . . ." She half sang the Bonnie Raitt lyrics while lifting the large skirt encircling her. What she was now wearing certainly beat a runny key lime pie any day! She was actually looking forward to showing herself off.

He laughed at loud with her. "You are truly . . ." He hesitated, as a quizzical expression grew on his face. ". . . most extraordinary, Mrs. Gilmore."

She batted her eyelashes furiously and with a playful curtsy replied to his comment in the best Southern accent she could muster, "Why thank you, Mr. Gilmore."

Again, they both burst out in laughter.

Her mind swirled as she continued to gaze up at him while he shook his head in comic disbelief. Was he thinking what she was thinking? Were they both mad? Delirious with happiness? Or were they just suddenly content? After so many years of aloneness for both of them, was this the beginning of a "happily ever after" ending?

She mentally slammed the book closed on that fairy tale. "Okay, I think we need some fresh air," she finally breathed.

"Right. I'll have Andrew bring the carriage around." Smiling, he bowed slightly and added, "If you will excuse me, madam?"

She grinned in return and watched him leave. "Oh, Daniel," she called out and he spun around in expectation.

"Thank you for everything. The garden looked absolutely lovely, and the luncheon was delicious."

Again, he bowed with a smile. "It isn't every day that I get married."

"So I've heard," she whispered as she watched him disappear beyond the hallway. So she had made quite a match, capturing the elusive Daniel Gilmore, huh? The thought pleased her, even if it was only business. She had to agree with Mrs. Holden. He was quite a catch.

Daniel led her through the city, and together they visited the finest shops. She was surprised at the low cost of goods, and when she told Daniel that the same leather gloves would cost well over fifty dollars in the year 2001, he was shocked. She giggled like a schoolgirl when he said she could have free rein in choosing her gifts and once let loose in the hat shop, she choose one for herself with silk flowers and netting and another for Lizzie and one for Clara. When Daniel led her to the toy store, she only purchased books, for she thought Lizzie was getting too old for toys and, besides, she had so many that she didn't touch. And then, she asked to be led to a jeweler. There she purchased two small gifts and felt very fortunate to have come upon them, for they were perfect.

On the ride back to the town house, Kelly leaned against the leather seat and sighed.

"Sounds as though you may be exhausted, madam. Perhaps you would care to dine alone in your room this evening."

She felt so close to him during the shopping spree that the thought of being alone was very unappealing. "Not really," she answered, then hurried to add, "Unless you want to be alone."

He chuckled. "No, madam. I do not. I was merely trying to be considerate. This has been a very full day for you."

"Well, I thank you, but I . . . I don't want to be alone," she quietly stated.

"Good. Perhaps our exhausting day has caused us to misread each other. Pray, madam . . . speak your mind. How else am I to know what you are thinking?"

"Okay, well then the first thing I'd like to say is please stop calling me madam when we're alone. In my time, that form of address is usually reserved for . . . a . . ."

"A what?"

She laughed. "Well, a woman that runs a house of prostitution." Now that certainly was speaking her mind!

He stiffened, and his expression revealed his shock. "Surely, you jest!"

Her laughter increased. "Surely, I don't. Well, only someone being extremely formal would address another with that term. Usually someone in service to another. The more common use of 'madam' would be what I just described."

"How can forms of address have become so convoluted?"

"Well, in most formal situations, it's still a form of respect. Yet, you would be surprised at how convoluted nearly everything has become in the twenty-first century compared to now."

"How so?"

"Okay, for instance, take this dress I am wearing," she said, inhaling deeply against the stiff bodice. "Clothing, at least for women, has changed drastically. If I were dressed like this in the year 2001, people would stare at me, some might even laugh, but everyone would think I was dressed for a costume party, or a parade, or think I was an actor in a theater show. It would, quite frankly, be considered outlandish attire. I'm not saying I don't appreciate it, or the fact that you were so kind to provide me with new clothes, but it definitely has a time and place, if you know what I mean. You see, in my time, dresses have been hiked above the knee . . . sometimes way above the knee." She gazed at him as he continued to look forward and watched his expression widen with shock. "In comparison to this day and age, everyone's attire has become less . . ." She paused, struggling for an appropriate word. ". . . less puritanical. Though I will say the complexity and artistry of women's fashions in this time are extraordinary."

"It truly is unbelievable to think of life and customs changing so much," he said, shaking his head in obvious wonder.

"Yes, and ironically I'm learning quite a bit, having been tossed back in time." She paused, shaking her head at the reality of her statement, then continued. "In the future, it's widely accepted to expose much of the human body, even publicly." Okay, she supposed she'd better clarify that statement for him. "Well, what I mean to say is, we wear less and less clothing, comfort taking precedence over bulky fashion, which isn't to say we don't have beautiful clothes, we just wear less of them. Suffice it to say *you* would certainly be shocked if you were tossed into the future, Daniel Gilmore."

"By the way you've described many things, I am certain you are correct. I would be most astonished, indeed. Yet, tell me of men's clothing in the future. Are we as barely clad as the women?"

"Well, comfort is still the biggest consideration, but men's clothing basically remains the same. The only thing that really changes is the style of the tie and the width of the lapels on jackets."

"Hmm . . ." He paused as though pondering her comment. "I find it disheartening to learn that ties are still male fashion. I've always considered them society's nooses."

This time she laughed. "I'd have to agree with you. Doesn't seem fair that a man has to start his day by putting a noose around his neck."

They grinned at each other.

"You know, women even wear pants, or trousers, sometimes a complete suit, just like a man, including a tie. We wear sleeveless blouses and makeup. Some women even wear their hair shorter than yours."

"They wear trousers?" he asked with shock. "Why?"

"Ah, tell me . . . when's the last time you tried to walk around in a getup like this? Why, even breathing is a strain. For comfort's sake, Daniel. You have to admit, pants are comfortable, and I wore them all the time."

"I simply can't imagine a woman wearing trousers."

"And I can't imagine spending a lifetime binding myself like this. You know, it's incredible what women have done to themselves in the name of fashion throughout history."

"Are you saying that you wish to wear trousers?" His

voice was half-teasing, as though he was hoping she would say no.

"Well, that remains to be seen. If I'm to be here for any length of time, I would imagine that I could find a seamstress who could make them for me."

"You wouldn't be seen in pubic wearing them, would you?"

She laughed. "No, I wouldn't embarrass you, Daniel. We have an agreement. I will play the role of a proper wife. Today, I was a bit overwhelmed, and I'm afraid I wasn't very social. I'll get better as I become more accustomed to the etiquette of the past."

He turned to her as the carriage slowed in front of the town house. "Please, do not berate yourself so, Kelly. I was, in fact, quite proud to present you as my wife today around town. You have done me more than a great honor."

In the moment of pause between them, he smiled tenderly at her. Swallowing down the lump in her throat, she smiled back into his deep blue eyes. "Thank you, Daniel . . . for everything. I don't know what I would have done without you. It terrifies me even to think what would have happened to me if you hadn't come with me to New Orleans." Her smile widened, as she thought of something very nineteenth century. "Why, you're my hero."

He threw back his head and laughed. "Now you flatter me, Mrs. Gilmore, for it is every man's secret desire to be regarded as such by a woman."

As the carriage came to a halt, Daniel hopped down and held out his arms to her. She hesitated for just a moment, then leaned forward as he put his strong hands on her waist and lifted her to the ground.

When they stood face-to-face, he smiled, and said, "Thank you for a wonderful afternoon. For so many years . . ." He hesitated as though uncomfortable with his own thought, then quickly offered. "I cannot recall a day I have enjoyed so much in a very long time."

Just as he finished, Andrew came out of the house to assist with the carriage and, nervously, they broke apart.

"Welcome back, Mister and Missus Gilmore." The kind

man smiled with a beam of happiness that couldn't be con-
cealed.

"Thank you, Andrew." Daniel then instructed the man to
bring all boxes into Kelly's room. As she walked into the
house next to him, Daniel leaned close and mused, "It is
quite evident we have dazzled more than a few with our sudden arrangement. The accolades from everyone, including
my staff, seem never-ending."

"Maybe they're just happy for you, Daniel. I mean, it has
been a long time for you . . . err, what I meant to say was,
you've been alone for a long time." At this point, with one
foot in her mouth, she'd might as well insert the other and
start chewing! Grabbing the railing to the staircase, she
thought she'd best be ready for a quick exit.

"Yes, it is true. I have been alone for a long time," he said,
placing his top hat on a table in the foyer. Turning back to
her as he removed his driving gloves he added, "There is one
thing of which I'm certain . . . I know a young lady who will
to be truly overjoyed by this unprecedented news."

She was very glad to hear him say that, since she wasn't
quite sure where her Freudian slip might have sent him. A
part of her brain knew that again he'd said it to change the
subject and save her the embarrassment of another faux pas.
There was so much more to this man than magnetic Southern charm. In addition to being kind, generous, intelligent,
well-off, and handsome, he was extremely intuitive. Daniel
Gilmore was made of the stuff that melted women. She
couldn't become that kind of mess in a *business agreement*.
She had her end of the bargain to hold up. Lizzie.

Quickly, she shifted her thoughts and remembered the
way the child had run along the bank of the bayou, waving
madly. Kelly grinned, and murmured, "I made a promise to
her that I would return, but I never thought it would be this
soon . . . or," she paused at her own bold thought, then decided to complete it by adding, "as her stepmother."

He stood only a few feet from her, and she could see the
sudden look of sincere tenderness in his eyes grow. In a low,
quiet tone he said, "Again, I am indebted to you, Miss Kelly.
Thank you for coming into my—" he paused, then supple-

mented, "*all* our lives . . . and bringing such goodness. Your contemporary expertise and loving nature is truly a gift to us all." Then he bowed.

Okay, now she was melting. "You're very"—she cleared the dry whisper from her throat—"welcome, Daniel, and thank you for such a beautiful compliment."

As gazes locked, the pause of silence between them seemed eternal to Kelly. Her brain began to overload, searching for possible nuances in his words. Was it more than a mere compliment? Could she read between the lines? Was he trying to seduce her? *Should* she be reading between the lines? Was he feeling anything like she was feeling? Did he want to be close to her, as she wanted him? Were there any lines? Those kisses had to mean something!

"Right. Well, if you will excuse me, I shall leave you to your repose," he finally said. "Presently, I must attend to the details for our departure in the morning." He smiled.

"Yes, of course." It was all she could think to say. Her mind was still awash with thoughts of leaping from her grip on the railing, closing the space between them, and throwing her arms around his neck to kiss him. Frozen with one foot on the first stair of the sweeping staircase, she simply smiled back to him.

Nodding, she watched him turn and begin to walk toward his office, when he suddenly spun around. "Oh, and Kelly?"

This time she let go of the banister.

"Weather permitting, shall we meet for dinner in the garden at seven this evening?"

"Sure. I would like that, Daniel," she said, clasping her damp palms together. The way she was feeling was so indecent, considering their agreement, that she wanted to smack herself. Slamming an iron lid on her emotions, she turned back to the stairs again and began to ascend them.

"Rest well, my dear."

Her brain seemed to freeze this time with his endearment, and, stopping midway, she turned to look back down at him. Of course, she knew in this time it was nothing more than a form of address. All of it was simply propriety. "Thank you," she whispered in resignation.

At that moment she saw Andrew enter the foyer through a side entry, carrying the boxes from their shopping excursion. Daniel turned away again and walked into the hall to his office. Could he be even slightly aware that just being near him sent warm rushes of pleasure through her? She was certain he must have felt something during that moment of silence between them only seconds ago. Adding all this to the memory of those kisses, days ago, was throwing her off-balance and wreaking havoc with her self-control. Okay, so maybe she was going to need a padlock for that iron lid imprisoning her emotions.

Continuing up the stairs, she pictured Lizzie, wrapped in her arms and wishing five times with all her might that Kelly would come back. How powerful a child's wishes, she thought. For she was coming back, and, for however long it lasted, she was now not only playing the role of wife, but also Lizzie's mother.

It was as though she were following some map, and being led, step by step, along the way. And everything pointed to the child who had found her. All she had to do was follow the signs as they appeared and not lose her head. As crazy is might seem, in every moment she was taken care of, with shelter, food, even clothing and gifts. Yes, it was scary, and no, she hadn't clue where the next turn was leading . . . but she was all right. There had been moments when she felt terrified and thought she was losing her mind, yet there were also moments of great joy and companionship . . . moments she hadn't enjoyed in many years. Still, a part of her sure wished she knew who was drawing this map, for she had more than a few questions. The first one was *why*? The next, why *her*?

She was still asking those questions in her mind hours later while sitting across from Daniel in the garden. Andrew had set a small table in the center of the courtyard by the fountain. The lanterns were lit, and crickets were chirping their songs of courting. The meal they had just consumed was deliciously prepared, and the wine was heady. Her dinner companion was, as always, devastatingly charming, and Kelly thought that it must all be a dream, yet she knew she was very much awake, for she hadn't been this happy in over thirteen years.

Could she have traveled back in time to find happiness, to remember what it felt like?

Shaking the thought out of her head, she concentrated on Daniel's words.

"And so, I have purchased whitewash and paint to be delivered in three days. You once joked it was about time I learned how the other half lives. At the time you were referring to washing dishes. Now I have the entire exterior of the house to transform in less than two weeks. I do hope to change your opinion of me. I am not such a dilettante that I would sit back and watch another do my work."

He was smiling, and Kelly assumed he was talking about the country house. She would have to stop daydreaming and pay attention. "I can help," she offered. "I've painted before, and if I may say so, I am quite good at it."

"My dear lady, I am speaking about painting the exterior of a house."

"Did you think I meant painting a watercolor?" She laughed. "Unfortunately, I have no creative ability in the finer arts. I know what you meant. I'm strong. I've painted walls before. As a matter of fact, when I started my business, I not only painted all the walls, I put together six desks. I even learned how to snake a wire through a wall to relocate a thermostat, though I will admit I had help on that last one. I really can be of assistance to you, Daniel."

He was staring at her, and suddenly Kelly thought she knew what the problem was. "Doesn't sound very ladylike to you, does it? I can't help it if the thought of sitting around all day looking pretty makes me think I'd wither away from sheer boredom. I like to keep busy, my mind and my body. I used to put in at least a twelve-hour day at work."

"You are a constant source of amazement for me, Kelly," he said with admiration.

She felt better and sat up straighter.

"Women are permitted to work such strenuous hours?"

"It was my choice, Daniel. No one made me. In the beginning when I was starting, I had to do it just to keep up.

More recently, I did it because . . ." Her words trailed off.

"Because . . . ?"

She inhaled and spoke the truth. "Because I didn't really want to go home to an empty house."

"Surely, a woman such as yourself, had many opportunities for . . . social pursuits."

She grinned. "Are you asking if I dated?"

"Dated?"

"Yes . . . ah, how would you put it? Have gentleman callers?"

He looked suitably embarrassed to have been found out. "I suppose I am trying to find out why such a lovely woman would be alone."

"It was my choice."

"I see."

"I think you know how I felt." She sipped her wine and smiled into his eyes across the candlelight. "Today, Mrs. Holden told me I snared quite a catch in you. She said many a family has been trying to get you married for some time."

He grinned. "I will admit that I am happy to put those days behind me. It was most awkward being on the receiving end of so many blatant social pursuits." It was obvious to Kelly that his inflection was meant to show he could laugh at himself. Another great quality.

Kelly chuckled. "I know! I had friends who tried for years to fix me up with men. It is embarrassing, isn't it? I guess they finally gave up."

"Fix you up?"

"That's what it's called in the twenty-first century. Like you're broken, or something, because you choose to remain alone, and many believe marriage is going to fix everything."

"Exactly!" Daniel agreed, joining in her laughter.

She sighed. "So here we sit. Married. Foiled all attempts at capture, only to enter into a business deal."

He stopped laughing. "Does it feel like a business deal now?" His voice was low and his gaze intense.

"No, it doesn't," she replied. "I'm confused, Daniel." It just slipped from her lips.

He stared at her for a moment longer, then looked down into his glass as he sipped. Placing it lightly on the table, he began thoughtfully. "I'm certain, for anyone to have gone through what you claim to have done, that is to be expected." He looked to her and his expression was serious. "When I say 'claim to,' I want you to understand it doesn't imply that I don't believe you. To the best of my knowledge, you have never exhibited any displays of hysteria or dementia, for that matter . . . at least in my presence. Quite to the contrary—"

"That's encouraging to know," she interjected.

"Please, Kelly . . . wait, and let me finish," he softly chided.

She nodded with a slight sigh and folded her hands on the table.

Leaning forward, his face was so close to hers, she could feel his breath when he continued speaking softly. "I am quite willing to accept that you have indeed traveled from another place and time . . . which could very well make me question my own sanity . . . however," he said, tenderly touching her chin to lift her gaze to his, "you are an attractive, intelligent, and rational woman. Nothing about this entire situation is fictional, in my opinion." Lowering his hand, he gently covered both of hers with it. "You sit before me, more real than any woman I have known for over ten years. For a reason, or perhaps many reasons—that we may never know—you have ended up in this place now. It is foreign and strange, and most likely will be for quite a while." He appeared almost reluctant as he released her hands and leaned back against his chair before adding, "You have every right to be confused. In all honesty, there have been many moments when I have been also."

What the hell just happened? She now felt even more bewildered and lost as though he'd moved a thousand miles away from her. Was she intoxicated by his words and actions or just the wine? Probably both.

The sensation that lingered in her fingertips from his touch still buzzed wildly. She wasn't really sure if he'd given her the complete response she wanted to hear, but damn, it was a good one. For now she'd have to accept his words, for she didn't think she was in the proper frame of mind to read anything more into it. She had to remember this was a business deal, and she had a task at hand.

Suddenly, those incredible kisses he'd given her in the country house came fleeting back into her brain and she considered the entire situation to which she'd agreed. What was she thinking anyway? It should have been so obvious, he'd simply mistaken her for his wife, a woman with whom he was still in love. Kelly couldn't compete with a ghost, and didn't want to. This man had already married a woman once for love, and she understood that, for didn't she feel the same way about Michael? Didn't she? But again she noted that she hadn't really thought all that much about Michael since she'd been here. That was strange. . . .

It was all too much to assimilate now.

She turned her attention back to the man sitting opposite her in the candlelight.

"You must be tired," he said softly and smiled.

"Just lost in thought for a moment."

"Perhaps it's best that we retire now."

Kelly nodded and waited as he stood and pulled back her chair. Not a word more was spoken between them as they walked to the doors leading into the house. She was wondering how they were going to say good night. After all, as insane as it seemed, this *was* their wedding night.

Once inside the darkened home, Daniel escorted her to the stairs, finally breaking the silence by saying, "Sleep well, Kelly. I wish you a peaceful rest." He took her hand and lightly kissed the space just under her knuckles. "I shall always remember this day."

"As will I," she murmured, sure her rest would not be so peaceful since threads of desire seemed to race up her arm and shiver down her body from his touch once more. "Good night and thank you again for everything, Daniel."

"All thanks goes to you, my dear . . . for today you have agreed to join your life with mine. I do keep my promises, Kelly. You won't regret it."

She deeply inhaled and simply smiled as she began to walk up the stairs, hoping she wouldn't trip up now.

Regret . . . ? Right now the only regret she had was that this was a business deal and she was walking up these steps alone.

Ten

"Lordy be . . . *married*!"

Clara threw her arms in the air and continued to praise God at the news. Kelly and Daniel glanced at each other and laughed with Clara's enthusiasm, and Kelly knew she didn't have the heart to tell the old woman it was all merely a business arrangement.

"Thank you for your seal of approval, Clara," Daniel said with a smile as he placed the last stack of packages on the dining-room table. "Miss Kelly has done me a great honor by becoming my wife. We came back to tell you and Elizabeth right away. Where is she, by the way?"

Clara lifted the edge of her apron and wiped at the corner of her eyes as tears of happiness flowed. "Oh, that chile is out there in them woods again. Lordy, she done moped around this house for two whole days after y'all left, 'til I couldn't stand it no more and had to shoo her out."

Daniel patted Clara's shoulder sympathetically, and replied, "I'll go and find her."

When they were finally alone, Kelly looked at the sweet older woman and announced, "I need a hug."

"Oh, chile . . ." Clara opened her arms. "C'mere to Mammy Clara."

Enveloped in the woman's warm embrace, Kelly felt her throat tighten with emotion. "I'm still reeling from everything that's happened to me."

"You can let it out now," Clara soothed, rubbing Kelly's back with a gentle motion. "I reckoned the city wasn't gonna be what you was expectin'."

"Everything's gone, Clara . . . my world . . . all gone . . . or, it hasn't even happened yet. I'm stuck here, in 1888 . . . and Daniel, he said . . . well, he said he would take care of me and I could stay with . . ." Her words were choked off with tears.

"Hush now," Clara whispered. "You is where you is supposed to be, and that's the plain fact of it. My heart is burstin' with gratitude for it, too. You coulda done mighty worse than Mistah Daniel, that's for sure."

Kelly sniffled and pulled back. "He's been wonderful. It's just that everything I've known is . . . gone, and now all this is happening so fast. Somehow I've got to fit in here . . . in this time, this place . . . to be his wife and . . . and I don't know if I can."

"Now that's sheer nonsense if I ever heard it. You're gonna fit in just fine," Clara said with a gruff voice of encouragement. "And you know that chile is gonna be overjoyed when she hears she finally got herself a momma."

"Oh, Clara . . . Lizzie's grandparents are coming from England soon, and somehow I've got to help her become a proper young lady. How will I ever manage that in such a short time?"

Clara chuckled as she let go of Kelly and shook her head. "Aw, don't fret so now, Miz Kelly. Greater miracles have occurred in shorter amounts of time. But I will reckon that's a tall order to fill . . . have some hope and just keep the faith," she said, patting Kelly's hand. "It's all in the great plan, and I'm sure this one's gonna be mighty interestin'," she added, as she nodded toward the kitchen. "Sounds like your miracle is a comin' now."

"What surprise, Daddy?"

Kelly could hear Lizzie's muffled voice as they made their way through the kitchen.

"You'll see," Daniel answered in a happy voice. "Now stop here, close your eyes, and I'll lead you into the dining room."

"Oh, Daddy, I'm not a baby."

"Close your eyes. I promise you won't be disappointed."

Kelly heard their footsteps and soon she saw Lizzie, dressed in her bib overalls, hair hanging down in her face as she pressed her little hands over her eyes.

"All right, Elizabeth . . . look what your father has brought you." Daniel beamed over Lizzie's head to Kelly.

Lizzie dropped her hands, and the look on her face was priceless. First gasping shock, then surprise, then absolute joy. *"You came back!"* she yelled, scrambling across the room.

Kelly caught her as the child slammed into her waist and hugged her so hard she had to hold her breath until she was done. "Hiya, Lizzie," she whispered and bent down to kiss the child's head. "It's so good to see you, too." Kelly almost started crying again as she looked up to Clara and Daniel.

"You came back! You came back!" Lizzie lifted her head and stared into Kelly's eyes. "I always believed you would."

Smiling, Kelly said, "You have some mighty powerful wishes, young lady."

"And we have another surprise for you," Daniel stated, moving to stand at Kelly's side. He placed his hand upon her shoulder then announced, "Miss Kelly and I were married yesterday."

Lizzie stood very still and stared at them both. "Married?"

Smiling, she and Daniel nodded in unison.

"Then you is my momma now?"

Kelly looked at Daniel, not sure what to say.

"Yes, Elizabeth . . . if you wish, Miss Kelly may be addressed as your new mother, for she has married your father."

The look on the small girl's face didn't indicate that everything had quite registered in her mind yet.

"Honey, you can still call me Miss Kelly since this is so new for all of us," she said, picking up Lizzie's hand. "Here, look at all the presents we brought for you." She turned toward the dining-room table, hoping to divert attention from the awkward situation. Lizzie had enough to assimilate. Besides, Kelly didn't know how long she would remain here, so how fair was it to ask the child to call her mother? She didn't have the answer.

"These are all for me?" Lizzie asked in wonder.

"Well, all but two of them." Kelly picked up a heavy package and a large hatbox, then placed them in front of Clara.

"What's this . . . for me?" the old woman asked in surprise, then turned toward Daniel.

"Yes, for you," Kelly answered with a wide grin.

"Miss Kelly insisted and picked them out especially for you, Clara," Daniel said with an approving laugh. "Open the package first."

"Open it! Open it, Mammy Clara, so's I can open mine next!"

"Now you just hush, chile. Ain't every day that I gets a present. I wants to savor it," Clara whispered, carefully untying the twine around the brown paper. She pulled back the wrapping and brought her weathered hands up to her mouth, while tears filled her eyes. "Oh, Lordy, you shouldn't have, Miz Kelly."

"What's in it?" Lizzie demanded, almost jumping up so she could see over the paper. "What is it? Show me!"

Clara's hands were shaking slightly as she lifted the pale blue cashmere robe. "Oh my, I ain't never felt anything so soft in my whole and entire life," she breathed in awe.

"As soon as Miss Kelly saw it, she just knew it was for you, Clara," Daniel said, beaming at Kelly.

Kelly grinned widely, then said to Clara, "Here, take it all the way out. There's more."

"More?" Clara carefully pulled the robe out of the package and set it almost reverently on the dining-room table.

"Slippers! My, and fine kid they are, too! And what's this . . . ?" She held the slippers in the crook of her arm, as though too precious to part with, and slowly lifted the soft cream-colored cashmere shawl, and the tears started once more. "Oh, this is too much," she protested.

"Do try it on, Clara," Kelly insisted, removing the slippers from underneath the old woman's arm.

Clara sniffled back her tears and put the shawl over her thin shoulders. She rubbed her hand over her covered arms. "What is this? It sure don't feel like no wool I ever felt."

"It's cashmere, Clara," Kelly said, "and you deserve to have the finest, softest shawl in the whole wide world."

"Well, I ain't never . . ." Clara kept shaking her head, as Lizzie reached up and also began stroking the material.

"I told you it was time you were pampered," Kelly said with a wink. "Now, open the big box, Clara."

Leaving the shawl over her shoulders, she lifted the lid and let out a squeal of pleasure as she viewed a navy blue velvet bonnet with a matching rosette on the side, amid a spray of white and yellow silk flowers. Clara touched the fine netting that would fall over her eyes and said in a shaky voice, "Oh my, this is just too fine . . ."

"Try it on," Daniel encouraged.

"Yes, put it on, Mammy Clara! I wanna see!"

She turned to the group. "Wherever am I gonna wear it?"

"Oh, I have plans, Clara . . . believe me, you'll wear it."

Clara lifted the hat and placed it on her head.

"Why, madam," Daniel proclaimed with a slight bow, then added, "you look absolutely stunning!"

Kelly laughed. "Wait, wait . . ." She rummaged through the satchel that Daniel had purchased for her things and brought out the mother-of-pearl hand mirror. "Look at yourself, Clara. See how beautiful you are."

Kelly held up the mirror for Clara and watched as the older woman looked at her reflection. "My, I ain't seen myself close in so long," she murmured, touching the lines on her face. "I sure done got old."

"You are beautiful," Kelly insisted. "What do you think of the hat?"

Clara adjusted the netting over her eyes and almost giggled. "Now, ain't I somethin'? But where am I ever gonna wear such a lovely thing?"

"We've got places to go, things to do, and people to see, Clara. I promise you'll get good use of it. Do you like it?"

"Do I like it?" she repeated with awe. "Why, I just love it. It's the prettiest thing I ever did see," she whispered, smiling at her reflection as she fastened the long hat pin. "But you really shouldn't a done all this, Miz Kelly."

"Actually Daniel was with me and we both picked it out. We knew it would be perfect for you." Kelly smiled and winked up at Daniel.

Clara turned to the man. "Oh, and thank you, Mistah Daniel," she said with genuine appreciation. Spinning back to Kelly, she added, "Miz Kelly . . . I ain't never gonna forget all your kindness."

Kelly hugged the older woman and, over her shoulder, said to Lizzie, "Okay, now it's your turn, Miss Elizabeth. You've been very patient."

"Which one?" the child asked, looking over the packages before her. Of course she grabbed the largest, the hatbox, waiting for consent to open her choice. Before Kelly could finish her nod, Lizzie was lifting the top off the box.

Kelly was pleased with Lizzie's intake of breath as she pulled out the wide straw bonnet with a profusion of purple and white flowers at the back. Long white-satin ribbons flowed gracefully from under the flowers. With anticipation, Kelly couldn't wait for a response. "Do you like it?"

Lizzie grinned. "Sure is pretty. Looks like a grown-up-lady hat."

"It's a proper young lady's hat. I think that maybe it's time you started wearing one, don't you? Go ahead, try it on."

Lizzie placed it on her head, and Kelly handed her the mirror. "Don't you look lovely," she murmured, as Daniel and Clara agreed.

Lizzie stared at herself, turning her head first one way and then the other. "It's pretty," she said to herself, then quickly turned back to the other parcels. Unwrapping the next package, she found a pale lavender dress with a white collar of embroidered cotton and white-satin ballet slippers. She touched the soft leather soles, and remarked, "I'd hurt my feet in these outside."

"You won't be climbing any trees in them," Daniel said with a laugh. "They're for when we entertain."

"Well I'm still gonna climb trees, Daddy," the child insisted while digging into the next package. She brought out the books. *Alice in Wonderland. Through the Looking Glass.* There was a book of poetry by Elizabeth Barrett Browning. "I think you'll like this one, Lizzie," Kelly said as she picked up *Little Women.* "There's a character in it, a girl named Jo, who is based on the author herself. She liked to climb trees and leap fences, too."

"Really?" Lizzie asked, thumbing through the pages.

"Yes. It was one of my favorites when I was a young girl." Kelly pulled the next largest gift toward Lizzie and said, "Now open this one."

Lizzie placed the book on the table and untied the twine around the present. There was a brown box inside and when she opened it, she reached in and brought out another box, this one painted white with a fine rendering of flowers around the base. "What is it?" she asked

"Open it," her father instructed.

When she did, music began playing, and her face lit with pleasure. There was a mirror on the inside lid and another tiny package lay in one of the velvet compartments. "What's it for?" Lizzie asked with wonder as she touched the velvet.

"It's a jewelry box," Daniel said.

"But I don't have any jewelry," Lizzie answered.

"Maybe you do," Kelly pointed out. "Open the next one."

It was obvious Lizzie was trying to keep her excitement under control as she caught her bottom lip between her teeth. She quickly unwrapped the last present and brought out a fine gold chain with an exquisite pendant attached.

"It's a fairy!" Lizzie announced with a squeal of delight.

"Here, let me help you," Kelly said, taking the necklace

and putting it around Lizzie's neck. The pendant fell right next to Lizzie's heart. "There, now you have your very own gold fairy."

Lizzie quickly wrapped her arms around Kelly, closed her eyes, and hugged tightly. "Thank you," she said with heartfelt gratitude. "But you're the queen of fairies, and now I really do have you forever and ever!"

"Thank your father, too," Kelly said, trying not to knock off Lizzie's hat as she hugged the child back. She wouldn't even comment on the queen of fairies remark and whether she would be staying permanently with this family.

Lizzie turned to her father and said, "Thank you, Daddy . . . this is the best day ever!"

Daniel held out his arms and Lizzie went into them. Kelly watched as he hugged his daughter and told her there was yet one more surprise.

Delighted, Lizzie looked up to him.

"Your grandparents are coming from England to meet you."

"My grandparents?"

"Yes. Your mother's parents. I've told you about them. They should be arriving within two weeks."

"Well, it looks like we're going to be right busy here," Clara declared. "And, as I wasn't expectin' you *and* a bride, I best be gettin' supper started."

Everyone turned to Clara as she picked up her gifts from the table. "Thank you from the bottom of my heart for such fine, fine things." Shaking her head, she added, "I will treasure them always."

"Enjoy them," Daniel said with a warm smile.

Kelly smiled as the older woman kept her hat and shawl on, muttering as she walked out of the room, "Umm, umm, umm, ain't things just a wonder now . . ."

"Come on, Lizzie," Kelly said, "I'll help you put your presents away, and you can help me with mine. Wait 'til I show you what I got!"

The two of them gathered up Lizzie's things and just as they were about to leave the room, Kelly turned around to Daniel, and said, "Thank you again . . . for everything."

" 'Tis I who thanks you, my dear, for this joyous home-coming."

Another moment of silence played between them. "I made the right decision," Kelly admitted in a whisper, and smiled tenderly. Once she felt the comfort of being back in this home she knew how right she was to say yes. For however long it lasted, she was happy.

Imagine that!

Dinner that evening became quite a celebration and was served in the kitchen upon Kelly's insistence. It was her way of commemorating the occasion and because she wanted Clara with them. Kelly and Lizzie had set the comfortable table. They all helped Clara with cooking and serving, and Daniel had even brought wildflowers in from the garden for the centerpiece. There was an air of renewal among this family, and Kelly felt grateful to be part of it. Several times during the night, she found herself pausing to take in the shared joy. At one point everyone became nearly giddy, as they gently teased Clara, who'd refused to take off her new hat. Able to laugh at herself, too, the Grand Dame lively paraded in her own defense and said she'd sleep in it if she could, but didn't want to spoil the flowers. Everybody helped with the dishes, and when Clara announced she was retiring early, merely so she could wear her new robe, they all followed suit. Lizzie wanted to start reading *Little Women*, and soon it was just Kelly and Daniel in the hallway.

He held the lamp high to light the way. "You must be exhausted, Kelly."

"I am," she admitted. "I think it's all catching up to me."

There was a moment of awkwardness between them and Kelly decided to end it. Impulsively, she stood on tiptoe and quickly kissed his cheek. "Good night, Daniel."

"Good night, my dear," he whispered, appearing pleased by her action. "Sleep well."

Once alone in her room, Kelly looked around and suddenly thought how lonely it seemed. She undressed and slipped on a negligee, turned down the oil lamp on the table, and climbed into bed. As her head sank against the pillow, she exhaled. Here she was, back again. In the same house, the same room, the same year . . . and yet there was no denying her present situation was entirely different. Kelly recalled when she had come upstairs with Lizzie earlier, she'd found that Daniel had put her clothing and other packages into this room and she actually experienced a moment of disappointment. But what had she expected? That her things would be in his bedroom?

Shaking her head, she tried to empty her mind of all thought. Better to get as much sleep as she could to wake fresh in the morning and begin tutoring Lizzie. That was the deal. Seducing a man who was still in love with his late wife was not part of the agreement.

Seduce?

She laughed out loud as she stared into the darkness. When was the last time she'd seduced a man? She knew. It had been Michael. Suddenly, her heart became conflicted with old emotions. Her mind drifted to pictures of her late husband, and she remembered their time together. A smile, filled with memories, played at her lips. But she'd been young then . . . young and in love and so sure of herself. Was she holding herself back now out of loyalty to her memories? How did one even begin to seduce a man when it had been years since a man had been so attractive to her? She knew Michael, knew his mind and his body, what to say, where to touch. Tonight she'd been shy about a simple kiss good night on Daniel's cheek! He'd been pleased, though. That much she had seen in his expression.

It was so hard to know what to do. Did he really want this to be just a business deal? Was he still in love with Lillian and only attracted to her because she reminded him of his first wife? Did he merely want someone to be a mother to Lizzie, to stand by his side when the grandparents visited, to be a charming companion? Was *he* satisfied with that? In an attempt to relieve her own anxiousness, she exhaled. Then she mentally practiced.

Excuse me, Daniel, but does your heart race whenever I'm around? Does your body throb with desire when our skin touches? Do you daydream about what real intimacy between us could be like? She didn't even have the courage to ask that of a man in the year 2001, let alone Daniel Gilmore with his nineteenth-century sensibilities.

Yawning, Kelly pulled the coverlet up to her neck and blinked tiredly with resignation. So she was flying by the seat of her pants—well, if she had pants in this day and age—and if anything was going to happen, she'd just have to wait for him to make—

Her thoughts were immediately suspended when what appeared to be two minuscule lights began twinkling at the foot of her bed. Blinking in disbelief, she willed her eyes wide open to stare at them in defiance. They didn't disappear. Nearly mesmerized, she could only watch as they grew in size, sparkling with an amazing luminosity. Against the darkness, brilliant trails of light dissipated behind them like melting stardust as they gracefully wove about each other. Now frozen in absolute awe, she heard herself breathing shallow and knew she wasn't dreaming. She was very much awake and could only liken them to dancing fairy lights, so exquisitely stunning, so entirely compelling, that she found herself caught in childlike wonder, willingly opening up to them as they grew even greater in size and slowly began making their way around the side of the bed toward her.

There was no sound, yet she sensed a communication as though from one she understood acceptance and from the other great love. She also got the impression they were a life force of some sort and that it took tremendous effort to make themselves be seen. She sensed it was a huge gesture on their part and she should feel privileged to witness the spectacle. None of it made sense. Now just a few feet from her, she suddenly recalled Lizzie and Clara talking about ghosts, and all her senses were immediately seized with fear.

Instantly, they were gone.

Stunned and rigid, Kelly lay in bed, entirely unsure of what had just happened. Her eyes darted about the lightless room, and she blinked repeatedly to be sure she was truly awake and hadn't dreamed the whole thing. Oh, she *was* awake, wide-awake, and now terrified of seeing things in the night. She wanted to jump out of bed, but was too scared to move. Her heart was pounding. Her skin was tingling with fear. She stared at the door, trying to judge how far it was and how fast she could make it. She had seen something, something absolutely irrational, something that was not of this world and she wanted *out*!

Enough was enough . . . she had time traveled, gotten married, and now she was seeing ghosts or apparitions? Oh, no . . . she might have lost just about everything in her life, but she would put up one hell of a fight for her sanity! Holding her breath and summoning every ounce of courage she had, Kelly flung the covers off and leapt from her bed. Bolting in one giant sprint, she jerked the door open and was down the hall pounding against Daniel's in time that would have surely won her an Olympic gold medal.

Waiting the few seconds it took for him to respond, she felt as though eternity was passing as she dared not look back in the direction of her own room. When his door opened, Kelly threw herself into his arms and began ranting . . .

"Something happened! I don't know what it was, or what they were! I was just . . . lying there in the dark, thinking, and all of a sudden they were there at the foot of my bed! Two of them!"

"What?" Daniel demanded, holding her in his arms and looking down the hallway. "Animals?"

"Not animals! Not vegetable, or mineral, either! Something! Some lights, and then they communicated to me, or something and . . . and then I got scared and they went away."

"Kelly, what are you talking about?"

"I'm talking about something, ghosts, lights that were visiting me, and . . . and I'm not going back in there. I can't!"

He rubbed her back, soothing her like she was a child, and she clung to him, burying her face into his chest. It was then she realized that he was wearing underclothes, some kind of short-sleeved cotton shirt and pants that reached his upper thighs. She pulled back, and pushed her hair from her face. "Oh . . . I'm sorry, but I'm scared, Daniel, and . . . and I didn't know what else to do and . . ."

"It's all right," he whispered, pulling her back into his arms.

Kelly listened to his heart pounding. She inhaled the scent of vanilla and a citrus spice and suddenly she realized this was exactly where she wanted to be.

"I'm afraid to be alone," she whispered. "I'm sorry to be such a coward, but nothing like this has ever happened to me."

"You said there were two of them?"

"Yes," she answered, still clinging to him as her teeth started to chatter. "Daniel, am I losing my mind?"

"Shh," he whispered against her hair. "You're not losing your mind. I know what you're talking about."

This time she pulled completely away and stared into his eyes. "You do?"

He nodded. "Though I've only seen one light, never two. I thought it was my wife . . . well, Lillian," he corrected himself. "Come, you're shaking. Let me get you a robe."

"I'm not going back there, Daniel," she protested. "I can't!"

He took her hand and led her into his room. In the low light from the oil lamp, she could see it was decorated in dark colors of brown and burgundy, with heavy carved furniture and a huge bed. "Here," he said, letting go of her hand and picking up his robe from a chair. "Put this around you."

He draped it over her shoulders and Kelly wrapped it tightly, as her teeth continued to chatter. "You've seen this, and you aren't scared?"

"I should have warned you. I'm sorry. I didn't think . . . it's been many months since the last time I saw it. I know it is shocking, Kelly. I, too, was shocked, but I don't think you have to be afraid. It's gone now."

She stared right at him. "I'm not going back there!"

"You don't have to. You can stay here."

"In your room?"

"Yes. I can sleep on a sofa downstairs and—"

"You can't leave me alone!" she protested, feeling her eyes begin to burn with tears. "What if they come in here?"

"What would you have me do, Kelly? Should I sleep in the chair?"

"No . . ." she answered, taking a deep breath. "We can share the bed. Don't worry, I probably won't sleep a wink as it is, but I would feel better if you were here. Do you mind?"

"Not at all," he said, closing the door and coming back into the room. "We are married, after all," he said with a slight grin. "Anyway, Clara would not be shocked. Are you sure, though, that you wouldn't rather have me sleep in the chair?"

"No," she answered, scrambling into his bed. "I want a big strong body next to me if they come back."

He chuckled. "Did you feel threatened?"

Knowing she was being pretty brazen, but not caring, she pulled the cover over her body and held it under her chin as she laid against the pillow. "Not when they were there, I didn't. Just when they left . . . I don't know . . . I was terrified. I mean more frightened then I have ever been. It was like my mind couldn't deal with it. After everything, Daniel . . . the time travel, the marriage, and now *this*!"

"Yes," he murmured, sitting on the edge of the bed. "I understand. Rest easy, my dear. You are safe now. Nothing is going to hurt you." He came into bed, and looked down at her as he slipped the cover over him. "Not ever again, Kelly. I promise you that."

She stared at him, wanting to be back within the warmth of his arms, yet didn't dare make that move. It was more than enough that she was in his bed! And she'd been shy about giving him a chaste kiss on the cheek!

"Look," she began, feeling a flush of embarrassment creeping up from her neck. "I really want to apologize to you for barging into your bedroom like this. I mean, we hardly know each other and—"

He held his hand up to interrupt her. "There is no need for an apology. I remember the first time I saw the light . . . I, too, was terrified afterward. We're not taught to believe that such a thing is possible and then when we know we've seen it, we can't help but wonder if we're losing our minds."

"Exactly! You hear stories about people seeing things and you think they're weird . . . and then it happens to *you* and you're blown away by it."

"Blown away?"

"It means your mind is blown because it can't comprehend it. There is no reference, no way to catagorize it in your brain. It's . . . too incredible." She sighed deeply. "But this stuff really happens!"

"Yes, Kelly. It really happens. You are not alone."

"You said you were scared when it happened to you?"

"Oh, yes . . . though not while it was happening. And only that first time. After that, I felt it was a . . . a visit from Lillian, and it never lasted very long."

"So now Lillian is visiting me," Kelly murmured.

"But you said there were two lights."

"Yes," she asserted as she leaned up on her elbows. "Two of them . . . I think . . . well, I know . . ." she said softly and began shaking her head at how crazy she must sound admitting it. "I know what I saw, but I'm not sure what I know." She shook her head with confusion.

"What do you think you know?" Daniel asked softly.

She didn't answer immediately, wondering if she should continue telling him her unearthly thoughts. Deciding at this point it really didn't matter, she whispered, "You know what? I think the other light was Michael."

"You do? Why?"

"I don't know. I could feel such love coming from it and . . . and it reminded me of him. I know it sounds crazy." She dropped back into the soft feather pillow and sighed. "I mean here we are, each reminding the other of their dead spouse and seeing lights . . . and this time travel fiasco and—"

He chuckled sympathetically. "It's no wonder you're frazzled, Kelly. Believe it or not, I understand. You poor thing," he added, reaching out and tucking the coverlet more firmly around her shoulders. "You've really had quite a time of it, haven't you?"

She nodded. "I don't want to whine and have a pity party for myself, but I *have*!" It was her turn to chuckle. "Really!"

He smiled so tenderly at her, with a look of such understanding and compassion, that her worries seemed to melt in the warmth of the amber glow on his handsome face. A moment of silence played between them, then he slowly began leaning over her. Her eyes darted from his lips to his deep gaze and back again to his lips. Her heart began to race and her mind began swirling with thoughts of another breathtaking kiss. He raised his hand and reached out to the lamp on the table beside her. Turning the flame down to a faint glimmer, his face was just inches from hers as he began to speak softly. "Try and rest now. I promise no harm will come to you, my dearest." Leaning back onto his side of the bed he added, "I am right by your side, if you need me," he whispered as he lay back against his pillow.

If she needed him?

Oh, if he only knew how she was interpreting his words!

Eleven

In some faint distance she heard a bird chirping and smiled, though she refused to open her eyes and give up the wonderful dream. She felt the warmth behind her and arched her back against it, rubbing her bottom in exquisite pleasure against the firm pressure. Heat permeated her skin where this dream lover spooned her and she felt so protected, so secure in the strong arm that wrapped around her. She imagined taking his hand resting at her waist and raising it up to cup her breast. She pressed the strong, warm hand on her breast and again she arched her back. Hearing herself moaning with such pleasure at the searing contact, a tiny part of her began to realize this dream was becoming too vivid, and it would soon end.

Disappointment was mixed with a revelation. In that half-awake state, Kelly saw how she had missed this intimacy and was now opening to it again. Dear God, it had been so long since she'd felt like this. Even if it was just a dream, then she must be preparing herself to reenter the relationship arena through her dreams and . . .

Wait a minute. She could feel legs, skin and hair on those

legs behind her own, since her nightgown had risen to her upper thighs sometime during the night. Hair . . . real hair! She ran her fingers over the hand beneath her own then peeked with one eye to see a strong male hand at her chest! With nearly a jolt, she drew in a quick breath and looked away.

Blinking, she stared at the wall and, not recognizing it either, she looked back down to the hand cupping her breast. Dear God, this wasn't a dream! This hand was real! *Real!*

Her brain seemed to crash, unable to integrate the bizarre situation.

"Good morning, Kelly."

A low rough voice whispered behind her head, and she stopped breathing as she slowly turned her face toward it. This can't be happening! It *can't!* Yet her senses could no longer deny the actuality. Daniel was right up against her and smiling sleepily.

"Oh my God," she exhaled while scrambling away from him to her edge of the mattress. "I am *so* sorry! I . . . I thought I was dreaming and . . . I didn't realize. Please . . ." She clutched the covers to her chin and stared widely back at him. "I didn't mean to—"

"Don't apologize. You were sleeping so soundly, I didn't have the heart to wake you. In all fairness, I should be the one apologizing to you," he said with a boyish smile, then quickly added, "But really, I don't think either of us should be held responsible for what happened in our sleep." He sat up, running his hands through his dark hair, and yawned.

"That's right," she said, pulling the cover up tighter against her neck. "We were sleeping. At least, I was. So, it doesn't mean anything."

He laughed. "Don't sound so relieved, madam . . . you injure my pride."

She remembered that she had been the one to arch against him. She had been the one to take his hand and place it at her breast. He was still smiling and now staring at her. A flush of humiliation crept up over her face and she covered it with her hands. "I am so embarrassed."

"You have no need for embarrassment, Kelly. Obviously,

during the night, we simply gravitated to each other for warmth."

She knew what he was saying had nothing to do with her back arching and the hand business, but she lowered her hands from her face and looked at him. "You really are a true gentleman, Daniel Gilmore."

"Why, thank you, Mrs. Gilmore." He smiled widely at her.

Now she couldn't help but smile back. She understood his point. "Yes, technically, we are married." But she still wasn't quite sure where cuddling came into the agreement.

"Exactly. There's nothing immoral happening here, madam . . . and yes, I remember you had asked not to be called madam, but it is a habit I am not willing to lose. It *is* a form of respect, and be assured, I do respect you, Kelly." He threw his portion of the cover to the foot of the bed and swung his legs over the side of the mattress. "I smell coffee brewing. May I bring you a cup?"

"Here?" she asked, looking around his bedroom, yet glad he'd changed the subject.

He grinned, and looking at his tall figure, Kelly thought he appeared way too handsome in that old-fashioned underwear. She averted her gaze before it lowered beyond his waist.

"Yes, here," he answered. "If I might have my robe?"

"Oh." Kelly immediately pulled her arms out of the sleeves and yanked the silky material from under her bottom. Handing it to him, she said, "I'm sorry I got it so wrinkled."

"No harm done," he replied, taking it from her and putting it on. "I'll be right back, please stay where you are." Tying the belt around his waist, he added, "Well, unless you would rather go back to the room across the hall?"

"No," she answered quickly, not wanting to deal with that room, even in the daylight. "I'm fine right here."

"Good. I shall return with coffee in a few minutes." He went to his dresser and pulled a thick hand brush through his hair, then winked at her as he left the room.

When the door closed, Kelly immediately got out of bed

and tiptoed across the room to look at herself in the mirror above the dresser. Her hair was a tangled mess. Her face was a flush of color. She picked up his comb and quickly pulled it through her hair. She fluffed it out as best as she could, rubbed the sleep from her eyes, and hurried back into bed. Arranging the covers over her, she thought how ridiculous it was for a woman of her age to be acting like this . . . afraid to sleep alone in her own bed . . . needing a big, strong man to feel safe. And now *this*!

But they had slept together, and truth be told . . . Daniel Gilmore's virility gave him away, even if his intentions were above reproach. She remembered having felt him behind her as they spooned. When she'd arched her back, she felt him instinctually push back. How else could it be? He was a man, like any other, with needs. A low moan of pleasure escaped her lips. At least his body desired her . . . his mind and his heart were another matter entirely.

Kelly decided to get busy and began fluffing all the pillows, placing them against the massive dark wooden headboard as a back rest for them both. She leaned back into her own, tucked the covers around her hips, and placed her hands on her lap. After a few moments, she looked at his side of the bed. Nervously, she sat up and straightened his side of the cover and folded it back like turn down service in a hotel. She paused, staring at the neatly made bed. Maybe that was too obvious. *Geez, Kelly, get a grip*, she mentally reprimanded herself. She lifted her legs and began to flail them underneath the cover to ruffle it about. Looking at his side of headboard, she knew it was too perfect. She punched his pillow to take the plump out of it. There. That's better. Flopping back against her own pillows, she exhaled. "Now relax," she advised herself in a whisper, and closed her eyes.

Unwillingly, her mind took her back to last night in her bedroom. She *had* seen those lights. They had moved toward her and had communicated something to her. They definitely contained an intelligence. It couldn't have been a reflection of the moon, or any type of lighting outside the house. There was no mirror in the bedroom, no reasonable explanation for them. Plus, Daniel admitted he'd seen a light once or twice, too, so she couldn't be crazy.

What if it had been Lillian . . . and Michael?

Now that sounded crazy, especially for a woman who came from the year 2001 where such things were heralded in publications you find at the grocery checkout line. She'd always questioned the validity of such stories, but she knew what she'd seen. She was absolutely certain of it, and at least Daniel believed her. She still didn't think it would be a good idea to go around broadcasting her latest experience to anyone else.

Okay, maybe she was qualified to sell a story to the *National Enquirer*.

The door opened and she saw Daniel gracefully balancing a tray with one hand as he closed the door behind him. "Here we are," he announced while holding the tray up in achievement. "You see, I am very talented and quite capable of serving others with ease." He began theatrically gliding across the room, and added with a grin, "Have I mentioned I do dishes, too?"

Kelly laughed out loud. "Yes, I can attest to your astounding agility and domestic abilities, sir," Kelly said, still giggling at his playfulness. He came to her side of the bed and placed the tray on the mattress near her feet. She moved over a little to make more room.

"Coffee. Cream and two sugars." He winked at her, then admitted in a whisper, "I asked Clara."

"Why, thank you, sir. It's been some time since I was served in bed."

He handed her the cup and saucer, and said, "Perhaps you will allow me to serve you more often. Coffee in bed is a small luxury . . . and you deserve it, madam."

"That's very sweet of you, Daniel, and I appreciate your kindness. Especially this morning. I am sorry for barging in here last night." Deep down she new her last words were only a half-truth now. At this moment, she was very glad to be right where she was.

"Please, madam. I say again, we have already concluded there is no need for an apology . . . for anything." Picking up his own coffee, he settled comfortably at the edge of the bed and leaned against the high corner post. "Let's discuss itineraries for today, shall we? I shall begin preparation of the house exterior for whitewash. What are your plans?"

She sipped her coffee, noticing it was just the way she liked it. Even the chicory taste didn't bother her as much. "Well, let's see . . . without my little black appointment book with me, I can only guess," she said with a sly grin, then added, "You know it's such a busy social schedule I keep." She averted his gaze and sipped her coffee again as though contemplating. She could almost feel his smile from across the bed. Suddenly she was reminded of mornings just like this that she'd spent with Michael. The memory went down hard with her gulp of coffee. Clearing her throat, she began again. "Okay, in all seriousness, I am going to begin tutoring Lizzie today. You know, the sooner the better. We don't have a lot of time if your in-laws are arriving in a couple of weeks."

"Very true," he agreed with a nod as he sipped his coffee again.

"Actually, I'm trying to think of ways for it to be fun so she'll go along with it. Just don't expect immediate miracles, Daniel, and I'm open to any suggestions you might have, too," she added with a soft smile.

"I think you have great influence with my daughter and your expertise is greatly appreciated, Kelly. Any improvement I'm certain will be wonderful." He smiled at her reassuringly. "Tell me what you have planned so far."

As she was answering him, she had the oddest sensation of really *being* married, of waking up with another, sharing morning coffee and the day's agenda. It truly was odd, and it was also wonderful.

"Yes, we're going to dress up in our best clothes, wear our new hats, and pretend we're entertaining your grandparents. It'll be like a game, and it'll be fun. C'mon, Lizzie."

"I don't see why I have to get all dressed up when it ain't even dinnertime and I could be outside playin'." Lizzie jammed her hands into the pockets of her overalls and pouted.

"Okay," Kelly answered, "I'll make a deal with you. You play my game, then I'll play one of yours. I'll even climb a tree with you, if you want. But make no mistake . . . your grandparents are coming and your father and I both want you to make a good impression and you are going to learn how to behave in front of them. I promised, Lizzie. Please, won't you let this be fun, instead of fighting it?"

"You'll climb a tree with me?" Lizzie asked in surprise and grinned wickedly.

Sighing, Kelly nodded. "It's been years since I've done it, but yes. I'll try to climb a tree, if you try to learn manners. Do we have a deal?"

Lizzie stuck out her hand. "Deal, but I ain't doin' it all day."

Kelly shook her hand, saying, "Deal, and the first thing we're going to work on is eliminating 'ain't' from your vocabulary. Try saying 'isn't.' For every 'ain't,' we have to play my game five minutes longer and your game five minutes less."

"Now that ain't fair!" Lizzie clamped her jaw shut when she realized what she'd just done.

Laughing at the child's expression, Kelly said, "Okay, we'll let that one go and start now. Let's go upstairs and get ready. Remember, hats and everything. I'll meet you in the drawing room as soon as you're ready."

"How you gonna climb trees in that dress?" Lizzie demanded.

"How am I *going* to climb a tree wearing this dress?" Kelly repeated.

"Okay, how are you *going* to climb a tree wearing that dress?"

Kelly curled her finger, motioning for Lizzie to come closer. "All right, this is a secret. Deal?"

Lizzie nodded.

"Last night, I saw some old pants of your father's that Clara was going to give away with a stack of clothes you and your dad had outgrown. I took them up to my room before dinner last night. I'm going to wear that, and an old shirt of his."

"You gonna wear Daddy's trousers?" Lizzie demanded with a giggle.

"Yep, but you can't tell anyone."

"I won't! Boy, you sure is gonna . . . er, going to look funny. Let's hurry up with these manners lessons and then go outside!"

Kelly couldn't help laughing with her. "Then you'd better run upstairs and get changed," she said to the giggling child.

Watching Lizzie race from the room, Kelly took a deep breath and followed her up the stairs to get her own hat. She had scoured her brain for a way to excite Lizzie about changing her habits and had come up with the idea of climbing trees with her as a reward. The clothes had been right by the back kitchen door last night, and Kelly had finally seen the way. Even if she would look like an idiot, she was willing to risk it. Besides, it might just be fun. Once she had loved climbing trees, but she wasn't kidding herself. Lizzie's habits were pretty ingrained, and this wasn't going to be easy.

A little over three hours later, Kelly and Lizzie sneaked out the back door while Clara was in her room and Daniel was repairing one of the shutters on the front of the house. Kelly realized if any adults saw her, they would probably be scandalized in this day and age, so she kept to the woods that bordered the property.

"You look real funny," Lizzie whispered with a giggle.

"So you've said, at least ten times. Come on, let's hurry before we're caught."

Kelly had rolled up the cuffs on the pants, used a ribbon as a belt to keep them up, and had tied the tails of Daniel's old shirt into a knot at her waist. Her hair was pulled back into a ponytail with a ribbon, and she was wearing the green clunky heels from Mel's wedding.

"I look like Ellie May," she muttered and laughed at herself, as she held back a branch. "Gone mad . . ."

"Who's Ellie May?"

"Never mind," Kelly whispered back. "You'd never understand. Even I have trouble believing it. Are you sure there are no snakes in here?"

"The water mocs like to keep close to the water. That's why they're called *water* mocs."

"Right. Of course. Okay," Kelly muttered, still cautiously watching where she stepped. "I can't go real far in these shoes, Lizzie. Keep that in mind."

"Ain't far . . . dang! *It isn't* far," she corrected. "That one count?"

"Yes, that one counts. Better get there soon, now we've only got fifteen minutes."

"How you gonna . . ." Recognizing her mistakes, she started over. "How are you going to know when it's fifteen minutes? You don't have a watch."

"I have a good internal clock," Kelly answered, feeling a bit more free now that they were far enough away from the house. "I'll be able to tell."

"Here it is," Lizzie pronounced, standing below a tall tree and looking up. "There's a better one, but I don't reckon we have time to get to it now."

"You don't *think* we'll have time today," Kelly responded almost absentmindedly as she looked up.

"Oh yeah, sorry. I don't think we'll have time today," Lizzie repeated quietly.

The tree was huge, and she had to agree it was a pretty good one for climbing. The branches were close enough so it shouldn't be too much trouble. What she wouldn't give, right now, though, for a pair of Nikes. "Okay, you first."

"No, you go first," Lizzie said.

Kelly stared at her. "You just want to laugh at me."

Giggling, Lizzie nodded.

"Hmm . . . well, I'll show you." She pushed up her sleeves and rubbed her hands together. "I used to be a great tree climber." She didn't want to add that it had been over twenty years ago.

Stepping up to the tree, she stretched out her arms and used the third branch to pull herself up until her foot could reach the first. It was fairly easy and Kelly continued up the tree, carefully placing her feet so her heel wouldn't catch.

She could hear Lizzie giggling and could just imagine what she looked like from below, yet now it was a matter of pride. She had said she could do it, and she'd give it her best shot. The higher she got, the harder it became, for the muscles in her legs were straining with each effort. Her mind might still think like she was a teenager, but her body was definitely shouting her age. She was beginning to wonder how much she was going to regret this act later that night. Situating herself on a branch, she held on to the trunk and took a deep breath. Looking down to Lizzie she yelled, "Okay, your turn!"

Kelly watched in amazement as Lizzie jumped up, grabbed a branch, and swung herself onto the next one. The child climbed with the agility of a money, quickly, efficiently, and in no time at all was directly opposite her.

"Wow," she said to Lizzie's smiling face. "That was something! I think you're even better than I was at your age."

"Let's go higher," Lizzie insisted, already climbing to the next branch.

Kelly inhaled deeply and followed her. Four branches later, she stopped and clung to the narrowing trunk. "That's it, for me," she called up. "I don't know if those branches up there will support my weight."

"Oh, come up," Lizzie said. "You can see the house from up here and the bayou. It's real pretty."

"Are you trying to kill me, young lady?"

"You're just scared."

"I'm just sensible," she answered with laugh. And then as the words left her mouth, she suddenly thought of how sensible she had been in her life, of all the things she had not done because of what someone else might think, or what she had been programmed to believe might not make sense. Well, here she was in the year 1888, married, seeing ethereal lights in the night, climbing a tree . . . none of it made sense, but it had happened. What did make sense? What was *normal*? She wanted someone to define that for her. Was normal following the rules, not making waves, believing what you are told? She'd done all those things and now saw there were no rules! Waves were meant to be ridden, and the only thing she could believe in now was herself . . . because her life was definitely *not* normal!

"You comin' up?"

She glanced up to the child who was smiling down at her, and forced her aching muscles to move. Lizzie was right. It was fear that was holding her back. Determined to get past it, she started to move. It was a struggle, and she proceeded much more slowly, but soon she reached Lizzie and leaned against the trunk as she caught her breath. "It's beautiful," she whispered, looking over the tops of trees to the panorama spread out before her. She could see the winding bayou and the house.

"Look, there's Daddy!" Lizzie said, pointing.

Kelly squinted her eyes and made out Daniel's form as he worked in the yard. "You know, this visit with your grandparents is very important to him, Lizzie."

"Yeah, I can tell. He never fixed up the house before."

"He wants to make a good impression."

"That's 'cause they . . . they never seen me."

"Because they *have* never seen you, Lizzie. It's not easy to come all the way across the Atlantic Ocean," she answered, though she'd wondered the same thing herself. Why hadn't they come to see their daughter's child? Maybe it was grief. "Well, they're coming soon, and your father wants everything to go smoothly, especially their visit with you."

"That's why I have to learn all them manners and stuff. I think it's stupid. Rules for the way you walk and sit and eat and talk."

"You want to know something?" Kelly asked, leaning closer to the girl. "I agree with you to a certain extent. Good manners don't mean you're a good person, it just shows you've learned to act in a way that is acceptable to the majority of people. And that's all I'm trying to do with you, Lizzie . . . to help you fit in. This is where you find yourself right now, and it's more trouble to you if you don't act the way everyone expects. Manners aren't going to make you a better person. Inside, you're just fine the way you are, and that doesn't have to change. It's all on the outside that people are looking at you, and, unfortunately, that's their first impression of who you are. You know it isn't so. I know it. Clara knows it. Even your daddy knows it, but your grandparents don't know you. Most people look at the outside of a person and then form their opinions."

"That don't sound fair."

She sighed, thinking it was hypocritical. "I know. So why not just make it a game? You know you are loved by those who really know you, so for right now you can pretend to play the game of the adults . . . this manners thing, and it will only make your life easier when you're around them. Believe me, one day you'll find yourself acting like them, and it will seem natural. You'll even like it that people don't talk when their mouths are full." Smiling, she reached over and brushed a strand of hair behind Lizzie's ear. "Then you'll be doing it because you want to do it, not because you have to do it."

"Will Daddy love me more?"

Kelly's heart felt a deep tug, and she quickly answered, "Oh, honey, your daddy loves you right now. You want to know what I think? I think your daddy is a little scared."

Lizzie stared at her and then to her father in the distance. "Scared? Daddy?"

"Yes. He loves you so much and wants you to make the best impression and he's scared that your grandparents won't think he did a good job raising you."

"Because of these manners?" Lizzie asked.

"Yes. Unfortunately, that will be their first impression. Remember, your grandparents loved your mother very much and raised her a certain way. Manners are very important to them. They would expect her daughter to be raised the same way. You are expected, Lizzie, to be a young lady."

"I don't want to be a lady. They don't have any fun."

Kelly grinned. "Well, someday you will be one, Lizzie Gilmore. And I think you'll find that being a woman can be a lot of fun. Your body changes. Your interests change and then—"

"How does your body change?" Lizzie interrupted.

Kelly took a deep breath. She didn't expect *this* conversation. "Well . . . you begin to develop breasts for one thing. Your hormones kick in and then—"

"What's hormones?"

"Hmm . . . let's see . . . this can be pretty confusing, but it's a chemical that's produced in your body, sort of like a messenger that sets into motion when it's time for your body to grow . . . your breasts become larger, your hips widen, you grow hair under your arms and between your legs."

"Eww!"

Kelly laughed at Lizzie's reaction. "I know how you feel, but you'll get used to it and, truthfully, there's nothing to be done about it. It happens to everyone. No one's talked to you about any of this yet? Not Clara, or your father?"

Lizzie shook her head. "I wouldn't want Daddy to ever talk to me about it!"

Kelly nodded. "I know it can be embarrassing, but you should know what to expect. Don't you think?"

Shrugging, Lizzie looked out to the treetops and muttered, "I think something is happening to me anyway. My chest hurts, and there's like stones under the skin."

"Stones?"

"Yeah, real hard, and they hurt when you touch them."

Smiling, Kelly said, "See . . . it's already started, that's the beginning. Your breasts will soon start to grow. You should know what else happens so you are prepared."

"What else happens? My titties get big like yours and I get hair all over the place and it's all so stupid."

"Who told you to call your breasts titties?" It didn't sound like something either Clara or Daniel would ever say to her.

Lizzie shrugged. "I just heard it. I want to stay like I am."

"Honey, you can't stay a child. You are going to grow, and one of the ways you'll grow into a woman is preparing yourself to have children."

"I can't have children," Lizzie said with a laugh. "I'm still little."

"Well your body is preparing you for when you grow up. There's something called menstruation."

"Menstru . . . what?"

Laughing, Kelly couldn't believe she was having this conversation. Ten minutes later, she looked at Lizzie's shocked expression and wanted to hug her. "It's not as bad as it sounds, and it's only once a month and—"

"You mean I can't cross my legs and stop it?"

"Nope. Nothing will stop it, except becoming pregnant. As hard as this is to believe, what comes from you would be nourishment for the baby, so if you aren't pregnant, you don't need it and the body flushes it out."

"That's disgusting!"

"I can see why you think so; I did, too, when I was your age. But isn't it better to know what is going to happen to your body? This way you won't be scared."

"I ain't scared!" Lizzie protested. "I just think it's disgustin'. And that ain't don't count, 'cause we been up here for more than fifteen minutes."

"Okay, that doesn't count and you have every right to feel the way you do," Kelly placated. "You just need some time to get used to it."

"I ain't never gettin' used to it. I'll just have a baby and stop it."

Kelly wondered how wise she'd been in her explanation. "It will just come back when the pregnancy is over, and do you really want to stop playing and take care of a baby? It's a whole lot of work, Lizzie, to raise a child. That's why you wait, until you are an adult and so much in love with a man that you want to share that love with another. Besides, there's so much for you to discover before you even think of getting married and having children. Just take my word for it. There is nothing you can do to stop this process, and every woman alive goes through it and survives. It isn't as bad as it seems right now. It's just a shock because you can't control what's going to happen to your body."

"I want to be like Peter Pan and never grow up then."

Kelly smiled sympathetically. "Peter Pan wasn't real. You're real, Lizzie. Your body is going to grow up. It's starting now, but your heart can stay young. You can still see the wonder in nature and laugh at the silliness adults put themselves through. Look at me, you can still climb trees . . . just don't let the adults catch you."

A tiny smile played at Lizzie's lips. "So you think all these manners and growing up is silly, too?"

Kelly shrugged. "I guess some of it's pretty silly when you think about it, but that's the way it is, Lizzie. At least in this time and place, but to tell you the truth, most of the time I like being around people who have manners . . . and I'm very glad I grew up and became a woman."

"You love my daddy? Is that why you got married?"

Shocked, Kelly didn't know what to say. Finally, she decided on the truth. Just because Lizzie wasn't an adult didn't mean she deserved less. "I think I'm falling in love with your father, but we haven't known each other that long and . . . and I guess that's what we're doing now . . . getting to know each other better."

"You gonna have a baby then? I always wanted a sister to play with."

Kelly grinned. "I was an only child, too. It can be lonely sometimes, huh?"

Lizzie simply nodded.

"And as far as having a baby is concerned, well I don't think either your father or I am ready for that just yet and—"

"Hey, Lizzie Gilmore! Who's that up there with y'all?"

Both of them were startled by the shout and looked down to the ground. A young teenager dressed in overalls and a straw hat was looking up to them.

"Hey, Will Hoskins!" Lizzie yelled down, and started to descend.

"Where are you going?" Kelly asked as Lizzie climbed past her.

"Goin' down to see Will," she stated, and continued her descent.

"Well, be careful," Kelly cautioned and started lowering herself, too. She had managed three branches when her legs began shaking. She looked down to see Lizzie swinging from the last branch and allowing herself to fall to the ground. Dizziness almost overwhelmed Kelly, and she

quickly looked up and hugged the trunk of the tree for support. Going down was not so easy as going up! Fear, that
was all it was. She was scared of falling, and her body was
rebelling. Taking a deep breath, she lowered her leg to the
next branch and commanded her body to stop shaking.

"She is so my new momma!"

Kelly heard the anger in Lizzie's voice, and all thoughts
of fear for herself ended as she quickly became more sure-
footed and lowered herself.

"Is not!" the adolescent voice protested. "Ain't no
momma gonna be climbing trees!"

"Just shows how ignorant you are, Will Hoskins," Lizzie
answered. "She is so, and there *isn't* such a word as ain't!"

Kelly almost grinned, except she was concentrating too
hard on getting safely out of the tree. When her feet finally
hit the ground, she had to hold on to the trunk to steady herself. "Hi," she said with a smile to the boy, who wasn't wearing a shirt. His face was dotted with pimples, and his hair
looked filthy under the straw hat.

"Hey," he answered with a scowl. "Y'all is Lizzie's new
momma?"

Kelly pushed back a stray lock of hair from her face and
straightened away from the tree. "Yes, I am married to Mr.
Gilmore."

"See!" Lizzie said and stood taller. "I told you."

Shrugging, Will kicked his weathered boot into the dirt,
then looked Kelly up and down. "She don't look like nobody's mother, that's fer sure."

A part of Kelly wanted to thank him for that statement,
yet she could see the resentment in the boy's eyes, and she
certainly didn't like the way his gaze remained on her
breasts. This kid was way too old for Lizzie to be playing
with unsupervised. "Well, it was nice to meet you, Will, but
we have to get back home now. Come, Lizzie. We've been
away far too long as it is."

She reached out to take Lizzie's hand and lead her away
when Will's hand shot out and grabbed Lizzie's shoulder.
"Me and Lizzie are goin' fishin', ain't that right?"

Lizzie stared at Will and shook her head. "I have to be going. We never said we would be fishing."

"Come on, Lizzie," Kelly said, forcibly grabbing the girl's wrist and pulling her away. "You know, Will," she said to the teenager, "the next time you want to play with Lizzie, you come to the house and ask her father or me or Clara."

The boy almost snarled at her. "I ain't askin' no nigra for permission for anythin'!"

Kelly was taken aback by his anger and didn't like the fact that they were alone with him in the woods. She decided the worst thing she could do was show any fear. Even though Will was her height, she straightened even more and stepped up to his face. "And until you can show some respect for your elders, don't bother to knock on the door." Pulling Lizzie with her, she said, "Now let's return home, Elizabeth. It's time to dress for dinner."

"Elizabeth . . ." Will taunted as they walked away.

Lizzie turned once and yelled back, "Shut up, Will Hoskins. You *are* ignorant."

"Ignore him," Kelly commanded, taking long strides to put distance between them. "He doesn't deserve your attention."

"But he was rude to you and . . . and we're walking the wrong way. This way," she said, and pulled Kelly to the right.

Kelly allowed the child to lead her out of the woods. When she thought they were far enough away, she asked in a low voice, "Lizzie, has Will ever . . . well, done anything inappropriate with you?" Call it instinct, but something was bothering her about the way he had handled Lizzie and the way he'd looked at her.

Lizzie didn't answer.

"Please tell me. You won't get in trouble. I promise. Has he ever touched you in a place that made you uncomfortable or embarrassed?"

Lizzie held a branch aside, and said in a worried voice. "It weren't nothing. I push him away, and he stops. He just wants to go fishing cause he thinks I'll go swimming with him, but I told him I wouldn't."

Kelly could hear Will's footsteps breaking the fallen branches behind them and knew he was following. Realizing he was trying to intimidate her, she refused to give him that power.

She abruptly stopped and turned around. She spotted Will about fifteen feet behind them. He stopped, too, and stared at her with a sullen expression.

"Stay here, Lizzie," she commanded. "I don't want you to move."

"What're you gonna do?" she asked in a worried voice.

"Just stay here and promise me you won't move," Kelly said, without breaking eye contact with the teenager.

"I promise, but . . ."

"Stay," Kelly interrupted before Lizzie could say anything else. She walked up to the boy and stood in front of him. Something protective and primitive filled her senses.

"No."

Will just stared back at her with that glowering expression of a male who didn't like females. She had seen it too many times not to recognize it, and the time period didn't make any difference. It was an intense dislike made all the more ugly because he wanted them and hated them at the same time.

"You know the meaning of that word? No?"

He didn't answer.

"Okay, you listen to me, you little shit . . . if you ever in this lifetime put your hands on Lizzie again, you won't just deal with her father, you'll have to get past me and don't let my size fool you. Now, get out of here."

"You ain't gonna do nothin'," he sneered.

She leaned her face closer to his and whispered, "No, you aren't going to do anything . . . ever again, or I'll have the law after you. Now, *move!*" She yelled the last word at the top of her lungs and startled him so that he took a step back. "Don't kid yourself, Will, into thinking I'm just some woman without any real power. Believe me, you've never met a woman like me in your whole life. I know now what you're up to with Lizzie. You try and even talk to that girl again, and I'll make your life a living hell . . . beginning with Mr. Gilmore paying you and your family a visit along with the law. Now, in case you didn't hear me the first time . . . *move out!*" Again, she yelled like a drill sergeant into his face.

She watched him step back a few paces and could read the hatred in his eyes. She knew she had made an enemy, yet she didn't care. The thought of this pimply-faced punk trying to paw Lizzie for a thrill nauseated her. She turned around and walked back to Lizzie. Surprisingly, she was too angry to be fearful.

Picking up Lizzie's hand, she said, "You are not to feel bad about any of this, Lizzie." They began walking, and Kelly added, "I'm going to give you my first request as your . . . your stepmother. Do not ever be alone with Will Hoskins ever again. Do you understand?"

"No," Lizzie answered. "I pushed him away all the time, and I could beat him up if he didn't stop and—"

Kelly tugged on her wrist to stop her from talking. "Listen to me. He outweighs you by fifty pounds, and what Will was trying was inappropriate and has to do with what we were talking about earlier . . . about growing up and hormones kicking in, and his are raging. I want you to stay away from him. He could hurt you, honey, and I won't have anyone hurting you."

"But he's my only friend."

"He's not your friend, Lizzie," Kelly said as they broke out of the woods. She looked down to the child. "Was he your friend three years ago?"

Lizzie thought for a moment. "No. He wouldn't even talk to me cause I was little."

"Exactly, and now that you're beginning to grow up he wants to touch you, right?"

"Well, not all the time, just when he starts askin' if I started gettin' titties and then he will try and touch them and . . . between my legs." Lizzie looked down to the grass in embarrassment.

Kelly clenched her teeth together with renewed anger, yet she took a deep breath and tried to calm down. "You did the right thing to push him away, and I don't want you to feel bad because he had no right to do that to you or to anyone else. Will Hoskins is trouble, and you should stay away from him. Promise?"

Lizzie looked like she wanted to cry. "Promise," she muttered.

Kelly put her arm around Lizzie's shoulders, and said, "Besides, you won't even miss him. Look at how well I climbed that tree. We'll have fun, Lizzie. I promise you that. Come on . . . let's go home. You have to help me sneak back into the house before anyone sees me."

Together they walked away from the woods. Kelly kept her arm around the young girl and vowed to speak with Daniel about getting Lizzie away from this place. She needed to make friends her own age, and New Orleans was the perfect place to do it.

So this what it's like to be a mother, she thought, knowing she would have wrestled that teenager to the ground and pummeled him for mistreating an innocent.

She was a wife and now a mother.

Life was full of surprises.

Twelve

As they all sat down to dinner that evening, Daniel was in high spirits. He was anxious for the whitewash to be delivered the next day and made it known he was very pleased with himself for repairing all the damaged shutters. He'd even weeded the front garden beds. Kelly and Lizzie applauded the man for his accomplishments, but despite her efforts to genuinely share his delight, the evening remained quite somber for Kelly. Her heart ached for a little girl and her father. But for the sake of the moment, and her determination not to embarrass Lizzie, she withheld the lurid information she knew she must eventually break to him.

Although he hadn't said a thing, Kelly realized she must not be hiding her feelings too well, as Daniel's mood became dispirited halfway through dinner. She'd caught him staring at her once or twice with a very concerned look on his face, as though he knew that something was not quite right. Everyone finished without much of a word between them, and they all seemed relieved when the meal was finally over.

After dinner, Lizzie went upstairs to continue reading her

book and Clara dismissed Kelly from helping with the dishes to join Daniel in the sitting room. She couldn't help but wonder if even Clara knew something was awry, when the kind old woman explained she'd already set up the coffee and brandy there. *Bless her sweet, all-knowing heart*, Kelly thought as she slipped out of the kitchen.

Standing for a moment between the open double doors of the elegant room, she gazed at Daniel, who was on one knee at the hearth, lighting a fire. It was her favorite room in the house for its size and comfortable furnishings. All the ornately carved pieces were made of blond fruitwood, rather than the dark English walnut throughout the rest of the house.

The full-size sofa with tufted medallion back and elongated wings was covered in a light, pleasing tapestry fabric. The coffee and end-table tops were made of thick white marble with fine gray veins, all polished to a glass finish. Tall shield-backed chairs were placed on either side of the fireplace, one a gentleman's and the other a lady's style, both covered in a tasteful dusty green brocade satin. A huge Persian rug covered nearly the entire wood floor.

From a heavy brass chain in the center of the ceiling an eye-catching, floral-painted glass-shade oil lamp hung, dripping with lead crystals from two tiers. Its amber light shed a soft glow on the upholstery and floral wallpaper, which Kelly figured under electrical lighting might otherwise have appeared gaudy. Another frosted-glass-shade-and-bowl oil lamp on one end table was also lit.

Beside her, against the wall of the entry where she was standing, loomed a moon-dial grandfather clock that stood over seven feet tall and chimed softly every quarter hour. It wasn't a cluttered room, but rather open and airy, with a romantic ambience of a bygone era, and Kelly thought it very inviting. A man at the fire was also an appealing feature, but she'd have to savor that impression another time. Right then she needed to talk very seriously with him.

She entered the room and immediately went to the high butler's table behind the sofa. She poured them both a coffee and a brandy. When she was placing Daniel's cup and glass by a chair in front of the fireplace, she saw him rise and look into the flickering flames.

"Daniel, I need to speak with you."

He turned and smiled at her with affection. "Yes, I could tell something was on your mind all evening." He strolled to an ornately carved wooden box on the table by the chair and, as if thinking better of it, turned away.

"Have your cigar," she said with a smile, guessing what he was about to do. "I really don't mind."

He looked pleased by her words. "You are sure?"

"I'm sure."

"Lillian always hated the smell and . . ." His words trailed off. "I'm sorry."

"Don't be sorry. Lillian was a major part of your life. I certainly don't mind if you speak about her."

He lifted the box lid and pulled out a thin cheroot. Using a small device, he cut off one end and struck a match. When he sat down in a chair by the fire, he picked up his brandy and exhaled with contentment. "Thank you, Kelly. This is very nice. I hope we do this often."

"Yes, it is nice," she responded, looking into the fire and sipping her coffee.

"Now, what has taken away your usual smile this evening? What's troubling you?"

She took a deep breath and said, "Lizzie and I were in the woods today. We had a long talk about . . . well, about her becoming a young lady. I guess you could say it was a prelude to *the* talk, about the facts of life. She's starting to develop, Daniel, and I thought it was time. The opportunity presented itself and well . . . I just went for it when I realized she had no idea about what was happening to her body."

"You don't think she's a bit young for that?"

Kelly shook her head. "She's almost twelve years old. Her body directs the timing, and since she's beginning to develop, it was time for her to know. Don't worry, I didn't tell her everything . . . about how babies are conceived, but honestly, I think that talk should be very soon, too."

"I appreciate that you have taken such an intense interest my daughter, Kelly, and I do thank you, for it would have been an embarrassing discussion had I tackled it. This is what's bothering you?"

"No. What's bothering me is that I met Will Hoskins today."

"You did? I will admit that he's not the ideal playmate for Elizabeth, but—"

"No, he's not," Kelly interrupted, feeling that it was time to bring it all out into the open. "Daniel, what I'm about to tell you is upsetting, but I want you to know that I handled it, and there's no need for you to—"

It was his turn to interrupt, as he leaned forward and narrowed his eyes. "What happened?"

"I found out through my talk with Lizzie that Will has been trying to touch her inappropriately."

"Inappropriately? Where?"

She swallowed deeply. "Her breasts and . . . and between her legs."

Instantly, he stood and stared at her with such anger that Kelly shrunk back.

"I'll kill him!"

Kelly got up quickly and raised her hand in a feeble attempt to placate his anger. "Daniel, please calm down. Rage right now is not going to help the matter. I confronted him and told him if he so much as even tried to talk to her ever again, you and the law would pay his family a visit. He knows he's been found out now. He probably won't try it again."

"How long has this been going on?"

"I don't know," she answered, sitting down again and picking up her own glass of brandy. She swallowed the alcohol and nearly gasped as the heat of it slid down her throat and burned her chest muscles. "Personally, I feel it's imperative we get her away from here as soon as possible." She looked up and stared directly into his eyes. "Daniel, she needs to make friends her own age, of her own sex, with common interests. Perhaps we should go back to New Orleans after the house is painted. All of us, even Clara."

She watched as he slowly sank back down into the chair and stared blankly at the fire. "I truly have been a poor parent, to have allowed this to happen . . ."

She rose from the sofa and sat in the chair opposite him. "Don't think that, Daniel. Without talking to Lizzie I wouldn't have known it happened. The important thing right now is that she realizes she did nothing wrong. In fact, you would be proud of her. She told me she's been slapping his hands away and that if it had ever come down to it, she thought she could beat him up." She tried to encourage him with a nod.

In spite of everything, Daniel smiled sadly. "She is quite a hellion. So unlike her mother. Perhaps that's why I don't really know how to deal with her."

"Well, let's just be glad we found out before it got any worse. I wouldn't have been so worried except Will is as tall as I am and full into puberty. That boy is trouble, and I think we should get Lizzie far away from here. And the sooner, the better."

"Yes, I agree, Kelly," he said with a sigh. Daniel stared into the fire for a moment, then drew in a sharp breath. "Regardless, I'm going to pay a visit to the Hoskins place and speak with the boy and his father to reiterate your threat. Nothing will save him if that boy so much as gets near my daughter again. I will do whatever I feel is necessary to protect my family and those I love from the deplorable acts of such people . . . and be assured, no jury of my peers would convict me, either."

Kelly knew this man was dead serious. As he stared into the fire, she watched the muscle in his cheek move as he ground his back teeth together in anger. "I'm sorry, Daniel. I just thought you should know."

He looked up to her and nodded. "You were right to tell me. It's not your fault that I'm filled with more rage and shame toward myself for not protecting my daughter better." He drew in a great breath as though trying to calm himself before adding with a sigh, "How her mother would be disappointed with me."

"I'm sure if Lillian had lived, many things would have been different, but that's not the way it happened, Daniel. You were left to raise Lizzie alone, and . . ."

"And I did a terrible job of it," he said, finishing the sentence for her.

"That's not what I would have said," she insisted. "I'm sure you did the best you could. You were just overwhelmed with . . . well, a lot of things. Grief, I imagine, was the leading culprit."

"It's no excuse," he said, obviously disgusted with himself now.

Kelly thought back to when she told Lizzie that she was falling in love with her father. She'd been honest with the child, but she didn't want to fall in love with a man who was still in love with his dead wife. If it happened, she wanted it to be for the right reasons, and she wanted her love returned. "Tell me about Lillian," she whispered. "I'd really like to know who she was."

He glanced up to her. "Why? What good would it do to bring up old memories?"

She smiled at his confused expression. "Well, for one thing it appears I'm stepping into her role here, and, for another . . . I, too, have put my life on hold, Daniel, because of grief. Maybe it's time we both got it out . . . just let it go, so we can get on with living. I can't explain why I'm here with you and Lizzie and Clara. I only know that I've started to care very much about all of you. Clara thinks I've come here, to this time, for a reason. Maybe the reason was finally, once and forever, to get rid of this heaviness I've been carrying around like a ton of bricks in my heart. What about you? Do you think it's time to let it go now?" She took a deep breath. "To begin again?"

She saw the muscle in his cheek moving again, only this time it wasn't from anger. This time she could see he was trying to control his emotions. "What would you like to know about her?" he asked in a rough voice.

"Well, what was she like? Where did you meet her? When did you get married?"

He stood up and poured himself another brandy. Relighting his cigar, he puffed on it a few times as he brought his thoughts together. He stood before the fire and spoke so softly Kelly had to listen very carefully as he began. . . .

"I believe I told you that my father had seen the war coming and didn't agree with secession. When I was ten, he took mother and me to England. I spent the rest of my youth there, being educated and growing into manhood. After I'd graduated from the university, my father insisted I then begin lessons in the proprieties of social grace, including dance. As a young man, I felt I was rather clumsy, and needless to say, I was none too eager to step onto a dance floor, but again, my father insisted I attend the Ridgeways' Christmas ball. They were good friends of my parents," he explained, then paused to take another puff on the cheroot.

Kelly nodded as she settled back in her chair and waited for him to continue.

"It was there I saw Lillian Howe for the first time across the ballroom . . . she was wearing a white-and-red dress. Her hair was pulled up, and she had a wreath of holly around her head. I thought she looked like the most beautiful Christmas angel, and I knew . . ." He turned his head and looked at Kelly. "What I mean is, I just *knew* she was the one for me, the one with whom I wanted to share my life. It's hard to explain."

Kelly smiled gently. "No need to explain. I know exactly what you mean. Go ahead."

He looked back to the fire and a small smile played at his lips as he remembered. . . . "We danced all night together, even though her dance card had been already filled. She was sure it would be a scandal she'd never live down, and, yet, she also realized something wonderful was happening. She flaunted convention and allowed me to stay by her side all evening. We both knew by the end of the night that we would be married. It happened so fast. Her parents were shocked, as were my own . . . since Lillian was not yet eighteen years of age." He paused, lifting the snifter to his lips with a knowing smile, then swallowed another sip of brandy. "Altogether youthful and impatient then, how I endured the following four months, I'll never know." He shook his head as though it might clear the blush from his face. Taking a deep breath, he continued. "The wedding plans took up most of her time, but we were finally married on March 8 and, miraculously, the sun was shining. It was a gorgeous spring morning, and there was no need to wear coats. It was as though nature celebrated with us such a joyous union."

Again, he turned his attention back to Kelly. "Would you like to see a picture?"

"Very much," Kelly answered, being drawn into the love story.

He walked over to a chest against the wall and withdrew a silver frame from a drawer. Handing it to her, he said, "To me, she was more exquisite that day, even if a bit fragile, as the picture may depict. She was dainty, like a butterfly."

Kelly took the frame and looked down to a sepia-toned picture of Daniel as a young man standing next to a small, lovely, dark-haired woman who was staring into the camera lens with a startled expression. She knew in most old photographs people rarely smiled, but Kelly immediately felt sorry for the young girl. She looked overwhelmed. "She's beautiful," Kelly remarked, studying the elaborate gown and the long veil of intricate lace. Daniel was in a formal tuxedo and looked very proper and somber for such a happy occasion.

"There's another," he said, now eager to share his life with her, as he went back to the chest and withdrew a second picture.

This one was of Daniel and Lillian in front of Notre Dame in Paris and both of them were smiling. Kelly could now see how happy they were. "What a wonderful picture of you both," she said, grinning as she handed it back. "Was it your honeymoon?"

"Our wedding trip was to Paris and Vienna. We had a wondrous year together before she became pregnant with Elizabeth. In the beginning it was dreadful for her and she was sick for almost four months. There were many days she couldn't even get out of bed. When she eventually started to feel better, I asked if she would come with me to the States, for I desperately wanted to attend the Centennial Exposition in Philadelphia in 1876." He placed both photographs on the mantel and stared at them.

"I begged Lilly to go. She didn't want to leave England and her family," he whispered, catching his breath as memories flooded back. "She wasn't a strong woman, and she hadn't a head for current events, but she could see what it meant to me. The war was long over, and I really wanted to return to my country at such an important time, and I believe that's the only reason she agreed."

The sound of the grandfather clock ticking permeated the silence as she watched him pause with the glass to his lips, as though gathering the courage to continue. "It's obvious she loved you very much," Kelly offered with sympathy.

"Yes, she did, as I her," he confirmed, then took another large gulp. Placing the empty glass down on the table, he began again. "I booked the finest stateroom on the ship, yet it was a horrible crossing for her." He looked down to the fire. "She was too delicate, like a fragile flower, and basically, transplanting her shocked her system. She was never the same. After the expo, I wanted to show her where I had been born and spent my early childhood. I also thought the warmer weather would revive her, so we traveled to New Orleans, and that was where Elizabeth was born. Unfortunately, it was then she became even weaker. I brought her here to this house with the baby, sure the fresh air and quiet would help her, but it didn't, and she asked that we all return to the city again where she could be readily seen by her doctor if need be."

Kelly rose and refilled his brandy glass. Handing it to him, she whispered, "I am so sorry, Daniel."

"No one could be more sorry than I am. I have spent the last eleven years of my life regretting all those decisions, but I took her back to New Orleans as she wished." He lifted the snifter then lowered it as though he'd thought better of taking another sip before he began again. "In October of 1878 an epidemic of yellow jack hit the city. It was beyond anyone's worst nightmare." He shook his head in obvious disbelief of the all-too-intimate reality.

"I won't go into the grotesque symptoms, but suffice it to say, people were falling over dead, right in the streets. They had wagons that constantly patrolled the city to collect bodies that had to be immediately cremated to ensure no further contamination. There wasn't time for funerals. Over twenty-seven thousand people contracted the disease, over four thousand died, and that was just in New Orleans." This time he raised the glass and swallowed a very large gulp.

"Oh Daniel . . ." Kelly whispered through fingers pressed against her lips in horror.

Clearing his throat, he set the glass back down on the table. "But I'm getting ahead of myself here. I should explain that when one of our maids became ill, I knew I had to get Lilly and Elizabeth back out of the city posthaste in hopes of protecting them. We came here again, but it seems even this wasn't far enough. The disease was spreading like wildfire all along the Mississippi, so transportation anywhere else was virtually impossible, if not futile."

"Oh, Daniel, it must have been hellish."

"Yes . . . it was hell on earth, for everyone." He placed both hands on the mantel and leaned, as though holding on for strength to continue. Kelly felt helpless as she watched his eyes fill with tears despite his attempts to blink them away as he stared at the picture of his dead wife. "Lilly, my dear, frail Lilly, was struck down the next month. It's impossible to describe her physical misery as she lay in that bedroom upstairs. It was a horrid sickness, and yet a blessing she died quickly."

Kelly could see the whites of his knuckles as he tensed his grip on the thick wood above the fire. She, too, was trying vainly to hold back tears as she stepped close behind him.

Inhaling through his tightly clenched teeth, his voice was nearly hoarse when he spoke again. "The night I buried her, I tried to burn this house down. Clara, who was hired to take care of Elizabeth, stopped me." Pausing, as though to calm himself, he freed one hand from grasping the wood and wiped tears from his cheeks.

Kelly didn't think anything she could say at this moment would help this man's inner agony. All she felt she could do was raise her hand to his shoulder and gently squeeze, letting him know she was there.

At once he exclaimed, "And so, I blame myself . . . God, I blame myself!" With the last word, he pound the mantel with his fist. "Lilly never wanted to come to this country . . . she did it for me, and what have I done? I have stayed here, in this . . . this place of her death, living each day with intolerable remorse, shutting myself off from my daughter, keeping myself occupied with my business in town, not wanting to accept responsibility for the death of my wife, but knowing I must!" He pressed his fist against the dark wood again. "I must," he finished with a whisper of resignation.

Tears now streamed down Kelly's face in empathy, for she truly felt his anguish. She tenderly rubbed his back and began to speak softly. "I can tell you, Daniel, you aren't to blame for an epidemic, but believe me, I know what you are feeling. I have lived with nearly the exact same feelings for almost half of my life."

When he turned his head, she saw his eyes were red and his expression still tortured, as though he were fighting for control. "Why?"

"My . . . my husband," she said, trying to make the words come past the thickness in her throat. "Michael and I were only married a year, but it was the best year of my life . . . like the one you and Lilly had. We were both late for work this one morning, and I begged him to run down to the store to pick up a pair of panty hose for me as I couldn't find a good pair. I'd meant to buy them myself the night before, but I was too tired and just wanted to get home. Then we started talking after dinner, and I forgot about it until the next morning."

He had a bewildered look on his face. "Pick up panty hose?"

She half laughed through her tears. "Yeah, hose and underwear sewn together . . . it doesn't matter. I should have done it myself. Michael was always so giving, so protective of me. He woke up a half hour before me and brought me coffee every morning. He was a businessman, but he was also a musician. He played the guitar," she muttered, as fresh tears welled in her eyes. "He'd sit on the side of the bed, behind me, and wake me in the mornings with the most gentle music . . . and my eyelids would flutter open and I would look out the window and hear birds singing, I'd smell the aroma of fresh coffee . . . and then I would turn my head and see him . . . smiling at me with such love, and . . ."

Her throat tightened and made it impossible for her to continue. She couldn't breathe through her nose and sucked in air through her mouth as her body started to shake with sobs.

Openly allowing his own tears, he reached for her, and whispered, "Kelly, you don't have to—"

"No," she managed to whisper as she held up her hand. "I . . . I have to say this . . . to get it out . . . God, it's been inside of me like a cancer for the last thirteen years!" She pressed her fist against her mouth to stop it from quivering and took a deep breath through her fingers. "Don't you see?" she cried, lowering her hand. "I sent him there! He would have done anything for me, and I sent him to buy a goddamn pair of panty hose and he . . . he never came home. There was a robbery taking place at the store, and he walked right into it. The man just shot him, right through the heart . . . like target practice! He died before I ever got to the hospital . . . all because of me, Daniel. Because of me . . . oh God, how do I say it out loud? I live each day knowing it. *I sent my husband to his death because I was too damn lazy to run an errand for myself the night before!*"

"Kelly, it's not your fault," Daniel said, pulling her into his arms. "It was a terrible, unfortunate accident."

She clung to him, sobbing, finally letting it all out as she buried her face in his chest. No longer did she have to keep it inside of her, hidden like a horrid secret. She had confessed it. It was out of her . . . this great sin she had committed against the man she so loved.

"And that's why I, too, worked so hard, building my business, putting in twelve-hour days . . . to . . . to prove I'm not lazy, never to ask another to do what I'm capable of doing for myself."

She felt his hands rubbing her back in soothing circles while his other hand stroked her hair so gently that she burst into more painful sobs. "I deserved my penance."

"Haven't you been paying a penance for thirteen years? Isn't it time to end it?"

She stopped crying, thinking of his words and slowly, miraculously, she felt a lightness in her chest, as though the weight of guilt had lifted. Sniffling, she wiped her face with her hands and looked up to him. "Haven't you paid long enough too?"

He stared into her eyes, blinking back his own tears, and whispered, "For the first time in over ten years, I think I have. What have we done to ourselves, Kelly?" he asked with wonder, as though the realization hit him that his mourning had now, finally, ended.

"I don't know," she whispered back, staring into his eyes. "I guess we allowed ourselves to be consumed with guilt?"

He reached into his breast pocket and withdrew a white handkerchief. Dabbing at her face, he smiled a little, and said, "I think we have allowed guilt to punish us for far too long."

"That's it, Daniel, isn't it? We've allowed it. Lilly didn't blame you, and I know Michael didn't blame me. We . . . we did this to ourselves, didn't we?"

He thought for a moment, then nodded. "Why did we do it? Whom did it serve? Not those we loved, and certainly not us . . ."

She took the handkerchief and blew her nose. When she was finished, she looked up to him and said, "Suddenly, it all seems like such a waste of energy, doesn't it?"

"That's a good way of putting it. You're right, it does seem a waste of energy," he said with surprise.

"I think there's a difference between taking responsibility and wallowing in guilt. We got stuck in guilt. I mean, Lilly could have said no, Daniel. She could have just stood up for herself and said no, I'm not going across the Atlantic. Michael could have said no to me, and I would have just picked up what I wanted on my way to work. But they didn't because they loved us. We've taken their acts of love and spent years soiling it with useless guilt, instead of . . . instead of celebrating it. That's not paying tribute to them at all." She was stunned by what she was feeling and thinking.

He was looking deep into her eyes as though reaching her soul. "Kelly . . ."

She saw something in his eyes that made her want to heal. "For the first time in thirteen years, Daniel," she whispered, "I want to be whole again. I want to live fully."

"Yes," he whispered back. "I want that, too, now. I want to love again."

It was a moment of tenderness, friendship, bonding . . . allowing another beyond the barriers to reveal their true selves. Through his eyes, Kelly saw the woman she was meant to become.

They held each other before the dying embers of the fire, whispering words of encouragement, releasing the hold they had put on Lilly and Michael, allowing themselves to move beyond the tightly held memories and, in the gentle process . . . freeing themselves and those they had loved.

Finally, almost miraculously, together they found closure.

Much later, Kelly looked up to the mantel and said, "Leave Lilly's pictures there, Daniel. I don't mind, and Lizzie should see them."

He kissed her forehead. "Yes, I think I can leave them out now. Thank you . . . for everything. I feel . . . renewed, is the best way to explain it."

She smiled tiredly. "Me too. It's been a long time coming, for both of us."

"You must be exhausted, madam. May I be so bold as to invite you once more into my bed? My chaste bed, if that be your choice. I can't rightfully speak for you, but I don't believe either of us wants to be alone this night."

She sighed and placed her head on his chest. "Thank you, Daniel. I am wrung out and would love to be held in your arms while I fall asleep." She lifted her head and looked into his eyes again. "Do you mind if we go slowly? I mean I know we're married, but it's like tonight is the first time that . . . I don't know, I feel we've come to something beyond our initial agreement. That there might just be something more."

"Absolutely, my dear. In time, I most certainly hope there will be something more, but I understand we have not had the proper courtship that you, my fine lady, so justly deserve."

"How long is a proper courtship?" she asked with a tired smile.

"How long would you like?"

Hmm . . . she'd better not answer this one truthfully, or his decency would be thrown for a twenty-first-century loop. "Um, how about a month?"

"Agreed. Considering the circumstances, my dear, a month seems perfectly appropriate and quite adequate to me," he answered with a devastating smile.

She shyly smiled back up to him. "Okay, just one more thing . . . you're sure it's okay if I sleep in your bed . . . I mean, if I get scared again?"

"Oh." He laughed. "I didn't know a torture clause would be added to this agreement."

Kelly pushed against his chest in mock protest. "C'mon," she grinned. "I'll behave if you will."

"Of course, yes," he reassured her with a sincere nod. "I shall prove to you that I am an honorable man and will not break my promise of a month's courtship . . . though in my recollection, no proper courtship ever occurred after a marriage, with both parties sharing the same bed, and remaining chaste. I don't believe I've ever heard of such a thing."

She stared up at the handsome, grinning man and couldn't stop the smile on her face from getting wider. Feeling a lightness that had been missing in her life for over a decade, Kelly giggled at the perfect silliness of the entire situation. "Ah, but then you never believed I would waltz into your life from out of the future, now did you?"

"I know exactly why you were sent to me, madam."

She grinned teasingly. "Oh, you do?"

"Indeed. And in one month, I shall tell you."

Playfully slapping his shoulder, she laughed at his attempt to torture her. "Fine. Let's go to bed now, Mr. Gilmore."

Not taking his eyes from hers, he slowly raised her hand to his lips and ever so teasingly kissed her fingers. "As you wish, Mrs. Gilmore. As you wish . . ."

Okay, fair was fair.

Thirteen

"That's right, Lizzie, after you serve Clara, then you serve me. You can do it."

Kelly watched as Lizzie carefully poured tea into the dainty cups. All three ladies were gathered in the sitting room and dressed to the hilt, even Clara was so very proper with her new hat on as she sat on the edge of the chair and waited while Lizzie very carefully brought her the cup of tea.

"Thank you, chile," Clara said, accepting the offering. "You did that real well."

"I still don't know why all this is so important and—"

"Thank Clara, Lizzie," Kelly interrupted, before the girl started another rant.

Lizzie stopped and did a small curtsy. "Thank you, Miss Clara," she mumbled reluctantly.

"Oh, come on, Elizabeth Gilmore. You can make it sound a bit more genuine," Kelly teased.

Sighing, Lizzie again curtsied, then thanked Clara with more enthusiasm. Turning to Kelly, she asked, "How's that?"

Kelly beamed at her. "Perfect! You're doing so well. Now you may serve me."

"It's right in front of you," Lizzie answered, pointing to the coffee table and the silver tea service.

"Yes, honey, but you are the hostess this afternoon, and when your grandmother arrives you want to be able to serve her correctly, don't you? This is practice."

"Well, she's a grown-up and should be able to pour a cup herself," Lizzie muttered, coming back to the table and flopping down on the sofa.

"Look, I know we've been at this for over two hours, but once you get it right we can stop, and then I have something special planned for us."

Lizzie eyed her suspiciously. "What?"

"It's a surprise," Kelly answered. "Now, serve me my tea, please."

Lizzie reached over and was about to pick up the cup when Kelly rubbed her hand on the girl's slumped back. "Sweetie, try to sit up straight."

"I'm *tired* of all this!" Lizzie whined, but did straighten her spine.

"You're almost finished."

Sighing, Lizzie picked up the dainty cup and saucer and handed them to Kelly. "Your tea, madam," she said in a very proper voice.

Grinning, Kelly accepted it, and said, "Thank you ever so much, Elizabeth." After taking a sip, she added, "See? That wasn't so difficult, was it?"

"Hmm . . . seems like a whole lot of work to me for people just to drink some tea."

"Just pretend it's a game, chile, like Miz Kelly says. You gots to know the rules before you can play."

Kelly smiled gratefully at Clara, then looked at Lizzie. "All right, you may pick up your own cup, now that everyone has been served. Remember, always serve your guests, and anyone who is older, before yourself. As the hostess, you are always the last."

Lizzie picked up her own. "Doesn't seem fair, since I'm doin' all the work."

Chuckling, Kelly sipped her tea. "That is how a hostess acts, Lizzie. Your guests' needs always come before your own . . . in everything."

"Well, I wanna be the guest then."

"You will, when we go into New Orleans. I plan to visit Mrs. Holden, and you can accompany me. You'll see how it's done when you're the guest then."

"Eww, why do we have to go to her house? That won't be any fun!"

"Because I promised when I met her that I would visit, and your father gave them his word that you would, too."

"I'm not going to that Sunday school again. They made me sit for hours and hours and just listen to that old man talk about God. He said to me that God would punish me because I was wicked. I ain't . . . er, am not wicked . . . am I?"

Kelly ground her back teeth and shook her head. "No, you are not wicked, Lizzie. Don't ever believe that. I'll talk to the Reverend, and he won't say such things about you again. Now, if you're finished with your tea, you may go upstairs and change. Put on your oldest pair of overalls."

"We gonna climb trees again?" Lizzie asked with a gleam in her eye as Clara clucked her tongue.

"No . . . we're going to do something else that will be just as much fun, if not more."

Lizzie started to run from the room when Kelly called out to her. "Elizabeth Gilmore!"

The girl skidded to a stop and turned around.

"Is that how you leave a room? Remember what we practiced?"

A loud sigh escaped the child's lips, and she asked in a low voice, "May I be excused?"

Kelly smiled. "Yes, you may. I enjoyed our afternoon tea, Elizabeth. Thank you again."

"As did I, madam." She curtsied and slowly turned around to walk quietly out of the room.

When Kelly heard her running up the stairs, she sighed and looked to Clara, who was observing the scene with her usual serene expression. "Sometimes I wonder if I'm doing the right thing with her."

"How's that?" Clara asked, continuing to enjoy her tea.

"I don't know. Sometimes I look at Lizzie and wonder if I have the right to try and break something wild and wonderful and free. It's like breaking a wild horse, breaking her spirit, making her into someone else who's just like everyone else. I don't want her to lose what makes her unique."

"You sound just like a mother to me," Clara murmured, standing up and placing her empty cup back onto the silver tray. "And Lizzie Gilmore ain't no wild pony. She's a young girl who is expected to grow up into a young lady. That's her role in life. Now, she don't have to accept it when she gets older, but she ain't even been exposed to it, and she deserves that, don't she? So's she can make up her mind herself, knowin' both sides of the matter?"

Kelly smiled at the older woman. "Thanks, Clara. You always make sense."

Clara waved her hand in dismissal. "I'm just speakin' my mind, is all. You is doin' real good with the chile, Miz Kelly. She be one lucky girl to have you as her new momma."

"That's kind of you to say, Clara, but I'm merely going by instinct right now. I just hope I'm not pushing too hard. We don't have that much time before her grandparents arrive."

"She's gonna be just fine. Don't let that chile fool you. Lizzie is one good actress, and since you made this into a game, she'll do it. Deep down, she wants to please you and her daddy," Clara said, looking out the front window. "And speaking of the man, I ain't never seen him work like this . . . paintin' and fixin' up everythin'." After shaking her head for a moment she turned back to Kelly. "What kind of magic you got, Miz Kelly?"

"I don't have any magic," she said with a laugh.

"Um, um, um . . . there I have to disagree. Ever since you came, this house and everybody in it has been transformed. And I ain't never heard such laughter either. I'd reckon that's some kind of magic."

Kelly's heart was touched by the kind woman's thoughts. Smiling, she admitted, "I'm glad you're coming with us to New Orleans, Clara. I'd miss you if you didn't."

"Well, I could still stay here and catch up on my pressin', but since you say it means so much to you, I'll come. Been years since I was there though. You sure they gots room for me at that town house? I don't want to be an old woman in the way."

"Yes, there's room. Besides, I want to pamper you. It's about time somebody did."

"There you go again with that sweet talk," Clara exclaimed with embarrassment. "Lordy, ain't nobody ever pampered me."

"Well guess what, Clara?"

"What?"

"It's your turn."

Clara's eyes suddenly got red, and she blinked furiously. "You best get a move on it your own self, Miz Kelly. That chile is gonna be stompin' down them stairs any minute now and you is sittin' here talkin' nonsense with me."

Kelly stood up and grinned. "Okay, Clara, I'll let you off the hook this time. We won't talk about what a wonderful friend you have been to this family, going far beyond the duties of a housekeeper. We won't mention that you have worked long and hard and now it's time for you to take it easy just a bit, and heaven forbid I mention that I *want* to pamper you because it would please me greatly. I'll run upstairs and get changed, but I want you to promise me something."

"And what is that?" Clara asked, trying to hold back a chuckle.

"That you won't laugh too hard when you see what I'm wearing when I come back downstairs."

"What you got planned, Miz Kelly? I can see in them eyes you is up to mischief. Ain't no wonder why that chile loves you so. You is just like her."

"Maybe that's why I don't want to see her spirit broken by the rules of society which, when you see me in a few minutes, you'll agree I'm about to flaunt."

Clara shook her head as she reached for the silver tray. "It's for sure and for certain this old place ain't boring no more . . . since you came, and for that . . . I thanks you."

"I can carry the tray, Clara," Kelly offered.

"I ain't bein' pampered just yet," Clara stated, taking possession of the silver tray. "I have supper to make, and you have to go upstairs and get wild, or somethin'." She chuckled under her breath, still shaking her head as she left the room.

Smiling with excitement, Kelly picked up the hem of her wide skirt and took the stairs two at a time. She hurried into her room and changed quickly, hearing Lizzie run down the steps. When she was finally dressed, Kelly tied her hair back with a ribbon and took a deep breath. Actually, it wasn't Clara's reaction she was worried about. . . .

Her mouth hanging open at the sight of Kelly, Lizzie swallowed hard as she whispered, "You're gonna get caught."

"I'm not," Kelly answered, picking up Lizzie's hand and walking her through the hallway and into the kitchen. "Because I'm not going to hide it anymore."

She stood at the entrance to the kitchen and just waited until Clara turned around from the sink. The woman stood for a few moments and stared, and then brought her apron up to her mouth as she giggled like a teenager. "Look at you," she mumbled from behind the material. "Yes, ma'am . . . you gots a wild streak in you for sure!"

Grinning, Kelly walked farther into the room and spun around, like she was strutting her "stuff" on the end of a runway. "May I present this fascinating ensemble, the very latest in lady's fashions? Notice the ease of movement, the uncluttered lines of the pant legs, showing just a hint of ankle." Using her hands like a model's she waved them gracefully down her leg and then at her waist. "And for that most important decorative touch, you will observe the satin ribbon replacing the stuffy belt nestled behind the flair of a perfect bow which is achieved by tying the ends of an oversize shirt. Together, both pieces create the modern woman's ideal for painting a house."

Lizzie giggled at Kelly's silliness. "We gonna be paintin' the house?"

Kelly finished her pirouette and looked at the child. "I

thought we could help your father." She glanced at Clara, who was still holding the apron between her hands. "So what do you think, Clara?"

"My, my, my . . . but ain't you somethin'! Now I know where them clothes disappeared to. You gonna show Mistah Daniel this?"

Kelly nodded. "I certainly am. This is much more practical than wearing a dress, isn't it? I mean, for painting a house that is. Daniel would agree, I'm sure."

Clara's eyes widened. "I wanna see this."

"Well, then come along," Kelly invited as she walked out the door and down the steps.

He was on a ladder, painting the side of the house, and Kelly walked up to him with her hands on her hips. "You have two workers, reporting for paint duty, sir!" she called up. "Just tell us where to begin."

Daniel looked down and didn't say a word.

He just stared for a few moments. "What are you wearing?" he finally demanded in astonishment, as though he couldn't believe his eyes.

"Your trousers, sir," she called up. "And your old shirt. What do you think?" She spun around, giving him the full effect.

"I think, madam," he called down, "you look . . . highly unusual!"

Kelly could see he was trying not to smile, and she grinned back at him. "I see I was successful in coordinating my costume then . . . thanks to you. So what do you say? Miss Elizabeth and I desire to be your assistants this afternoon. I see you have the paintbrushes, and we are two willing bodies eager to make this task easier."

He started to lower himself down the ladder.

"Pick up a paintbrush, Lizzie," Kelly muttered, as she picked up one herself. "Now stand at attention." Kelly held the paintbrush up at her side, like a sword, and watched as Lizzie followed suit.

When Daniel finally stood before them, he shook his head. "What if someone should see you?" he demanded.

"Someone already has seen me. Clara. And she laughed. I'm okay with that. Are you?"

Daniel glanced at his housekeeper, who was standing on the porch and grinning at the scene. "What if someone else saw you? How could you ever explain your attire?"

"I would simply say that I am eager to assist my husband in finishing the painting of this house, since it takes his attention away from me and his daughter. Many hands make light the work," she argued convincingly.

"Or spoils the broth," he added with humorous sarcasm.

"Oh, come on, Daniel," she cajoled. "Let's just do it and have fun."

"It appears I am outnumbered."

"You are. Just say all right, then show us what to do."

He sighed deeply with resignation, as though he knew any further debate would be futile.

"We can do the lower parts of the house and you can do the top. How's that, Daddy?"

"Wonderful suggestion, Lizzie, you have a great mind for delegating," Kelly affirmed, saluting her with the paintbrush.

The child laughed and performed her own salute in return.

"Okay, I'll need two more pails then, one for each of you," Daniel mused, looking toward the back of the house.

"I'll get them," Clara volunteered, and scurried around the side of the porch.

"Go help her, Lizzie," Kelly directed. "We're volunteers in action!"

Beaming, Lizzie ran off after Clara.

Daniel turned to Kelly and shook his head. "Well madam, it appears you fill my clothes far better than I do. Tell me, are you doing this to torture me further?"

She playfully appeared shocked. "Why, sir . . . I only wanted to save my new dresses from any mishap that might occur. I would never want to cause you any discomfort. In fact," she lowered her voice and smiled teasingly as she released the top button of the shirt, and then the next one, "what I'm attempting to achieve . . . would be anything but discomfort."

A low growl resounded deep in his throat, and he pulled her to him. "That's an invitation you don't have to make twice," he stated firmly, holding her tightly against his chest. "With such extreme tests of willpower, how is it that you would expect me not to breach my promise of a full month's courtship?"

"Hmm . . . one month is a very long time, isn't it?" she asked, studying his lips. "Well, I'm sure the original agreement could be renegotiated, if given the proper—"

Moaning deeply, he lowered his mouth to interrupt her words. Kelly gladly surrendered to the passionate kiss, the breathless merging as his teeth gently tugged on her bottom lip, yet they quickly and most reluctantly broke apart when Lizzie was heard yelling that she had the pails. Pretending to look chaste, she and Daniel glanced at each other, and all hopes of chastity seemed to vanish with the memory of that kiss branding their minds and their lips.

Standing back, he cleared his throat. "Well. Now you're sure you want to do this?" he asked, holding up a large container of whitewash.

"You think we donned this fashionable attire for any other occasion?" Kelly asked with a mock curtsy and grinned at Lizzie before connecting her gaze once more with the man who was capturing her heart. "We're more than ready, willing, and able, sir."

A moment of silent communication passed between them as her last words became a double entendre, and she watched Daniel's lips curve into a sexy smile.

"Yeah, Daddy. We wanna help," Lizzie offered.

As if bringing himself back to the task at hand, Daniel replied, "All right, while I finish the second story, you two can begin on the lower half of the house. Lizzie, since you're the smallest, if you would paint the lattice around the base of the porch, that would be a very big help. Kelly, if you would be so kind as to begin on the siding around shoulder height, I can get the rest. This is the last side of the house and, if we all work together, we just might finish the project today."

"Oh yes, I quite agree. Finishing that which we've started

sounds like a perfect plan to me," Kelly replied with a mischievous grin.

"You, madam, are a very adept tease," Daniel muttered with a smile as he bent over and began pouring paint into their pails. Standing upright, he handed her a full pail, but didn't release his grip as she began to take it.

Looking into his eyes, she was sure he was silently telling her that had his daughter not rushed back onto the scene, he would still be holding her in his arms. Kelly returned his conveyed message with a knowing smile. "Thank you, Daniel. I really do think I'm going to enjoy this."

He bit his lower lip, and she figured it was to hold back another response. As he simply nodded, she turned toward Lizzie. "Shall we begin?"

"Um, okay," the young girl replied with a slightly confused tone as she picked up the other full pail.

Kelly could still feel his gaze as she and Lizzie stepped away, and she was seizing the advantage. She was a twenty-first-century woman who was definitely making her mark in history.

"Um . . . Kelly, what's the lettuce at the base?" Lizzie whispered as she tugged one of Kelly's shirttail knots.

Chuckling, Kelly pointed to the bottom of the house. "It's lattice, honey. That's what the crossed pieces of wood are called that make a fence under the porch."

"Oh. So, I have to paint behind all them bushes?"

"Here," Kelly offered, holding back an azalea. "I'll show you how. It's not hard."

Soon all three were working diligently. After instruction from Kelly and several reminders to "mind the drips" from her father, Lizzie was tediously applying whitewash to the lattice. It was a good place for the young girl to work, for where her paintbrush dripped, the garden bed could be turned over later to hide the spots.

Daniel was on the ladder, having finished painting the second-floor siding and was now putting the final coat on the eaves of the porch roof. Kelly was busy painting the railings and posts of the wraparound porch. As the hours passed, they shared stories and laughter, and moments of comfortable silence.

There was a genuine feeling of camaraderie, and the time went quickly. Lizzie and Kelly made good progress and applauded each other as more and more of the house was covered in fresh whitewash. Making her way slowly, Lizzie moved her pail toward the last corner of the house, where they were all converging as the job neared completion.

No one was prepared for what happened when the man stepped off the last rung of the ladder.

"Arg!" Daniel blurted as his foot sank into his daughter's pail of whitewash.

Kelly and Lizzie both looked up from their painting in shock. Daniel stared at Lizzie, his face red with a quick anger and then his gaze slowly came to rest on Kelly's eyes.

She tightened her smile in a grimace, trying not to laugh. It wasn't successful. "I . . . I'm sorry," she muttered, attempting to hide her mouth with her forearm.

Daniel balanced himself on one leg and slowly pulled his dripping trouser cuff, sock, and shoe out of the white mess. It was obvious Lizzie didn't quite know what to do as she quickly glanced from one adult and back to the other. Kelly had to look away to stop herself from bursting out in further laughter.

"Daddy, don't!"

Kelly promptly turned back, to see Daniel grinning wildly as he flicked his own paint filled brush toward his daughter. Lizzie's overalls were instantly splattered, and the absolutely stunned look on the child's face was all it took. Kelly now roared with laughter at the two.

Lizzie began giggling nervously as Daniel dipped his paintbrush again, smiled at his daughter and implied she follow suit and take aim elsewhere.

"Wait a minute!" Kelly protested. "I won't be part of this debacle!"

"Fair's fair, ain't it, Daddy?"

He turned to Kelly and meekly shrugged his shoulders. "She has a point, you know. It's not polite to laugh at someone else's misfortune. It's just not good manners." He glanced back to his child, and calmly added, "It seems our Miss Kelly is in need of a lesson today, too. You may go right ahead and instruct her, Elizabeth."

"Danie—" she couldn't finish shouting his name fast enough before having to shut her mouth to stop from swallowing the glob of whitewash.

"Oh, good aim, Elizabeth," her father verbally applauded.

Pointing at her, Lizzie held her stomach and laughed even harder. Kelly quickly dipped her brush into the pail and flung the whitewash across the small distance separating them. Lizzie got splattered again and, as Daniel was laughing, Kelly turned her brush on him.

Stunned, he blinked at her as paint dripped off his nose and chin.

"My aim's not so bad, either, is it, dear husband?" Kelly asked, now bending over with gut-wrenching laughter.

"Yes. I'd say quite on the mark, dear wife," he answered, quickly scooping up a large amount of paint onto his brush. Squishing sounds from his one soaked shoe as he clumped across the yard made Lizzie point and laugh hysterically. He was slowly advancing toward Kelly and she clearly saw the devilish look in his eyes. It was obvious this man intended to even the score.

"I mean it . . . don't do it, Daniel," she warned through her own barely repressed giggles as she backed up.

"All for one, and one for all, I say. Lizzie's had her two, I've had mine, but you've only had one good splattering. This is a democracy, and I feel it's only fair we each have an equal share."

"Do it, Daddy!" Lizzie encouraged, jumping up and down.

"Gee, thanks for the support, Lizzie!" Kelly laughed. From the corner of her eye she saw Clara walking around the side of the house with a pitcher of lemon water. Scurrying across the yard in her direction, Kelly ran behind the shocked woman and peeked at Daniel.

"Ha! You won't do it now," she teased. "I've found sanctuary."

"Have you now?" Daniel asked, as though her words meant nothing.

"You wouldn't!"

"Justice will always prevail, madam. I most certainly would," he said with a laugh and flung the paint right over Clara's shoulder.

"What in heaven's name is goin—" She was quick for an old woman, Kelly would give her that, but not quick enough to escape completely unscathed. Clara shifted her weight just in time for the majority of the whitewash to hit Kelly smack in the face, yet her own had more than a few speckles.

The three of them must have seemed completely certifiable to Clara as the terrified look on her face was so comical it made them laugh even harder.

"Mistah Daniel! You done gone crazy, or what?" Clara demanded. "What you doin' to these womenfolk?"

"Wha—*Me?* I'm the minority here! It was the *womenfolk* who started it!"

"We did not!" Kelly retorted with a giggle.

"Oh, and who put the pail of paint directly beneath my ladder?"

"That was an accident!" Kelly protested, looking at Lizzie, who was holding a painted white hand over her mouth to stop laughing.

"Well, everybody hold on right now!" Clara ordered with a stomp of her foot. "Just look at all of you! Like a wild bunch of children you is. Lord have mercy. I reckon I'm gonna have to be the adult here . . . why if I had my way, I'd be sendin' y'all upstairs without supper and—" Her words were stopped short as she looked beyond Daniel and Lizzie to the pair of men coming through the woods.

Everyone remained silent as Daniel picked up a rag and wiped his face and hands. A part of Kelly's brain registered that everyone was standing perfectly still, as if frozen, as an older man and Will Hoskins came closer to the house. She didn't like the expression on either of their faces.

"My woman tells me that you was lookin' for me an' my boy," the older man said. He was dressed in a dirty undershirt, with brown stains under his armpits and filthy overalls. His hair was dark and matted and he looked like he hadn't had a bath in over a month . . . but what really frightened

Kelly was the way Daniel's face became rigid with anger.

"Yes, Rufus. There is a matter that we need to discuss." Daniel turned to Kelly and said, "You and Clara take Lizzie inside, please."

Rufus Hoskins sauntered up to them and eyed the paint-splattered scene. "You lets your nigra talk to you like that?" he asked, then added with a sneer, "What y'all doin'? Tryin' to make her white?" The hideous man laughed, showing several missing teeth.

Kelly put her arm around Clara and tightened her hold. "Come along, Lizzie," she called out. "Let's get cleaned up and ready for supper."

Lizzie slowly walked up to Clara and Kelly.

"That your new missus?" Rufus asked, nodding toward Kelly. "My boy told me 'bout her. Didn't believe him when he said she wore pants like a man . . . but now I sees my boy speaks the truth."

Kelly's spine stiffened and she was about to open her mouth and say something when Daniel turned his head, and ordered, "Get in the house, please."

She took a deep breath, trying to calm herself, and put her other hand on Lizzie's shoulder as she turned Clara and began walking to the rear of the house. When they were about to turn toward the back door, Kelly looked over her shoulder and could see Daniel in a heated discussion with Rufus Hoskins, while Will continued to stare at her and Lizzie with absolute contempt. Shuddering, Kelly said to Lizzie, "Honey, you go up on the porch and I'll pump some clean water. We can get cleaned out here and then we'll take a bath inside."

"Why are Daddy and Will's pa so mad?" Lizzie asked in a frightened voice.

"This is between your father and them, Lizzie. Don't you worry about it." Kelly turned to Clara, who was wiping her face with her apron. "I'm so sorry you got hit with paint. It was just silliness."

"Ain't no mind, Miz Kelly," Clara answered, untying her apron and staring into her eyes. "Better'n what's takin' place out there now."

Kelly could read the concern in Clara's expression and nodded. "Do you have any rags we could use to clean ourselves? I don't want to track paint into the house."

"Just you wait. I'll bring 'em," Clara said, first checking her own shoes to make sure they were clean. Taking off her apron, she handed it to Lizzie. "Use this," she directed the child. "You've got it on your hair and everythin'. Um, um, um . . . Lordy." Shaking her head, she disappeared into the house.

Kelly was anxious about what was taking place in the side yard but didn't dare peek. Daniel had made it clear he didn't want her around for it. "Stay here on the porch, honey," she said to Lizzie, and stepped down the three stairs.

Walking stiffly to the water pump, she nearly had to force herself to keep from turning around. She didn't know what difference her presence would have made, but she really wanted to be at Daniel's side for this confrontation. She was married now, and she knew what it was to be a wife. Okay, so she hadn't successfully omitted the word "obey" from the ceremony, and it irritated her even to think it, but she knew she if she disobeyed Daniel in this matter, he would be furious. She had to remember this was not her time. She was living in an era when man reigned supreme, a time when women didn't have the right to vote, to own property, or even have custody of their own children.

Sure, slaves had been emancipated and the males given those rights . . . but not women. Women in this time were given two choices: to be a drudge or a doll. Without money, a woman could only clean *his* house, raise *his* children, become totally dependent on the male's whims. Her very life was dependent on him. It didn't matter if he beat her and her children. If she left, it could only be with the clothes on her back and without her children. In this day and age, a woman was forced to stay.

With money she became a plaything, there for the comfort and amusement of man, yet beyond the money she still was denied basic human rights her husband and sons enjoyed.

There was no such thing as an equal partnership in this

time. She knew things would eventually change, but the history she knew would be a long time coming, and that really peeved Kelly.

Pumping the water, she recalled the way Rufus Hoskins and his son had looked at her. She wondered about his wife and felt sorry for the woman . . . for all women of this time who would never experience, even for a period of their lives, the feeling of independence . . . freedom to make their own choices about their own lives. Shaking her head, Kelly picked up the heavy bucket and walked back to the house where Lizzie had waited for her.

She looked at the young girl and her heart ached that Lizzie was growing up in a time when women were not recognized as equals. She vowed, should she remain here, to teach the young girl about independence and to join the struggle for suffrage. Again, she was reminded of everything she had taken for granted in her life. She never really thought about women like Elizabeth Cady Stanton, or Susan B. Anthony, women who had made it possible for her to have enjoyed the freedoms of the twentieth-first century.

Suddenly, as she stepped up onto the porch, she realized she just might not want to leave, to return to her old life. It was a startling and bittersweet revelation. Could she just say good-bye to her friends, her business? A part of her ached for the modern world and everything she had left behind. A larger part wanted to remain with Lizzie and Clara, and especially with Daniel. Dipping one of the rags Clara had left on the porch into the bucket of water, she wondered how this could be possible. When she'd arrived here, she would have done anything to leave, to get back to her own time . . . and now, now she couldn't even imagine leaving this family.

"Here," Kelly whispered, reaching out for Lizzie. "Let me clean your face."

Gently, she washed the paint from Lizzie's cheeks. "Close your eyes, sweetie."

As she was wiping the child's forehead, Kelly listened as Lizzie started talking in a low voice.

"Is everybody mad 'cause of me? Cause of what I told you about Will?"

Kelly took a deep breath as she dipped the rag again into the water. "Honey, no one is mad at you. This isn't about anything you've done. This is something between your father and Mr. Hoskins . . . and Will," Kelly added, not wanting to lie to the girl.

"But they never came to the house to talk to Daddy before." The child's expression clearly showed confusion and worry.

"This is probably the first and last time they ever will, Lizzie. Hey, wasn't it funny the way your father stepped into that pail of paint and then splattered it on you?" Kelly figured a change of subject might distract her.

Lizzie, with the agility of a child maneuvering moods, giggled at the memory. "I thought he was gonna be *so* mad at me and then he flung that paint at me and then you done it to me and then . . ." She stopped speaking when Kelly wiped at her chin.

"And then we all got into a hilarious paint fight," Kelly finished for her. "Including Clara, though now she wants to send us all to bed without dinner." She smiled encouragingly at the girl, then added, "I hope she doesn't, cause it sure smells good, doesn't it?"

Nodding, Lizzie muttered, "She always says she's gonna do that to me, but then she gives in. Though I ain't never heard her say that to Daddy."

Kelly grinned. "Hmm, maybe it's been a while since your daddy played, too."

"I ain't never seen him play before. Never . . ."

"Okay, I allowed the first ain't, but that's a second one now. Try saying, 'I have never seen him play before.' Really, Lizzie . . . it's only a habit, and you can break it if you want."

"I have never, ever seen him play before."

"Who?"

They both turned when Daniel asked the question. He was standing on the steps in his paint-splattered clothes.

"You," Kelly finally answered to break the silence. "We were just saying how much fun we had playing with you."

Clara opened the back door, and said, "Miz Lizzie

Gilmore, I gots your bath ready now. Leave them dirty shoes on the porch and come in this kitchen. Hurry, chile," she added as Lizzie fumbled with her shoes. "There's gotta be two more baths after you, and my supper is gonna be ruined if we don't get this done in good time."

Before Lizzie stepped into the kitchen, Daniel called out to her. She turned around with an expression of remorse on her face, as though she figured she was in trouble for something. "Yes, suh?"

"Thank you for helping paint the house, Elizabeth. You did a fine job, and we had a good time, didn't we?"

The child's face lit with pleasure. "Yes, suh! We sure did!"

Clara looked at Kelly and an unspoken communication passed between the women. It seemed the decade-old gap between father and daughter was beginning to heal.

"Hurry with your bath now," Daniel said with a smile, then added, "as Clara said, we don't want to spoil supper."

Lizzie skipped happily into the kitchen and when the door was closed, Kelly looked into Daniel's eyes and saw the anger return. "Are you all right?" she asked softly, handing him a clean rag, dipped in water.

He took it and wiped his face and hands. "All right? No, my dear, I am most certainly not all right, yet I will not have my daughter thinking anything else. You were right about Will. He denied everything, and I have made an enemy of Rufus Hoskins by calling his son a liar. I told him the next time his son even approached my daughter we would involve the law, and if it happened again, I would deal with it myself."

"Oh, Daniel . . . I'm so sorry about all of this. I was right to tell you, wasn't I?"

"Of course you were. And, I agree about moving her to New Orleans for a few weeks. In addition to removing Elizabeth from the possibility of any retaliation, it will also take her mind off this situation."

"Yes, let's hope out of sight, out of mind."

He threw the rag back into the bucket and tilted his head slightly. "Speaking of sights, Will informed me he witnessed my new wife climbing out of a tree in those very same trousers and proceeded to . . . oh, how did he put it?" Daniel paused and looked up as though trying to recall the exact words. "Yes, that was it. He said she screamed at him like a banshee from hell."

Kelly was glad to see the slight hint of a smile at his lips. "Well, I did tell him in no uncertain terms that I knew what he was doing and he was to stay away from Lizzie."

"But climbing trees? Kelly, you simply can't go around the countryside dressed like a man. It is unseemly, and you could be badly hurt."

"Well, at the time, I didn't think anyone would see me. I told Lizzie that if she went along with the tutoring, I would play one of her games. I've only done it a few times and hey," she said flopping a rag against his paint-covered chest. "I'm no doddering old biddy. I'm still pretty agile. Why, you'd be amazed at my physical prowess."

He raised one eyebrow. "Oh, I intend to learn about all your fantastic abilities, my dear," he said, softening his gaze. "Just promise me you won't be climbing any more trees."

She stared into his sincere, beautiful eyes. "C'mon, Daniel, how can I promise that? Never again to climb a tree? I mean, what if I'm walking in the woods and . . . and an alligator or a water moccasin or . . . or a wild boar comes along?" Okay, she was grabbing at a straw on that one, but damn it, she was going to defend her right to be free.

"You know what I mean, Kelly," he answered with a grin. "I don't really wish to explain to anyone why my wife chooses to wear pants, instead of a dress. I know you've told me that wearing trousers in your time is acceptable, but it is not here, and here is where you find yourself now."

"All right, Daniel," she said in a low voice. "To honor your concern for my well being, I won't climb any more trees . . . unless it's absolutely necessary." She looked back up and held eye contact with him to make her next point very clear. "I don't like it that what I wear defines me and how I'm expected to conduct myself, but I will *honor* your request and wear dresses so as not to embarrass you again."

She wanted him to hear the distinction she'd made by omitting the word "obey."

"Thank you, Kelly," he said, picking up the wet rag and wringing it out. Gently wiping at the paint on her face, he added, "However, I must admit that seeing you in one of my shirts doesn't exactly displease me."

"Oh?" Her smile couldn't be hidden.

"But only for my private viewing, Mrs. Gilmore." He tilted her chin up. "Can you promise that?"

"That I can promise," she answered, staring at his lips.

He lowered his head and softly kissed her. "Now, madam, I shall leave you to your ablutions while I finish the last of the house painting."

She watched him walk back down the steps and fought the urge to follow him. She knew, deep inside, that she had changed. No longer could she envision a future without him. With everything in her heart she wanted to play this out, however it was written, for she had fallen in love with this family . . . and she was making a difference in their lives, just as they had completely changed hers.

Clara was right . . . she didn't have to understand it all, for there was a reason for everything. Even happiness.

Fourteen

"Lordy, this is much too fine for me!" Clara protested, as she looked around the stately guest bedroom. "Maybe it's better I stay downstairs . . . with the others."

Kelly smiled tenderly. "Well, unfortunately, Clara, there's no room for you downstairs. Do you think you could manage suffering through your stay with us up here?"

"Sufferin'?" The old woman's eyes widened with disbelief. Shaking her head, she walked up to Kelly, and softly said, "Listen, Miz Kelly, I knows you is bein' real kind to me an' all, and I sure 'preciates it more than I can say . . . but the sufferin' may be yours. You really don't know 'bout the way it is. Here, a Negro woman sleepin' upstairs around the white folk is gonna be trouble you don't need."

Kelly could feel her jaw clenching at the implication and had to remind herself to relax it. "Let me explain to you what I do know, Clara. I am the lady of this house now, and therefore, I've decided it's more than right for you to be here. It's not my intention to make you or anyone else uncomfortable, and I don't want trouble for anyone, but I'm not about to back down on this simply for the dictates of a prejudiced society." Kelly inhaled and took the old woman's hand into her own. "Clara, in case you haven't realized it yet, I'm very fond of you . . . I consider you family. And as a family member, I want you to enjoy your stay here in the city. I have a lot planned for us, lady," she said with a smile to comfort the woman then added, "but, I can see the long trip has tired you, so right now you just unpack your things and get lots of rest. Tomorrow, we have a busy day of shopping ahead of us. Any arguments?"

Sighing heavily, Clara pulled the cashmere shawl from her shoulders and placed her knitting bag on the floor. "Mm, mm, mm . . . the way you talk, Miz Kelly. Does anybody argue with you, and win?"

Kelly laughed and quickly hugged the older woman. "Don't be upset with me. I only want the best for you. It makes me happy."

"I knows that," Clara murmured, nodding.

Pulling back, Kelly grinned. "Okay, I'll let you get settled in while I check on Lizzie. I'll come back and see if you need anything a little bit later. I want you to rest, Clara. There's nothing for you to do here, except enjoy yourself and, if it makes you more comfortable, think of it as a holiday, one that's well deserved."

As she closed the door behind her, Kelly overheard the woman mumbling about how she'd never had a holiday in her "whole and entire life." Pausing for just a moment, she smiled, then continued down the hall to Lizzie's room. The child was already lying on her bed, reading *Little Women.*

"I can see you're right at home," Kelly whispered, coming into the room and sitting on the edge of the bed. "I'm glad you like the book."

"I like Jo the best. She's like me."

"Yes, she is," Kelly agreed. "But you'll see that Jo also knows how to act in front of company. Are you excited about being here in the city for your grandparents' arrival?"

Lizzie shrugged. "There's no trees good enough to climb, but it's all right, I guess. And I don't even know my grandparents, so there's nothing to be excited about."

"Hmm, I guess I can see your point. Still, I'm sure they're excited about meeting you."

Lizzie simply nodded.

"Hey, listen," she began enthusiastically. "Tomorrow, we're going to have quite an adventure." Kelly paused for a positive reaction from the child. None came. She continued anyway. "You and I and Clara are going shopping."

Lizzie only nodded again. "It's not the same as climbin' trees, though."

"C'mon, I think you'll have fun. We need to look for a present for you to give your grandparents. And, when I was here last, I think I saw a shop that might have just the thing."

"Oh, what's that?"

Kelly grinned. "Another surprise. You'll see tomorrow."

"Okay," Lizzie sighed with a blasé tone.

"All right, I'll let you get back to your book. Right now there's something I have to do. If you need me, I'll be downstairs."

She left Lizzie reading and made her way through the elegant house. She much preferred this house to the one in the country. Maybe it was because Lilly seemed to be so much a part of that house and her presence was missing in the city. There were other reasons she was glad to be in New Orleans, too. She wanted to help Lizzie make friends her own age and learn to socialize. There was only so much she was able to do with their limited tea parties in the country. Now it was time for the real thing.

Taking a deep, steadying breath, she entered the kitchen and watched as Andrew, Delia, and Mary came to attention, as though her presence was startling to them.

"Excuse me," she said with a smile. "I just want to speak with you about our present houseguest. Miss Clara. I know it may seem unusual for her to occupy an upstairs room, but she is an old family friend and I just want to make her stay as pleasant as possible. If there are any questions, please don't hesitate to ask me. Mr. Gilmore and I will also be expecting another couple, Mr. and Mrs. Howe from England in a few days. I would appreciate it if the guest bedroom, the one I occupied on my last visit, is prepared for their arrival."

"Yes, ma'am," Andrew answered. "It'll be done this afternoon."

Kelly held up her hand. "Tomorrow will be fine. Our surprise arrival has given you enough to do today." She smiled again. "Are there any questions concerning Miss Clara?"

"No, ma'am," Andrew answered.

Delia and Mary shook their heads.

"Good. Please make her as comfortable as possible. Oh, and should she wander down here, I'm certain she would enjoy your company, and she may even prefer to take her meals here, if that's all right with you."

"It'd be our pleasure, Miz Kelly," Andrew replied, as they all nodded in unison.

"Thank you for being so kind." Kelly smiled to the trio and stepped out of the room.

She walked through the house until she came to the alcove that led to Daniel's office. Before peeking in, she stopped to view her reflection in a large mirror on the foyer wall. Tugging at the tight corset beneath her dress, she had to admit she actually thought the dated fashions she now wore were rather becoming, even if a bit uncomfortable. Determining no further adjustments were needed, she turned to the open door.

Unlike his study at the farmhouse, this room was kept orderly. The afternoon sun was beaming through the grand floor-to-ceiling French doors that led out to the patio. Against the almond-painted wood panel walls were several tall stacks of barrister bookcases made of lightly stained oak. Hundreds of books and odd mechanical objects were displayed behind the glass doors. There were several comfortable chairs and small tables grouped together, and Kelly figured it was probably set up that way for meetings and to entertain his clients. That would also explain the neatness of the room, she mused.

He was standing at a tall, antique drafting table looking over some papers. His back was to her, and he seemed lost in concentration.

Knocking softly on the doorjamb, she said, "Daniel, I'm sorry to interrupt, but may I discuss something with you for just a few minutes?"

When he turned to her, she saw his face light up. "Your presence is a welcome interruption at any time, my dear."

As she entered the room, she smiled and walked up to him. "Thank you for the compliment," she replied. Leaning with her hands on the edge of the table, she added, "You are *such* a gentleman, Daniel Gilmore. You know, I think that's one of the things I most enjoy about this time. Your innate charm is a refreshing change from twenty-first-century men." She smiled warmly.

"Ah, it's quite evident you are not without your own beguiles, madam." The twinkle in his eyes told her he was genuinely pleased by her visit.

"Oh, I haven't begun truly to flatter you, Daniel," she murmured teasingly, "but that isn't what I came in here to do . . . not that I won't at a later time, but right now I need your feedback about something."

He blinked with an amused look on his face. "I am entirely enchanted with you, Kelly, and all that I have is yours, including whatever is my 'feedback.' "

"Oh," Kelly laughed, realizing the term was futuristic. "It means your thoughts on something."

"I see. I shall gladly share my thoughts with you. What would you like to know?"

"It's about the guest and sleeping arrangements here."

"Is there a problem?" he asked quickly.

"No, I don't think so . . . I just hope you don't think so either."

"What is it, Kelly?"

"It's about Clara. There was no room downstairs in the servants quarters, so I put her upstairs in the second guest bedroom. Well, she seems to think it's improper and may cause problems. I want everyone to be comfortable and I'd just like to know how you feel about it."

He inhaled deeply and put his hands in his trouser pockets. "Hmm . . . I see."

Although he paused, the kind smile never left his face. He

seemed to be gathering his thoughts carefully before speaking again.

"Kelly," he began in an understanding tone, "I appreciate that you are accustomed to ways that are liberated and unconventional in comparison to our nineteenth-century standards, but Clara is correct. Unfortunately, it's true that if word of her position got out, and where she was staying in the house, there would be more than a few scandalized here."

"Position has nothing to do with it, Daniel. She's absolutely devoted to you and Lizzie. She could have left at any time, but she stayed to help raise your daughter. She's like a member of the family, and we're about all the family that kind woman has. I refuse to accept that just because the color of her skin happens to be different than ours, she should be segregated in this household. No. I won't let that happen," Kelly said, shaking her head with conviction, before adding, "That's not my idea of family values, Daniel."

"Kelly, I agree with all you're saying, and I feel the same way about Clara. However, you must understand the war may be over and some laws may have been changed, but regrettably, not everyone's mind has. Remember, you are in the South, the Deep South, and there is still a great feeling of resentment and a lot of bitterness yet to heal."

"Did your family own slaves?" It was a question that had been burning in her mind for days and she didn't have the courage to ask until now.

"Yes. Not many, just house servants. When my father moved the family to England before the war, he gave them their freedom and supplied them with funds and safe passage to Canada. Believe me, slavery is not something I'll ever condone, but the reality of it is, at one time not so long ago, it was an accepted way of life for everyone, Kelly."

She shook her head. "And you must believe it when I say I am from a different time and a completely different way of life. There's over a hundred years of history that stands between us, and therefore, I know what happens. There will be more than a few people who stand up against injustices everywhere, a good few who will fight for equality; some giving their lives for it. They will inspire others to change their minds, and they will make a great difference in this world."

Daniel smiled warmly and came around the drafting table to encircle her within his arms. "It seems no age is without its struggles. History does teach us that. I guess you might call it evolutionary growing pains." He kissed her forehead. "I am inspired by your perspective and beliefs, madam. How do you propose we change some minds?"

She gazed up at him. "Well, I don't want to start a revolution or anything, I'm just asking that if anyone objects, you'll support me in this decision. I really want to reward Clara for her years of service to you and Lizzie. Besides, she's fragile and tires so easily now. Did you notice when we got to the house how exhausted she was from the trip?"

"Yes. She is up there in years, but I think Clara's got more spirit than most folks half her age. Pamper her as you wish, my dear . . . do whatever makes you happy, save parading down Royal Street in my trousers."

Kelly laughed and playfully slapped at his chest. "Okay, I'll only parade in front of you, and I won't say exactly what I'll be wearing. How's that?"

"That sounds like a very interesting proposition, madam," he said, raising an eyebrow.

Kelly felt his body tense against hers as he drew her more closely to him. Gently halting any further advances, she pressed both her hands on his chest. "Daniel," she began, "thank you for your feedback and support on this issue with Clara. It's very important to me to take care of her now. I want you to know that."

"It is abundantly clear to me, Kelly, that you are of pure heart. Another attractive quality I'll add to the many I've already discovered in you. As a matter of fact, every moment I've spent with you shows me even more how blessed I am that you accepted my proposal."

She raised her face to his and studied his eyes, seeing in them such love that it nearly took her breath away. How could she ever leave him, even if it were possible? How odd that thoughts of the world she had left behind were quickly fading. Nothing seemed to matter, save right now . . . this wondrous moment. Raising her hand to his face, she caressed his cheek and ran the tip of her finger over his bottom lip. "And more and more I am seeing how blessed I am that you asked me," she murmured, right before his head lowered and he captured her mouth with an impassioned kiss.

To Kelly it suddenly seemed as though everything around them ceased to exist. There was only the moment of wonder as she felt their connection becoming even deeper. Kelly clung to him, allowing him further access as he ran his hands over her back, around her waist, up her sides and against her breasts.

When they pulled apart, she stared into his eyes once more, and whispered, "I had my things put into your bedroom."

She watched as his eyes lit with pleasure again. "Though it be torture to hold you chastely each night, I wouldn't want you anywhere else save beside me in bed."

"Honestly, I've been waiting almost thirteen years to feel this way again, Daniel. I don't know if I can wait another month to express it."

His devastatingly sexy grin played on his lips. "And trust me when I say, the anticipation of intimacy brings an unbearable ache to me, yet I promised you a proper courtship, and you shall have one. Now, my delicious time traveler, as the possibility of my disgracing us both becomes greater with each moment you're near me, I must suggest you leave. I'm expecting a business associate in a few minutes and, as it is, not even my jacket will be effective enough to conceal the evidence of what your presence arouses."

His meaning was clear, and Kelly found herself giggling like a teenager as she kissed his cheek and backed away from him. "Why, Daniel Gilmore," she said, attempting her best Southern accent, "I do believe you are making me blush."

"Oh, I intend to do more than make you blush, madam," he answered with a laugh and took her hand before adding, "All in good time, my dear. All in good time."

"I . . ." She hesitated when she realized what she was

about to say. Instead, she said, "I guess I'll see you again at dinner later tonight."

"Yes, until then," he said, not taking his eyes from hers as he gently kissed her hand.

When she closed the door behind her, Kelly stood for a few moments in awe. She kept her focus on the center of the garden as she walked past the staircase and stepped out into the late-afternoon sunshine. Hearing only the streams of water dancing rhythmically into the fountain pool, she felt she could almost be floating as she went over in her mind the words she had just deliberately withheld.

I love you.

Like the sprays of water before her, it had nearly flowed as freely from her lips. It had seemed such a natural response, and that shocked her. She hadn't said those words to a man in thirteen years.

Attempting to bring Michael's image into her mind, she found he was becoming faint, like a fading photograph. That truly shocked her. Suddenly, she realized she couldn't recall the sound of his voice. She had been able to hear it every time she thought of him before, but she sensed something was changing within her.

So this is healing, she pondered.

Deep inside she knew she would always love Michael and the time they had, but she was releasing him now and making room within her heart and mind for Daniel. It was the closure she'd needed, and in that discovery she found it provided a whole new opening.

With those three words she'd almost whispered, she knew all those years of grieving had finally ended. Taking a deep breath, she noticed her chest felt more expansive and her heart felt lighter. Her mind marveled at the idea that she had to travel back over a hundred years to realize she had sealed herself off from love and, in so doing, she'd almost allowed her heart to die with Michael.

She exhaled. She was more *alive* now than she had been for many years.

"Mrs. Gilmore, ma'am?"

Spinning around, she saw Andrew standing at the French doors.

Smiling, she walked closer to him. "Yes, Andrew?"

"I was wondering how many place settings I should use in the dining room for dinner."

She knew what he was asking and thought it was a very tactful way of putting forth his inquiry. Thinking about it for a moment, she answered, "Three. Miss Clara will eat in the kitchen with you and the girls, if that's all right."

"Yes, ma'am." He bowed slightly and left.

Looking up to the bedrooms that bordered the garden, Kelly thought of Clara and knew the woman would feel more comfortable in the kitchen. If she had refused to dine with them in the country, she certainly wouldn't want to here in the city. Besides, even in her own time, servants didn't dine with their employers . . . but Kelly simply couldn't think of Clara as an employee. She was a member of the family and neither Clara's position nor the color of her skin made her any less loved.

Kelly reminded herself that she would simply have to be more careful now, here in the city. Certainly she didn't want to make life more difficult for Clara by creating any friction with the other servants. Her good deeds could be interpreted as favoritism and alienate Clara from the staff. It was a delicate balance, and Kelly vowed to be more aware.

Running a household in the nineteenth century sure was a different challenge, but she could do it. She had to . . . for, as incredible as it seemed, it was now her life.

Many hours later, she was snuggled in bed next to Daniel, feeling his strong, warm body next to hers. His arm was wrapped around her shoulder and back and her head was resting on his firm chest. She sighed deeply with contentment and ran her hand over his shoulder.

"You sound tired," he whispered to her in the darkness.

"I am . . . a little. Aren't you?" She loved this part of the evening, settling in bed next to him and talking. It brought them closer each night to knowing one another, and she realized Daniel was using any discussion to distract himself from more intimate thoughts. If he only knew how her body was aching with desire as she lay so close to his.

"Yes, I am a bit . . . we've all had a very full day. Elizabeth did well tonight at dinner. She is making wonderful progress with your tutelage, Kelly. I didn't hear a single 'ain't' the entire evening."

Kelly chuckled along with him. "She is trying so hard, Daniel. I just hope the Howes don't expect this perfect little robot when they arrive."

"Robot? What is that?"

She shook her head and grinned. "Well, 'robot' is a term that means someone devoid of human feelings. I used it to describe a child who is so well behaved, they don't seem like a real child any longer, they act more like a little mechanical thing . . . A robot."

"What an odd term. Ro-bot," he practiced.

Kelly giggled. "The way you say it, it does sound automated."

"Well, that's one thing my daughter will never be. She's very strong-minded."

"In the long run, that's going to be to her benefit, Daniel."

"I hope so." He sighed. "To tell you the truth, with all the technological advances we're making even today, I worry sometimes about what the future holds in store for all mankind. Do machines such as these things you call robots actually exist in your time?"

"Yes they do. When they're invented, they'll be designed and programmed to perform a variety of tasks, doing much of the work of humans."

"We have that now. We call it industrialization."

"Yeah, well, the future takes it a whole lot farther. Robotics will eventually lead to artificial intelligence, which is an even scarier reality if you ask me."

"There is so much about the future that I should like to ask you, Kelly," he said with excitement. "Can you tell me more?"

She yawned and closed her eyes. "I can't think anymore."

He began stroking her hair. "Does this help you think?"

Again, she chuckled against his chest. "That will only put

me to sleep," she said with a sigh. "But if there was one thing I have missed, it was this."

"Someone stroking your hair?"

She nodded. "I'm a sucker for it."

"How interesting. Here," he said, and used both hands. "More."

She laughed. "No . . . it's not so much 'more' . . . I don't know . . . it's soothing, if it's done gently and slowly, almost absentmindedly."

"Ah, yes. The whole point would be to soothe you, madam." He dropped his other hand and resumed his previous stroke.

"Now, who's the tease?" she asked, again closing her eyes and absorbing the wonderful feeling.

"I'm not teasing you. I'm *soothing* you so you will tell me about the future and these robots."

"I can't tell you about robots. I'm not a scientist."

"Tell me what you can. For instance, what is their power source?"

She thought about the effort it would take for her to explain things, then realized that Daniel, being an architect and having worked on the New Orleans Expo of the future in 1884, had a genuine interest in the future. Tired as she was, she would try to make as much sense as she could for the man to understand her rather limited, if not elementary explanations. "Well, let's see . . . they are run by computers and—"

"I remember you mentioning them. A machine that calculates and stores information."

"Yes, exactly," she said, perking up with a smile. "Hey, you really do listen to me, don't you?"

"Your every word, madam," he replied softly as he continued gently stroking her hair.

"Mmm." She sighed with deeper contentment. "Okay, where was I? Oh, storing information. Well, all the books in your library could be stored on a disk, which basically, is something the size of a bread plate, and there would still be room left over."

He stopped stroking her hair. "No!"

"Yes."

"How?"

"That's just it. I don't know *how*. But take my word for it. I could just slip a disk into a small machine and sit in front of a monitor, a glass screen, and direct the machine to find . . . let's say," she said, pausing to think of an example he could mentally grasp. "A copy of Edward Bellamy's book and, within seconds, I could be reading it, or I could print it out and save it to read later."

"You have a printer working in your home?"

"Sure, I have a printer. It's attached to the computer with a cable."

"Wait, I'm confused. You have a person attached with a cable to . . . to this machine?"

She raised her head slightly and looked at him in the soft moonlight. "Daniel, the printer is another machine. That's what I was saying . . . machines are taking the place of people."

"Fascinating," he mused, beginning to stroke her hair again. "Then what do people do for employment?"

"They adjust to the use of this machine in their own field, or they're forced to learn a new skill. Computers are everywhere, but they need people to operate them, to instruct them in what to do. They're used to design houses, to send bombs across continents, and to put men on the moon. More things than I could ever relate to you."

His hand stopped stroking her and just rested on her head. "Men on the moon? You are saying that . . . that men have been to the moon?"

She giggled. "Yes, Daniel, I am saying that."

"How ever did they get there?"

"Oh geez," she said, pausing to recall the scientific part of her education she now wished she'd paid more attention to in her youth. "Well, they went up in a rocket, fueled by boosters made of atomic energy . . . and there were computers to carry out the flight plan . . . and they had to wear special suits with air tanks that allowed them to breathe. Daniel, there's only so much I can explain, I'm not an expert. You'll just have to take my word for it, men have been on the moon and space is now the new frontier to explore."

"Men on the moon . . ." His voice was filled with awe. "What was it like?"

She thought about it, trying to bring a picture of it into her mind. "There's no water, or oxygen, so it's very dry with no life. It's a desolate place. You wouldn't want to go there."

"Oh, but I would!" he proclaimed. "I would love to ride a rocket to the moon."

"It must be a guy thing," she muttered. "And it's called the space shuttle now. I guess I wouldn't mind a ride in that myself, come to think of it."

"Tell me, have these 'space shuttles' traveled anywhere else? I mean, do you know if they have discovered life on any other planets?"

"No, not yet. But they're still trying."

"So we are alone in this universe."

Kelly shrugged and settled back against his chest as he continued to stroke her hair. "I don't know, Daniel, but I think it's pretty arrogant to think that we on Earth are the only intelligent life out there. We just don't have the technology yet to travel to many planets. And don't ask me to explain light-years because I can't."

"You have given me much to think about, but how boring life here in this time must seem to you." He bent his head and kissed the top of hers. "I applaud you, my love, for adjusting so well to what must appear a primitive culture."

He called her his love!

She couldn't think about his compliment, or about computers or space travel. He used the word love . . . and it had slipped from his lips so naturally. Knowing she should say something, she snuggled closer to him, and whispered, "As long as you're by my side, Daniel, it is an easy adjustment."

"Good. Then I am fulfilling my duties as a honorable husband."

As a dutiful husband he was doing very well, but she really wanted the man in him right now. "Yes. As a matter of fact, I can hardly wait for the next adjustment, Daniel. I'm certain it will be very comfortable with you."

He chuckled and then, squeezing her, said, "Okay now,

tell me more about the future. How can bombs travel continents? Is it on rockets through the air? And I must know how these machines design houses. Can you tell me more of that?"

Her head sank heavily on his chest, and Kelly wondered what she had just started. She absolutely knew she couldn't take a month of *this*! She was about to ask him if it wouldn't be easier to just make love, when she realized that he wanted this courtship more than she did. He thought he was honoring her by it and all these questions were occupying his mind, keeping his thoughts away from his body . . . and hers.

But a month?

She had been celibate for thirteen years, and this last month seemed as though it was going to be longer than all of them put together. Perhaps because for the first time in all those years, she had met the right man, even if she had to travel back in time to do it.

There was no doubt in her mind any longer.

Daniel Gilmore was the right man.

And she wasn't waiting . . . she counted it off in her head . . . three weeks and two more days. Her feminine wiles might have been put on hold for over a decade, but she still had them, and it was definitely time to bring them out of hiding.

She almost giggled at the thought of seducing a man again. She might be rusty, but once she had been fairly good at it. All she needed was some practice.

"Kelly? Are you sleeping?"

"Just thinking," she replied softly, and snuggled more closely to him. Bringing her leg up over his in a slow seductive movement, she murmured, "What was the question again?"

There was a prolonged pause after she heard him take a deep breath.

"I forgot," he muttered.

"Mmm, me too," she whispered, very pleased with her new plan of seduction.

"Oh . . . you were going to tell me how these computers

design houses. Yes. That was it." He sounded almost relieved to have remembered.

She nearly groaned as she closed her eyes. Okay, so maybe she need a bit more practice.

Fifteen

"Come on, I promise this will be fun," Kelly said, tugging on Lizzie's wrist.

The girl looked into the dressmaker's window and sighed. "I don't need any more clothes."

"Yes, you do. You're almost grown out of the ones we brought from the house in the country. Honey, you're growing fast now and, besides, it isn't only dresses we're going to order."

Lizzie looked at Clara and then back to Kelly. "What else?"

Clara, wearing her best dress, her new hat and shawl, just shrugged.

"You'll see," Kelly answered. "Now, come on."

As the trio walked into the shop, a bell above the door tinkled and a woman, hair swept up off her face and neck, wearing a pretty lavender-and-white gown greeted them. "Good afternoon, ladies. How may I help you?"

Smiling, Kelly walked past bolts of material and ready-to-wear clothes on headless mannequins. "Good afternoon. My name is Mrs. Gilmore. This is," she said, placing her hand on Lizzie's shoulder, "Miss Elizabeth Gilmore, and this is Miss Clara Walker."

"How do," Clara added with a polite nod.

"It's a pleasure to meet you ladies. My name is Mrs. Robelier."

"Likewise, a pleasure, Mrs. Robelier. Are you the seamstress of this shop?" Kelly inquired.

"I am one, madam. I employ three others."

"Do you make special orders?"

"Why, yes, ma'am."

"Wonderful," Kelly declared. "I'd like to look at some fabrics, please. I have several items I'd like to have made as quickly as possible."

The woman appeared delighted and showed her to a table with a chair on each side. "Please, do sit down. I'll bring you some dress patterns and bolts of our fabrics. We have selections of the finest silks from China, satins from France and Italy, wools from Scotland and—"

As she sat down, Kelly held up her hand. "Actually, I'm looking for someone who can be . . . creative. Someone who can make her own patterns."

"Have you a design already?"

"Well, in my head, I do. Really, what I desire is very simple." She hesitated for a few moments and then said, "I'd like some pants. Trousers . . . for the female form."

"Uh-oh," Lizzie muttered, and turned to look at Clara. The older woman just stood stoically.

"Pants, madam? You mean, bloomers, I'm sure."

"No, not undergarments. Not quite bloomers . . . I mean long, loose-fitting slacks."

"I'm afraid I don't understand, Mrs. Gilmore."

Kelly again smiled to the woman, trying to appear friendly. "Yes, I know this is highly unusual, but I am seeking someone who can sew something like lounging trousers with jackets, made out of silk and satin and other soft materials. Do you think you can do this?"

"This *is* a highly unusual fashion, madam. You are speaking of these for women?"

"Yes. For myself, my daughter, and Miss Walker."

Clara clucked her tongue and looked away. Kelly tried not to laugh as Lizzie came closer to the table.

"For me, too?"

"Yes, for you too, sweetie." Kelly turned to look at the seamstress who still appeared to be digesting the entire concept. "They could be made simply, with a drawstring waist, and the jackets could be collarless, so it shouldn't take too much time. The hardest thing to make would probably be the sleeves. Would you be able to accommodate me?"

The woman thought for a few moments, as though envisioning it in her head. Suddenly, her eyes took on a glint of enthusiasm. "Yes, madam. I do think I should be able to help you. First," she said, bringing over a large paper and charcoal pencil to the table, "we shall sketch it, then I will take all the necessary measurements."

"Wonderful!" Kelly exclaimed, anxious to begin this project. "And besides the delicate fabric, I'd also like some made with heavier material for the winter. But those can wait. What I really need as quickly as possible are the ones made of silk. Now, this is the way I'd like them to fit . . ."

For the next hour and a half they were busy selecting fabric, being measured, and laughing over Mrs. Robelier's shocked, yet excited, expressions. When Kelly told them that they were to be called "pajamas," Lizzie kept repeating the word and giggling. Mrs. Robelier seemed delighted, remarking how she had been wishing for something to inspire her and *voilà* her wishes had walked in the front door.

Kelly really liked the woman, who appeared to get over her reservations quickly. Mrs. Robelier didn't hesitate in taking Clara's measurements, and even helped her pick out a soft blue-silk material Clara thought would match her robe. Lizzie would not be budged from the bright green satin, and Kelly chose a lovely cream-colored silk. When they finally left the shop and were standing outside it, Clara again shook her head.

"Miz Kelly, if that woman gets to gossipin', you're gonna be known in New Orleans as a loon. You knows that, don't ya?"

"I figured sooner or later the diagnosis would be in."

Kelly laughed more to herself for the thought, but added, "Really, Clara . . . I think Mrs. Robelier seemed excited to start a new project . . . why, I'll bet she starts singing my praises and, before you know it, all the women will be wearing pajamas. Just you wait and see."

"Uh-huh," Clara muttered, looking away. "The future of women's fashion is prancing in *pah-jam-ahs*."

Chuckling, Kelly leaned closer to the older woman. "That's right. We're just a little ahead of the times, is all. It *is* going to happen."

"Women wearin' pants?" Clara finally appeared shocked.

"Yes, though it does happen slowly. I think it's in the 1920s that they get popular. And it's just nice to have the choice to wear them when it's more comfortable . . . not that women have to wear them. Wait until you try them on, Clara, and then you'll see how freeing it is."

"Freein', huh? And just where am I gonna be wearin' them?"

"Well, I wouldn't suggest walking around on the streets. We'll wear them in the house and—"

"Mrs. Gilmore! What a pleasure to see you again."

Kelly turned her head and recognized Mrs. Holden approaching with another woman. They were dressed nearly identically in somber gray dresses, high-collared white blouses with narrow black ribbon ties. Each had a little black hat, and each held a small, wrapped bundle in their hands. She couldn't help thinking they looked like an etching out of an old storybook, but politely Kelly held her grin and returned the greeting. "Yes, Mrs. Holden, it's a pleasure to see you, and so soon again, too."

The minister's wife smiled with friendliness and nodded to Lizzie. "Elizabeth."

Kelly looked at the young girl and silently begged her to behave. A surge of loving pride ran through her as she watched Lizzie make a small curtsy.

"Good afternoon, Mrs. Holden," she said in a polite little voice.

Mrs. Holden glanced back down at Lizzie with a pleasantly surprised expression, and said, "Your new mother told

us you'd be coming back to New Orleans. We're looking
forward to seeing you in Sunday school again very soon."

"Yes, thank you." Lizzie's tone was less spirited, but she
managed a strained smile.

Mrs. Holden turned to the tidy woman at her side. "Allow
me to present a leading citizen of our city, and president of
our garden club, Mrs. Deaveroux."

Kelly extended her hand, and the surprised Mrs. Deaveroux accepted it. When Kelly shook it firmly, the woman's
eyes widened even more.

"I've heard wonderful things about your gardening club,
Mrs. Deaveroux. It's a pleasure to meet you."

"And you, Mrs. Gilmore," the woman muttered, looking
askance at Mrs. Holden.

Then Kelly did something she knew wasn't acceptable,
yet felt was only right. "And may I introduce Miss Clara
Walker?"

Both the prim women appeared startled, especially the
older Mrs. Deaveroux, yet to their credit, they did nod.

"How do," Clara offered with an anxious smile.

Okay, that was all Kelly wanted, an acknowledgment.
She didn't want to embarrass Clara, but she refused to be
rude, even if it meant going against societal programming.
To leave the kind old woman standing to the side, as though
her presence wasn't worthy even of a simple acknowledgment, was just something Kelly wasn't willing to abide, no
matter what the social consequences.

To fill in the awkward silence, Kelly said, "Elizabeth and
I look forward to calling on you, Mrs. Holden . . . at your
convenience, of course."

Mrs. Holden's demeanor brightened considerably. "Why,
I would enjoy that very much, Mrs. Gilmore. Shall I plan tea
for tomorrow afternoon, say three o'clock?"

"That sounds lovely, Mrs. Holden," Kelly answered with
a smile. "And perhaps Mrs. Deaveroux might join us. I do
so want to learn all I can about my new home, here in New
Orleans. I'd be grateful if you shared your expertise with
me."

The stuffy Mrs. Deaveroux gave a tight-lipped smile and

nodded. "Pending no other engagements on my social calendar, it would be a pleasure, I'm sure."

"Wonderful," Kelly confirmed, then added, "until tomorrow then." She figured she'd been polite enough and hoped she'd made a fairly decent impression. Besides, she, Lizzie, and Clara had one more stop on their own excursion.

After bidding good day to the two women, Kelly turned to her companions, and said, "Okay, guys . . . just one more place and then we're finished."

"Why did you say we would go and visit Mrs. Holden for tea? And now that old Mrs. Deaveroux is gonna be there, too!" Lizzie was decidedly not pleased.

"Honey, listen . . . this is a game we're playing because of where we find ourselves right now, and this is simply one of the ways it's played. It means a great deal to your father, and I don't mind going along with it if it will make him happy. Do you?"

Lizzie shrugged.

Smiling, Kelly touched Lizzie's shoulder. "Underneath all these stuffy rules, you and I both know who we are. When you grow up, you'll watch as the rules change. Sometimes they're for the better, giving you more freedom . . . and sometimes you miss some of the manners that have gone by the wayside. It's a form of people dealing with each other in a civilized way."

"But there's so *many* rules. I'll never learn them all."

"Yes you will. You've already learned so much in such a short while. Look how well it went with Mrs. Holden today, and tomorrow, she'll play hostess to us. It's the same game we played, just the roles will turned around."

"Oh, goodie," Lizzie said, obviously perking up at the idea. "Is Mammy Clara gonna come too?"

Kelly looked up sympathetically from the young girl to the older woman. "Um, no, Lizzie, I . . . I don't think—"

"I got's things I gotta do tomorrow, chile. I'm sorry I can't go, but y'all go and have a good time. Tell me all about it when y'all get back, okay?"

"Okay," the young girl replied reluctantly. "But it won't be any fun without you."

Clara smiled with tender understanding, and Kelly felt honored to stand next to such a dignified woman. "Thank you, Clara," she whispered. Looking down at Lizzie, Kelly prompted, "Okay, we need to get moving, or we're going to be late. We still have to get that gift I told you about for your grandparents."

She hurried Lizzie and Clara through the streets until they were in front of a door with an engraved brass sign.

"What's that say?" Lizzie asked, pointing to the word under a name.

"It says Leonard Collins. Photography." Kelly looked at Clara and Lizzie and announced, "We're going to have our pictures taken!"

Lizzie's jaw dropped in surprise. "Does it hurt?"

"Of course not," she answered with surprise. "You've never had your picture taken?"

Lizzie shook her head.

"Well, it's about time you did. You just have to hold really still for a minute. Do you think you can do that, Lizzie?"

"Yeah, I guess so."

"I'm just comin' in with you," Clara stated very suspiciously.

Kelly turned to the older woman. "Clara, we're all going to have our pictures taken. Even you."

Clara shook her head as she eyed the sign once more. "That chile's grandparents don't want no picture of me."

"No, not for them," Kelly said with a reassuring smile. "Your picture will be for me, Daniel, and Lizzie. We'll also get an extra copy for you, too, if you'd like. Lizzie will have hers taken for the Howes and we'll get a copy of that for you, too, and another for me and her father. I'll get mine taken for Daniel and Lizzie, you can have a copy of that one, too, if you'd like. This way, we'll all have copies of each other. See?"

Clara continued shaking her head. "The only thing I see is that this is confusin'."

Kelly laughed. "Come on, we'll have fun. I had Andrew stop here yesterday and make an appointment for us. We're expected." She opened the door.

"Expected . . . well, they may be expectin' you, but I don't think they's expectin' me!"

Kelly tried to hide her laughter, for it was obvious that Clara wasn't thrilled with the idea. She placed her arm around Clara's shoulder and tenderly applied pressure. "Oh, Clara," she whispered, "you look beautiful, don't you know that? This picture will show everyone who sees it the loving soul that you are. Besides," she added with a chuckle, "you're wearing your new hat and shawl. Let's commemorate the occasion. It'll be fun . . . I really think you're going to enjoy this."

Before Clara could respond, a short, balding man came quickly out from behind a dark curtain that was draped across an entryway. "Good afternoon, ladies," he said, briskly rubbing his hands with a dirty towel. "How may I help you?" His voice was so wispy, Kelly nearly had to strain to hear him.

"Good afternoon. I'm Mrs. Gilmore. I have an appointment."

"Oh yes, Mrs. Gilmore," the man said and hurried to a desk, grabbing a small book from it. Rapidly flicking the pages, he seemed to find what he was looking for. "Yes, here it is. You were interested in having several portraits taken today, is that correct?"

"Yes, three in all, but I'd like a couple of copies of each. Can you make copies?"

"I can take as many plates as you'd like, madam. You just tell me how many of each."

"Great," Kelly responded enthusiastically. "What do we do to get started?"

"Allow me to get the necessary supplies from the other room. Please, make yourselves comfortable, and I'll be back momentarily," he said, dashing away.

"Thank you, Mr. Collins," Kelly called to his retreating back. Pausing for a moment, she then asked, "You are Mr. Collins, aren't you?"

The man spun back around and hustled back up to them. "Forgive me, ladies! My apologies for not introducing myself," he said, vigorously shaking each one of their hands.

"Yes, I am Leonard Collins. Welcome to my studio."

Kelly found she liked this busy little man. He might be a bit nervous, but he seemed genuinely kind, and he showed no prejudice toward this trio for age, sex, or color.

After all introductions were made, he hurried back to his task behind the curtain, leaving them alone in the large room.

"It smells funny in here," Lizzie whispered.

"That's normal, sweetie," Kelly said, reassuringly. "It's the chemicals used to develop the film."

Leonard Collins was a middle-aged man of good taste, and Kelly was glad she had chosen him. He understood her immediately when she explained what she wanted, yet seemed surprised when she made her last comment. . . .

"And I know that all portraits seem formal, but I would like to dispense with that today."

"I'm sorry, Mrs. Gilmore, I don't understand what you mean."

Kelly smiled and said, "I want these to be more natural. Instead of stern expressions, I'd like us to be smiling."

"Smiling?"

"Yes. Smiling, even laughing if that happens. I'd like you to capture that, if you can."

Mr. Collins thought for a few moments, then issued a genuine smile himself. "I think it would be delightful. Spontaneous, you say?"

She nodded.

"Capture a spontaneous moment. This, madam, is why I became interested in photography. However, following fashion has been . . . how might I put it . . ."

"Financially rewarding?" Kelly offered.

Mr. Collins looked a bit embarrassed and nodded. "Thank you, Mrs. Gilmore."

"Well, Mr. Collins, if there's anything I'm finding out in my own life lately, it's that there has to be someone to break with what is fashionably accepted. How else would change occur? This should be a wonderful session for us all. You'll be doing something you love, and we will be getting something we desire. And, you'll be getting paid for it!"

Mr. Collins burst out laughing, and Kelly couldn't help

grinning herself at how well she was transacting her business. First the dressmaker and now this. Somehow, she was managing to maneuver in the nineteenth century pretty well.

"Well said, Mrs. Gilmore," Mr. Collins answered eagerly. "Shall we begin?" He waved his hand toward his studio.

Kelly held her arm out to Clara and Lizzie, motioning them forward. "The first picture I'd like is one of the three of us together. That way everyone can get comfortable with the process before we have portraits done."

"Oh, very good," Mr. Collins agreed, moving an ornately carved pedestal to the center of his backdrop. "If all three of you would stand here. Perhaps the child in front . . ."

He arranged them with Kelly and Clara behind the pedestal and Lizzie beside it, in front of Clara. He then walked back to his camera on a wooden tripod and began adjusting lenses.

"Now think of this as a present to each other, all right?" Kelly asked. "This is something we'll always have to remember this time together."

"Well, I don't need no pho-to-graph to remind me of being with you, Miz Kelly. Though it's hard to keep up with you, I'd *never* forget our time together."

"Oh good," Kelly answered with a chuckle, and put her arm around Clara, who was holding back a nervous laugh. She reached down and touched Lizzie's hand that was resting on top of the pedestal. "We have had a good time together, haven't we?"

Lizzie looked up and gave Kelly a beautiful smile. "I knew you were special when I caught you. You have magic."

"Oh, come on, Lizzie . . . I'm not any more special than you are, or Clara is, and you know it. And if there's any magic at all, it's what we can make together. I don't know how to do it alone."

"That's perfect, ladies!" Mr. Collins shot out in excitement, and all three of them jerked toward his voice with frozen expressions.

The man's shoulders slumped as he held a long cord and was about to press his thumb on the shutter-release button. "Now, we've lost it."

The three looked at each other and sighed. "Okay, I have an idea," Kelly noted. "Mr. Collins, on the count of three we all say a word, then you take the picture."

"A word? Like smile?"

"I have a better one. Pajamas."

Clara kept shaking her head and clucking her tongue, yet Kelly could see she was trying very hard not to smile.

"Pajamas!" Lizzie said with a giggle.

"Yes, pajamas," Kelly stated. "That's our word, Mr. Collins."

The man shrugged his shoulders and then smiled, as though throughly enjoying the session. Poised once more with his thumb, over the button ready to capture the moment, he said, "When you are ready, ladies."

"Okay," Kelly said to Clara and Lizzie. "Take a deep breath and when I count to three we all say pajamas. Ready?"

Clara reluctantly nodded and Lizzie bobbed her head, completely enjoying the adventure.

"One . . ." They each took a deep breath.

"Two . . ." They all held it.

"Three . . . !"

"Pajamas!"

The picture was taken on the end of the word, when they were laughing and smiling at their own silliness. "Perfect!" Mr. Collins proclaimed in a puff of sulphur smoke.

Kelly, Clara, and Lizzie were still laughing at themselves when Clara asked, "And *that's* the first picture I ever had taken of me. You was right, Miz Kelly, you do have one wild streak!"

"Aw, Clara, it wasn't that bad, and you know it. You had fun." Kelly pointed to the camera. "We even have proof!"

Clara shook her head, while trying unsuccessfully to look stern. "You be turnin' me into a child again."

"What's wrong with playing? Who said it had to stop?" Kelly countered then realized that when she had been in her own time, she hadn't played either. She spent all her time working, but now she knew the working was to keep her busy, so she wouldn't have to be with her own thoughts. It was Lizzie, this child, who had taught her that it was okay to play again.

"Now, for the portraits," Mr. Collins announced. "Who shall be first?"

"I will," Lizzie volunteered, completely into the project now that all her fears had been allayed.

She was so glad she had thought of this adventure. Maybe it was seeing the picture of Lilly that made her think of it. She wanted to give Daniel a picture of her. It would be her wedding present to him. When it was her turn, Kelly stood next to the pedestal and looked into the lens of the camera. Instead of glass, she imagined Daniel's face in that moment when he looked at her with his foot in a bucket of paint and made the decision to play instead of getting angry. That was when she had completely fallen in love with the man . . . this same man who could hold her so gently in his arms through the night and then pull her behind a wall to steal a passionate kiss. Daniel Gilmore, who had captured her mind, her heart . . . and very soon, she hoped, her body.

A month of prolonging her years of chastity!

It was so ludicrous that Kelly couldn't hold back a chuckle.

Leonard Collins captured the moment and called out that it was perfect.

Walking toward her friends, Kelly sighed and thought no matter how the picture turned out, she would give it to Daniel and hope he could see the love in her eyes. Bringing herself back into the moment, Kelly patted Clara's back and said, "Now it's your turn."

"Hmm . . ." was all Clara would say as she slowly walked up to the pedestal. She looked very uncomfortable as Mr. Collins arranged her hands and tilted her hat back into place.

"Think pajamas," Lizzie directed in a loud whisper.

Clara barely cracked a smile.

"Think of all of us *wearing* pajamas," Kelly said.

The smile widened a little, but it wasn't enough.

"Think of someone explaining to *me*," Mr. Collins offered, "these pajamas . . . whatever they are!"

Kelly and Lizzie looked at each other and burst into

laughter. That was enough for Clara, and she couldn't hold back her own. Within a brilliant momentary flash, an image of Clara's spirit was captured for posterity.

It had been a good day and, as Kelly was getting ready for bed that night, she was still marveling at how well she had adjusted to the nineteenth century. It was at moments like this when she didn't even miss the hustle and bustle of 2001. Brushing her hair in front of the mirror, she thought back to how rushed and stressed she had been, always trying to fit more into the day. Time, itself, seemed to be speeding up, and it wasn't until now, when she was thrown back to this place that she had no choice but to live each moment as it unfolded in front of her. She couldn't really make plans, for she was never sure where she would be when she woke in the morning. She had been thrown back in time, but could it mean that she could be taken forward again in a flash? That thought, one that she had prayed for not too long ago, now seemed like the last thing she wanted.

She knew then that she couldn't leave Daniel, or Lizzie, or Clara. Somehow, she was tied to this family and it was here she wanted to remain. Incredible! She would miss many things from the year 2001, but this time contained the one thing that made her feel alive. Love. And she was willing to sacrifice anything for it. How freeing it was to know that she loved Daniel for himself, not for any reminders of her past. And she now knew that Daniel had healed his wounds and was ready to begin a new life together. What had begun as a nightmare had turned into a blessing.

Lost in thought, Kelly didn't hear Daniel coming into the room or walking up behind her. "Allow me," he said, holding out his hand for the brush.

Startled for a moment, Kelly smiled and extended it to him. "Thank you."

He sat on the edge of the bed and patted the mattress before him. "Sit down and relax."

Dressed in her negligee, Kelly did as she was asked, very

pleased by the offer. She waited in anticipation and was rewarded as Daniel ran the brush very gently, very slowly, down her hair. Her scalp tingled with pleasure and it was as though she could feel it all the way to the ends of the strands. She sighed with deep contentment. "That feels wonderful," she murmured, closing her eyes as he continued.

"I'm glad," he whispered back. "You have such beautiful hair."

"Thank you," she said, pleased by the compliment.

No more words were spoken as Kelly was enveloped in a sense of peacefulness. Her mind shut down as she allowed herself to be drawn into the pleasure she was receiving. Minutes later, she sighed, "This is heaven. It's been so long . . ."

He brushed her hair to the side and softly, tenderly, kissed the side of her neck. "You are so lovely," he whispered against her skin.

She felt tingles race all over her body and shivered in delight as she shifted slightly and turned to look at him. "I don't know how this happened, but I look at you and feel ever so grateful, Daniel, that we are together right now."

He released his hold on the brush and it fell onto the bed. Cupping her face in both his palms, he leaned forward, and whispered, "I don't know how it happened either, and I'm no longer questioning it. How can I question a miracle?" He kissed her then, running his lips across hers, tenderly nipping her bottom lip. When he heard her moan, he deepened his kiss and she opened up to him, accepting his offer and giving back in return.

She wound her arms around him, cradling his head in her palms, touching, stroking, feeling the silkiness of his hair, inhaling the scent of him, tasting him with her mouth. Within moments, he laid her back upon the bed and she stared up into his eyes, eyes that were inflamed with passion. "Why are we waiting?" she begged.

He was breathing heavily as he continued to study her face. "Because I promised you a courtship. When we join, Kelly, I want us both to want it more than we've ever wanted anything in our lives."

"I'm there; I feel that now!" she blurted out, and laughed at herself.

"No, you don't," he whispered, stroking back her hair from her forehead. With a sexy smile, he added, "Not yet . . ."

"You want to drive me mad with desire?"

"Yes."

Her eyes widened. "Really?"

"Isn't that what happens in a courtship? It's a building up to the union. I am courting you, Mrs. Gilmore . . . in the only way I know to court someone I am already married to. You must admit it is a highly unusual situation."

Chuckling, she agreed. "Yes, it is. But this . . . this waiting seems like we're denying ourselves what's right here in front of us."

He groaned and shook his head. Smiling, he answered, "You are not making this easy."

"I have no intentions of making this easy for you, Daniel Gilmore. In fact, I think I should try even harder to make this . . . this state of celibacy even more difficult."

He laughed and rolled over onto his back, staring up to the ceiling.

With the ease of a cat, Kelly slid herself over him and sat there, looking down at him. She could distinctly feel his arousal beneath her, and situated herself upon him. "Now what do you say, Daniel Gilmore?" she asked with more than a hint of challenge in her voice.

He reached up and grabbed her waist and pulled her to his side. "I think, Mrs. Gilmore, that you are a terrible tease, and I will have to be more careful around you."

Laughing, she snuggled up against him and, lifting her head, slowly whispered into his ear, "Why? Just surrender."

He turned his head and stared into her eyes with such intensity that Kelly held her breath.

"Don't you know I have already surrendered to you? I can't explain it. You have captured me . . . my mind, my heart . . . I can think of little else, no matter how hard I try to distract myself. I love you, Kelly. Don't you know that?"

She slowly let out her breath and felt tears forming at her

eyelids. "I do now, Daniel," she whispered through the thickness in her throat. "Thank you for loving me. Somehow, I feel as though I've loved you forever . . . and . . . I can't explain it either. I just know how I feel. All of this . . . you and I . . . it seems so natural. There's no struggling to make it fit. It just does . . ."

"Yes, my beloved . . . you and I *fit* together well. No struggling. Just love."

"Just love," she repeated, lifting her face to his.

This time the kiss was filled with reverence, as though in declaring their love they had acknowledged a deep commitment to each other, vowing to honor that love and nurture it. It was a moment of awe, and Kelly knew that no words spoken by anyone official could possibly make it more real.

"This is our wedding night, isn't it, Daniel?"

He brushed a tendril of hair behind her ear. "This is the night we have declared our love, Kelly. To me, it is far more important than a wedding night. It has been a long time in coming to this place, where we could say those words to another."

"Yes," she agreed, placing her head upon his shoulder and sighing deeply. "That, too, is a wonder. I never expected *this* . . . this . . ." she struggled for a word to describe it.

"This miracle? For that is how it feels to me." He cradled her within his arm and began stroking her back. "You, my wondrous time traveler, came into my life and turned it upside down, challenging all my beliefs. I finally feel alive again. You have given me this gift of resurrection. I call that a miracle."

She hugged him. "I didn't even fully realize how much I was sleepwalking through my life until I came to this family, to you, Daniel. I don't ever want to leave."

His hold on her tightened. "I do not think the fates would be that cruel, my love. Especially since we are just beginning our life together. We have both suffered loss, Kelly, and know we can survive it. We know what it is like to hold on too tightly to the past. I say we embrace this moment and envision our future together. I am committed to us."

Her heart seemed to open like a lush flower as she listened to his words. Imagine being this blessed to experience love like this again. She clung to him and prayed that he was right. "So am I," she whispered. "So am I. I love you, Daniel. For however long it lasts . . . may it be a lifetime."

Sixteen

Kelly and Lizzie sat together on a sofa in Mrs. Holden's living room. Mrs. Deaveroux and Mrs. Holden were in chairs, politely making inquires into Kelly's background. She tried to be as inventive as possible. So far, she had managed to make up a plausible story of meeting Daniel through family, which was the truth, and their quiet and unexpectedly quick decision to marry . . . all of which worked out wonderfully well, and Kelly hoped she had put their minds to rest. Truth be told, she didn't know how much longer she would be able to take the scrutiny, but she knew this was important to Daniel, so she smiled at Lizzie, who was displaying her very best manners. If she had given birth to the child, she couldn't be more proud of her.

"Please tell me of your garden club, Mrs. Holden," Kelly asked, to change the subject. "The inner courtyard of our home has a lovely one, and I would be most interested in maintaining it."

Mrs. Holden seemed pleased with the question and looked to Mrs. Deaveroux. "As president, perhaps Mrs. Deaveroux might enlighten you."

The older woman straightened in her chair and nodded. "Of course, Mrs. Holden." She looked to Kelly and began speaking . . . "Once a month we hold luncheons, subject to the weather conditions, and we discuss many subjects besides horticulture. We are interested primarily in various charities that benefit the city, such as . . ."

Kelly held the woman's attention and smiled politely, yet her mind drifted to last night in Daniel's arms. There she had found peace. It was as though she had been walking in a desert of aloneness and finally had found an oasis, a place of comfort, where she could rest and be rejuvenated, where her thirst for harmony was fulfilled. There she had found companionship, tenderness, strength, creativity, humor. Grace, integrity, charm, intelligence. It was everything she ever wanted, and even though it was something she had experienced before . . . she had to admit that right now, in this time, the *love* was even more intense.

"Would you be interested in joining us?" Mrs. Deaveroux asked, penetrating her thoughts.

Kelly really had to bring herself back into the moment. Blinking, she straightened her spine and answered, "Yes . . . yes, I would." She had only a vague idea of what she was joining, but somehow knew she would soon find out.

Both women looked pleased, and Kelly smiled. Trying to seem more interested, since she'd zoned out earlier, she said, "And in addition to horticulture and various charities and cultural events, is this group involved with any . . ." she tried to think of a way to phrase it . . . "civic movements?" There, that was perfect and she surprised herself by finding the phrase. Not bad for a time traveler.

"Civic movements?" Mrs. Holden asked, appearing confused.

"Yes, any organizations for women that are interested in issues of . . ." She thought for a moment. ". . . of equality, for example."

Mrs. Deaveroux inhaled sharply. "You can't mean you are interested in the suffrage movement?"

"Why, yes, I am. Very interested," Kelly answered, not wanting to offend them, but there was only so far she was willing to play this game. She also had some integrity. That was another thing she was learning in Daniel's arms. To acknowledge in herself those things she was finding in him. Yes, she had some integrity, and she intended to put it to use. "Why? Is that a problem?" she asked with a smile, hoping not to appear defensive, for she was more curious about their reaction to her question than anything else. "Isn't it permitted to join two clubs?"

Mrs. Holden looked to the president for an answer.

Taking a deep breath, as though needing her patience, Mrs. Deaveroux sat up more formally, and said, "Yes, it's permitted. There is nothing in the bylaws that say one may not join another organization, but Mrs. Gilmore, it is . . . how shall I say this . . . is it a woman's place to be involved in such things? Politics is such a tedious and nasty business."

"It is, isn't it?" Kelly answered, realizing it didn't matter what year, that subject always brought up the same description and the same reaction. "Maybe it's time for a change."

"Change?" Mrs. Holden said, and held her hand to her heart. "We have had enough change in the last thirty years!"

"That's true," Kelly stated, seeing how these women must feel. They were afraid. Why else would they not want the same rights as men? Full freedom? Because you pay a price? She wanted to tell them it was worth it, that women's lives had improved, that they could earn their own living, only stay in a marriage where two partners were committed to its growth and if not, retain custody of their children. Yes, there was a price to pay as men became comfortable with the concept of equality, but it was worth it. Before she knew what she was saying, Kelly blurted out something she had once heard . . . "Is it true that it is lawful for a husband to beat his wife as long as what he beats her with is no bigger than the width of his thumb?"

Both women looked at each other with shocked expressions.

"Truly, I'm merely curious. I had heard that once, and I wondered if it were true. Mrs. Holden, have you ever heard that?"

The minister's wife looked exceptionally uncomfortable.

"I'm sorry," Kelly said when she saw how she was putting her hostess in a poor position. "You don't need to answer. It was just a curiosity of mine."

"Do you think this is a suitable subject for a child?" Mrs. Deaveroux asked, nodding to Lizzie, who seemed very interested in the conversation and the reactions of the adults around her as she munched on her tea cake.

Kelly smiled down at the girl, and said, "I think Elizabeth is coming of an age when she has the right to know about the possibilities in her life." She turned to her hostess. "By the way, Mrs. Holden, Elizabeth's grandparents are coming from England for a visit. I would like to hold a dinner party for them, since this is their first visit to New Orleans."

"How simply wonderful for you, Elizabeth." Mrs. Holden said, giving Kelly a look of gratefulness for changing the subject.

"I would ask a favor," Kelly continued. "If you could recommend a florist . . . either of you."

"Well, Mr. Cameron, down on—"

"Oh, Mrs. Holden, his petals drop before the day is over. She should go to Alexander's on Royal Street for the best flowers," Mrs. Deaveroux declared, with a final nod of her head.

"Mr. Cameron and Alexander's," Kelly repeated. "I shall remember those names."

She then proceeded to ask their advice on everything from table arrangements to the menu, fully aware that these grand old dames had something to offer her. Besides, if she was going to infiltrate their camp, she would really need to fit in. She knew exactly how Lizzie felt. It was asking someone who *knew* freedom, had tasted it, lived it, enjoyed it, to give it up and *pretend* it was only foolishness. Somehow, she would find a group of women who were interested in change. There must be one in the city.

There, in the parlor of a minister's wife, Kelly felt a strange sensation pass through her body. It was a recognition, maybe an instinct, that kicked in and reminded her that there was something she could do here in the past, something that really would make a difference in a lot of lives sometime down the road. She had never been a joiner, or a crusader. Those concepts were uncomfortable for her. That was something she had in common with Mrs. Holden and Mrs. Deaveroux. Now she realized all she needed was the courage not to care what anyone else thought, but to follow what her gut was telling her.

Be of service . . .

She didn't have to become Susan B. Anthony. All she had to do was take advantage of the opportunity to speak her heart when it came to her. Maybe it wasn't just to discover an oasis of love. That was a big part of it . . . but maybe it was also to help bring about change in her own small way? All she knew was that it felt right.

An hour later, after they had finished their tea and cucumber sandwiches, Kelly said good-bye to her hostess.

"Thank you so much, Mrs. Holden, for having us this afternoon. It was a delightful and informative visit."

"You are very welcome, Mrs. Gilmore. I, too, enjoyed the time we spent together."

Kelly nodded to the other guest. "Mrs. Deaveroux . . . it was a pleasure to see you again. And thank you for all your suggestions. I do hope you and Mr. Deaveroux would be free to join our dinner party."

"We would be honored," the stout woman proclaimed, very satisfied to have received the earliest invitation.

"And thank you for all your entertaining wisdom. I'm a bit nervous and appreciate your help."

"Never fear, Mrs. Gilmore . . . it will be splendid." Mrs. Deaveroux stated. "You have a fine home, a decent staff, and I shall send over my girl with the recipe for that entreé we discussed."

"You are very kind," Kelly said, meaning it. She hadn't even thought of giving a big dinner party for the Howes until it came out of her mouth. She did need help!

Without being told, Lizzie performed a perfect curtsy, and said, "Thank you, Mrs. Holden."

"You're very welcome, Elizabeth. My, what a fine young lady you are becoming."

Turning to her left, she duplicated the curtsy to perfection. "Good day, Mrs. Deaveroux."

"Good day to you, Elizabeth. We'll be seeing more of each other, you and I, for your stepmother will soon be hosting a luncheon." She looked up at Kelly. "And that, Mrs. Gilmore, is in the bylaws. Each new member is required to host the next meeting."

Kelly grinned. "It would be my pleasure." She was in!

Mrs. Holden led them out of the sitting room and to the front door. When Lizzie walked out onto the porch, Kelly looked once more to her hostess, and said, "Thank you again. I really did enjoy myself."

Mrs. Holden seemed to clench her jaw momentarily, as if making a decision, before whispering, "I have heard of a group, the National Women's Suffrage, that meets in the small Quaker church. That's all I know."

Startled, Kelly impulsively touched the woman's shoulder. "Thank you. You're very kind."

Mrs. Holden looked embarrassed and shook her head. "I'm probably just a silly woman. Do not say you haven't been warned, Mrs. Gilmore. It is not an easy road you are about to walk."

Kelly understood what the woman was saying to her. "I know," she whispered back. It was an uphill road that would take a lot of energy to climb, but she knew something these women didn't. It was going to happen . . . for their daughters and granddaughters and great-granddaughters. Change was inevitable.

When the door was closed, Kelly turned to Lizzie, who was staring at her.

"What was that about?"

Kelly grinned and held out her hand. "That was about making friends, Lizzie Gilmore. And sometimes they are found in the most unexpected places. Come on, I saw a park on the way here. Let's go find it."

Within ten minutes they had found an empty bench and sat down, watching the people stroll before them. "Oh, isn't that pretty?" Kelly asked. "See that woman's outfit? Look how simple it is and yet how elegant. Except for the hat . . . wow, how does she handle it?"

Lizzie looked to the woman dressed in a gown of black-and-white stripes with an enormous hat stuffed with flowers and plumes. "Looks like she's wearing a flowerpot on her head."

Kelly laughed. "I guess from your view, it does. Anyway, I was just admiring the way she moves. So gracefully."

Lizzie suddenly giggled.

"What?" Kelly asked, grinning before she even heard what the child was thinking.

"I was picturing Mrs. Deaveroux with that hat. She'd look like she was under a toadstool."

Still grinning, Kelly shook her head. "Well, I don't know about that, but you would have to be tall like that woman to be able to carry it off."

"Do you really like them ladies?"

Kelly looked down at the girl and nodded. "Yes, I do. Especially Mrs. Holden."

"I like her better, too. I thought one time Mrs. Deaveroux was mad at you, and then she wasn't. What happened?"

Chuckling, Kelly said, "That's what's called successfully changing the subject. Most people, especially women, don't like talking about politics. I didn't either, until recently."

"What's politics?"

Kelly relaxed against the back of the bench. "Do you remember the night we all did the dishes for Clara?"

Lizzie nodded. "That was when I broke the dish."

"That's right. But that's over," she said, reaching down and gently holding Lizzie's hand. "That night your daddy and I were talking about the suffrage movement. Remember?"

"Daddy said you were one of them suffrages, and I would be one, too, someday."

Laughing at the memory, Kelly nodded. "Yes, he did, didn't he? Well, it was that subject that made the ladies uncomfortable."

Lizzie shook her head. "No it was when you said a husband can beat his wife and something about his thumb."

"Right," Kelly acknowledged. Trust a child's memory to keep it straight. "Obviously, it wasn't the right question."

"Is it true?"

Kelly looked down into Lizzie's eyes and saw an honest question that deserved an honest answer. "Honey, in this time where we find ourselves it isn't against the law for a man to beat his wife. I think you have a right to know the truth."

"Does that mean it's all right?"

"No, Lizzie . . . it is definitely not all right. It's politics, laws that need to be rewritten."

"Then why don't Mrs. Holden and Mrs. Deaveroux like politics, if it will keep them from being beat?"

"Good question, Lizzie," Kelly answered, patting the child's hand. "I think your daddy was right. You are a budding suffragette."

"If you're one, I want to be one, too."

Kelly stuck out her hand. "Deal."

Grinning, Lizzie shook it. "Deal."

They sat back in a companionable silence until Lizzie said, "They didn't want to talk about that in front of me. They thought I was too little."

Kelly nodded. "Yes, they did. I don't. I think now that you're growing up, you should be prepared."

"You mean like that stuff you were telling me that day in the tree."

Smiling, Kelly again nodded. "Yes, like that stuff."

"What's that got to do with suffrage stuff?"

"I think it's all got to do with being female. Look out there," Kelly directed, casting her gaze once more to the passing scenery. "Every single person out there, and all over the world, came through a female."

"Through a female? Like when my momma had me?"

"Yes. Without the special way we are formed, there would be no life. Do you see how wonderful it can be to be a girl, Lizzie?"

Looking out to all the people, Lizzie nodded.

"But we can't do it alone."

"Like the magic you said needs more than one?"

"Exactly. To make the magic of life, we need men."

Lizzie crossed her arms over her chest. "I'm not gonna let any man beat me, even if it is with his thumb!"

Kelly laughed. "Oh, honey . . . I don't think you ever would." Wrapping her arm through Lizzie's, she continued, "Listen, you have every right to know that there are men who get angry, who think the way to solve a problem is with violence. You can make life with them, but it's real hard to make magic happen with them. But there are many men, like your daddy, who aren't like that, and then the magic is easy. You'll know. You'll feel it inside of you whether it will be hard or easy."

"How?" Lizzie asked in a small voice. "Love?" She said the word almost with distaste.

Kelly's smile widened. "Well it doesn't start with love. First there's an attraction, you really, really start to like being around him. Then there's a . . ." She thought of Daniel's word. ". . . a courtship, a time for the two of you to get to know each other, what the other person thinks about things that are important to you both. That is where love grows, and it's there you will trust yourself and see the man for who he is, not who you want him to be."

"Sounds hard," Lizzie muttered.

"Nah, it's easy. The hard part is being honest with yourself, I think."

"Well, how do you make the magic then?"

Kelly released her breath slowly and deliberately. The time had obviously arrived, and she inwardly prayed for some guidance. "You know, now that we're having this discussion about life and how the magic happens . . . there's more you might want to know about the way females and males are designed. Remember when I spoke to you about how your body is now preparing you for when you become a woman?"

They talked for over an hour going from the birds and the bees right up the food chain until they came to humans. Lizzie had plenty of questions and was horrified by most of the answers. Kelly remembered how she had felt when her best friend in sixth grade had told her about the facts of life. She called the girl a liar, never believing that anything so ridiculous and disgusting could be true. She then went home and asked her mother, which necessitated an even more uncomfortable discussion. Well, she never would have seen herself in this position now, as a stepmother, but here she was. Realizing how difficult this information was to integrate, Kelly tried especially hard to be as gentle and truthful as possible.

"I'm never gonna do that," Lizzie pronounced with defiance. "I won't have no babies. Not ever."

Biting the inside of her lip to keep from smiling, Kelly nodded. "I can understand how you feel now, but maybe one day you will feel differently. This isn't something you have to decide for many years, Lizzie."

The girl again crossed her arms over her chest and held them tightly together. "Then I wish my body would just stop growing. I don't want to be a woman!"

"Oh, Lizzie," she said, poking her arm into Lizzie's shoulder. "You sound like Peter Pan, and you know that it was just a story. There's nothing you can do to stop it. You are already starting to become a woman, and it's wonderful to be one. Trust me." And then she thought about being a woman in the nineteenth century. "Besides, we made a deal. We're suffragettes, right?"

Resigned, Lizzie nodded.

"Why, Elizabeth Gilmore, I didn't know you were in town!"

They both looked up to see a woman walking toward them, holding a parasol, and keeping a young boy about twelve years old in tow behind her. The boy was carrying three packages.

"I wish I wasn't," Lizzie answered under her breath, though the boy heard her and brought the packages up higher to hide his grin.

Kelly observed all this and stood up to greet the woman, who seemed to be around her own age.

"And you must be Mrs. Gilmore. Forgive me, but I seem to have the advantage. I'm Mrs. William Tyler." The pretty blond woman actually extended her hand in greeting.

"It's very nice to meet you," she said, gladly shaking the woman's hand. "I'm Kelly."

Mrs. Tyler appeared surprised and then pleased as she said, "And I'm Susan. You must forgive me, but Mrs. Holden has already spoken of you with high regard."

"I just came from Mrs. Holden's home. She was kind enough to have Elizabeth and me to tea. Mrs. Deaveroux was also there."

"Oh, she was?" Susan asked, with a sympathetic grin. "And are you now a member of the garden club?"

Kelly grinned in return. "I think I am."

"I am too," Susan said, arching an eyebrow. "I've lived in this city my whole life and still can't manage to escape that garden club."

Chuckling, Kelly immediately decided she liked the woman. "And here I thought it was an honor."

"Oh, it is," Susan quickly agreed. "Heaven forbid you don't make the grade." She shook her head while laughing. "Well, I am happy to have made your acquaintance, Kelly. May I introduce my son, Christopher Tyler?"

The young boy came forward and shifted the packages under one arm. He extended his hand and held Kelly's very briefly while saying, "It is a pleasure to meet you, Mrs. Gilmore."

Kelly noticed that Christopher sneaked a glimpse at Lizzie before he backed up behind his mother again. "Thank you, Christopher. It's a pleasure to meet you, too. Do you know my daughter, Elizabeth?"

"Yes, ma'am . . . from Sunday school," the boy answered, keeping his gaze on his shoes.

Kelly nodded and looked at Lizzie, who was staring down at her hands in her lap. "Elizabeth . . . aren't you going to say hello to Mrs. Tyler and her son?"

Lizzie pushed herself off the bench and did a quick curtsy while muttering, "Good afternoon, Mrs. Tyler and . . ." She paused for a tense moment. ". . . Christopher," she finally added, as though with great reluctance.

Kelly and Susan exchanged glances and grinned even more widely.

"Well, I hope to see you again," Susan said. "It was a pleasure to meet you."

"And you, Susan. Thank you for stopping."

"Please feel free to call upon me, Kelly. I'm sure this adjustment to your new home can be confusing at times. Here's my card." She reached into her drawstring purse and withdrew a calling card.

"It is," Kelly agreed, realizing there was no way for Susan to know how true that statement was. Accepting the card, she said, "I'm afraid I don't have one to give to you yet."

"I know where you are. Our husbands are business acquaintances."

"Oh," Kelly answered, brightening with the thought. "Then I'm sure we will see each other again soon."

The woman and her son left, and Kelly was very pleased with the encounter. She liked Susan immensely. Even though it was a short meeting, Kelly could tell they would become friends. "Wasn't that nice?"

Lizzie shrugged. "We'd better get home."

She put her arm around Lizzie's shoulders and tugged gently. "Come on then, kiddo. You've had quite a day." They started off in the direction of the town house, and Kelly added, "We won't discuss it again until you're ready, but I want you to know that you can always ask me any question, and I promise I'll tell you the truth. All right?"

Lizzie didn't say anything for a few moments, then she nodded. "All right."

"This is something that is private, between us," Kelly added, picturing Lizzie walking into Sunday school and blurting out what she'd just learned. "It wouldn't be appropriate for you to speak with anyone else about this right now."

"I don't even want to think about it," Lizzie exclaimed. "I'm not gonna talk to anyone." The girl actually shuddered.

"Good. By the way, you handled that encounter with Christopher and his mother pretty well. I like her."

"You're making new friends real fast."

Something in Lizzie's voice made Kelly look down at

her. She stopped walking and waited until Lizzie glanced back. "It doesn't matter to me how many people I meet, you will always be the first friend I made here. And my best."

Smiling shyly, Lizzie nodded and started walking again.

Joining her, Kelly looked out to the park, and asked, "So what do you think about these trees? Any of them look good enough for climbing?"

Lizzie looked out to the trees and shrugged her shoulders. "What's it matter? You can't climb them."

"Hey, who knows? Once we get our pajamas, we could do all sorts of things. Just you watch."

Lizzie reluctantly giggled. "Pajamas . . . what a silly name!"

Seventeen

"The day after tomorrow?" Kelly felt her stomach muscles tighten with fear.

Holding the telegram in his hand, Daniel nodded. "Yes. Before noon on Thursday." He reached out and touched her arm. "My love, you knew the Howes were arriving soon."

"I . . . I know," Kelly answered, running her hand over her stomach as she looked around his office. "I guess I'm just nervous."

He pulled her into his arms and stroked her back. "Now, now . . . you have nothing to be nervous about. I'm very proud to present you as my wife. And Elizabeth has made great progress. Even Mrs. Holden said her behavior at Sunday school was remarkable. Everything will go well."

She hugged him back and nodded. "I have to believe that. Oh, why did I announce I would have a big dinner party for them? Now, I'm obligated to do it!"

Daniel chuckled. "I'm sure you will be a splendid hostess. I will help in any way I can. Have you sent out the invitations yet?"

"No, I'm still writing them. Now, I'd better hurry. Ten guests! What was I ever thinking?"

Still chuckling, Daniel pulled back and looked into her eyes. "Forgive me, but I haven't seen you this rattled since you first saw New Orleans from the packet. Why are you worried? You have your menu. We will have additional staff. All you have to do is be your ever-charming self."

"Well, my ever-charming self has to watch her mouth around people. I told you about Mrs. Deaveroux's reaction when I asked about the suffrage movement. What if I offend the Howes?"

"You will do no such thing," he answered, kissing the tip of her nose. "So I have a . . . a progressive wife. I'm happy you aren't a shrinking violet, Kelly. I enjoy your vibrancy."

She smiled into his eyes. "You're such a charmer, Daniel Gilmore. You know exactly how to calm me down. You're right. I can only do my best, and if it isn't good enough, then—"

"Then the fault will be in the eyes of the beholder," he interrupted, "not with you, my dear. Worry not. We shall make a fine presentation, and perhaps even enjoy ourselves."

"How can you be so confident?"

He grinned. "Because everyone who meets you falls under your spell."

Chuckling, she lifted her face and lightly kissed his chin. "Oh, so I have you under a spell, huh?"

He nodded. "I have succumbed to your magic, Mrs. Gilmore." He paused. "Not that I fought it very hard."

Laughing, Kelly wrapped her arms around him and rested her head against his chest. "Neither did I, my love. There wasn't much to fight, for it happened so naturally. Sometimes I wonder if . . ."

"If . . . ?"

She swallowed deeply. "Well, sometimes I wonder if all this wasn't orchestrated."

"By whom?"

She shrugged. "I don't know. Maybe by Lilly and Michael. That sounds ridiculous, doesn't it?"

Again, he stroked her back, and Kelly could hear the steady beat of his heart against her cheek. She loved being held in his arms, feeling his warmth, his strength.

"To someone not in our position, I would say it might be considered ridiculous. But you and I, Kelly . . . we are in an unusual position. Who knows what is behind it all? Something wondrous has happened to us. How many time travelers do you think there are?" He squeezed her with affection.

She pulled back and looked into his eyes. "I don't know. I never thought of it before. This must have happened to more than just me. What if there are others?"

"I was trying to make you smile, not to set your mind off wondering about other time travelers. I don't know the answer to that question. A month ago I would have laughed at it, and now I find an incredible woman who has traveled through time to be right here in my arms, and I'm not about to question it." He looked deeply into her eyes. "I am too grateful for the gift to examine the way I received it."

"I love you, Daniel," she whispered, touching his cheek. "Sometimes, I can't believe it's all true."

"Perhaps this will help," he whispered back and lowered his lips to hers. It began tenderly, yet quickly built in passion. She moaned when his hand slid around her waist and traveled up to capture her breast. Threads of pleasure raced through her body, and she vowed enough was enough.

When they broke apart and were breathing heavily while staring at each other, Kelly murmured, "How would you like to have a private dinner tonight in our room?"

"The two of us? Alone?" he asked with a sexy grin.

She nodded and smiled back. "All alone. I'll ask Andrew to arrange a small table and chairs. Lizzie can eat with Clara in Clara's room. We'll have a very relaxed informal evening."

"Considering the excitement to come, I think it sounds like a splendid idea. You do remember I have a business meeting with William Tyler at four this afternoon, don't you? It would be a late dinner, I'm afraid."

"I'll wait for you," she whispered, as details of a plan came into her head. "Always, Daniel."

He groaned and pulled her back into his arms, grinding his mouth against hers until she was the one to push at his chest, breathless and dizzy with excitement.

"If you keep that up, sir, you will have to cancel your meeting," she stated, patting her upswept hair back into place. "And you call *me* a terrible tease!"

Laughing, Daniel kissed her forehead and released her. Turning back to his drafting table, he began rolling up blueprints. "Far be it from me, madam, to have caused you any discomfort."

Kelly's jaw dropped right before she burst out laughing. "You will pay for that remark, Daniel Gilmore!"

He glanced at her and winked. "I am counting on that, Mrs. Gilmore."

She spent the remainder of the afternoon writing out her invitations, speaking with the florist, going over the seating arrangements with Andrew and the menu with Mary. Checking the guest bedroom, she made sure everything was in readiness to accommodate the Howes. Tomorrow morning, fresh flowers would be delivered. She had tea with Clara, who was so tired that she simply stayed in her room and knitted. The fact that pampering wasn't restoring Clara's vigor nagged at Kelly's brain, but she put it down to the unusual circumstances. Clara probably just preferred the country and found the city to be too hectic and exhausting.

Lizzie was playing in the courtyard with a small kitten she had heard mewing outside the back gate. And . . . she had a friend. At Sunday school, Lizzie met young Catherine Halewood, who had just moved to New Orleans with her family. The newcomer and Lizzie had bonded quickly and Kelly watched with great satisfaction as the two girls giggled over the kitten's antics with a ball of Clara's yarn.

"She's going to be okay," Kelly whispered to herself, feeling tears of gratitude coming into her eyes. Leaning against the French door and observing the girls at play, she wanted to kiss young Catherine for befriending Lizzie. It was an important beginning.

Kelly turned from the courtyard and headed for the

kitchen. There she instructed Andrew in her plans for the evening.

"Miss Elizabeth will take her dinner with Miss Clara. I've already spoken to Miss Clara about this and she will see to Elizabeth's bath and tuck her in for the night."

"Yes, ma'am. I put all the white candles in your bedroom, as you instructed, and the table and chairs from the garden are already set in front of your terrace. Will there be anything else?"

Kelly smiled. "Just a wonderful dinner, Andrew. Something cool, like fried chicken and a salad, since I'm not sure exactly what time it will be eaten. Make sure Mr. Gilmore's brandy and cigars are there."

"Yes, ma'am. I will do that now."

"Then, that's it. Don't bother to collect the dirty dishes until tomorrow morning. If we're not already awake, ask Delia to bring coffee no later than eight o'clock."

"You will not be disturbed, Mrs. Gilmore, until the morning."

"Thank you, Andrew. I would like you to know how much I appreciate your attention to details, and next week there will be a bonus for you and Mary and Delia. I realize how much I am depending on all of you to pull off this large dinner party."

Andrew seemed surprised, yet pleased. "Thank you, madam."

"You are most welcome," Kelly said, and turned to leave. So much for being the lady of the house. Now she had her own plans to see to, for she had every intention of making sure that payback was indeed sweet tonight.

It was as though she were preparing for her wedding night. She bathed in scented water and rubbed almond oil onto her skin . . . every inch of skin that she could reach. She brushed her hair a hundred strokes and was pleased to feel it spring into curls that fell to her shoulders. Sitting on the edge of the mattress, Kelly opened the box she had been saving since yesterday afternoon. Inside, nestled in tissue paper, was the loveliest set of lounging pajamas that she had ever owned. Simple and yet elegant, long-sleeved, with a V neck and tiny pearl buttons, the top was perfect. Kelly tried on the pants, and the cream silk felt so soft against her skin. She tied the drawstring loosely, allowing the waist to ride her hips. Picking up the top, she slid her arms into it as she walked to the mirror. Mrs. Robelier had done a wonderful job, for when she buttoned the top three buttons, a sufficient amount of cleavage was exposed and when she walked . . . why, her belly button showed. Kelly grinned.

Three more weeks of celibacy, huh?

Well, if tonight Daniel Gilmore didn't throw that idea out the terrace window, then she was going to give up. As far as she was concerned, this courtship had gone on long enough. Kelly looked around the room. Everything was perfect. The iron table from the courtyard was covered in a long white tablecloth. Flowers, silver, crystal, and the best china graced the top. Fourteen white candles were scattered around the room. Kelly had counted them when she'd lit them. The lighting was soft and romantic.

Now all she needed was her man.

She strolled over to the small table by the window and pictured Daniel when he would walk into the room. Should she be draped over the bed, legs free to sprawl, smoking one of his cigars?

Too obvious.

She wanted to seduce the man, not scare him.

Suddenly she realized how long it had been since she'd been intimate with another, and all her self-confidence plummeted. She was thirty-six years old and she hadn't had sex since . . . since the morning she became a widow. Thirteen years. It was like riding a bike, right?

She had no more time to ponder the thought as the door was opened. Spinning around, she simply faced him as he just stood at the doorway, staring at her.

"Kelly . . ."

He called her name in a whisper of wonder, and she found herself smiling. "Welcome home, Daniel." She waved her hand toward the table. "Are you hungry?"

She watched as his gaze lowered to take in the way her top fluttered open to reveal her skin.

"Absolutely famished," he stated in a hoarse voice, as he closed the door behind him.

"Oh, good," she said, walking up to him and holding out her arms. "Let me take your jacket."

"What are you wearing?" His eyes widened even more as she moved closer to him.

"Lounging pajamas. I had them made. Don't you like them?" she asked, coming up behind him and assisting him in removing his jacket.

He slipped his arms out of the sleeves and turned his head to her, again sweeping her with his gaze. "Madam, you leave me breathless."

All her self-confidence immediately returned when she saw Daniel's expression. He looked like someone had just hit him in the head with a baseball bat. "Why, Daniel, my in-tention is not to cause you any *discomfort.*"

He stared at her for just a moment as if he remembered his own words earlier in the office. A light seemed to come back into his eyes, and he grinned. "And this," he asked, nodding to her and sweeping his hand toward the room, "and this is the retribution I must suffer for a simple re-mark?"

"Ah-ha," Kelly whispered, giving him a sexy grin as she took his coat and left him at the door. She opened his wardrobe and hung up the jacket. Slowly closing the heavy wooden door, she leaned against it and watched as he crossed the space between them. "Would you like to eat? Or would you care to bathe? I've prepared a bath for you. The temperature should be just right by now."

Shaking his head, he chuckled as he reached for her. "You are a temptress, madam!"

She allowed him to take her into his arms, yet held her head back to stare into his sexy blue eyes. "I'm just making this courtship interesting, Daniel." She ducked out from his hold just as he was sliding his hands down her back, and walked toward the bed. Wrapping her arm around the carved wooden post, she examined the fine work and murmured,

"It's entirely up to you, but it would be a shame to waste the warm water. Your robe is there."

"You are aware, madam, that every time you move your arms, you are exposing yourself?" He took a deep breath and unbuttoned his collar.

"I am?" Kelly asked in feigned surprise and looked down to herself. "But I'm so modestly dressed. My legs and arms are completely covered." And she lifted her arms to show him, completely aware that he could now view from under her breasts to her hips.

He groaned and headed for the bathroom. "I hope that bathwater is now cold."

Laughing, Kelly said, "Take your time. Relax. I'll be right here . . . *waiting,* Daniel."

He glanced over his shoulder and, grinning, muttered, "You don't play fair. I should douse you with cold water!"

She giggled. "But I've already bathed. I've even used scented almond oil all over me. Would you care to smell it? It's wonderful." And she raised her arm to him, revealing more of herself.

He slumped against the doorjamb. "Have mercy, Mrs. Gilmore."

"Take your bath, Mr. Gilmore. The evening is just beginning . . ."

Shaking his head, Daniel almost fell into the bathroom and, as he closed the door behind him, Kelly wanted to rub her hands together with glee. It was working! When she heard him enter the water, she waited a few minutes . . . walking to the narrow terrace and looking up to the moon, just making its way from behind a cloud. She stood there, allowing the air to softly caress her skin, and deeply inhaled the fragrance from the courtyard garden below.

This is what it's like to feel like a woman, she thought, staring at the moon . . . remembering this power from when she was young. How strange that time hadn't diminished it. She had simply shut it off for thirteen years. If anything, it was stronger now, having been dormant for so long. Now the sensation was back, in full force. Once more she felt like a sexual creature and realized what a gift it was. In a flash of insight she saw how sexuality was the basis for life itself, and from it everything was defined. It was the most powerful creative force on the planet, and women held that power.

Edward Bellamy was right. Women could change the world by changing how they used their power, and not giving it away to men who weren't *their* equals. Grateful for the man in the bathroom, a man who respected her interests and wasn't intimidated by change, Kelly turned around and walked back into the room. She poured two glasses of brandy and placed them on a silver tray. She then opened the cigar box and brought out a thin cheroot. Placing a box of matches and a crystal ashtray on the tray, she lifted it and headed for the bathroom.

Knocking lightly on the door, she waited for Daniel to answer.

"I'm almost finished," he called out.

She opened the door and slowly walked in. "I told you to relax, my love," she whispered, noticing that he sat up straighter and looked a bit shocked by her entrance. "Here. I've brought you a brandy and a cigar."

"Such service," he mumbled, running his hands through his wet hair. "I am impressed."

"I think I'm getting the hang of Southern hospitality." Kelly smiled politely and placed the tray on the floor. Sitting down crossed-legged, she handed him the crystal glass. "Your brandy, sir."

"Thank you," he whispered, accepting it.

Kelly smiled and thought how handsome he was in the candlelight. She was glad she had placed two candles in the small room. Reaching down, she withdrew a match and struck it against the side of the box. Picking up the cheroot, she held it to her mouth.

Daniel started chuckling as she puffed to get it started.

"Your cigar, sir," she said, handing it over. She tried hard not to make a face and reached for her glass of brandy to take the taste from her mouth.

"To courtship," Daniel said, lifting his glass.

Kelly raised her glass and, looking deeply into his blue eyes, whispered, "To ending courtship."

His grin widened. "I do believe, madam, I am going to enjoy the rest of my life with you." He touched his glass with hers.

Swallowing the liquor, Kelly placed her glass back on the tray and pushed her sleeves up to her elbows. She stood up and sat on the back edge of the tub. Holding her hand out over Daniel's shoulder, she said, "The sponge, please."

"I thought you said you had already bathed."

From the sound of his voice, Kelly could tell that Daniel wasn't sure of anything she might do next. Stifling another giggle, she answered, "I have. I'm simply going to wash your back. Now, relax, my love . . . drink your brandy. Smoke your cigar. And allow me to bathe you."

"You are making this very difficult, Kelly," he whispered in a husky voice, as he handed her the sponge and then the soap.

Bending down, she kissed him behind his ear and whispered back, "Why, Daniel, I have every intention of making this as difficult as possible."

He laughed and shook his head.

She began washing the strong muscles in his back, admiring the shape of his body. This man she had married was exceptionally well built. Another bennie! She peeked over his shoulder, seeing his long legs, and a surge of yearning began low in her belly, and she dropped the sponge and used her hands. She simply *had* to feel the texture of his skin. Her soapy hands caressed his shoulders, his neck, and he moaned with pleasure and dropped his head toward his chest.

"You're spoiling me."

"You deserve it," she whispered, massaging his tight muscles.

He moaned again.

Smiling, Kelly continued to slide her hands over this man who was now her husband. She might have married him in haste, yet no decision in her life felt as right. Her fingers memorized each muscle, every contour, and she had to remind herself to go slowly, for she wanted to explore the rest of him. Daniel, however, was a nineteenth-century man, and

she was sure she had shocked him already with her bold-
ness.

"Are all women from your time like you?" he asked, as
though picking up on her thoughts.

"I don't know about all women," she answered, running
her hands over his shoulders and down the front of his chest.
"I only know about me . . . how I feel about you."

He made a guttural sound of pleasure as he puffed on his
cigar. "What have I ever done in my life to deserve you?"

She grinned. "I could ask the same question," she whispered, picking up the sponge and rinsing him off. She allowed the water to trickle slowly over his neck, his
shoulders . . . over and over, long after all traces of soap had
dissipated. Leaning closer to his ear, she whispered, "Are
you relaxed, Daniel?"

"Oh, yessssssssss," he answered, dragging out the word in
appreciation.

"Good," she replied, standing up and dropping the
sponge into the bathwater right in front of him.

He appeared startled as he opened his eyes and looked up
at her.

She took his empty glass and handed him the ashtray.
"Our supper is waiting." Grinning, she jerked her head toward the bedroom. "Don't look so startled, my love. I would
just hate to cause any discomfort. I'll meet you on the other
side." She picked up the tray and closed the door behind her.

Kelly was seated at the table, with her legs crossed, waiting for his appearance. The front of her silk top was wet and
clung to her breasts, yet she merely leaned one arm over the
back of the chair and stared at the bathroom door. The next
move was his . . .

The door opened slowly and he emerged, wrapped in a
brown robe with darker brown-velvet lapels. His face looked
serious as he closed the distance between them. He didn't
stop staring into her eyes as he came up to her and, without
a word, lifted her right out of the chair.

"Daniel!" she protested. "Our supper!"

"I am starved for something beyond food," he gritted out
between clenched teeth, while slowly walking over to the bed.

"What about the courtship?" she asked, clinging to him as water from his damp hair sprinkled onto her sleeves. It had been more years than she could remember since she had been carried by a man, and never had she been scooped right out of a chair!

"Can you not tell, madam, it has ended?" He dropped her onto the bed, then knelt between her legs. "I surrender. The white flag is flying. No man alive could resist you as long as I have!"

Kelly burst into nervous giggles. As she opened her arms to him, her voice suddenly became more serious. "Come, Danny Gilmore . . . let us make magic together."

It was as though words were no longer necessary as Daniel slowly untied the bow at her hips. Kelly sucked in her breath between her teeth as his hand began to lightly caress her skin. When he reached down and kissed her belly button, and then slid up her body, Kelly could no longer contain the moan of pleasure.

He stared into her eyes for just a moment, reaching inside of her and bringing forth even more intensity, before capturing her mouth in a passionate kiss. They tasted each other, quickly, voraciously, building even more intensity between them as hands became instruments of pleasure, stroking, kneading, almost pleading to shed the barrier of clothing that separated them.

She slid her hands between them and pulled his robe apart. He deftly unbuttoned her top and cast the material aside. Daniel drew in a quick breath.

"You are so beautiful," he murmured, taking in her nakedness and lowering his head to her breast.

Kelly ground her head back into the pillow and sucked in her breath as his lips kissed her lightly, then more urgently. "Daniel . . ." she whispered, arching her back. She pulled him up to her and wrapped her arms under his robe to cling to his shoulders, running her hands over his damp skin, his lower back, the firm roundness of his bottom. Her legs became tangled with his, and she pulled him closer. "I want you more than I've ever wanted anything in my life."

He was breathing heavily, staring once more into her eyes, a look of wonder upon his face. "That's all I want, Kelly. Let us make this magic . . . together."

He knelt between her legs and pulled off his robe. When he threw it to the floor, Kelly gasped at the naked power of the man before her. Taking control now, he slipped her pants down her legs and flung them behind him. Once more sliding up her body, he moaned with pleasure as their skin met without any barriers.

"Daniel," she whispered his name in awe, feeling delicious rivers of fire racing through her. She wrapped her legs once more around him, pulling him in closer and gasped when she felt the heat of him throbbing against her. "I don't want to wait any longer."

"And I can't wait any longer, my love," he whispered back, arching his back, thrusting his hips, and parting the soft folds of her flesh. "Heaven knows I've tried . . ."

She gasped at the searing contact as she took him within her, and Daniel closed his eyes briefly, as though in wonder. When again he looked at her, his breathing became heavier, and he clasped her hand in his and began a slow, hypnotic movement.

Kelly quickly matched his rhythm, and, together, they began the dance of ancient magic, using the fire of their passion, the moisture of their bodies, and the scented air they inhaled to perform the most sacred ritual on Earth. It was as though they had done this before, knowing the ache within each breast that yearned to be eased, the desire within each body that fit together so well, building to a feverish pitch, craving release. Together they conjured anticipation, wonder, magic . . .

He slowly led her onward to heights she had never before dreamed existed, and she gladly followed, marveling at how her body responded, crying out her need as astonishing waves of rapture started to build and cluster within her. It was as though everything in the world ceased to exist, save for that moment, when the love within felt like it exceeded her capacity to contain it any longer.

"Daniel . . ." She breathed his name, calling out to him to come with her as their ritual became frenzied and she surrendered . . . over and over . . . in a brilliant flash of primal magical joy. The sensation saturated her body like stardust cascading over her until every fraction of her seemed to sparkle with a white-hot light. Rapture spread over her body like warm honey as Daniel clasped her tighter, burying his face into her shoulder and moaning against her skin when his body went rigid in release.

"My beloved . . . my love . . . Kelly . . . I . . . adore you . . ."

She clung to him, wrapping her arms around his shoulders, pulling him in closer, as frizzles of astounding aftershocks continued to contract within her while accepting his gift. It was a glorious and profound merging, combining their power, wedding them in union. Slowly, she was transported to a place of exquisite peace as she kissed his damp temple and stroked her hands down his moist back. She opened her eyes and stared at the ceiling and felt tears of gratitude gather. She felt whole again. Safe, secure, loved. It was like she'd come home.

"Thank you, Daniel," she whispered against his hair.

He slowly raised his head and looked into her eyes. "I will always love you, Kelly," he whispered with near reverence. "I owe you my life. You brought me back."

She smiled with the sweetness that filled her heart. "We made some powerful magic together, didn't we? We're both alive again."

He sighed and closed his eyes before muttering, "God help me, but I can't get enough of you. I want you again."

She did a mental scan of her body and his, and her grin widened. "I can tell," she murmured, running her heel over the back of his thigh and squirming under him. "Now aren't you lucky I have all those years to make up for?"

He chuckled and captured her mouth in a breathtaking kiss. "Yes, my love," he breathed beyond her lips. "I am the luckiest man on the face of this planet. And I never asked you properly . . . Kelly Brennan Gilmore . . . will you honor me and be my wife for the rest of your life?"

She swallowed down the lump in her throat and nodded. "Yes, Daniel Beauregard Gilmore, I will. Gladly, for the rest of my life."

And the magic continued to build. . . .

Eighteen

"Y**ou is gonna wear a groove in them tiles, Miz Kelly, if'n you don't stop that worryin' and pacin'."

"But Daniel is going to tell them about me on the ride here from the dock. Why did Lizzie have to go with him? What if they're really upset? I mean, they're coming here to meet their granddaughter. The marriage of their daughter's widowed spouse is not something they are expecting!"

"Now what's that worry gettin' you? It makin' you feel any better?"

"No, but—"

"And you think it's doin' any good for them peoples coming all the way from England?"

Kelly stopped and looked to Clara. The sun was shining over the woman's thin shoulder onto the knitting in her hands. "I can't help it," Kelly declared, resting her fists on her hips. "They'll be arriving any minute."

"You can help it," Clara pronounced firmly, then gentled her voice. "You'll do just fine. Why, look at you . . . all dressed up in that fine gown. You look beautiful. You ain't got nothing to worry about at all. They is gonna be mighty impressed."

Kelly lowered her gaze to her gown of pale yellow shot-silk taffeta. It was lovely. Mrs. Robilier had done a wonderful job, accenting the dress with fine white-lace trimming on the round neck and the fitted sleeves. She was learning fairly well to maneuver the muslin petticoats underneath, and she actually liked wearing her hair up.

She felt . . . very feminine and, suddenly, she was filled with a surge of the most pleasant frizzle of electricity. Hadn't last night taught her anything? She had felt power last night. Not *over* anything, but being herself . . . a woman.

She found that for the first time in an awfully long time, she enjoyed being in her own skin. She wasn't concerned with doing it all by herself, pleasing everyone, playing some game that she had tired of long ago. That's what being around Lizzie had taught her. It was the interaction of a child growing into a woman that allowed her to see herself, and the choices she had made. She had recognized that she had lost something, never saying *no* to anyone and trying constantly to please. She had forgotten how to play, how to *enjoy* life. She had given up on her own dreams, not believing that she was powerful enough to bring them back.

Playing again had taught her how to really feel like a woman!

Why, she'd just gotten *way* too serious!

She burst out laughing.

Grinning, Clara peeked up over her new glasses, and said, "What is it that's makin' you laugh, chile?"

Kelly suddenly stooped down. Placing her hands on Clara's knees, she looked into the woman's dark warm eyes, and said with wonder, "That's just it, Clara . . . I had forgotten I was a child. That it was okay to have dreams come true! Do you remember what it was like?"

Clara's smile lessened only slightly. "Remember what, Miz Kelly?"

She rose and sat on the edge of the opposite chair. There was over a hundred years separating them, yet Clara was one of the wisest women she had ever met in any time, any place.

The sun was shining on her skin, warming her, and Kelly took a deep breath to steady herself and collect her thoughts. "I don't know how else to describe it, except to tell how it felt to me."

Clara nodded. "Sounds sensible. Go ahead, chile, speak your truth."

Yes, Kelly thought. Telling how it felt was her only truth if she really wanted to communicate with Clara. How else could she relate this to a woman who had been a slave?

"Okay," she began, "did you ever feel like this?" Kelly thought back . . . "It was a beautiful Saturday in early summer. All your work was finished. You had fulfilled all your responsibilities, what everyone else was trying to teach you, and you flung open the back door and thrust yourself into the day? It was time to *play*, to just allow the day to unfold around you? To have an adventure . . . and it turned out to be magical in some way just to be in your own skin?" She stopped speaking for a moment, then asked, "Did you ever have a day like that?"

Clara put her knitting in her lap and took a deep breath, as though going in her head to some memory. She looked up to the tree at the back corner of the courtyard where Lizzie's kitten was playing, and sighed deeply. Nodding, she said, "I have. Once when I was a little girl, no bigger than a young saplin'. I had such a day. I tasted magic. And then the day Mr. Gilmore done paid me for the first time, cause I was a free woman and I had reaped that payment. I went out and bought myself a new shawl and sat right back over that fence, by that very tree, and looked up to the stars and laughed at the moon. I was comfortable to be in my skin that day, too."

Kelly smiled, picturing a younger Clara, huddling by the tree in her new shawl and looking up to the moon. Yes . . . she could see it and knew Clara would understand. "Didn't you feel, I don't know . . . in touch with everything?"

The older woman sighed and slowly smiled. "Yes . . . good memories."

"Well that's how I feel now, Clara. Ever since I came back here, to all of you . . . I guess I've learned how to play again, to *be* me. I never really lost what Lizzie has. I just tried to make myself believe that I couldn't get it back because I was a *grown-up*. I forgot what real freedom tastes like."

"That's it, chile. Freedom . . . precious freedom."

"Freedom," Kelly repeated, tasting the word on her tongue. "Wow . . . I traveled back in time to find freedom?" She shook her head. "So why come to this time when women are denied it?"

Clara shrugged, again picking up her knitting and examining the stitches. "I don't know, maybe to encourage them to seek it? You know, I do have to thank you again for these spectacles, Miz Kelly. I didn't even know how bad my eyes were, until you told me about these, but I sure likes bein' able to see now."

Kelly blinked, trying to digest all of Clara's words. Why was the first thing she thought of when Clara answered . . . the suffrage movement? She shook her head and tried to focus on the knitting Clara was holding up for her to see. "Yes . . . it's lovely," she said, noticing that Clara was making a shawl of soft wool, dyed slate blue. "And I'm glad you can see now."

"Looks to me like you can see some things now too, Miz Kelly."

She stared at the old woman and grinned. "You know, you're one wise grande dame, Clara."

"Grande dame," Clara said the words with a chuckle. "Whatever is that?"

Kelly laughed. "You," she said, pointing with her finger. "It means the great woman, the wisewoman, the matriarchal figure in a family, and you're certainly that."

"Now, ain't that sweet of you to say. A great woman . . . go on with yourself." Clara shook her head good-naturedly. "I'm just an old woman who's seen too much of life, I think, but I do agree with you about dreams. They is powerful, and they can come true, chile. Mine did, when you showed up. I'd been prayin' for help."

Chuckling, Kelly nodded. "Funny how it all works out in the end, isn't it?"

"Makes a body wonder why they would worry at all, don't it?"

Grinning at her dear friend, Kelly said, "Oh, you're good Clara. See? That's why you're a grande dame, and I'm still learning." Sighing, Kelly sat up straighter and lifted her chin. "I shall not worry," she stated, like she was repeating a new commandment in Sunday school.

"Good," Clara pronounced with a strong nod. "And you is a woman, Miz Kelly, one who remembers the magic of freedom. Don't you go denyin' that, either. To some that might be childish, but you knows it's true . . . 'cause you've lived it. You knows how to play the game now."

"The game?"

"Of life, Miz Kelly. Ain't that what we been talkin' about, and ain't that what you been teachin' Miz Lizzie?"

"I guess it is," Kelly murmured. Suddenly, she really felt like a mother. She had so much she wanted to teach Lizzie, and somehow she had to be careful in her responsibility. She wanted to laugh at the incredible situation she found herself in . . . captured by a lonely little girl, allowing love to fill her heart again, and now . . . to find herself a mother.

"Yup, you is right," Clara declared. "Life sure can be funny sometimes in the way it all works out."

"No kidding!" Kelly said with a laugh. "I have so much to learn!"

"You is learnin' just fine, Miz Kelly. You is simply re-memberin' who you are."

"Yes, remembering . . . putting it all back together again," Kelly murmured. "I guess I just stopping believing in myself. I listened to others and started to believe what they said, and before I realized it, the part of me that knew about magic got so far away I thought it disappeared. Why did I—"

She stopped speaking when she heard Daniel's voice as it carried out to the garden. Startled, she glanced to the French doors and realized that at any moment the Howes were going to walk through them. "They're here!"

"So they is," Clara said in her calm voice.

Kelly shot to her feet and smoothed down the material of

her gown. She touched her hair, making sure the ribbon holding it back off her face was securely in place. "Do I look all right?"

"I done told you, you did."

"Right . . . right . . . that's right. What should I do? Walk in to them, or wait until Daniel brings them out here?"

Clara didn't answer and Kelly looked down.

The older woman dropped her knitting to her lap and folded her hands over it. "Now, why is you goin' and makin' this more difficult for yourself by all that worry, chile? Believe in your power," she added, reaching up to remove her glasses.

"You're right," Kelly agreed, watching as Clara rose and pushed herself upright.

"Um, um, um, sittin' on that there metal chair don't help my hip none. I'll be goin' up to that soft chair in my room."

"You're leaving me?" Kelly demanded while Clara gathered her yarn.

"Best place for me is to be in my room and—"

Daniel's voice interrupted anything else Clara might say. "My dear, our guests have arrived," he announced.

Kelly looked to her left and saw her handsome husband behind an older woman who was holding Lizzie's hand as the group walked through the opened French doors. An older man with a shock of white hair stood beside Daniel, looking very formal in a dark suit with a gray brocaded vest. She noticed the sun glint off the gold chain of his pocket watch.

With a brisk stride, Kelly closed the distance between them. She noted Mrs. Howe's polite smile when their gaze met and Kelly was grateful that there was that simple invitation for friendship. "How do you do, Mr. and Mrs. Howe," she said as sincerely as possible. "Welcome to our home and New Orleans." There was a moment when the Howes just continued to stare at her with surprise and Kelly knew she had to do something.

She held out her hand in a simple gesture and Mr. Howe stepped forward to take it.

Bowing, he said, "A pleasure, madam."

Kelly looked to Daniel, who smiled reassuringly. He must have told them, and it went all right. Breathing easier, Kelly asked, "How was your trip?"

Mrs. Howe, dressed in an expensive traveling outfit of deep navy, put her free hand to her chest and sighed. "What an adventure, madam. Ships, trains, and more ships, but all worth it to look into the eyes of my sweet granddaughter." The plump older woman gazed down at Lizzie.

"Well, we are very glad you have arrived safely. You must both be exhausted," Kelly said, waving her hand toward the house. "Would you care for a light luncheon? I can have it brought to your room, if you would prefer."

Mrs. Howe glanced at her husband and made a decision. "I think a rest would be refreshing. And a light repast would be most welcome . . . only on the condition that dear Elizabeth join us."

Kelly looked to Lizzie, who was grinning and nodding. Obviously, she was delighted with her grandparents. "I think that can be arranged."

"I want you to meet Mammy Clara," Lizzie announced, pulling on her grandmother's hand. "Mammy Clara!" she called out.

Clara turned from the table and held her knitting in her arms as she smiled and slowly walked up to the group.

Daniel came forward, and said, "This is Clara, our good friend, and housekeeper when we are in the country." He paused, then added, "Quite frankly, Elizabeth and I owe our lives to this woman."

"How do you do, Clara?" Mrs. Howe asked. "What a lovely piece you are working on. Whatever shall it be?"

"Thank you, ma'am," Clara said, and then looked down to her arms. "It's gonna be a shawl."

"Well, that color is just beautiful," Mrs. Howe pronounced and shot Kelly a quizzical look.

Kelly realized the woman was questioning Clara's position within the household. Inhaling deeply she said, "We have all been looking forward to your visit, Mr. and Mrs. Howe and wish to make you comfortable. May I show you to your rooms?" It was best not to deal with that issue yet.

"That would fine, my dear," Mr. Howe said.

Daniel spoke up. "Andrew should have your luggage settled by now."

"Wait . . . wait," Lizzie exclaimed, breaking with Mrs. Howe and running toward the back of the courtyard. "You have to meet Peter Pan!"

Kelly grinned as she watched Lizzie collar the kitten and cuddle him in her arms while walking back. "Elizabeth has just adopted this kitten," she said to the group and observed the child holding up the soft bundle of fur for her grandparent's inspection.

"I call him Panny."

"How adorable," Mrs. Howe remarked, sticking out a gloved finger and touching the kitten's nose.

"Yes, Elizabeth," Mr. Howe murmured with a smile, "very nice, indeed. Do not forget we have brought you a gift all the way from England."

"Yes, Miss Kelly," Lizzie said, turning her head to smile up at Kelly. "Grandfather Howe made sure it arrived safe, too. Kept it with him on the ship and the train and everywhere."

"I can't wait to see," Kelly said, smiling at Daniel as he came up to her and slipped his arm behind her. "And don't forget you have a present for your grandparents, too."

Running his palm over her back in small circles, Daniel asked, "Shall we go inside?"

Everyone followed Lizzie through the house and up the stairs. Bringing up the rear, Kelly smiled at Daniel, who lowered his head to her and whispered, "It's going better than I had expected."

Kelly let out her breath in relief and squeezed Daniel's hand as she continued to climb the stairs.

She was not going to worry.

"What a lovely room," Mrs. Howe exclaimed, walking into the guest bedroom. Delia was already unpacking their trunks.

To Kelly, it looked like they would be staying for some time. "We're glad you like it," she said, relieved that the room was suitable.

"Where's my gift?" Lizzie asked, looking at all the clothes and boxes.

"Elizabeth!" Kelly scolded gently. "Don't be impolite. Perhaps you should first give yours."

Mr. Howe patted his granddaughter's shoulder. "She's just eager, for I'm afraid I have been whetting her curiosity all the way from the dock. Here it is, my dear." The man lifted a heavy box and set it on the bed. "There, now have at it."

Lizzie looked to her father and Daniel nodded. She handed Kelly the kitten. Hurrying to the bed, she ripped at the box and peeked inside. "What is it?"

"Perhaps your father would help you take it out?" Mrs. Howe suggested.

"Certainly," Daniel answered. "I would be happy to assist."

It was a large circular stage, with red-velvet curtains. When Mr. Howe cranked the small handle, music was heard as the curtains parted, showing twirling ballerinas.

"That is just so adorable!" Kelly murmured, watching as the scene changed.

"How ingenious!" Daniel exclaimed.

Lizzie was mesmerized and, when it began to slow down, she cried out, "Crank it again!"

Everyone laughed, and Daniel did as she asked. Kelly looked up to the Howes and saw the great love they had for their granddaughter. Mr. Howe was softly patting Mrs. Howe's arm as tears came into the woman's eyes. Suddenly Kelly realized how strange this situation must be for them . . . to have lost a daughter across an ocean, never to see her again, and now to meet her child must be both painful and joyful at the same time.

She tugged on Daniel's arm, and whispered, "Perhaps we should allow Lizzie's grandparents to get acquainted with her now."

Nodding, Daniel placed his hand over hers, and said, "We shall leave you to get settled in comfort. Now, Elizabeth, don't you wear your grandparents out. They've had a very long trip and need to rest."

"Oh, Daniel . . . thank you, but this child is exactly what we need," Mrs. Howe answered, beaming at Lizzie. "She can assist me in sorting through all this . . . for there are more surprises to come."

Lizzie turned her head. "More surprises?"

Mr. Howe smiled and nodded. "Yes. Your grandmother packed some things of your mother's . . . books, jewelry she had worn when she was about your age, and some other small gifts she thought would be appropriate."

"We'll leave you now," Kelly said diplomatically when she saw that Mrs. Howe was getting filled up again. "We shall see you when we dine tonight." She touched Lizzie's shoulder. "Don't overstay your welcome, young lady, and don't forget to give them your present."

"I won't," she whispered. She walked up to Mrs. Howe and took her hand. "Don't be sad, Grandmother."

Mrs. Howe shook her head. "Oh child . . . I am not sad. I am overjoyed just to look into your beautiful face. Do you know how much you resemble your mother when she was your age?"

Lizzie shook her head.

"Well, you do . . . and I have brought some things that will show you what I mean. Come, let's look . . ."

Kelly motioned to Delia to follow them from the room. When she and Daniel were in the hallway, she said to Delia, "Please see about bringing up a light lunch for the three of them."

"Yes, ma'am." Delia answered, and headed for the stairs.

Kelly turned to Daniel and sighed. "Everyone has been so concerned with Lizzie, but how are you doing?"

He gathered her into his arms and inhaled deeply. "I'm fine, my love, now that I'm holding you. I will admit to some anxiety as Elizabeth and I were waiting at the dock, but it appears Grace and Anthony have fallen in love with their granddaughter." He kissed the top of her head and leaned back to see her face. "Now, how are you taking all of this excitement? I am sure it has been awkward for you."

"You mean because of Lilly?"

He nodded.

She thought for a moment, and then said, "I understand how the Howes feel." Looking deeply into his eyes, she whispered, "We all know about grieving. I'm glad they don't seem to resent me."

"How could anyone resent you, my love? You are an angel."

She chuckled. "I thought I was a temptress."

Grinning, Daniel kissed her forehead, and whispered, "Don't remind me, madam, or I shall take you into our bedroom and ravish your luscious body once more."

She thought back to the three times last night that he had ravished her body, and a rush of desire swept through her. Placing her hand over his heart, she whispered, "It appears we have a free afternoon, sir."

"You are serious?" he asked, suddenly still.

"Very serious," she answered, raising her face to him. "Besides, I have a present for you."

He stared into her eyes, and muttered, "God help me, I feel like a young man around you. What magic have you cast?"

Her smile was slow and seductive. "Why, it's called love, Daniel. The best magic of all."

Minutes later, he was sitting on the edge of the bed and unwrapping his present. "What have I done to deserve this?" he muttered with a pleased grin as he tore through the brown paper.

"Why, you married me and brought me back to life," Kelly whispered as she sat down next to him and watched as he turned over the frame. "It's my wedding present to you."

She heard his quick intake of breath as he viewed her portrait and waited for his reaction. It really was a very good picture, exactly what she wanted. Finally, she couldn't take it anymore, and asked, "Do you like it?"

When he looked up to her, Kelly could see that he had tears in his eyes. "It's beautiful," he breathed, smiling and looking down to it again. "You look so . . ."

"In love?" Kelly supplied.

"Yes . . . breathtakingly in love."

Grinning, Kelly said, "I was thinking of you when Mr. Collins took it."

Daniel placed the picture on a bedside table, and announced, "I want a copy for my office and one for the country house. If I'm not in your presence, I want to be able to see you like this." He turned to her and caught her in his arms. "Thank you, Kelly. No other gift has pleased me more." Glancing once more to the picture, he held her closer. "Save for the miraculous gift of your love." He turned his head and stared deeply into her eyes. "I hope you weren't just teasing me about your earlier offer of how to spend our free afternoon."

Giggling, Kelly wound her arms around him and offered her mouth. "Teasing, sir? When have you ever known me to tease?"

He threw back his head and laughed before growling as he brought her in closer to him. "And last night wasn't precipitated by an agonizing amount of teasing?"

She lifted her eyebrows in an attempt at innocence. "Well, if I hadn't done something, we both would have spontaneously combusted."

They laughed into each other's eyes until their laughter eased into silence. It was a moment of wonder, of seeing beyond all the barriers they had erected over the years into the soul of the other. There were no secrets left, nothing to be hidden, nothing to guard against. There was only the beauty left of their true natures, and an eternal bonding happened in that wondrous, timeless moment. In that instant, they saw what was always there behind all the illusions. The true magic of love.

The dinner party seemed a huge success. Kelly, dressed in her elegant gown of pale gray, sat at the table and looked around at the assembled guests and smiled. Great food. Great conversation. She resisted touching the string of pearls Daniel had given her as a wedding present. After viewing her photograph, he had rushed to the jewelers and presented her with the necklace and earrings in a black-velvet box. How was it possible to be this happy?

"There's a man in Baton Rouge," William Tyler said with

a grin, "a Mr. Frank Wallace, who pulls teeth free as a way of getting people to buy his extract, called Wild West Bitters. He not only pulls teeth, he also presents a vaudeville show that includes comedians, jugglers, and banjo players."

Kelly smiled at Susan's husband, and asked, "Can it be true that this man uses entertainment as an anesthesia?"

"I believe William is merely entertaining us with this bit of . . . of unusual information," Susan said with a slight shake of her head. "He does so love these odd bits of trivia."

William looked suitably shocked, then grinned back to Kelly. "I assure you, Mrs. Gilmore, I am telling the truth. Why the local dentists created quite a stir of complaints, but Mr. Wallace pacified them by telling them when he pulls teeth, it gives the good dentists the chance to replace them."

Everyone laughed.

"Such an interesting country," Anthony Howe remarked with a smile. "When I arrived in New York City, I was reading in one of your newspapers that a certain congressman from a place . . . I believe it was called Minnesota . . . has just published a paper called 'The Great Cryptogram,' arguing that the identity of the Shakespearean works is open to question."

"Yes, I have heard of this," Daniel said, sitting back in his chair. "What are your thoughts, Anthony, as someone who has lived in England his entire life and is well versed in Shakespeare?"

Kelly watched Mrs. Howe sigh, and quickly interjected, "Excuse me, before Mr. Howe answers, may I suggest that we ladies leave you gentlemen to your cigars and brandy and your great debates."

Daniel nodded graciously and rose from his chair, as did the other men who assisted their ladies in rising. "Thank you, my dear. We won't be long."

"I hope not," Kelly said with an answering smile, as Andrew pulled back her chair. Looking to the Mesdames Holden, Deaveroux, Howe, and Tyler, she added, "Shall we retire to the garden?"

Everyone nodded and followed her from the dining room. Well, she had just pulled off the dinner part of this party, and it was now time for the real entertainment to begin. Thankfully, she had something to help her. Leading the ladies out into the garden lit with many lanterns, Kelly deeply inhaled the warm night air. They were blessed with a gorgeous Indian summer, and Kelly had decided to bring everyone outdoors to enjoy it.

"I had forgotten how lovely this garden is," Mrs. Deaveroux observed, looking around the courtyard.

"Yes," Susan murmured, "it is beautiful. So peaceful."

Kelly smiled at Susan, and a silent moment of friendship passed between them.

She stopped at the fountain and turned around to the ladies. "Mrs. Howe was kind enough to bring Daniel and me a present and I'd like to show everyone," she said, nodding to a table set in the corner. "A gramophone."

There was a murmur of appreciation as all the ladies walked over to it.

"I have heard of these," Mrs. Holden remarked, staring at the large brass horn.

"As have I," Mrs. Deaveroux added. "My niece in Biloxi wrote to me saying she had ordered one that uses shellac disks instead of cylinders. She claimed that the sound quality is far superior. Is that true?"

"I would agree with your niece, Mrs. Deaveroux," Mrs. Howe remarked, looking well pleased that everyone was so interested in her gift.

"May we hear it?" Susan asked, looking very eager.

"Of course," Kelly replied. "That's why it's set out here. Once the men hear the music, I doubt they shall leave us stranded for very long."

"Music hath charms to soothe the savage breast," Mrs. Holden murmured, and all the women laughed at the perfect quote.

Mrs. Howe added, "Carlyle says 'Music may well be said to be the speech of angels.' "

"Listen," Kelly whispered, cranking the windup motor. She placed the needle on the turning record.

Soon the strains of a Strauss waltz filled the night air, and all the women stood in silence, listening to the magic that engulfed them.

Susan placed her hands to her chest, and whispered, "I do believe you are correct, Mrs. Howe . . . for this sounds like the angels themselves are right here in this garden."

Mrs. Howe nodded and smiled with approval at Kelly.

Perhaps it wasn't so strange that Kelly really did want this woman's approval. She was, after all, Lizzie's grandmother. But it was more than that . . . she wanted Grace Howe to know that she respected her role. So far the visit was going smoothly, with Lizzie taking up much of their time as they explored the city together. Meals were pleasant and lively, and neither of the Howes seem to resent her. All her worrying . . . and for what?

The men burst through the French doors, carrying their cigars and brandy. "Since this musical interlude is to be outdoors, we thought we might join you," Daniel called out.

Susan clapped her hands and looked at Kelly. "It worked!"

Kelly leaned down, and whispered, "Now if we can only get them to leave their smelly cigars and dance with us."

Susan laughed. "Do you think we can?"

Kelly looked up at the sky. "Dancing under the stars? Who could resist it?"

The men joined their wives and everyone just stood and listened to the melodious strains fill the air and their hearts. When it ended, all seemed deflated and Daniel quickly cranked the mechanism again. No one was more surprised than Mrs. Deaveroux when her husband placed his brandy and his cigar down on the table and extended his hand to his wife.

"Will you join me, madam, for it has been many years since I danced in the night air."

Mrs. Deaveroux looked positively flustered as she stammered, "Why, Hugh . . . Mr. Deaveroux . . . we have just finished our meal and it would be most unseemly to be prancing about out of doors."

"May I have this dance, madam?" Hugh repeated, stoically ignoring all her stuffy excuses.

"Wonderful idea," Daniel chimed in, placing his crystal glass with Hugh's and his cigar in the ashtray he had brought out with him. Turning to Kelly, he said, "Will you grace me with a dance, my love?"

Grinning widely, Kelly opened her arms. "Why, thank you, sir. It would be my pleasure to dance with you."

Together they glided across the tiles, and Kelly marveled at how well they danced together for the first time. There was no hesitation, just a smooth elegant merging as she allowed him to lead her in the graceful waltz. She stared into his eyes and couldn't believe how blessed she was to be in his arms. He was so handsome, so intelligent, sexy, and witty, and filled with integrity . . . and he loved her. She never felt so cherished in her life. Even when she was younger. Filled with happiness, she whispered to him, "I love you, Daniel Gilmore."

He smiled down into her eyes and whispered back, "And I adore you, Mrs. Gilmore . . . look . . ." and he nodded behind her.

Kelly shifted her view and saw that not only the Deaveroux couple was dancing but everyone else. Even the Howes. Laughing with delight, she lifted her vision to the stars and was filled with gratitude for this evening. Something caught her attention, and she lowered her gaze to see Lizzie leaning on a terrace railing upstairs, watching the scene.

She smiled up at her, and Lizzie shyly waved back. A surge of happiness filled her being as the record ended. She and Daniel broke apart, just as Susan and her husband did the same.

"Kelly, you are a huge success," Susan said, smiling with happiness. "I haven't enjoyed myself this much since I was a young girl."

"She has this . . . magic," Daniel offered, reluctant to let go of his wife's hand. "She seems to rejuvenate everyone around her."

Kelly laughed at his silliness, yet his words touched her heart. It was as she had said to Lizzie. You can't perform magic alone. You need somehow to be connected.

"Crank it again, Daniel," Hugh Deaveroux called out. "I was just getting started!"

Everyone laughed, and Mrs. Deaveroux appeared suddenly as shy as a new bride, as she fanned her throat with her hand. "Really, Hugh!"

Keeping Kelly's hand securely in his, Daniel walked over to the gramophone. Soon, they were all dancing once more, and Kelly realized that her role as hostess within New Orleans society appeared to be established. She had love, family, friends, security . . . it was more than she'd ever hoped to find again in her life.

Wouldn't Mel be lime green with envy?

Nineteen

She was seated at the table in the garden with Mrs. Howe, enjoying afternoon tea while Lizzie played hide-and-seek with Panny around the large potted urns. It was a pleasant interlude and one that she thought was missing from modern society. Taking time in the afternoon to relax, instead of pushing through the day until one was so stressed out that one forgot how to enjoy simple pleasures, was a lost art in modern society.

"I was wondering, my dear, if I may have a frank word with you?"

Kelly pulled her thoughts together and smiled at the older woman. "Of course," she answered politely, curious as to what Mrs. Howe was about to say.

"Your . . . marriage to Daniel took us by surprise, as I'm sure you understand."

She nodded and tried to steady her nerves. How had she hoped to avoid this conversation? Of course Lizzie's grandmother would have questions. Wanting to avoid a direct interrogation, Kelly said, "Certainly I understand, Mrs. Howe. I think our marriage took us by surprise, too." She smiled, and added, "We were introduced by family, and it was a whirlwind romance. We love each other deeply and didn't see a reason to delay. I am honored to be Daniel's wife."

"It is obvious the man adores you," Mrs. Howe commented. "Daniel told us you are from Philadelphia, and that your parents are no longer alive?"

"That is correct," Kelly answered quickly, not wanting to get into a discussion about her earlier life. What could she possibly say to this woman? *I traveled back in time to find love?* "I only have cousins remaining. Daniel and Elizabeth are my family now." And with that statement, Kelly realized she had actually shut the book on her past.

Mrs. Howe nodded.

"I have been wondering for some time now why Elizabeth calls you Miss Kelly. Have you asked that she not address you as her mother?"

Letting out her breath, Kelly smiled. "No, I haven't asked, but I thought it might be an easier transition as I entered the family. I respect your daughter's role, Mrs. Howe, and I wouldn't want to replace her. How could I? I'm a different person."

"Thank you. That is all I wanted. You would be surprised how much you are alike," the woman said, and hesitated. "You bear a resemblance to her, you know."

Kelly nodded. "Yes, I have been told, and I did see two photographs of her. She . . . she was lovely."

Grace Howe sighed deeply and sadly, as though picturing her daughter. "Yes, she was. I just wanted you to know that you would not receive an objection should you ever wish Elizabeth to call you mother. She is so attached to you."

Smiling again, Kelly said, "Thank you, Mrs. Howe, but I think I'll leave that up to Elizabeth to decide. I wouldn't want to press the issue."

"Yes . . . you are like my Lillian. She was also very kind and patient. Perhaps too kind at times. She never really learned to take a firm stand."

Kelly straightened and picked up her cup of tea. "You mean she found it difficult to say no?"

"That is exactly what I mean," Grace Howe answered,

folding her hands together in her lap. "She should have stayed with us in England to have her baby, instead of coming to this wild country with all its strange maladies. She wasn't strong, you know, unlike you in that respect."

Kelly could tell the woman wanted to speak her mind. "Don't most women find it hard to say no?" she asked quietly. "Aren't we taught from an early age to please everyone around us? To feel as though it's selfish for wanting our own wishes to be fulfilled?"

Grace sat back in her chair and watched Lizzie. "I believe you are correct, my dear. I had to take a stand against Mr. Howe, who thought us too aged to make such a long voyage, yet I was determined not to leave this life without ever seeing Lillian's child. I said no to all his objections."

"And now you're here," Kelly added with a grin, glad the subject of her background had changed. "It appears you made a wise choice, Mrs. Howe."

"Yes, I did . . . didn't I?" The older woman chuckled. "I should have learned to say no many years ago."

Leaning closer to the table, Kelly whispered, "I had the same problem . . . the inability to say no, but I do think women are beginning to band together now and voice their wishes. Change is coming, Mrs. Howe."

"You can't be speaking about the odd movement in this country for women to be granted the right to vote. I read about it when we landed in New York City."

"Yes, I am," Kelly answered. "Look at your granddaughter, Mrs. Howe. Do you want her to grow up without the freedom to make choices in her life that are appropriate for her to live a long and happy one?"

"Well, of course I don't, but politics, my dear . . ." She shook her head. "Leave that to the men."

"Mrs. Howe, we *have* left it to the men, and look where it's gotten us. Laws that deny us the right to live our own lives with freedom. Is it any wonder we hesitate to say no, and if we do, most men don't take us seriously?"

Mrs. Howe took a deep breath. "I can see this is an impassioned subject for you."

"You're right," Kelly answered, placing her cup back

onto the saucer and realizing what a debt of gratitude she owed to the female population of this time who, despite ridicule, championed women's rights, the rights that she and every other woman in the twenty-first century had enjoyed. "It wasn't always so, believe me. I guess when I really agreed to mother Elizabeth, it became very important to me. I don't want her to live her life depending on the good moods of a man. I want her to be free and protected under the law so that no matter what happens to her, she will at least have choices."

Mrs. Howe reached across the table and patted her hand softly. "You will make Elizabeth a fine mother. I am happy you are in her life."

Smiling, Kelly finally relaxed and said, "Thank you. I love her very much."

"I can see that, my dear. So, as a mother, now you might understand my next request."

Kelly waited . . .

"I would like to see where my daughter is buried. I understand her grave is in the country. Would it be possible to arrange for us to visit?"

She shouldn't have been surprised. It was a natural request. "Of course," she replied. "Though I must tell you that we don't have room for the staff there. Only Clara. I'm afraid you might not find it as comfortable."

"Nonsense. I survived an ocean voyage. Do I look fragile to you?"

Kelly burst out laughing. She really liked this straightforward woman.

Preparations were quickly made, and two days later they were leaving the small dock and walking up to the country house. Lizzie was so excited to be back that she placed Panny on the ground and started running ahead of them.

Mr. and Mrs. Howe were walking with Daniel, while Kelly pulled up the rear with Clara. "I promise I'll help you with everything," Kelly said, noticing that Clara looked kind of gray. The packet trip must have been too much for her. "As a matter of fact, we have the food Mary packed for us, and tonight I'll take care of supper. You rest."

"Now you know I ain't gonna lie about in bed while you go servin' them folks, Miz Kelly."

"I think you should rest, Clara," she said with more firmness. "You look tired."

Clara inhaled deeply and looked toward the house. "I will admit I likes bein' back here and sleepin' in my own bed."

Nodding, Kelly said, "This is your home, Clara. I can understand that."

"Home," Clara repeated the word, and slowly shook her head. "Now don't that sound good?"

Kelly smiled as she looked at the freshly whitewashed house with the neatly weeded garden beds. "Yes," she murmured. "It sure does." So why was she suddenly filled with a sense of dread, as though something was going to happen that she had no control over? Knowing she didn't want to be pulled from these people for any reason, she tried to shake off the weird feeling. It was probably because this visit of the Howes was one of mourning. Well, she would try to be positive about it all. Straightening her shoulders, Kelly put her arm through Clara's and continued to walk toward the house.

After she had settled everyone into bedrooms, Kelly presented Mrs. Howe with some wildflowers she had picked and had tied with a white-satin ribbon. The woman had thanked her profusely, then Daniel and Lizzie led Lillian's parents to her grave.

She was secretly glad her presence wasn't required, for she had no desire to entertain thoughts of death. It seemed like she had just freed herself from years of grief and, more importantly, this was a private moment for them. She busied herself in the kitchen, pulling together a meal with Clara's help. Several times the older woman had to sit down at the table to rest, and Kelly made a mental note to ask Daniel about getting Clara a medical checkup. What were doctors like in this time? Did they even understand the aging process?

"Your arthritis bothering you again, Clara?"

"Oh, it's always there," the woman said, snapping the ends off the string beans. "You learn to live with pain you can't do nothin' about. Sometimes, it's just hard to ignore this arthur of mine."

"That ointment I found in the city isn't helping?"

"Shucks, Miz Kelly . . . this is deep in the bones, but I thanks you kindly for thinkin' about this old fool."

Kelly glanced up from the sink, where she was pumping water into a pot for rice. "I've told you before, Clara, you're one of the wisest women I've ever met. If you're a fool, then I want to be one, too."

Clara chuckled, as Lizzie came running in through the back door.

"You seen Panny?" she demanded.

Both Clara and Kelly shook their heads.

"I can't find him," Lizzie said, looking very worried.

"He probably just walked off to explore, honey . . . he'll be back," Kelly said, wiping her hands on a dish towel and walking over to the girl. She put her arm around Lizzie's shoulders, and added, "If he's not back after supper, I'll help you look."

"I can't wait!" Lizzie answered. "What if a gator gets him?"

Daniel walked into the kitchen and Kelly noted that he, too, looked tired.

"Panny's lost! You didn't see him, Daddy?"

Shaking his head, Daniel said, "He'll come back, honey. Cats wander off all the time. He's probably just exploring."

"But he's only a kitten! I have to go look for him," she exclaimed, and ran out of the house. They could hear her in the yard calling, "Panny! Panny! C'mere, kitty!"

Daniel looked at Kelly and answered her unspoken question. "I thought I should give the Howes their privacy."

Nodding, Kelly poured him a glass of lemon water. She handed it to him, and asked, "How are you doing? I know this can't be easy for you."

He swallowed the cool water and ran his hand through his hair as he smiled at her. "I'm fine, my love." Looking around the kitchen, he added, "How's supper coming along?"

Kelly sighed and grinned, filled even now with more love for this man. He was walking a delicate line between the past and the present and doing it gracefully. "Clara and I are pulling together here. We'll manage."

"I am so sorry there was no room for the staff. You must be tired yourself."

"Don't be silly, Daniel," Kelly reprimanded, with a kiss to his cheek. "I'm used to working, and this is nothing. Clara and I have a system going."

"You are a remarkable woman . . ." Turning his head, he added, "Don't you agree, Clara?"

"Yes, suh," Clara answered with a nod. "Remarkable, for sure. You is one blessed man, Mistah Daniel."

Daniel smiled and gathered Kelly into his arms. "You know that's the second time someone said that to me recently."

"Best you be believin' it then," Clara murmured, with a crisp snap of beans. "You been given a second chance, Mistah Daniel. Ain't many folks that gets such a gift as you."

Daniel nodded, hugging Kelly closer. Kissing her forehead, he whispered against her skin, "A precious gift, indeed."

Kelly felt such love rushing through her that she laid her head against his chest and closed her eyes in deep gratitude. She was the one who was blessed, the one given a gift. In the past thirteen years she had learned how to make a living, but not really a life. She'd found that here. Here, she had learned to open her heart again. She felt loved, connected . . . *alive.*

Raising her head, she smiled into the eyes of her husband. "We've all been given gifts, I think."

Daniel nodded and was about to answer her when a loud, agonizing scream rent the air, and everyone froze. It was Lizzie!

Immediately, Daniel hurried from the house, and Kelly followed, picking up her skirts to run after him.

"Elizabeth! Where are you?" Daniel called, standing in the middle of the backyard.

Kelly caught up with him and clutched his arm. *"Lizzie! Where are you?"*

Clara, panting from the effort, held her chest as she stood next to them and looked out to the woods. "Somethin' terrible frightened that chile," she muttered.

"Elizabeth!" Daniel again called out.

"Daddy!"

They heard her scream, and all ran toward the sound of it as the Howes hurried to join them. Daniel kept calling out to her, and they could hear her desperate sobs.

"What's happening?" Grace Howe shouted.

"We don't know," Kelly answered, trying to slow the pounding of her heart. "It's Lizzie."

Pushing back branches, they entered the woods and nothing could have prepared them for what they saw. Lizzie, in her white dress, was down on her knees in front of a tree . . . her head hanging in despair, her shoulders shaking as she continued to sob.

Daniel ran to her and grabbed her into his arms as the rest of them caught up. Kelly was holding Clara's hand, trying to help the older woman keep up. When Clara stopped and froze, Kelly turned her attention to the ground.

Kelly's eyes widened in horror and she held her hand over her mouth to stop a scream of denial. The tiny kitten was lying on the ground lifeless, its neck grotesquely twisted by a thin rope.

"Oh my God," she muttered behind her palm, sickened by the sight.

"Heaven help us," Mrs. Howe choked out. "Who would do such a horrid thing?"

Daniel, holding his daughter in his arms, looked up, and his face took on a mask of anger. "I know exactly who did it," he growled, lifting Lizzie as he rose.

Kelly looked into Daniel's eyes and saw something that made her heart lurch with fear.

"Let's get the child away from here," Anthony Howe suggested gently, nodding to Kelly. "You ladies return with Elizabeth, and I shall stay here until Daniel returns. If you might give him a small blanket or towel, Miss Kelly?"

She simply nodded, leading Clara and Mrs. Howe away from the grizzly scene. Her heart was breaking as she listened to Lizzie sobbing in her father's arms. Clara stumbled, clutching the dress material at her chest, and Kelly reached out to steady her.

"Are you all right, Clara?"

The old woman nodded and set her expression with determination as she straightened her back and walked from the woods. "It's time to go home," she muttered, blinking back the tears in her eyes.

"Yes," Mrs. Howe murmured, lifting her skirts as she walked over a fallen branch. "Let us leave this place and take care of the child."

They followed Daniel from the woods, listening to Lizzie's whimpers of sorrow as she buried her face in her father's neck and clutched his shoulders. Kelly's heart was breaking for her, and she didn't know what to say to make any of it better. It was such a cruel act. How does an adult explain cruelty to a child? She didn't know.

When Daniel deposited Lizzie on her bed, he kissed her cheek and backed away to allow the women to come forward. Mrs. Howe immediately rushed to gather Lizzie into her arms. Kelly followed Daniel from the room and grabbed his arm in the hallway.

"What are you going to do?" she demanded, as he spun around to face her. "You have no proof."

"It was Will Hoskins," he spat out, clenching his jaw. "You know it, and so do I."

"Daniel, please calm down before you do anything in anger. Let me get you a towel so you can bring Panny back and we can bury him. Mr. Howe is waiting in the woods."

Daniel exhaled heavily and nodded. "All right . . . but then I am going to seek justice. He's not getting away with this, Kelly. I can't allow it."

She pulled him farther down the hallway, away from Lizzie's room. Opening up a small linen closet, she yanked out a towel and thrust it into his hand. "And what are you going to do?" she whispered, holding back her tears. "Wring his neck?"

Her husband didn't say anything.

"Is it worth it? Don't you dare do anything, Daniel Gilmore, that might take *you* away from this family. Remember that. We have enough trauma right now. Please don't cause any more."

He stood for just a few moments, breathing heavily, and looking into her eyes. "I cannot allow this to go unanswered. I must go there, Kelly."

Her eyes were burning, and she couldn't hold back the tears. "I understand, Daniel. Just be careful what you do. Calm down before you confront anyone. Please . . . ?"

"I will handle this, madam." He nodded quickly and turned to leave, as Lizzie cried out for Kelly.

She was torn between following her husband and going to her daughter. Rushing back into Lizzie's room, she met Mrs. Howe's gaze. "She wants you, dear," the woman said, tears of sympathy in her eyes.

Kelly walked over to Lizzie, whose body was curled into a fetal position as she hiccupped and stared at the wall. Nodding to Mrs. Howe, Kelly sat down on the edge of the mattress and reached out to stroke the child's back.

"I'm so sorry, honey," she whispered, wanting to lie down behind her and cuddle her into her body.

"Why'd he do it?"

"I don't know, Lizzie. Truly, I don't."

"Who did it?" Mrs. Howe asked, as she was walking to the door.

"Will Hoskins! I hate him!"

"Hush, now, Lizzie," Kelly whispered, "I know your heart is broken."

"How . . ." she hiccupped and sniffled, "how could he kill Panny?"

"I don't know," Kelly answered honestly, glancing at Mrs. Howe as she silently left the room. "Your daddy and your grandfather are bringing Panny back and together we'll bury him."

Lizzie started crying again when she moaned, "But Panny was just a baby! He did it 'cause I told on him!"

Kelly didn't know what to say. The only thing she knew to do was follow her heart. She lifted up her skirts and climbed into bed with Lizzie. Pulling the young girl's body against hers, she cuddled her and stroked her damp hair off her face. "Honey, some things just can't be explained. I wish I could take this pain away for you, but I can't. I don't know how. I can only hold you and love you . . ."

She allowed her own tears to mix with Lizzie's as she slowly rocked back and forth, allowing Lizzie to grieve for her little kitten. She listened as Lizzie's breath hitched and then as the child told her all about Panny, how smart he was, how funny his antics. She held Lizzie tighter when anger burst through her once more, then soothed her when the tears came back. They lay there for what seemed like an hour until Mrs. Howe returned.

"Excuse me," the woman said in a soft, hesitant voice. "Kelly, dear . . . you are needed downstairs."

Immediately, she thought of Daniel, and kissed Lizzie's temple before rising. She prayed that he was all right and hadn't done anything rash. "Would you stay with Lizzie, Grace? I'll come back up as soon as I can."

"Certainly," Mrs. Howe answered, sitting down on the bed and stroking Lizzie's shoulder.

Kelly rushed downstairs, calling out for her husband. "Daniel? Where are you?"

She entered the kitchen and saw Clara seated at the table amid the green beans, with her head down on her arms, as though she were sleeping. "Clara, have you seen Mister Daniel?"

"No, ma'am . . . he done left for the Hoskins place," the woman murmured, raising her head slowly.

"*Clara!* What's wrong with you?" Kelly was shocked by the ashen color of Clara's face and the weariness in her expression.

"I don't know, Miz Kelly . . . but I asked Miz Howe to gets you, 'cause I don't knows if'n I can reach my bed by myself."

Terrified, Kelly rushed to Clara and tried to help her rise. "Put your arm around my shoulders and lean on me. I'll get you there."

Clara tried to smile. "I'm sorry, Miz Kelly."

"Just hush," Kelly commanded, refusing to think of anything except getting Clara to bed. "Here," she whispered, "I'll pull you up." She wound her arm around Clara's waist, and together they slowly made their way into Clara's small bedroom.

Kelly sat Clara on the bed and knelt down to unlace her shoes. "What happened?" she asked softly as her fingers struggled with the old laces. Why hadn't she thought of buying Clara a new pair of shoes in the city? She shook the thought out of her head as she listened to Clara's answer.

"Just gots all weak of a sudden. Maybe I shouldn't been runnin' in them woods like I was a spring chicken, which . . ." She caught her breath. ". . . Lord knows I ain't."

Kelly smiled. "Well, we'll get you into bed and let you rest. I'll bring you something to eat later, if you feel like it." She pulled off one shoe and started on the other.

Ten minutes later Clara was lying in bed, wearing her silk pajamas, wrapped in her blue robe as Kelly pulled the old quilt over her. "Is there anything else I can get you?" she asked, wishing that the color would return to Clara's face. "A cup of tea?"

Shaking her head, Clara pointed to the wooden dresser along the wall. "In that first drawer, in the back . . . you'll find a little box. You can bring me that."

Kelly pulled open the drawer and searched through Clara's cotton underwear until she felt a small wooden box. Grabbing it up, she closed the drawer and handed it to Clara.

"I thank you, Miz Kelly, for all your help," Clara whispered, taking the box and holding it to her chest as she grimaced with pain. "You be a kind woman."

Kelly felt tears once more return to her eyes as she looked down at her friend. Clara looked so small and old suddenly. "Maybe I should call a doctor, just to make sure. He could give you something to regain your strength."

Clara closed her eyes briefly and smiled. "Miz Kelly, ain't no doctor can give me anythin' for where I'm goin'."

"Going? What do you mean?"

Clara opened her eyes and stared into Kelly's. "Home, chile. "I'm goin' home," she stated matter-of-factly.

"You *are* home, Clara," Kelly answered, refusing to listen to the meaning behind Clara's words. "Right here with us."

"No, *home*, chile . . . where I belongs."

"You belong with us. Don't talk foolishness. You just

need to rest is all, and then I'll get Daniel to find a doctor and he'll give you something and—"

"Miz Kelly."

Clara interrupted her, and Kelly stopped talking, knowing she didn't want to hear whatever was coming next.

Sighing deeply, Clara reached out her hand. "Come sit with me a moment."

Kelly clutched Clara's thin hand in both of hers and sat on the edge of the bed. "Let me get the doctor, Clara . . . please?"

Clara shook her head. "What for? I don't belong here no more. This ole heart of mine can't take any more of the mean ways of this world, and it's tellin' me it's time. I'm tired, chile. Weary to the bone. I wants to go be with my man and my boy Clevis. My work here is done."

Kelly realized that seeing Will Hoskins's handiwork had been the last straw for this gentle soul. Shaking her head, Kelly tried to settle her overloaded mind. She had a child upstairs grieving, a husband who was in a rage, and a dear friend who acted and talked like she was dying! How was she supposed to deal with all this? "Clara, you can't leave me. What will I do? I can't handle all this by myself."

Clara's breathing was labored, yet still the woman smiled. "Oh, you'll be jus fine. You . . . you's a fool like me, Miz Kelly . . . you'll do what's necessary to feed the children and love your man and keep your home as happy as you can . . . even when it looks like the world is fallin' down around you." She gulped for air. "You're a woman." She clutched Kelly's hand and looked directly into her eyes. "You carry hope in your heart, though it seems foolish sometimes."

Kelly tried hard to swallow down the lump in her throat, but the burning in her eyes was too intense and she couldn't stop it. Sniffling back her tears, she said, "I have hope now, Clara . . . that you'll get stronger and . . ." Her words dropped off as Clara began slowly shaking her head.

"Don't you go tryin' to keep me here," she muttered, closing her eyes. "I done prayed for you to show up. I made that promise to Miz Lillian to watch over her baby and her man, but now you's here. I wants to go home . . ."

Kelly just sat on the bed and allowed the tears to come. She had no answers anymore. Not for Lizzie or Clara or anyone else.

"Oh!" Clara opened her eyes. "You can gets me my new hat."

Sniffling, Kelly asked, "What?" She couldn't have heard correctly.

"I wants my pretty new hat."

Kelly swallowed down fresh tears. "You want to wear it now?"

Clara nodded, then winced as she pressed the box down on her chest. When she regained her breath, she murmured, "If I'm to be meetin' my man again, I wants to look nice."

In spite of everything, Kelly grinned as she stood and picked up the bonnet she had given to Clara. Very gently, she placed it on Clara's head. "There. You look beautiful."

"You is lying, but . . . I'll forgive you."

"Clara, please allow me to call in a doctor. He can give you something for . . . for any pain or—"

"No doctor, chile. Grant me my last wishes."

Kelly bit her bottom lip and felt the burning in her eyes return. "How am I supposed to do this?" she demanded. "I don't know how."

"Me neither," Clara gasped. "Ain't never died before. But it would sure help if I could stop talkin' for now."

"Okay, okay . . ." Kelly relented, anything to make Clara happy. "I'll just get a chair from the kitchen and sit with you and together we'll . . . I don't know . . . figure this out, I guess."

Clara opened one eye. "You go see to your chile and your man. I'll still be here when you gets back."

"Promise?" Kelly simply could not believe she was talking like this!

Clara nodded. "I just wants to rest now and . . . and prepare myself. Gots a lock of Clevis's hair in here," she said, patting the box still lying on her chest. "Took it before he passed. And the ribbon I wore when I jumped the broom with Lucius."

"You'll be all right?" What a stupid thing to ask someone who was preparing to die!

"I don't think I'll be goin' anywheres right soon."

Nodding, Kelly bent down and kissed Clara's forehead. "I'll be back."

Clara opened her eyes and, staring into Kelly's for the longest time, said, "I thanks you, Miz Kelly. I may not know how I'm gettin' there, but I ain't scared of where I'm goin'."

"I know," Kelly answered, feeling her chin begin to quiver with fresh emotion.

Closing the door behind her, Kelly leaned against the doorjamb and covered her face with her hands. This can't be happening! Clara could not be dying now! Where was Daniel? She looked to the ceiling and thought of Lizzie, already grieving for her kitten. How was she to tell her that the woman who had raised her was also leaving her life?

What answers did she have for any of them?

Suddenly, she realized what Clara meant by calling her a fool.

There were no answers. It was just the circle of life spinning around, and she somehow had to accept it, deal with it and do what needs to be done for her family.

Stumbling to the table, she clung to the back of a chair with one hand to steady herself and pressed her fist to her mouth to cover her sobs. Deep within her soul, she knew Clara was right. She was a woman. She would somehow manage to care for those she loved, even if it meant saying good-bye.

Twenty

"*Will Hoskins!*"

Daniel stood in front of the run-down house, littered with junk, and called out for the boy. "You come on out, Will, before I come in and drag you out here."

Anthony Howe murmured, "Are you sure you should attempt this without the presence of authorities?"

Daniel, never taking his eyes from the front door, shook his head. "This is between me and that boy."

"That's just it, Daniel. He is a boy and—"

"He's fifteen years old."

"But—" Anthony stopped speaking when the door creaked open.

A woman, blowsy and worn, pushed her coarse hair back off her face and yelled out, "What'd y'all want, Daniel Gilmore?"

"I want to see Will, Sarah. Where's your husband?"

"He's sleepin'."

"Then wake him. This is important."

Sarah Hoskins sighed deeply, and Daniel remembered her as a vibrant child who had laughed easily. A part of his brain registered that the life had gone out of her, and it was hard to see even a shadow of it within the shell she now wore.

"Can't wake him. He's lickered up and he won't wake till evenin' . . . if I'm lucky. Why you want my boy?"

He gritted his back teeth and tried to control his temper. He did not want to deal with a woman. "Will is responsible for a despicable act, and I intend to see that he takes responsibility for it."

"What act?" Sarah demanded. "What's that boy done now?"

Daniel motioned to Anthony, and Mr. Howe uncovered the body of Panny as Daniel walked up the three steps to the front door.

Sarah clenched her jaw for a brief moment. "What proof you got that Will done it?"

"Yeah, what proof you got that I done it?" Will demanded, suddenly appearing behind his mother.

Daniel instinctively reached over Sarah's shoulder and grabbed the teenager by his shirt collar, yanking him out the door past the woman. "Come out here from behind your mother's skirts, and I'll show you," he muttered, dragging Will down the steps and making him stand in front of Anthony's outstretched arms.

Holding the flailing Will with one hand, Daniel picked up the thin rope from the blanket with the other. He dangled it before Will's face. "See this? See the thread of red in the cording? When you and your father last spoke with me about a certain situation, you were using this to hold up your pants." With the speed of a magician, Daniel flicked the rope around Will's neck and used both his hands to tighten it. "How's it feel, Will?" he demanded, sensing the teenager's fear. "You feel powerful now? You think that's what it takes to be a man?"

Anthony called out to him, and Daniel vaguely heard Sarah screaming for her drunken husband. He could think of nothing as he watched Will claw at the rope around his neck, save those same hands touching his daughter, strangling the life from a small kitten. "Answer me, Will . . . you feel like a man now?" He glanced down to see that Will had soiled the front of his pants.

"You're not a *man*," he spat into the boy's terrified eyes. "A man protects the innocent; he doesn't destroy them. Do you understand?"

Again Will nodded in terror.

"I want you to know something . . . something very important . . . if you ever come near my daughter again or place your foot on my property . . . ever"—he tightened the rope—"I *will* protect the innocent. Do you understand?"

Struggling for breath, Will nodded quickly.

"Daniel . . . let him go!" Anthony called out behind him.

Through the haze of rage that coursed through his body, Daniel remembered Kelly's words before he'd left the house. He concentrated on her face, not the face of perversion in front of him, and in disgust cast Will away from him.

He watched as Will fell to the ground and pulled the rope loose from his neck, gasping for air. He wasn't worth any more anger.

"If you ever become a man, Will . . . if you ever know the honor it is to be one . . . you will understand what just happened here." He turned to Anthony and flipped the corner of the towel over the tiny body of the kitten. Suddenly, he was drained of all emotion.

"Let's go home."

Kelly held Lizzie on her lap by Clara's bed. Wrapping her arms around the girl, she breathed heavily, and whispered, "Thanks for being strong, kiddo, but it's okay to cry you know."

Lizzie turned her head slightly, her face a mask of sorrow. "Why's everything happening like this now? I don't want Mammy Clara to die." Her little chin started quivering as fresh tears gathered at her eyes.

"I don't want it either, honey . . . but she says it's time . . . and we have to respect her." She rocked Lizzie in her arms and looked once more to the sleeping Clara. The old woman had already said good-bye to the child and had closed her eyes and fallen into an exhausted sleep.

"Why does everything have to die?"

Kelly closed her eyes briefly. How was she to answer this one? She was so weary, and her brain was already fried. "Because it's part of being alive. Clara says it's a journey we're on, and she's tired now and wants to go home. She wants to be with her husband and her son who went before her."

"Is my mother home? Will Mammy Clara see her?"

"Yes, honey, she will," Kelly whispered, leaning her chin on Lizzie's shoulder.

"And Mammy Clara will take care of Panny?"

"Yes."

"Will she come see me, like my mother?"

"I don't know."

Neither of them said anything for a few minutes until Lizzie whispered, "I guess Mammy Clara is just lonely now for her family."

"Yes," Kelly whispered back with a sad smile. "I think she is. She hasn't been with them for a very long time."

"Then it's all right, isn't it? If she's tired and lonely and wants to go home to her family?"

Kelly took another deep steadying breath and felt the burning once more at her eyes. "Yes, honey . . . it's all right to let her go. You know something most people don't, Lizzie. You know you never really lose the relationship with the person you love. Your mother taught you that. You carry her in your heart and in your mind. You can feel their love whenever you want." She paused as a thought flitted across her brain. "Maybe the best thing we can do for Clara is not to try and keep her here with us by being so sad, but to send her off with love so she has a great homecoming."

"Maybe . . . but I'm gonna miss her."

Kelly nodded. "Me too . . . but we just have to think of her, and then we'll *feel* her love and we won't be lonely anymore."

The door opened and Daniel walked into the room with a shocked expression on his face. "Grace just told me," he whispered, looking down at Clara. "I can't believe this."

"Believe it," Kelly said, shaking her head and biting her bottom lip to stop any more tears. "Are you all right?"

Daniel nodded, placing his hand on Lizzie's shoulder. "I handled it."

Kelly saw the look of determination in his expression and decided to drop it. He said he had handled it, and he was safely back with them. She didn't need details right now.

Daniel bent down and kissed first Lizzie's forehead, then Kelly's. "You both look exhausted. Why don't you get something to eat?"

"I'm not hungry," Kelly answered.

"Me either," Lizzie chimed in.

"Your grandparents are in the kitchen waiting for you, Elizabeth. I'll stay right here until you get back."

"Yes, suh," she mumbled, sliding off Kelly's knees. She stopped at the doorway and looked up to her father. "You see Will? You make him pay for what he did?"

Gazing down at his daughter, Daniel caressed her cheek and murmured, "Will Hoskins will never bother you again. It's over, child."

Lizzie sniffled and nodded before walking out of the room.

Daniel knelt beside Kelly and reached out to stroke Clara's hand softly. "I still can't believe this. You're sure she . . . she's . . ."

"Dying. It's got to be okay to say it, if Clara can calmly talk about it," Kelly whispered, realizing in that moment that she was actually coming to accept it herself. "And I'm not sure about anything, Daniel. Clara refuses to call in a doctor. She says she's weary and just wants to go home."

Daniel nodded and smiled with sadness.

"I think seeing Panny was the last straw for her. She says her heart's giving out, and I believe her."

He turned his head and smiled to her while reaching out and running his fingers under her eyes. "You should eat something to keep up your strength. I'll sit with Clara. I have a lot to thank her for before she leaves us."

Kelly took a deep shuddering breath and nodded, realizing that Daniel wanted to say his good-byes privately. They had shared so much together, this old woman and Daniel, and Kelly turned her face into his palm and softly kissed it. "I'll go for a short while."

He looked deep into her eyes, and whispered, "I love you, Kelly. I'm so sorry this isn't a happier time for us to begin our life together."

She smiled with tenderness. "Oh, Daniel, I love you, too . . . and as far as being sorry . . . there's no point. This *is* life, a part of it, whether I like it or not, and in a strange way there is happiness for Clara mixed in with the sadness." She glanced to the woman in the bed. "Look at her. She wants to wear her new hat so she'll look pretty for Lucius."

Daniel smiled while turning his head, and whispering, "She's an incredible woman."

Nodding, Kelly stood up and waved her hand to the chair. "Then sit here and talk to her. Tell her that, Daniel. She's served this family so well."

"I can never express my gratitude."

"Try . . . This is your chance, my love."

He sat in the chair and pulled her back to him. Standing between his legs, she wrapped her arms around his shoulders as his wound around her waist. She felt the weight of him lean into her and the tension leave his shoulders as he silently allowed his tears to come. Stroking his head against her chest, Kelly closed her eyes and prayed for the strength to get through this night.

Everyone else was sleeping and the house was quiet and peaceful, save for Clara's labored breathing. The oil lamp was burning low, and Kelly laid her head down on her arms as she stared at the sleeping woman. After hours in the chair, Kelly's body had become stiff and she'd pulled two pillows from the sitting room and sat on the floor beside the bed. Though she hadn't been asked, Kelly vowed not to leave Clara, and Daniel said he wouldn't leave her, so he, too, was sleeping in a chair behind her.

Quiet and peaceful.

She smiled when she thought of that word . . . peaceful.

"I been . . . dreamin' . . ."

Kelly wasn't sure she heard the barely audible words and raised her head to look at Clara. The woman's eyes were still closed.

"Clara . . . you were dreaming?" she whispered.

"When I was that . . . that little girl . . . runnin' through the sugarcane . . ." Clara gasped for breath and Kelly held on to her hand. "I came to a big ole tree and just sat down . . . and the birds was singin' and . . . and I could hear the bugs in the grass . . . I felt . . . free."

Kelly smiled, picturing a young girl who was still a slave yet tasting a brief moment of freedom. "Yes."

"I wants you to do somethin' for me, Miz Kelly."

She raised her head slightly. "Anything, Clara. Just tell me."

And so the young girl who grew into a strong yet gentle woman told Kelly her last wish, and Kelly promised to fulfill it. When Clara stopped speaking, Kelly put her head back down on the edge of the bed and Clara lifted her hand to stroke Kelly's face. The tears she shed were soft and unbearably sweet. They remained silent for the longest time; words were no longer needed. The communication through Clara's touch was exquisitely tender, and Kelly closed her eyes, wanting to memorize the peaceful, loving moment.

She must have finally fallen asleep for she awakened with a start when Daniel placed his hand on her shoulder, and whispered, "*Look . . . !*"

Opening her eyes, she could barely breathe as she watched the dancing lights fill the room with a warm golden glow. There were two . . . no . . . *three* now, sparkling and glowing and moving about like fairies at play.

Astonished, she fell back against Daniel's legs and he held her tightly to him as, together, they watched in awe the amazing display move closer to them. Slowly the lights seemed to encircle them and a rush of pleasure raced through her body. Kelly breathed in deeper wonder as she started to smile. She couldn't hold back the surge of happiness, and she vaguely heard Daniel's gasp by her ear as the lights began spiraling around them and then move up toward the ceiling.

They disappeared so quickly that Kelly just blinked as she looked about the room. "Did . . . did I just see that?" she managed to say.

Daniel held her tighter and kissed her temple. "We both saw it, my love. It was amazing, wasn't it?"

"It was . . . *magical*," she breathed, then turned her head to Clara. "Daniel?"

Her husband checked Clara's pulse and then smiled sadly. "She's gone."

"It was her, wasn't it . . . with the other two lights? They came for her." Her body was still vibrating with wonder.

"I felt that way, too," Daniel murmured, pulling Kelly closer into his arms. "I kept thinking of Clara and . . . and imagining her ecstasy."

"She's free now . . . truly free," Kelly whispered, laying her head back against his shoulder. "All this time I've been so afraid of death, as though it were this dark specter waiting to take everything away . . . and . . . and it's not, is it?" She looked to Clara's body. "We just leave this . . . this costume we've been wearing. Once we shed it, and gravity, we become who we always were inside . . . and we're free to *fly!*"

"May Clara have a glorious flight home," Daniel whispered against her ear.

Tears came into Kelly's eyes as she nodded, yet they were tears of happiness for a dear friend, a wise soul and one hell of a woman. Neither of them spoke for the longest time as they settled into the peace that filled the room.

"Let's make breakfast," she said, suddenly hungry, and almost chuckled as Daniel helped her to stand. Surprisingly, shockingly, there was no grief.

He gathered her into his arms and rubbed her lower back. "You sound as practical as Clara."

Kelly glanced once more to the frame that had housed her soul mate, for that's what Clara was, a playmate for her soul. That was the past, though, and Clara had taught her something about being a woman and taking care of the present. There were things that needed to be done. "I sure hope some of her wisdom rubbed off on me," she whispered. Nodding toward the kitchen, she added, "You make the coffee, and I'll begin breakfast. We have a big day ahead of us."

Together they walked into the future.

"Take us back to where you found me, Lizzie."

"What're we gonna do with that?" the girl asked, looking at the oak sapling Daniel carried over his shoulder.

Touching the root ball of burlap, Kelly smiled. "We're going to be fulfilling Clara's last wish, honey. She wants a tree planted to remember the young girl she used to be. She left it up to me where to put it, and I want it in that grove where you first saw me."

"This way," Lizzie said, tugging on the rope attached to the new puppy the Howes had given her, right before they'd left New Orleans. "C'mon, Tinker . . . it's not a far walk."

Kelly strolled beside her husband as they passed the front of the house and made their way past the picket fence and down to the dirt road. "Do you want me to hold the shovel? That tree will get heavy soon."

Daniel looked down to her and grinned. "I think I can manage, my love."

She gazed into his eyes and smiled back. "I just want you to know I'm here to help, if you want."

"Thank you. What a great partner you are, Mrs. Gilmore. However was I so blessed?"

"*We* were blessed by second chances," she corrected, thinking of Clara's words the day she'd died. Every once in a while during the last two weeks, she'd walk into a room and expect to see Clara and her heart would feel heavy for a moment. Then, just the thought of her eased the weight and she'd feel the old woman's presence and be lifted.

Still, she missed her friend. Surprisingly, none of them were grieving, for they knew Clara wasn't really lost to them. It was just a different way of communicating now.

Lizzie ran ahead, and Kelly grinned as she watched the child and dog scamper along. The birds were chirping, and the sun was shining. It was a perfect day to fulfill a promise. How strange, she thought, as they entered the woods, to be going back to the place where it all began. She held some Spanish moss to the side for Daniel to pass and gathered her skirts as she stepped over a branch. She wasn't the same woman who had fallen into the nineteenth century. In the last month she had truly grown up. She felt very much a woman now, comfortable in her own skin as Clara had agreed. She was a wife and a mother, and she loved her life with her new family. She couldn't even imagine going back to the twenty-first century. That life seemed like a dream now . . . all that rushing around in order not to spend time with herself.

"Here," Lizzie said, stooping down to pet Tinker's back. "It was around here."

Daniel dropped the tree to the ground and Kelly looked out to the woods that surrounded them. It seemed the same, but even the memory of that was fading.

"Pick a spot," Daniel directed her, looking up through the branches to the sky while wiping his forehead with a handkerchief.

"I guess right where it is is fine."

Nodding, Daniel stuffed the handkerchief into his back pocket and began digging.

Kelly watched for some time until Lizzie walked up to her, and asked, "How come Clara wanted a tree to remind her of when she was a girl?"

Kelly put her arm around her daughter and smiled. "The night she died, she was remembering a time in her life when she was as young as that tree. Clara was born a slave, Lizzie, and on one day she felt the freedom you feel when you're here playing in nature and it was magical for her. Even though she was enslaved, she experienced freedom . . . and she wanted that oak tree to grow in her memory. It was all she wanted."

"She doesn't care if I bring flowers to her grave, like I do my mother's?"

"I'm sure she thinks the flowers are lovely, but you know Clara isn't there in the ground, don't you?"

Lizzie didn't say anything.

"She's like your mother . . . free now. You can talk to her anywhere, anytime."

Holding the shovel in his hand, Daniel stamped the soft earth around the young tree with his boot, and said, "Is it straight?"

Kelly and Lizzie stood back a few feet. "It's perfect," Kelly called out, and smiled as she walked back and wound her arm through his, bringing him closer to her body. "Thank you, my love."

He bent his head and kissed her cheek. "You know I would do anything for you, don't you? You're my life now, Kelly Brennan Gilmore . . . my beloved time traveler."

"I couldn't ask for a better life," she whispered, as Lizzie joined them in front of the tree. She took a deep breath. "This is for Clara. May it grow wild and strong, broad and wise, gently watching over all who come in contact with it."

Tinker lifted his leg and christened the young sapling.

Lizzie yanked on the rope, while Kelly and Daniel laughed.

"It's okay, honey," Kelly said, still chuckling. "Clara would love the gesture . . . it's *life*."

Standing with her husband and child, Kelly was filled with peace as she marveled at the mystery of this lifelong adventure she was on. She'd had to travel back in time to re-member freedom, to put it all back together again, and that's when the magic really unfolded as all the barriers dropped like filmy illusions and revealed what was there all the time . . . waiting for her. *Love.*

"I got all my wishes," Lizzie said, staring up at Kelly and her father with a look of happiness.

Kelly smiled down at the girl as she felt Daniel's strong arm against her breast.

"We all did, every single one of us, even dear Clara."

Daniel kissed her temple, and whispered against her skin, "Wishes do come true."

Sighing deeply with contentment, Kelly gazed at the tree that one day, over a hundred years into the future, would drip with Spanish moss and listen to a grieving heart that was yearning to heal on its endless journey. "You just gotta *believe*," she breathed.

And she did . . . with all her heart.

Epilogue

"Madam, you never cease to take away my breath!"

Giggling like a young girl, Kelly applied the brakes and brought the bicycle to a stop in front of her husband. "Remember, I've done this before. You really don't forget how to ride one, you know."

With his jacket flung over his shoulder, Daniel walked down the last step of the magnificent house and chuckled. "Now what if someone saw you in those trousers, riding a bicycle like a hoyden?"

Kelly grinned, slipping off the seat and standing with her legs on either side of the bike. "A hoyden, huh? I would think, Daniel Gilmore, in the last eight years you'd be used to people talking about me. Besides, I think I look quite . . . dashing."

Laughing, he leaned down and kissed her cheek. "So how many of your suffragist ladies, besides my daughter, have you converted?"

She fluffed up the huge leg-of-mutton sleeves on her white blouse and asked, "Converted to what . . . trousers, bicycles, or the protest march I'm organizing for next month?"

"I can't keep up with you," he murmured, gazing at her with such love that it was her turn to be breathless.

"Sure you can," she whispered back. "I keep you young, Daniel Gilmore." Her eyes took on a mischievous gleam. "Wanna ride back home on the handlebars?"

"You are a hoyden," he pronounced with a hearty chuckle.

"I know," she answered, glancing up to the house he had designed. "It's just beautiful, Daniel. Congratulations."

He turned slightly and looked back to the project that had taken well over a year to complete. "I couldn't have done it without your help."

Shrugging, she said, "I just gave you a few pointers, from what I could remember."

"It is a fitting home for my daughter to raise her children. I'm glad she picked this piece of property, so close to us."

It was only last week that Lizzie had married Christopher Tyler, after a four-year courtship that had taken root in Sunday school. She and Susan had discreetly nurtured the relationship for years and were thrilled now to be related through their children. "You know why she picked it," Kelly said, turning her head to look into the woods. "She wants to watch Clara's oak tree grow and teach her children and her grandchildren to climb it."

"She's become quite a young woman, thanks to you."

Kelly looked back at her husband and smiled with tenderness. The last eight years hadn't changed him, except for more threads of gray at his temples and a finer etching of laugh lines around his eyes. He was still the most handsome, charming, loving man she had ever encountered anywhere, in any time. "Lizzie is her own woman, and Christopher accepts that. You know he's joining us at the rally in six weeks when they return . . . hint, hint."

Daniel again laughed and shook his head. "I suppose Susan has talked William into this, too?"

"Of course. We're hoydens, don't you know . . . it's expected."

"You love that the newspaper called all of you that, don't you?"

"I do. The week before I was touted as the mother of the bride at one of the most fashionable weddings the paper has ever reported on, and the next week I'm a"—she raised her eyebrows dramatically—"a *hoyden* championing a federal women's suffrage amendment and rousing the gentle womenfolk to march on the streets like common workers. Oh, and a heretic, too!" She burst out laughing.

"And yet, all of New Orleans society clamors for an invitation to one of your famous supper parties. You are quite remarkable, my dear, but then . . . I know your secret."

"You do?" she asked with an arched eyebrow.

"Ah-ha . . . you're already a free spirit. You possess a strong feminine magic, and I, like most who meet you, am helpless to resist it."

"Hmm . . . you're right. I don't seem to recall you resisting too hard, sir."

"I just told you . . . I couldn't . . . ever. You're irresistible."

They stared into each other's eyes for a moment as a silent communication took place, a look that said what each other was thinking. It was Kelly who put it into words.

"We're both free spirits, Daniel . . . and we now have an empty house. I say we go home and make some magic together."

He kissed the tip of her nose. "Hoyden."

"I love you too," she whispered back. "Now, are you going to walk or ride? I was serious about the handlebars."

He sighed deeply. "I'll ride *you* home, madam. You get on the handlebars."

"Okay," she muttered, as they switched places. "You can be the big strong man, and I'll be the little woman, but just so you know I could do it." She didn't admit that it might be hard to look past his broad shoulders, plus this way seemed like much more fun, she thought as she climbed up onto the front of the bike.

"Are you ready?" Daniel asked, preparing to pedal as he leaned forward and placed a warm kiss behind her ear.

She shivered as threads of delight raced through her body. "Oh, I've been ready," she replied. "Why do you think I came to find you?"

He laughed. "I'm talking about riding, madam."

"So am I."

She heard his laughter and grinned broadly as they started off down the new road of crushed shells. Here she was, on the handlebars of a bike again . . . like she was a young girl. The man of her dreams was behind her, ready to make love to her. Her daughter had married a fine young man and was on her wedding trip to England. She had friends, a fulfilling life . . . the sun was shining and the birds were singing. What more could she want?

She just loved being a woman, for it truly could be magical. All she had to do was open her heart to life, and remember it was okay to play again.

Happiness. It was about time she claimed her birthright.

Afterword

Row, row, row your boat

gently down the stream.

Merrily, merrily, merrily, merrily

life is but a dream

Acknowledgments

Lyssa Keusch, my editor, for her expertise and her encouragement.

Colleen Quinn Bosler, my playmate, for the laughter and continued support.

Marcy Posner, a terrific lady. I enjoyed our time together.

Melissa Werner, a bright, warm star in my life and a shining example of courage. A star to the core.

Cristopher Sterling, my beloved, who reminds me that life is but a dream . . . a great one.

I would also like to acknowledge the staff of Avon Books/HarperCollins who contributed in any way to the publication of this book. It is appreciated.

"I need to get away from it all!"

*H*ow many times have you cried out these words? The chance to change your life and maybe even be swept away by romance is so tempting . . . And as everyone knows, there's nothing like a good vacation . . .

*T*he Avon Romance Superleaders are your passports to passion. As you enter the world created in each book, you have the chance to experience passion you've only dreamed of. Each destination is different—you might be whisked into Regency London, or perhaps to a secluded mountain cabin. But at each stop along the way, an unforgettable hero awaits to take your hand and guide you on a journey into love.

Imagine long, lazy summers in the country—the sun caresses your skin by day as you bask in its warmth in your favorite hammock . . . and each evening you curl up by the fire as contented as a cat. But something—or someone—is missing . . .

Then a compelling stranger comes striding into your life. And suddenly, a fire of a different sort begins to keep your nights hot.

He's all-male, he's all-trouble . . . and he's got you . . .

All Shook Up

COMING JANUARY 2001

by Susan Andersen

"**A**re you planning on stalking me around my office?" Dru asked. Then she lost it. "Who taught you your manners, anyway? It certainly couldn't have been Great-aunt Edwina."

A muscle ticked in his jaw. "No, the lesson I learned from Edwina was that talk is cheap, and in the end there's only one person I can depend on—myself."

"Indeed? You'll have to excuse me if I don't cry big,

sloppy tears over how misused you were. Because it seems to me that Edwina's talk wasn't all that cheap—for here you are, aren't you? Half owner in our lodge."

He took another step closer. "And that bothers you, doesn't it, sweetheart?"

She deliberately chose to misunderstand. "That you're bad-mouthing the woman who made it possible?" She ignored her reaction to his proximity this time and thrust her chin up. "Yes, I can honestly say I find that rather tacky."

For a moment his eyes went hot with some emotion Dru couldn't pin down, and she felt a burst of triumph that she'd managed to push one of his buttons. It was only fair, considering he seemed to have a natural facility for pushing all of hers.

Then his eyes went cool and distant. "Well, see, that's the thing about us lowlife types," he growled, stepping forward again. "Tacky is mother's milk to us, and we live for the opportunity to get something for nothing." He ran a rough-skinned fingertip down her cheek, leaving a streak of heat in its wake.

Dru jerked her head back, but he just moved in closer. "And we don't particularly care who we have to step on to get it either," he said in a low voice. "You might want to keep that in mind." His thumb rubbed her lower lip open, but he drew his hand back before she could slap it away. Giving her a slow once-over, he smiled insolently, and she saw that he didn't have bad teeth at all. They were maybe the slightest bit crooked—but very white and strong-looking.

The moment she dragged her gaze back to his eyes, he lifted an eyebrow. "The books?"

Blood thumping furiously in all her pulse points, Dru stalked over to the cabinet and pulled out the ledgers. A moment later she slapped them in his hands. "Here. These cover the past three years. Don't spill food on them and don't lose them."

"Guess that means I'd better not eat my peas with my knife again, huh?"

Embarrassed by her own snide rudeness, she resumed her seat, snatched up a pencil, and tapped it impatiently against the desktop, hoping to give the impression of a woman too busy for this nonsense. "Just be careful with them."

"Yes, ma'am." He gave her a bumptious salute and, with surprising grace for someone wearing several pounds of boot leather on each foot, strode out of the office.

Dru remained fuming at her desk long after he had gone. Things between her and J.D. were shaping up like Trouble with a capital *T*, but she had a bad, bad feeling that his being aggravating as all get-out was the *least* of her problems. She was more worried about the way she felt every time he was near.

Oh to be a Regency debutante . . . to wear beautiful gowns and to waltz (with permission, of course!) with a handsome nobleman, hoping he'll steal a kiss—and more—once the ball is over . . .

But what if your London season doesn't end in a spectacular match? Would you take the chance of traveling to the romantic Scottish Highlands and marrying a man you've never met? Who would want to be someone's poor relation anyway? After all, every woman needs a husband, and that's reason enough to sign . . .

The Marriage Contract

COMING FEBRUARY 2001

by Cathy Maxwell

"*That* is a wedding ring on your finger, isn't it?"

Anne had an unreasonable desire to hide her hand in the folds of her skirts. She clenched her fist. She wasn't ready for the confession, not ready at all.

He misinterpreted her fears, his gaze softened. "Your husband will be happy to know you are safe after such a bad accident."

"I hope he will," she managed to say. *Tell him*, her inner voice urged. *Now*.

Her husband looked down at the way he was dressed and laughed in agreement. He had a melodic, carefree laugh, for such a large man. Anne knew he would have a fine singing voice, too. And he didn't sound mad at all.

"It's a ritual I have," he explained with a touch of sheepishness over his peculiar dress. "Based on Celt customs. Well, actually, they are customs of our own. They make the sport more enjoyable. Adds to the game of the chase."

"Game?"

"Aye, a little danger is a healthy thing." He shrugged with a rueful grin, like an overgrown boy who couldn't help himself from pulling a prank.

Relief teetered inside her. Her husband didn't sound *raving* mad—just unconventional. He had a reason for being blue. Of course, she didn't know what to make of a man who considered it a game to fight a wildcat with his bare hands, a man who *enjoyed* danger—but then, this was Scotland.

And as long as he wasn't howling at the moon, her marriage might work.

Heat rose in her own cheeks. She attempted to make her interest a purely medical one. "Perhaps someone should put a salve on your scratches."

"They can wait." He abruptly changed the subject. "I'm sorry, I don't know your name."

She had to tell him before courage deserted her. This imposing man, clad only in a kilt, could overpower her merely by his presence. And they were alone together in the beautiful, but desolate Highlands, where no one could protect her. Still, she had to tell him . . .

"My name is Anne. I've come from London, sent by your sister. And I am your wife."

Most women would do anything to get out of wearing a hideous bridesmaid dress. Of course, leaving town is one thing—but leaving this century is quite another! But that's just what Kelly Brennan does . . .

And she ends up in sultry, steamy New Orleans, landing in the arms of a dashing, wealthy, and tantalizing man, who woos her like a lady by day . . . and someone quite different by night. But is it too extreme to marry someone from another era, even if he proves that he loves you . . .

Time After Time

COMING MARCH 2001

by Constance O'Day-Flannery

"Mr. Gilmore! Please."

Kelly heard him breathing heavily and, even through the darkness, she could see his shocked expression.

"Oh my God! I beg your pardon, Miss Brennan. I . . . I am mortified by my own actions."

Kelly pushed her hair back from her face. What could she say? She couldn't condone what had just happened, yet she was still reeling from the kiss, the first kiss in many years that felt as though it had awakened something in her she thought had died when she was twenty-three.

"I . . . I saw you standing there in that nightgown, and for a moment I thought . . . well, I thought you were someone else." He took a deep, steadying breath.

Kelly knew he meant his wife, his dead wife. This was becoming too uncanny, for in the darkness, he again reminded her of Michael. She couldn't help it. She giggled in nervousness. "You certainly surprised me, Mr. Gilmore."

"Please call me Daniel. And again, I implore your forgiveness. I most certainly am not the type of man who accosts his houseguests in the middle of the night."

"I didn't think you were." Now, why in the world did she want him to take her back into his strong arms? Craziness. Would it never end?

"I guess I shouldn't have been wandering around your home in the dark." She was rambling now, but who could blame her?

He'd kissed her! Just like that. *Kissed her and she'd liked it!*

"This is a most awkward situation, Miss Brennan."

"Call me Kelly," she whispered. "My husband died when I was much younger. I sympathize with your loss."

"You were married?"

"Yes. He died when I was twenty-three. Honestly, I don't know that I've ever really gotten over it."

"Was it the war?"

"The war . . . No, it was an accident. Something that never should have happened. Well . . . I guess I should say good night."

"Good night, Kelly."

He said her name . . . and she loved how it sounded coming from his lips. Lips that had felt so inviting, so impassioned . . . what was wrong with her?

"Good night," she whispered again and quickly opened the door to her bedroom.

Closing it behind her Kelly leaned against it and sighed heavily. She looked around and sensed a familiarity she hadn't felt before. How could she possibly know this place . . . this house and, somehow, him?

If a proper young English lady finds herself having the ill fortune to be confined with a stranger in a public conveyance, she must take special care not to engage this person in any way—either by speaking or staring.

It is true that a carriage can be rather small, making it difficult to avoid speaking to a handsome stranger—even if he might not be a gentleman. But as everyone knows, conversation can lead to so much more. And a woman can be ruined if it's known she's committed . . .

The Indiscretion

Coming April 2001

by Judith Ivory

She stared at his black hat tipped over most of his face. If he ever should play in a Wild West show, he'd be a stagecoach robber, she decided. Or a gunfighter with a "quick temper and a quicker trigger finger," which was a line out of one of her brother Clive's Buffalo Bill novels. She entertained this fantasy for a few minutes, smiling over it. Yes, something about him, a leanness, "a build as hard and dependable as a good rifle" (she, in fact, had pilfered one of Clive's contraband American novels just to see what they were about), not to mention something in his brooding attitude, spoke of a possibly harsh, very physical existence.

Her imagination put him in a big, tooled-leather saddle on a horse caparisoned in silver stars down its breast. To his black hat with silver beads she added silver guns in holsters at his hips and American spurs that jingled as he walked. She remembered what such spurs looked like and, more memorable, what they sounded like: a lot of metal to them, a silver band low on each heel, silver chains underneath, with jagged, spinning wheels at the back. Nothing like an English riding spur with its single, neat point affixed to an English gentleman's boot.

Something about his posture, his attentiveness, made her call over the road noise. "Are you awake?"

After a second, he pushed his hat brim up enough with a finger so that his eyes were visible, if shadowed. "Yes, ma'am."

He had a nice voice when polite, like a bow being pulled slowly over the lowest groaning strings of a bass. He took his time saying things, slow-talking his way over sliding consonants and drawn-out vowels. His diction was full of *ma'am*s, *thank-you*s, and *you're-welcome*s. A politeness that turned itself inside out when he used it to say surly things.

"Who's Gwyn?" she asked.

Sam sat there slouched, watching a lady he'd been sure wouldn't utter another word to him, while he chewed the inside of his cheek.

Why not tell her? he thought. "The woman I was supposed to marry this morning." He sighed, feeling blue again for simply saying it. Hell, what sort of fellow left the woman he'd courted for almost two years at the altar in front of all their friends and family? He expected a huffy admonishment from Miss Prissy Brit now—

"I'm so sorry," she said.

The coach turned sharply, and they both leaned to counter the force of the motion, him stretching his leg out to brace himself with the toe of his boot, her swinging from the handgrip.

Over the noise of their travel, she asked, "What happened?"

Sam frowned. Now where had this little lady been five hours ago? Because that was the one question he had been dying for someone to ask all day, though not a soul till now had thought to. Her concern and his needy longing for it from someone, anyone, shot a sense of gratitude through him so strong he could have reached out and kissed her.

He said, "I was on the way to the church, when out the window of my hackney, I saw the robbery I told you about. The fellow stopped the woman on a Plymouth street and grabbed at her purse. She fought him. He was puny but wiry and willing to wrestle her for it. It made me crazy when he dumped her over. I figured, with me being a foot taller and sixty or so pounds heavier, I could hop out, pin the punk to the ground, then be on my way with very little trouble. I wasn't prepared for his four friends." Sam sighed. "I spent the morning at the doctor's when I was supposed to be standing at the altar."

"But your bride—"

"My bride won't talk to me long enough to hear my explanation."

Their eyes met and held. Hers were sympathetic.

And light brown. A kind of gold. Pretty. Warm. He watched her shoulders jostle to and fro as she said, "Well, when she saw you like this, she must have—"

"She didn't see me. She only called me names through her front door. No one would let me in."

"How unreasonable."

"Exactly." What a relief to hear the word.

"You could send her a note to explain—"

"She returned it unopened."

"You could talk to someone, get a friend to tell her—"

"No one will speak to me. I had to bribe the stable-boy to get me to the coach station."

Her pretty eyes widened. "But people have to understand—"

Exactly what he wanted to hear, the very words he'd been telling himself all day. And now that he heard them, he realized how stupid they were. "Apparently not. 'Cause not a person I know does."

Bless her, her mouth tightened into a sweet, put-out line. "Well, how unreasonable," she said again. Oh, God bless her.

"Yes." But no. He looked down. "It is unreasonable. Until you realize that I left Gwyn at the altar once before, eight months ago."

She straightened herself slightly in her seat, read-justing her wrist in the leather strap. Aha! her look said. Maybe it just wasn't the right woman.

There's something about a man who works with his hands . . . his self-reliance and ruggedness—along with his lean, muscled body—make him oh, so appealing.

So if you're seeking a strong, silent type—a man of the land—you might want to check out Wyoming. Yes, this is someone who seems like he's only willing to speak when he's asking you out to a Saturday night dance—but once he takes you in his arms, you'll know he'll never let you down . . . and he'll probably keep you up all night long. Because this is the place you'll find . . .

The Last Good Man

COMING MAY 2001

by Kathleen Eagle

She heard the scratch of gravel, turned, and caught the shift of shadow, a moving shape separating itself from a stationary one. It was a horse.

"Where did you come from?" Savannah asked, approaching quietly, assuming it had wandered up there on its own, and she was all set to welcome the company. Then she got close enough to make out the saddle.

"The Lazy K."

The deep, dearly familiar voice seemed to issue from the mouth of the cave.

"Clay?" She jerked the hem of her skirt free from its mooring in her waistband and let it drop. Another shadow emerged, bootheels scraping with each step as though they were taken reluctantly. He looked bigger than she remembered. "Clay, is that you?"

"The real me." He touched the brim of the cowboy hat that was pulled low over his face. "Are you the real Savannah Stephens?"

She laughed a little. "I was hoping it wouldn't matter up here."

"It matters to me." He reached for her hand. "Welcome home."

He seemed to surround her entirely with a simple squeeze of the hand. She stepped into the shelter of him, her nose a scant inch below his square chin. She had yet to see his face clearly, to assess his life by counting lines, but it didn't matter. She knew Clay Keogh. Reflexively she lifted her free hand, her fingertips seeking something of him, finding a belt loop, a bit of smooth leather. All she wanted was a proper greeting, a quick embrace, but she heard the sharp intake of his breath, and she knew she had the upper hand. She'd turned the surprise on him. He was big-man sure of himself one minute, shaky inside the next, simply because she'd stepped a little closer than he'd expected.

A power surge shot through her.

She lifted her chin, remembering times gone by and aiming for a little humor with her old dare. "You can do better than that, Clay," she purred. Her own throaty tone surprised her. Having no humor in her, she couldn't help but miss the mark.

He touched his lips to hers, tentative only for an instant. His hunger was as unmistakable as hers. His arms closed around her slight shoulders, hers around his lean waist. He smelled of horsehide and leather, tasted of whiskey, felt as solid as the Rockies, and kissed like no man she'd ever known, including a younger Clay Keogh. She stood on tiptoe to kiss him back, trade him her breath for his, her tongue for his.

"Savannah . . ."

She couldn't understand why he was trying to pull away. There'd been a catch in his breath—she'd heard it distinctly—and it was that small sound that had set her insides aflutter. The surprise, the innocence, the wonder of it all. Good Lord in heaven, how long had it been since she'd been kissed?

"Shhh, Clay," she whispered against the corner of his mouth. "It's so good, finding you here."

"Glad to see—"

"But don't talk yet. Just hold me. It feels so good. You're not married or anything, are you?"

"I'm something." His deep chuckle sounded a little uneasy, which wasn't what she wanted. She wanted him easy. "But not married."

"Let me see you," she said, reaching for his hat. He started to duck away, but she flashed him a smile, and he stopped, looked at her for a moment, then bowed his head within her reach. "Girlfriend?" she asked as she claimed his hat and slid her fingers into the hair that tumbled over his forehead.

"No."

"Me neither."

"How about boyfriends?"

She laughed. "Completely unattached," she assured him, learning the new contours of his cheek with her hand.

"Well, I've never been to New York, but I hear there's a lot of variety there."

"There's variety everywhere, Clay. Don't tell me you've turned redneck on me. I won't have that."

"You won't, huh?" His smile glistened with moonlight. "Not much has changed here."

"That's what I was counting on."

It's one thing to get away from it all . . . and it might be another to visit the town of Gospel, Idaho. Still, even though it's not near very much, you can always have some eggs at the Cozy Corner Café and get your hair done at the Curl Up and Dye Hair Studio.

And there's the added attraction of Gospel's sheriff. He's easy on the eyes and not above breaking the laws of love to get what he wants. Before you know it, you'll have plenty to talk about in the way of . . .

True Confessions

COMING AUGUST 2001

by Rachel Gibson

"**C**an you direct me to Number Two Timberlane?" she asked. "I just picked up the key from the realtor and that's the address he gave me."

"You sure you want Number *Two* Timberlane? That's the old Donnelly place," Lewis Plummer said. Lewis was a true gentleman and one of the few people in town who didn't outright lie to flatlanders.

"That's right. I leased it for the next six months."

Sheriff Dylan pulled his hat back down on his forehead. "No one's lived there for a while."

"Really? No one told me that. How long has it been empty?"

"A year or two." Lewis had also been born and raised in Gospel, Idaho, where prevarication was considered an art form.

"Oh, a year isn't too bad if the property's been maintained."

Maintained, hell. The last time Dylan had been in the Donnelly house, thick dust covered everything. Even the bloodstain on the living room floor.

"So, do I just follow this road?" She turned and pointed down Main Street.

"That's right," he answered. From behind his mirrored glasses, Dylan slid his gaze to the natural curve of her slim hips and thighs, down her long legs to her feet.

"Well, thanks for your help." She turned to leave, but Dylan's next question stopped her.

"You're welcome, Ms.—?"

"Spencer."

"Well now, Ms. Spencer, what are you planning out there on Timberlane Road?" Dylan figured everyone had a right to privacy, but he also figured he had a right to ask.

"Nothing."

"You lease a house for six months and you plan to do nothing?"

"That's right. Gospel seemed like a nice place to vacation."

Dylan had doubts about that statement. Women who drove fancy sports cars and wore designer jeans vacationed in nice places with room service and pool boys, not in the wilderness of Idaho. Hell, the closest thing Gospel had to a spa was the Petermans' hot tub.

Her brows scrunched together and she tapped an impatient hand three times on her thigh before she said, "Well, thank you gentlemen for your help." Then she turned on her fancy boots and marched back to her sports car.

"Do you believe her?" Lewis wanted to know.

"That she's here on vacation?" Dylan shrugged. He didn't care what she did as long as she stayed out of trouble.

"She doesn't look like a backpacker."

Dylan thought back to the vision of her backside in those tight jeans. "Nope."

"Makes you wonder why a woman like that leased that old house. I haven't seen anything like her in a long time. Maybe never."

Dylan slid behind the wheel of his Blazer. "Well, Lewis, you sure don't get out of Pearl County enough."